D1585449

ACKNOWLEDGEMENTS

The act of writing the third book in a trilogy reveals several things. Firstly, the characters – the surviving characters – are almost like old friends. Well, maybe not friends, exactly, but certainly guys the scribbler's got to know pretty well. After that comes the realisation that by the end of the book, even the good guys may not make it, and killing them off – or worse – feels strangely personal and disturbing. There are also times when the scribbler – that's me – just wants to stop, shout 'Enough!' and write something else. It can feel like the world's longest obituary, and they're rarely entertaining. Support, comment and criticism are entirely invaluable at that point. So, thanks above and beyond my wildest expectations are due to RJ Ellory, who was right about everything. Every time. Ieish Gamah provided all the ordnance info, as well as displaying more knowledge of lethal weapons than any woman should. Meanwhile, despite admitting to a certain discomfort, Eden Sharp and Jane Risdon ploughed through an early version, then supplied entirely valuable – and at times remarkable – insights into what I'd meant to say all along... but I just didn't know it.

And, inevitably, all praise and cakes are due to Rowena Hoseason, without whom none of it would have happened. This may have been a good thing...

Oh. Of course every trilogy has a fourth book. It's just a matter of time, as you'll see if you make it to the end.

Frank Westworth,
Cornwall, 2016

1

AUGUST, THIS YEAR: OFF IN THE DISTANCE

Shots. Steady. One to twelve. Pause. Start again. One to twelve. Pause. Repeat. Repeat and repeat again, as necessary.

'It's the Brit.' A ring-pull bit the dust in a fizz of quick-flattening beer. A slender man dressed for hunting poured the can empty in one long swallow, ditched it into the back of the truck and another ring-pull bit the dust. Exactly the same time to empty the can as to shoot twelve shots, pause, shoot twelve more. 'He got a good rapid rhythm going there,' the drinker remarked.

His nearby companion grunted and sipped at his own can. 'Good practice with the reloading, too. How many magazines is that?'

'Ten. Maybe twelve.' The first speaker paused in his drinking, belched volcanically and studied the descent of the evening. 'That's a lot of lead. He got a one man war going down or what?'

Quiet descended with the evening through the trees. Then the shooting recommenced. The same rhythm, steady and metronomic. Trees moved in the falling dark to the right of the companions and their beer, their truck, their conversation. A third man joined them. No audible greetings between long friends. None necessary.

'Night sight.' The third companion remarked. 'He's hooked up a night sight. He takes this damn serious.'

The first speaker paused in his consumption. 'You reckon as he's shooting at cans? Reckon we should go offer him a few more targets?' he chuckled.

The third companion's voice stood out against the background warfare. 'You'd not want to sneak up, now. All the lights on the rig, maybe some music.' He sounded serious.

'Firecrackers too? Choirs of angels? Come on man. We know the hills, the country.' He paused. 'Do you know him? The trigger-happy Brit? Joshua?'

The more quiet of the three replied. 'His name is Stoner. He's on vacation. Has a visitor's visa and gun permits. He's a vet, big time, so we tread lightly if we intrude, gentlemen. Got that?'

'Gotcha, Joshua.' The third companion was standing with them now. 'He's counting cadence, for sure. Military. Sharpshooter. Didn't know the Brits still did sharpshooters. Cool. That's cool. We should, like, take him hunting. He'd never miss, we'd all eat better.' They laughed, as old friends, longtime companions do. 'But he's on a visitor visa? Been there a while, up on his hill. How long do they last? Thought it was less than a year. Thought the feds were heavy about that. Homeland Security. Those guys.'

Joshua cleared his throat. Both of the others stood very still for a moment, then turned to face him in tight familiar formation, peering through the gloom while the shooting continued above them, up and across the valley through the trees and into the darkness.

'Yeah. They are.'

'He's out of time? Is that it? Should you be putting on your shining shield and paying him an official visit, Joshua? We don't need no immigrants in the woods, especially not immies with their own private war. Just saying.'

'He's legit, Cole. Entirely legit. A vet with traction and a warm welcome from Uncle Sam. I called in his details about a month back. Got told that he was one of the good guys. Iraq with our boys, special forces, Airborne too. I said to the Feebs that maybe we should go visit and make like friends, but they suggested otherwise. Suggested that in addition to being a welcome guest of Uncle Sam he is also extremely armed and extremely dangerous. That something bad, very bad, had gone down in the old country and that he was here to rest. Recuperate. R and R. I told them that he shoots a lot. They told me that so would I if I were him. They wouldn't say why, but they weren't unhappy with him shooting up trees.'

'Wow.' Cole slapped his side and laughed, ripping open another can of Coors. 'We got us a cowboy, hey?'

Joshua didn't laugh. 'They called me back. The Feebs. They never did that before. Took their time. Friendly like. Told me they'd spoken with Mr Stoner the Brit's friends in the Bureau and they had advised him of my interest and my concern. Told me that our pet Brit understood my concern and was heading into town to see me. That I should be polite. I wondered then, and asked why the politeness? Not that I would be anything other than hospitable.' His companions chuckled. 'I always am.' They chuckled some more, maybe nervously. 'But why in particular? And what they said was a surprise.' He silenced, as did the repetitive shooting above them.

'Well?' Cole demanded. 'Morgan and me, we're waiting? He a one-man task force? He disfigured? He got no legs or no head or something?'

Joshua shook his head, the movement still visible though his features were unreadable through the darkness. 'They said if I piss him off he'll vanish. Go someplace else. He has a deal with them. He stays above ground, in plain sight while his vacation lasts, causes them no alarms and they maintain his welcome. And he is welcome. Figure that, if you like. Brit guy's shooting up half a hill, like he's ploughing for the Taliban or some such, and we just wave and smile. Somebody owes him a big one. Then the fed said that in any case this guy, Stoner, would be coming by the office. Going to say hi, shoot the breeze, so on.'

'When's the big day, Joshua?' Morgan spoke, his tone so painfully neutral that he sounded dangerous.

'In the morning. In about twelve hours.'

'You reckon the practice tonight is so he shoots straight when he sees you? He going to call you out onto main street? Gunfight in Sleepytown, hey?' Cole through the dark sounded genuinely amused, and relaxed, unlike Morgan.

'Reckon I'll find out in the morning. Meantime, how's about heading home. I need to polish my suit ready for my own funeral, maybe.' They laughed, piled into the big rig, switched on all of its many lights and drove back to town, a thin trail of ring-pulls in their wake.

***

'Mister Stoner, is it?' The small town's senior law enforcement officer held open the door to his office, allowing his visitor to enter. He called for coffee. 'Unless you want something stronger? We're pretty relaxed here,' he smiled and waited for a response.

'Coffee is fine, Officer. Just fine. Can you call for a

glass of water to chase it? Tap's fine.' He held out a hand, the policeman took it firmly, held it and looked face to face into his visitor, searching.

'Joshua. I'm not an officer, not as such. I'm the sheriff. Call me Joshua. Or sheriff. What do I call you? Is it Mister Stoner or do you do informal?'

Stoner smiled, withdrew his hand from the American's grip with a wrist movement which took the latter by surprise. 'Stoner. Jean-Jacques. Call me what you want. I'm easy. Informal is good. Most...' he paused, squeezed his eyes closed for a moment. 'Most people who know me well call me JJ. Easier than Jean-Jacques.' He stood like a brawler, arms hanging away from his sides, hands open, fingers spread.

'Your friends. What do your friends call you? And sit down, no need to be upstanding here. So. What do your friends call you, Mister Stoner, Jean-Jacques?'

'Friends, Lieutenant? That's a world of mystery, isn't it? Reckon I'm fresh out of friends for a while. Being a friend of mine is hazardous. Seems less unkind to keep away from them at the moment. Call me what you like.' He peeled off his jacket, a biker's black leather with the American legend 'Harley-Davidson' large in red and white across the wide shoulders, and draped it over a chair back, sat himself in the second visitor's chair and was motionless while the coffee was delivered by an unspeaking uniformed sergeant.

'OK. That sounds pretty unhappy, if you don't mind me saying so, Mister Stoner.' Joshua took in the man seated before him across the desk, an open appraisal. Tall, bearded, hard-muscled, thin, dry and weathered, wearing a black biker's T-shirt with the more local legend 'Harley-Davidson Detroit' written in script weaving through a fearsome image of TV biker fantasy violence. Leather jeans and heavy biker boots completed the ensemble.

'I shopped at the Harley dealership near the airport when I landed.' Stoner was suddenly grinning broadly. 'Cool threads, huh? Subtle. I got a selection of T-shirts, every one of them bearing a cheap image from hell.' He laughed, suddenly loudly and with a lack of relevance which shocked Joshua into observant immobility. 'I got Harley socks and pants. Would you believe it. This is why everyone loves America.'

'You got the motorcycle to match?' Joshua held neutrality comfortably close to his tone of voice.

'Couldn't talk the walk if I didn't walk the talk, sheriff, now could I? Got a couple up at the cabin. Hell, I got a Ford pick-up that pretends it's a Harley.' The smile was controlled now, subsiding into a nod of appreciation for the coffee, which was excellent.

'Excellent coffee, Sheriff,' Stoner said, catching his companion's eye and holding it. 'Officer. Sorry. Sheriff's better. I will remember. I'm a Brit. We call our policeman bobbies. You'll need to forgive me. Stranger in a strange land, all that.'

'You seem nervous of me, Mr Stoner,' the lieutenant held his gaze, unsmiling. 'Why is that?'

'Human contact, officer.'

'Joshua.'

'Joshua. You're the first local neighbourly official person – a person of authority – to share a conversation with me in almost a year, maybe. Long time, certainly. I've forgotten how to do it.' He corrected himself, shifted his gaze to the water cooler in the corner. 'Almost forgotten. Expected that I would, and that it'll all come back soon enough. You've got a lot of questions, I bet. Ask away. I'll be unable to answer some of them but the answers I give…'

'Will be the truth, the whole truth and nothing but the truth?' Joshua's smile had neither warmth nor welcome within it.

'It'll be true. Part truths are not lies. Only lies are lies. I'll not lie to you. Do you get more coffee while being interrogated in this place?' Stoner smiled again, controlled again, worked his shoulders. 'I left my helmet on the cycle. Is that safe?'

'You talk like a half-American, Stoner. Why is that?'

'I do? Cool. I pick up accents, relax with languages. And I've hardly spoken Brit English in a long while now. Not much at all. You want I should try harder to sound like a foreigner?'

'You are a foreigner, Mr Stoner. But you're not pretending. I have no concerns. A friendly remark, is all. You're just a partner in the special relationship, with only friends around him and nothing to hide.' He laughed, called for more coffee, raised an eyebrow, received the responding confirmation and added a long glass of water to the order.

'Lots to hide, Sheriff. Understand that, please. You might find talking about me with the FBI to be easier than talking about me with me. They know what they want you to know.'

'And you don't?'

'No. Not really.' Stoner gave thanks for the coffee, sipped it and placed the mug on the desk between himself and the law. Sank the big glass of water in one. 'I'm welcome in the USA, Sheriff. I've done service for the nation, and to my endless surprise it's proved to be a grateful nation. So far. You a military man?' He sat back, blew on his hands for no reason Joshua could see.

'Army. You?'

'Yeah. Your wars in several places.'

'My wars? I don't think so.'

'Mr Bush's wars, Sheriff. Hot lands far away, a lot of killing. Young men, blood in the sands.'

'You special forces? Some Brit outfit, SAS? Something like that? Fought for Uncle Sam?'

'In a way. But it was a very long time ago. More than ten years. Twelve, maybe more. Memory wanders. Like everything else.' He fell quiet, face and posture in neutral, idling, which Joshua found more un-nerving than anything he'd seen or heard to date. Including the gunnery displays.

Stoner shook his head, as if to clear it, and suddenly laughed again, pointlessly. There was no shared joke between them. The silence was louder when the laughter ceased.

'R&R,' he said. 'Rest and recuperation. Rebuild and rectify. Resurrection and recharge.'

'And a lot of shooting.'

'Yes. A lot of shooting. Recently. Hence your interest. Hence my sitting before you, being friendly and co-operative. Good coffee. Best coffee in the world outside of Turkey.' He looked up. 'Maybe outside Iraq, too. That's good for coffee. Better than Iran.' He pronounced them 'I rack; I ran.'

Joshua nodded his understanding.

'You and a couple of the guys were out on the slopes last night.' Stoner was matter of fact, sipping with appreciation. 'Good rig. Bright.'

Joshua leaned back in his lawman's chair, raised both his eyebrows. 'You saw us?'

'Yeah. Lit yourselves up like Halloween.'

'Where were you?'

'About a hundred yards, metres, paces away. You still

do yards out here in the colonies? Most of my sights are in yards.'

Joshua considered quietly. The quiet stretched towards becoming a silence. 'You were firing. Maybe a mile away. You got company? A friend?'

Stoner began to laugh again, caught it, controlled it. Squeezed both his hands into a grip of the desk's wooden edge. 'No company. Not at the moment. Not for a little while now. Earlier. Not now.'

'I heard the shots, Mister Stoner. A lots of shots. And I heard where they were coming from.'

'Yes you did. You did not hear any impacts. You heard a real gun firing real bullets. OK, it just wasn't being fired last evening. It was fired maybe a month ago, I think. Damn memory really can be inaccurate. It's getting better, but it's not good. Not yet. It'll get there. And when it does I'll be ready for it.'

'I think you need to explain this to me, Mister Stoner. Keep it simple, like I'm some kind of country hick sheriff and you're some very clever English guest.' Stoner smiled more normally. 'I recorded some shooting. Practice. Target shooting. Long gun. Very accurate.

'Twelve shot magazine.'

'Yeah. Holds more. I always did worry about jamming. Usually load just the twelve. Very accurate.'

'And I could hear you firing maybe a mile away. Care to explain?'

'Did it sound right to you? The right sort of sound level for the distance?'

'It did.'

'Good. Got it right then. Hard for me to tell, myself, ever tried to judge the sound of your own shooting, Sheriff?'

'Can't say I have. And you've still not explained.'

'I'm sorry.' Stoner nodded and spread his hands wide. 'Still finding it... strange to be talking civilised.' He paused, considered, spoke some more. 'A guitar amplifier, Sheriff. Couple hundred of your American Watts, RMS, courtesy of one of your fine American Marshall guitar amplifier stacks. Very crisp. The cabinets usually come with four twelve-inch speakers – I've no idea what that is in metric, I'm sorry – but I rebuilt them for six tens.' He sat back, nodding. Considered. Drained the last of the coffee and smiled. 'Celestions.'

'And why would you do that?' asked the Sheriff, ignoring Stoner's stranger statements.

'Do what?' Stoner stood and walked to the water cooler as though he'd only now noticed it, poured and drank. 'It gives the guitar much more bite. You lose some bass response, but hey...' He tailed off, observing the dry look from the sheriff. Walked methodically back to his chair, sat down. Paused.

'Why did you play back shooting?' asked Joshua, as to a dim child.

'To sow confusion among my enemies, Sheriff. There's only one reason for that. I prefer my enemies to be confused. Always.'

'You have enemies, Mister Stoner? Have you brought your enemies along with you?'

Stoner took the question entirely seriously. He swilled the remains of his drink around the mug and shook his head in quiet contemplation.

'Enemies I have. I do. That's a fact. Whether they're nearby I could not say. Paranoia keeps us alive on the battlefield, Sheriff. I see no reason why it should be different here, where all the fire is supposed to be friendly.' He stood once more, made ready to leave. 'Great coffee. Thanks for this.'

'Sit down.' Joshua sounded more irritated than he wished to. He softened his voice, waved a placatory hand. 'No no; sit, we're just getting acquainted, Mister Stoner. Don't leave me with more questions than I had before you arrived.' He attempted levity, succeeded somewhat. Stoner sat. Fiddled with the stitching on his black biker's jacket.

'Yeah,' he said, finally. 'Yeah. You want a story.' Not a question. No reply, just a tilt of the policeman's head.

'The first answer,' Stoner began. Paused. Restarted. 'The first answer needs a first question.' He stopped again. Adjusted internally, pressed his own personal reset. 'You don't know what to ask or how to ask it. OK. Here you go. Yes. Yes, I am a dangerous man. Anyone with extensive military training – specialist military training – is a danger to civilians. I guess our mutual host, the US of A, has trained more killers than any other nation in the history of the world.' He paused again. 'Don't look outraged... Joshua. It's just a fact. I've killed for this country, and I'm guessing you have too.' He looked up. The sheriff nodded, said nothing.

'After that it's just a question of scale, volume. The long dirty dry road from appropriate response to simple overkill.' He nodded, eyes elsewhere. 'And then we have the whole principle of deterrence. The pre-emptive strike. Killing someone because they're a perceived threat. A hard line to define, that one. The opaque transition from a dirty look to a physical assault. Self-preservation. To preserve ourselves we need to posture, to demonstrate our superiority and our invulnerability. We increasingly need to prove that inside our mighty trousers is a god-awful heavy weapon and inside our soul is the will to use it. To use it first. So we beat up on the innocent, because that's the easiest way of making sure that our perceived enemies get the message without feeling a need to return our fire. At us, any rate. We don't care if they also demonstrate their own trousers and soul by zapping another bunch of irrelevant third party innocents. I've killed a lot of innocents. Lots of Arabs.' He paused. Looked up.

'Am I boring you?'

The sheriff shook his head, silently poured more coffee for them both. Rose to his feet and walked around the desk and the chairs to the door, checked that it was closed. Then turned the key in the lock. Returned to his seat. Sipped. Nodded to his companion. 'Go on,' he said, quietly. 'I hear you.'

Stoner looked briefly into his eyes; the sheriff held his gaze. Stoner nodded, looked at the window.

'That was the army life. I killed a lot more innocents than combatants, Sheriff Joshua. A lot. A whole lot. And your boys, your fly-boys mainly, killed a lot more on my say-so. So it goes. Up and down. Around and around and around.' He sipped again. Water first, then cooling coffee, then water again.

'Out of the army into government work. The same work. Easier in a lot of ways. "Stoner," they'd say; "this is a bad guy. Go remove him." I'd do that. Always. Easier morally than calling in an air strike, killing dozens, hundreds in some dim hope that a guilty party or two might also cop the blast. Taking down a few a-holes at a time is more expensive and more risky and surely less televisually delightful, but there's no need for courts and lawyers, journalists and politicians. If everything's deniable, then everything's fine. You still awake?'

'Yeah. Surely. We should adjourn to a bar. Your talking is bringing on a thirst.'

'No. No bar. Here is fine with me.' Stoner's tone was dismissive, detached.

'Say why?'

'Weakness. Mine. In a bar I'd need to drink to talk this through, and the drink would always ease the grief and dampen down the controls, and there would be a need to fight, to hit or to get hit, and I am a dangerous man, like I said. OK if the bar is full of vets, bikers, whatever, because they'd give me a kicking and that would be OK. They'd kick some sense into me and nobody cares if a few wasted bikers kick the crap out of each other. Do they? No. No, they do not. And I doubt that you'd frequent bars of that lively kind. Although I could be wrong.' He looked up, a question.

'You're not wrong. I take your point, Mister Stoner. Please... continue.'

'To function like that – I made maybe twelve years out of it – you need to trust no one apart from those you need to trust. Get that? It's too tough a concept for civilian minds.'

The sheriff nodded. 'Gotcha.'

'OK. And the few you trust, you trust absolutely. One hundred percent. You do not need to like them, but you do need to trust them.' He paused. 'And when they decide that you've passed your sell-by, that a newer model would be cheaper, more reliable and more easily controlled, then they discuss the terms of your departure from the field, like civilised men, and all is blissful.' He stopped. Stalled.

Joshua leaned so far back in his sheriff's wheeled chair that he appeared in danger of capsizing, skating. 'That's not what happened?'

'Correct.'

'What did happen?"

'Betrayals, mister policeman. A lot of betrayals. A

whole down and dirty series of betrayals so complicated and so deliberately obscure that they near brought me down. And a mistake, Sheriff.'

'Yours or theirs?'

'Mine. An act of charity, Joshua. I allowed a man – the prime mover in the whole thing, probably the closest thing I had to a trusted partner; a professional friend, if you like – I allowed him to live. My last act. Charity, like I said.'

'Well. Good for you. Charity, as you say. Its own reward. It work out for you?'

Stoner barked. Abruptly. He closed his eyes and his face fell forward, his tears running freely, staining his dark Harley-Davidson shirt a deeper dark. He barked again, looked up, eyes straining, water running from around them, sweat providing an accompaniment on the brow above his eyes. A weary man on the edge, of something. The sheriff leaned forward, hands gripping the armrests of his chair, ready to raise him rapidly to his feet. Stoner barked once more; it was dead laughter, Joshua understood at last. The visible death of humour and belief.

'No,' said Stoner, shaking salt water from his face without lifting his gaze from his companion's eyes. 'No. Not at all. Which is why I'm here. Bring on the clowns.' He stood, held out his hand. The sheriff dropped the door key into Stoner's palm.

He turned at the door, flicked the key back to the sheriff, who made no move to catch it, letting it clatter instead between their cups.

'The irony, Joshua. The answer, if you need an answer to explain why I'm here, cluttering your carpet, is that I discovered friends where I never knew I had friends, like I discovered enemies where there should have been none. Balance in all things, they say. People – a very few – believed they held a debt. They did not. But I accepted their generosity. You know who I refer to, because they've been in contact with you and that is how and why we're here and why I've introduced myself. Sorry about the emotion shit. I'm just about ready to face the big bad world, and when I do I'll look forward to it with some little relish... but not yet. Not... quite yet.'

Sheriff Joshua stood, held out a hand. Stoner hesitated, then returned to the desk and took the hand. Held it. Gripped forearms as comrades sometimes do.

'I'll put out the word that you're to be left alone. Keep making with the fireworks and they'll stay away. I hope.' He dropped Stoner's hand.

'That is the idea, Joshua. Part of it, anyways.' Stoner pulled a cell phone from a pocket, keyed it. The sheriff's own phone buzzed, as it had, ignored, several times through their encounter. 'That's me,' revealed Stoner. 'You're welcome to drop by. Text me first. I tend to retaliate in advance; that old pre-emptive thing. Just text and call in, if you wish. Thank you for your time and for listening. G'day to you.'

The policeman watched him leave, and as the door closed behind him, he sat on the edge of his big wide policeman's desk and wiped the palms of his hands on the knees of his uniform trousers. His hands, he'd realised, were sweating, badly.

2

What had at first been a silence had grown into a comfortably constant envelope of background sound. The morning's skies had done with raining. Sunlight highlit the shimmering greens of the woods themselves, leaves and darker waters reflecting and reflected. A fox coughed, fish snatched flies from the surface of the lake and sank with them... separating food from water and air from water with an expertise of which they knew nothing. Fish are like that, Existence itself is quite sufficient to fulfil a fish. And when their existence is terminated, by fair means or otherwise, fish go into their own long night with equal understanding.

JJ Stoner absorbed the stillness. He sat in calm comfort, relaxed in the totally natural world surrounding him. The rifle had rested across his crossed legs through the night, through the early morning rain; the oil on its metalwork beading the water into reflecting jewels in the new sun's low light. He'd slept, and deeply, for the first time in several days; both legs were locked together and numb, a welcome numbness, the numbness before the ache. He'd woken before his body betrayed its patient presence by

16

cramping and shifting position. The shimmering drops on the rifle's metalwork confirmed this.

He laid the rifle down beside him. Leaned back, taking his body weight onto his arms and upper body, lifted his backside from the groundsheet and eased his legs straighter, then fully straight before him. Sighed, so quietly that the natural ambient was undisturbed. Finally, legs relaxed again and tingling with the return of movement, he let his attention drift back to the lake, to the long body of water stretching itself before him, its shores lost in reflections of the woods above them. Shadows of clouds drifted across the cold expanse, the glitter of the sun's own reflections lost from them. Beauty.

Stoner gently rubbed the muscles of his legs, encouraging the circulation, preparing to stand, to rise upright for the first time that day. It held a tiny but real significance for him. He had no idea why. Finally, he loosened his stance completely, then re-tied the laces of his soft-soled boots. He stood, his view of the lake changing slightly, pleased in a quiet way that his movement had caused almost no ripple in the steady beat of the natural activity surrounding and protecting him. The shift in his position allowed him to include the cabin in his wider view. His cabin, for the time being. Borrowed without formal consent. A lost haven, maybe. A place to rest and to recuperate, hopefully.

He wrapped the rifle into its soft, oily, waterproof carry bag – a well-worn gunny sack – and slung it over a shoulder. Checked himself for the reassuring presence of other weaponry, and scanned the ground surrounding him for a track to follow. Tracks are less noisy, less conspicuous than trekking through the wild. Human smells are lost when mingled with those of the more frequent mammalian inhabitants of the woods.

He breathed the clean, crisp air of the trees. Set out.

And walked steadily, smoothly, almost silently downhill and around the hill, following the contours and the animal track until it encountered the man-made track. The only vehicular access to this side of the lake, and only then for all-wheel drive machinery or committed trail bike riders. Both of which could not disguise the signs of their passage, signs which were welcome only by their absence.

Then along the track, keeping himself at the edge of the track, passing steadily through patches of light and dark, for maybe two kilometres until the track entered a gravelled parking area, once again empty of both vehicles and all signs of their recent presence. He emerged from the notional protection of the foliage and walked across the wide open space to the unoccupied hut, used by parking attendants in a more prosperous age but empty for several recent years. Checked his own markers around the hut for signs of interference, moved around to the rear of the unremarkable little building and stashed the rifle nearby. Walked to another location, removed his military pattern jacket and replaced it with a more civilian fleece, swapped soft-soled boots for trainers, leaving his socks in the boots, dropped to his belly and ran through a sequence of press-ups. Rolled to his back and ran through another sequence, stretches and pull-ups. Stripped off the fleece and repeated both sets of exercises; stripped off his T-shirt and repeated them again. Dressed again in T and fleece, and ran down the metalled road which left the old car park and ran down to the two-lane, maybe six, maybe eight kilometres distant.

At the two-lane, he rested. Ate a little, drank a little, then ran back, changing his clothes and collecting the rifle, returning at a comfortable energy-conserving pace to the lakeside, where the sun was approaching late morning and the tranquillity was complete. At the cabin, he disarmed, stripped, primed the paraffin stove and set the day's first coffee to brew, after grinding the beans by hand and using water he'd boiled the day before. Every day the same. Routines are killers, but he needed this routine to survive. A tiny conundrum.

While the cabin filled with the unmistakeable invigorating aroma of the coffee, he ran, buck naked, down to the lake, ran along the landing jetty and dived into the cold, smooth glittering water. No stylish dive, but his entry into the water made just a few ripples, no splash, and when he broke surface he was already mid-stroke, long limbs powering in unison as he back-crawled towards the far shore. Not fast, but mostly quiet. Muscle building, confidence building, life affirming natural exercise.

Then flipped over, front-crawl for the return, a wider loop through undisturbed water, his eyes always on the cabin and its surroundings, as they'd been as he'd back-crawled away from it. He had no concerns about the threat of an attack from the centre of the lake.

Back to the cabin. Dress in clean dry fatigues, borrowed like the cabin itself without the express permission of the notional owner, and the day's caffeine contribution. He allowed himself a smile. Every day now he allowed himself a smile. Life and his appreciation of life improving. Purpose to that improving and continuing life would come later. He assumed that it would. If it didn't, he had another dilemma to contemplate while sitting higher on the hill through the lengthening hours of the dark.

Every day the same. But not quite. Every day he grew stronger. Every day he felt the return of stability. Every day, he ran, walked and swam towards recovery. As the body revived, the mind followed. The body's demands dictated the routine of his life. And at some point that would reverse, his mind would resume control. At least, he presumed that it would. He'd worry about it when happened. If it happened.

3

AUGUST THIS YEAR: SPINNING LIKE A CANNONBALL

A hundred miles from home. Home? He smiled at himself. Home is where the hearth is. Home in this case was a borrowed cabin by someone else's wide lake in someone else's country. Stoner kicked down the motorcycle's kickstand and let the machine roll back until its rear tyre was resting against the kerbstone, then he stood and let the stand take the weight from his legs. He lifted his right leg over the low saddle, dropped his gloves onto the fuel tank, and used both hands to lift the helmet clear of his head. Shook out his hair, then ran the fingers of his right hand through it. A loose attempt at tidiness. 'Artisan Coffee and Net Café', read the sign in front of him. The modern neon sign of the times harmonised gracelessly with the horse tethering rail beneath it. That was worth another smile. He wondered whether he should hitch his own steed to the rail to complete the unlikely symbolism. Another small smile.

A short chorus of 'Hey!' surrounded his entry into the darkened and aromatic world of the connected café. The youth behind the counter added a final 'Hey!' and wondered whether he could help. He could, Stoner advised him, in non-threatening and quietly cultured

F/2378698

COUNTY LIBRARY

tones, with both internet access and coffee. Lots of both, the best strength available. Counter youth nodded indulgently at this latest take on a very old joke and wondered some more, about whether his customer took it as it came or sweetened and whitened, and whether he had a device of his own or needed to use one of the café's? Stoner was led to a quiet station with a set of privacy screens and a huge modern flat-screen display powered by some improbably heroic computer which could certainly land men on Mars as easily as it could handle email – the coffee, so the youth assured him – was yet more epic even than the computer.

Stoner produced a memory stick from around his neck, laid it on the desk and revealed that he was chasing up his office, needed some files from them and needed to send some to them too. 'Media shit,' he revealed. 'Been working on a couple of stories about bikers in the up-country culture, how stockbrokers on Harleys have replaced the meth-cookers as an indicator of shifting suburban alliances and...' His audience flapped a hand and retreated to produce coffee, as required.

Access to the global cyberworld was instant and clean; the coffee was hand-ground and disgustingly restorative. Stoner revelled in both, and opened a commercial website dedicated to selling flower arrangements to the recently bereaved. A fine line in black tulips, certainly, and Stoner clicked his desire to purchase three dozen of these unusual blooms, and when prompted to append any additional instructions to the expert florists he connected the USB device and left it to talk to whatever it wished. He sat back, pulled his untidy hair into a short and scruffy ponytail, and sipped. Counter youth appeared at his side and gazed in transparent confusion at the enticing displays of flower arrangements for the dear departed.

'Don't be fooled,' Stoner instructed him. 'There's more to this site than meets the eye.'

'It's all to do with... biker culture?'

'Sure it is. The site is a mask for my media contacts. Keeps everyone anonymous. I don't know who's the more scary, meth-cookers or stockbroker bikers, but I'd like to avoid the both of them. And editors are worse than them all!' He smiled. 'Do you have more coffee?'

'Yeah.' Counter youth collected Stoner's mug. 'Bring two, please. And take a ten for your time' – he handed over a note – 'I'll have company in a moment and would appreciate a little privacy. If that's OK? Say if not...'

'Not a problem. No worries.' The youth turned and walked straight into an older, unobserved black man, bounced comically off him, and saved the coffee cup from unwanted floor encounters only with difficulty. 'Sorry, sirs,' he muttered, and left, balance if not dignity restored.

'Hey,' announced the black man.

'Hey yourself,' Stoner continued the great American tradition of meaningless welcomes. He pointed at the screen, by now displaying a stylish array of petunias. 'This is taking time.'

'There's a lot there. A lot. How big's your stick?' American humour is hard to beat.

Stoner produced a handful of USB devices. 'I have more than one. I am a man of infinite resource. You know that.'

They shook hands as the coffee landed, while counter youth flapped around them like an improbably hirsute mother hen, and they shooed him away after a decently friendly interval.

Stoner raised an eyebrow at his companion's appearance. 'You look like the weekend fisherman from hell, Travis. Ivy League suits you better.' The black man beamed at him.

'And you're the backwoods biker crystal meth cooker from every deadwood movie ever made, JJ. Good to see you. You survived ordeal by county sheriff, I see?'

'He was fine. I made like the heavily damaged war hero you appear to have painted for me, which wasn't too tricky, considering, and he was fine.'

'Never mind him, JJ. How're you? You're sounding solid, but you look like shit – and I was worried you'd get shot to shit by some good old boys mistaking you for Armageddon, or something worse and more noisy. So.' He paused and sipped dangerously; 'How are you? Don't lie to me.'

Stoner untied his ponytail, shook his head as though attempting to stir up his brains, and re-tied it. 'Better. Not good. I won't lie about that. I can act like I'm good, but... it's on an edge. The slips are less frequent, but I still make them. The gaps between them are better, longer, but I still can't always predict them.' The computer emitted an electronic chime, maybe adding its own opinion to the conversation. Stoner removed the memory stick and logged out of the site.

'This... communication still secure?' Stoner slid the memory stick back onto its chain and hung it around his neck.

'It doesn't exist now.' Travis cracked the knuckles of his well-manicured fingers. 'Open it and see.'

Stoner did, called up the site he'd just closed. 'Error 404; file not found' announced the computer, also suggesting a long list of pointless strategies Stoner could employ in his quest to revive a dead entity. He shrugged and logged out.

Travis pointed at Stoner's chest. 'The new codes are on the device. Single use. Untraceable. Also on there are a stack of audio files, a pile of vids and a whole lot of data. You'll know what's useful to you and what's not. It's current as of this day, and we two are the only persons who know you've got it, and I don't have the time to analyse it all, to work out what it all means. Read it carefully. Act at leisure... if at all.'

'Pressure from London?' Stoner watched as the other inhabitants of the dark café went about whatever their business was. 'More or less intense and frequent?'

Travis spread his hands. 'Nothing unusual. An MI-something – not 5 nor 6 – tried the old-boy routine on a senator, congressman, some self-important asshole on the bipartite love-in committee or whatever they call the old boys' back-scratching post these days, but he didn't know anything anyway, and reported the contact like he should. Suspicious in itself...' both men laughed quietly, '...but not a problem. Last time my office was asked, we confirmed that we were still in contact with you, that you were one hundred percent inactive and so far as we could see intended to stay that way. It's been almost a year, JJ, they'll have given up expecting you to do the big bad wolf routine now. They chilled when we fed them the romance thing, the love interest. Plainly believed it.' He laughed again.

Stoner did not.

'Soul still on fire, big boy?' Travis's words were light, but the look he gave his companion was darkness itself. 'Do us both a favour and remember this needs to be a team game. Huh?' He tapped the table for a little emphasis and the café's counter youth steamed across to them carrying an appropriately puppy expression.

'Guys?' He beamed. Seemed that he could recognise

honest skullduggery when he saw it. 'Coffee? Something more... supportive?'

Stoner's smile was a wide and honest smile, which appeared to surprise Travis as much as it cheered the counter youth. 'You can do a spliff as well as the coffee? I didn't realise it had been legalised in this fine state.'

'Decriminalised for personal consumption, Sir,' confirmed the youth.

Stoner shook his head and spread his hands in a supplicant gesture. 'Then coffee for two, and something supportive just for me. Damn,' he turned back to Travis, 'I love America. You'd get locked up in England for that.'

Travis muttered, then let his wide white smile split his sombre black face; 'In America too, JJ. You must look trustworthy... to hippies at least. You look like an insane axe-murdering asshole to me. But I'll take a toke or two. It has been a while.

'Speaking of axes and murder, guitars and music, I'm heading to a festival in Texas in ten days. Austin. Some excellent musicians in Texas. You should join me.' Travis fell silent as counter youth delivered their refreshments, entirely legal and potentially otherwise.

'You are? I should?' Stoner did not sound convinced about the plausibility of either part of the suggestion.

'You should.' Travis tapped the youth's hand as it delivered the joint to Stoner. 'Bring another. I feel a need to be mellow.' The youth nodded and left them; a man on a mission. 'You should be there conspicuously. Play something. Start a fight or finish a fight. Steal someone's woman, get locked up. Be on the radar for a while, but making it completely plain that you're in the USA to stay.'

'I see a strategy.' Stoner inhaled, held his breath, closed his eyes, let go the smoke and reached for the coffee. Waved away the smoke cloud. He coughed a little and raised an appreciative set of eyebrows at the youth, who appeared suitably relieved. 'If I show no signs of taking the fight to the enemy, the enemy will leave me alone. Or something.'

'Or something. I do the something. In my version, the enemy sends their top troops to wait for you at your mountain retreat, and you repair to your native land and... well... do whatever you need to do to get closure. Completion.'

'Yeah.' Stoner coughed again, gently. 'Revenge. Say what you mean.'

'OK. Revenge. Oh, man...' Travis was developing his own art of relaxation. 'I should do this more often. The state should pay for this.'

'I don't do revenge.' Stoner's joint was burned down to the roach. 'I seek understanding.'

'Understanding as fatal as revenge, man?'

'Usually. But I need to understand what was done, exactly who did it and why they felt a need to do it.'

'Then what? You kill everyone who you decide is guilty? Sort of judge, jury and one-man hit squad? Or you attain ultimate enlightenment about means, methods and purpose, then fade back into the undergrowth like a good little spook. You can live in Uncle Sam's house for the remainder of your natural, y'know.' Travis leaned as far back as his chair would allow; it was a long way back. 'Or somewhere between the two.'

Counter youth delivered two more fat joints, neatly arranged on a chromed tray. 'On the house, gentlemen. My compliments. And it may be illegal to actually sell this stuff.' He smiled. 'Only rarely have I seen such appreciation on the faces of the older generation. No offence.' He smiled again.

'None taken.' Travis sighed. 'I am of the Woodstock

generation. Almost.' He produced a one hundred dollar bill from nowhere and dropped it onto the tray. 'One gift,' he intoned, 'deserves another. Please accept this as a donation to your worthy cause.' His eyes were closed.

'Woodstock?' Stoner smiled as he smoked, gently. 'I thought you saw all Glenn Miller's gigs. Certainly Paul Robeson. Thank you.' He waved away the youth.

'Seriously, Travis. I just want to understand.'

'No you don't.' Travis appeared to be asleep, but carried on talking anyway. 'You're feeling chilled because of some fine dope – Lebanese from the taste of it, certainly not Afghan or further east – and once you're confronted with your former realities your former priorities will reassert themselves and you'll... oh, I don't know... you'll kill everyone. Probably horribly. D'you think it's Leb Red? That was always my favourite, and it tastes completely familiar.'

'The coffee's Columbian. None finer. No idea about the dope. I never touch the stuff.' Stoner sounded strangely adamant, and both men fell to chuckling.

'Like the booze, huh?' Travis opened a single eye, partly. 'You alcoholic or abstinent at the moment, JJ?'

Stoner had opened the screen's windows again, had entered the information mountain that was Google, and was flicking through page after page of images. He stopped, pulled an image to full-screen, then closed it again. Repeated the procedure several times.

'Not sure,' he announced finally. 'Some days I really want a drink, so I take a drink, other days the opposite. Some days I really want a drink, so I run some miles, swim some more miles, shoot up a few dozen tin cans. You know?'

'No. I can't imagine. It's good that you're not bothered.' Travis sat up, rubbed his eyes. 'Time to return to Planet Earth, huh? How long do I have before you do something foolish, JJ? And is there any likelihood that you'll let me know what you're doing before you do it?'

'Little chance. And I don't know. Truth, Travis. That's just it; the truth. You Bureau guys are long on planning. I used to be. Now, I'm more... instinctive. Reactive. The time will always be right for something. Action or inaction. They're just the same thing, viewed from different perspectives. Doing nothing is usually harder than the opposite, and it takes a lot more energy. At some point I'll reach a position where I have to move, no matter how good or interesting or involving or intense are the distractions. When that point lands, then I'll move. I will tell you, somehow. A promise.'

Travis was looking around him. A man ready to move. 'What were you looking for in the vastness of Google? Porn?'

'Pictures of me; references to me.'

'What?' Travis's surprise was genuine. 'You can be found on a Google search? You? Mister Paranoia? No.'

'Looking for worknames,' Stoner revealed. 'Not just my own, but those of... other players. You'd be amazed at what Google turns up. Not everything out there is the truth, not everything out there gets hidden as well as it should.'

'Find anything?'

'Yeah. John Hand has a Facebook page, and it's even got some followers.'

'That's your ID, yes? One of them.'

'Sort of. I borrowed it from my deceased employer. Former employer. A decently wealthy man, John Hand, for a dead man. Active too. Demon in the sheets.'

'Hartmann? He's not very dead, JJ. Very hard to trace unofficially without arousing interest. I don't even try.

That's your war. Is he running under the John Hand jacket? Seems a curious call, you ask me.'

'Don't think so. Think it's a trawl. Think it's someone else. Are we ready to leave?' Stoner looked up from Facebook and waited for a response.

'Yeah, just about. Shame though. Enjoyed the... relaxation. And you need more of that.'

'OK. Let me try a little stunt.' Stoner dropped his hands back to the keyboard and typed, shifted screens and typed a little more. 'This could be amusing.'

Travis stood and looked over his shoulder. 'What you up to, compadre?'

'I just asked John Hand to be my very own Facebook friend. Me, Jean-Jacques Stoner, making friends with me, John Hand. Who can't be Hartmann, because he's officially not of this world.'

'You're nuts.' Travis turned and scanned the quiet café. 'What're you hoping for?'

'Hoping for? Nothing. I'm simply curious, in a cat-like sense.' Stoner collected his biker gear and approached the counter, tapped a couple of long fingernails to attract attention. Which arrived, the power of the mighty dollar bill being what it is. He smiled in a companionable way at the counter youth.

'You'll have noticed that my friend and I like to chill a little, to keep ourselves to ourselves?' The youth nodded, looking vaguely worried. 'Nothing to worry about. However, as well as my large and elderly friend here, a man you have certainly never seen and could not describe, mostly because I was here on my own playing with your excellent computers, there are another couple of guys who would like to find me. Nothing heavy, but it's always good to stay one step ahead. You savvy?'

The youth nodded, relaxing. 'Oh yeah. No worries.'

Stoner unfurled another large denomination bank note, rolled it into a neat tube and slipped it across the counter. 'I'll call tomorrow or the next day, just to check whether the other guys traced me here.'

'You reckon they can track you somehow?' The youth was plainly interested.

'They can certainly do that. What I'd like to know is whether they are doing it, and how long it takes for them to get themselves here. So. When they appear and ask after me, some Limey drinking a lot of your coffee and working on your terminals, just make a note of the time and date. I'll call. That OK?'

The youth scribbled a number and passed it across. 'My cell.'

Stoner took it, nodded thanks. 'Thanks. I'll call the shop, most likely, keeps you away from the Feds, which is a good thing for you, yes?'

'They're Feds? You got bad shit with them?'

'Not really. They just like to keep track, and I like to leave no tracks. That's a basic conflict of interest between us, which they do not appreciate and which I consider to be non-negotiable.'

'Like a game, then?'

'In a way. I want to stay private, they're nosey.' He laughed. 'But it's no big deal. I'll call in a day or two and see whether they show up. No probs either way. But if anyone lands asking for a Brit – that's me – just note the time. OK?'

'It's OK to tell them they you were here?'

'Hell yeah! Don't lie. They know already – like now – that I've been here. I just want to see how much they care about it. They're not heavies. Just a pain in the backside for a man who wants a little space. That's all.' He turned away, then turned back, Travis blocking his path to the door. 'The dope. What was it?'

'Lebanese, man. None finer.'

Stoner turned back to Travis. 'No one, but no one, no one at all loves a smart-arse.' Travis grinned wider than a smile, and they left together.

***

Beautiful midsummer. Roads in the American north-east ripe with family fun. Campers, SUVs, trailers toting everything from smaller cars to quad bikes, trikes, boats, jetskis and light aircraft. And motorcycles of every conception, size, shade and ability, ridden by riders of every size, shade and ability. Stoner rode within ten percent of the limits, positioned himself carefully and obeyed every traffic instruction. His Harley-Davidson, a current model Sportster – nearly-new, dammit – with few added extras and sporting the standard Federal silencing, was wholly unremarkable among the ragtag road rabble, ranging from serious long-haul tourists with their Gold Wings and Road Kings, to ace racers on their oriental rice-rockets and the statemental rebels of the road, helmetless, gloveless, clueless and slow. Stoner ignored them all, waved to no one, passed many along the road and was passed by many more.

The miles mounted, and after an uneventful seventy or so of them, he swung off at a wide interchange and headed for a rest area. Parked. Visited the restroom to return his cyber-café coffees to the grateful planet from which they sprang, and exchanged coins for a bottle of chilled water and some Trail Mix, a combination of nuts, fruits and seeds to fortify the inner man. The inner man who had the munchies. He was waiting; waiting for the evening to arrive and for the very few other travellers at the rest area to head out on their own highways.

He enjoyed the quiet, a time to sit, to think and to feel an increased confidence in his own returning sense of balance, of control. He sipped and chewed, while shadows stretched out around him and his inner calm expanded.

Another man joined him, unbidden and unwanted. Another biker. For solitary souls, bikers are often strangely gregarious. Stoner nodded an unspoken greeting and returned his gaze to the woodland countryside as though it were his favourite work of art. A painting of woodland countryside, maybe. His new companion was speaking. Stoner listened to none of it, just nodded, companionably but with no added encouragement. Another three bikers joined them, one man, two women. All of them wearing the patches, regalia and insignia of some apparently terrifying biker gang. Stoner waved a hand companionably, got up to leave.

The original intruder called out words to the effect that Stoner's bike was a girl's bike and that only a woman would ride a machine so devoid of charm, a machine which was uncustomised, was as it had left the factory in Milwaukee. Stoner turned back and smiled.

'It is what it is. It's how I want it to be. Ride safely, now.'

'Oh listen to him with the crazy Limey accent,' one of the women called out. 'Another weekend warrior pretending to be a bad-ass.' They all laughed.

Stoner bowed, politely enough, and widened his smile. To anyone other than Grade One assholes he would have appeared dangerously feral. His present companions were either blind or stupid. Both, maybe.

'We not good enough for you?' The woman was

incapable of leaving it alone. The men nodded, like chimps.

Stoner looked at her man. 'Not really,' he said, quietly. 'And I need to be going.'

The two men rose rapidly to their feet, moving fast, their movements familiar and co-ordinated. Stoner faced them. They were both big men, at least as tall as him, and much the meatier. He shook his head.

'We don't need this, guys. Let me by, and I'll be on my way. Live and let live, that kind of thing.'

'Thing is,' remarked the younger and larger of the two. 'Thing is, mister suburban hero, this is what you might call a polite request for some additional funding to help us on our way – our own way. An act of charity; a donation to assist your fellow bikers.' His sneer was a calculated insult. 'We accept all major currencies, but cash only, no cards.' The pair laughed at their joke with the familiarity of long use.

Stoner glanced around. The parking lot was almost empty apart from their small tableau, and none of the few others present showed any interest. In fact, the remaining tourists were leaving, plainly preferring to avoid any unpleasantness which might interrupt their holiday enjoyment.

'There's no help out there, mister,' continued the leader of the – small – pack. 'We don't want any grief, just whatever cash you have. Maybe your watch. You know how it goes down.' The women had joined their men, and appeared just as mean. The younger of them pulled what appeared to be a cosh from somewhere about her person.

'Come to momma,' she suggested in a voice that may once have sounded sweet.

'You'd not like that. Momma.' Stoner moved towards

the silent older woman, and punched her hard in the neck with his left hand. His right hand swung his crash helmet into her face. Her nose certainly broke, such is the contrasting solidity of nasal tissue and polycarbonate crash helmets. Maybe a cheekbone too. She screamed and reached for her face. Both men moved rapidly towards him, reaching inside their clothing for weaponry of some kind. Stoner kicked the woman he'd punched behind her knee and thrust her hard at the approaching men, dropping the helmet and turning fast, hitting the younger woman in the ear with his right hand and relieving her of the cosh with his left. Pivoting some more, he kicked her feet from under her and swung the cosh sharply against her head as she fell. A sickening, flat, hollow sound came from the impact. A wet sound. And he stepped backwards over her, facing the two men, who had stopped. One of them had pulled a revolver from his jacket, the other a knife. The two women were making a lot of noise.

'Shoot me now,' suggested Stoner. 'It's your only hope. I like to fight, and I fight to win. This is great. Thank you for the opportunity. You'll only stop me with a bullet. Shoot me now. Don't miss. A wounded bear is an angry and dangerous bear.' He held his jacket open, enticingly.

The would-be gunman raised the revolver, and stumbled, dropped the gun. His companion turned and stared at him. The black handle of a knife had sprouted in the gunman's neck; the black tip of the black blade protruding through the hair of his neck, lifting the leather of the black cap he was wearing. As the seconds lengthened, the tip of the blade incrementally sliced through the leather of the cap, alien black and gleaming, as the material parted before its hard edge, the last energies of the throw fading.

Stoner turned to the other man. 'Would you make a statement to the law that I acted in self-defence? It might help me a little. He'll die, I think.'

'Fuck you.' He ran at Stoner, who sidestepped and felled him using the cosh he'd taken from the woman. The last man fell silently. His impaled companion was still standing, eyes wide and pleading, fingers holding the handle of the knife as though wondering what to do with it. Both women were weeping, one of them more in complaint, in anger than in distress.

Stoner walked around the static grouping, up to the would-be gunman.

'This will hurt. It'll most likely be fatal if you can't call 911 soon. Hold your windpipe together with both hands and sit down. Keep your head up and wait for assistance. Do not fall asleep. Tell the paramedics that there'll be nerve damage in your neck, to be careful round back. And have a nice day.' He slipped the knife out, wiped it on the man's badge-bedecked jacket, collected his helmet, the revolver, and paused while the players in the minor tragedy before him collected what wits they had.

'Crash helmets save lives,' he revealed. 'Your thought for the day.'

He walked to his unremarkable and plainly style-free Harley-Davidson, fired it up and rode away, heading as raucously as the mufflers would permit for the highway and out of sight of the stricken outlaws. But before he reached the road, he swung the bike around, rode slowly and almost silently to the far end of the reservation, parked up by a dusty black pick-up truck and switched off. He could hear some unhappiness from the would-be bandits, but the approaching evening and the sounds of the traffic blanketed most of it, and the unfortunates would be unaware of his actions.

He unlocked the pick-up, dropped its tailgate, pulled out an aluminium ramp and rolled the motorcycle up it, into the bed of the vehicle, tied it down with strong ratchet straps. Pulled a vast and dirty tarp from the loadbed and shrouded the machine, tied it all down in its turn. Then he pulled a duffel bag from the cab, changed out of his riding clothing, with its leather and its protective Kevlar, replacing it with less restrictive denim and cotton, all of it still black and branded with the logos and slogans of his favourite motorcycle manufacturer.

The Ford's big petrol engine fired up instantly, and together man and machines left the scene. Quietly, unlit, unobserved and unremarked through the shading haze. Headed north, a little north-west, and north some more. It was developing into a beautiful August evening, and Stoner felt well. He felt more alive somehow, and he wondered whether the biker boy he'd knifed would die of it. He didn't wonder for too long, though. It was a fine evening for a drive. The perfect end to a perfect day.

4

OCTOBER LAST YEAR: PLENTY OF ROOM
DOWN ON THE FLOOR

Every day the same. The rhythm of life returning. Arise from another night on the forested mountain. Walk, swim, run, walk, swim. Exhaust. Relax. The peace of mind that comes from sheer tired-out exhaustion. Wash, swim, bathe, run. Eat and drink. The cabin's rations appeared to have been intended to feed a decent family – there were four beds – for maybe a whole summer, with additional dietary proteins provided by fish and rabbit, maybe deer. Stoner had managed fish and he'd managed rabbit. His running was much better now, smoother, quieter, faster, so maybe a deer would join the menu soon. But cooking on a paraffin stove, lighting by a paraffin lamp, no butter, cream, milk. The only dairy products in his regime were cheese and tinned milks; condensed, evaporated. No eggs, few fresh greens apart from wild plants he recognised. A hard regime, but healthy. His health was excellent, his weight falling steadily. Eyes clear, muscles hard, hair and fingernails growing at a scary rate. Mind screwed. Every way he looked at himself, every attempt at positive thought, he was simply screwed. Screwed and screwed up. Screwed tight.

Every pause in his routine, every attempt to consider more than his immediate situation, every relaxation resulted in chaos. Mental horror stories. Tears. Violence against trees, the cabin walls, but not against himself. The demand was there sometimes, a demand that he wreak vengeance upon himself for his blindness, his failures, his misplaced trust and his woeful over-estimation of his own abilities and judgement... but when it was at its height he would run again, swim again. Chase elusive deer, and stalk what he thought could be pigs. Distract the self-destructive drift of his mind by considering the ways of the theoretical wild pig.

As his mental balance improved, so he returned to the military mindset which had carried him safely through operational tours in several seriously unpleasant theatres. Observe, plan, investigate, conclude and summarise. Terrain, topography, patterns of light, darkness, sound and silence, and any unnatural interruptions and deviations. His routines were all centred around his base, his HQ and its immediate environment. After food, after a swim and the bracing bathing which was as close as he would ever get to godliness, he would select an animal track into the woods, and would orient himself with the sun, moving with ever-increasing strength, silence and purpose through the woods, keeping the slowly moving sun as his marker. He wore no watch, counted time only by the internal rhythms of his body; pulmonary resilience and the current state of his digestive process. Every day's outing on that day's heading lasted a little longer than the previous.

Then the turn, his mentally plotted arc, sun before or behind him, depending on his mood. He wanted no predictable patterns. There appeared to be no one there to observe and predict, but his horrid levels of insecurity and painful paranoia bred ghosts for him. He knew they were spectres, that they were unreal, and was grateful for that awareness, but the effect on his mind was as real and solid as if they'd been invading Viking hordes intent on his destruction. After maybe a month, he would have welcomed the Vikings; he spoiled for a fight. He was developing a passion, a need to kill. Which was how he brought down – ran down – his first small deer.

As the scope of his daily sweeps grew longer, as his strengths, both physical and emotional, returned from chaos and weakness to routine, rhythm and resilience, he became increasingly conscious that at some point he would encounter other humanity. Either other woodsmen or their properties. The area around the high lake was statistically unpopulated, but there's a margin of error in all things. In any case, there was a settlement – a town, maybe – as far away across the lake as it was possible to be. It was lit at night, so it plainly boasted streetlighting and the modern amenities demanded by urbanites. He occasionally saw lights in the distant woods at night, too, so there were some other active souls, hunters, nature lovers, independent mountain men, refugees from the law, whatever.

At some point, he knew, he would need to take a trip into town. But not yet. Not for a while. Not until he was more his own man and less the running coward of his nightmares. He wanted to fight someone. Anyone would do. But not here. He needed a plan. Any plan would do. But not yet.

After maybe thirty-five days of solitary manoeuvring, he found a track, wide enough for a vehicle, rough enough to discourage anything without all-wheel drive and decent ground clearance. He followed it, for maybe an hour, maybe three, four miles until it reached a metalled road. Then he aligned himself with the declining sun, and started to run. The angle of decline was correct, the solar orientation was correct, he knew where he would end up. And he did, reaching the old parking area where he maintained a change of clothing, ignored all that and ran back to his borrowed cabin. His base. Night was rushing in, now. he collected his rifle, his waterproofs, his groundsheet and a thermos flask of strong black coffee, and he returned to the hillside, constructed a fresh hide, a shelter, and settled down to watch the water. He half-dreamed of Vikings, and they always attack from the sea.

***

Another day, wet, cold, dark. Mists would lie on the lake all day. Any attack, any approach to his base would have the advantage that its sounds would be muffled by the mists and their drip, their constant slow inner rainfall. He calculated for that, though there was no need, as he was slowly understanding and accepting. No one was actually likely to attack him. He recognised that. However, the military synonym for paranoid is survivalist, and Stoner's military life had all been about surviving. And killing others. Killers understand and appreciate the great symmetry of their profession. To kill their targets they need to survive being targeted themselves. As in the military, more so on civilian streets.

He enjoyed his coffee. Contemplated the cabin's reserve of paraffin fuel and understood once again that a visit to a town was one day closer than it had been yesterday. He had no wish to visit a town. He considered burglary as a working alternative. It was, he decided, time to meet the neighbours. Or at least it was time to visit their empty properties. The dirt road he'd stumbled across hadn't been driven for quite some time. Hard to guess, as he wasn't entirely familiar with the growth rates of plants here in the mountain and upland lake country, but probably not for a year. At least. Maybe a couple of years. Maybe they'd have a few spare gallons of paraffin, and maybe they'd not miss them.

The chores. The mind-saving routines. The body cleansing and balance restoring rituals. He performed them all, recognising as he did so that his mind was healing as his body hardened. That as the fracturing inside his head knitted itself, so the flab of a civilised lifestyle was leaving his muscles, which were tightening and lightening, becoming tougher and stronger. Both his body and his brain were preparing for a fight. Flight was over; the time to fight was still over the horizon, but its presence was inescapable, looming insistent, and oddly welcome.

He set out. A different track to the previous day's, but heading in the same general direction. If his interpretation of the mountain topography was even approximately accurate, he could expect to encounter the rough road a little later, a little further away and a little closer to the human habitat which most likely was the road's destination. Which proved to be correct. He saw the cabin around a bend in the track, left the track edge and moved into the woods themselves, set up an observation post, an OP, smiled to himself as he recognised what he was doing, and resisted the temptation to discuss his strategy and approach with non-existent fellow combatants. He remembered that his days as a military team player were more than a decade behind him, but that the ghosts of his former comrades, some fallen, others fate unknown, would always be with him at times of stress and duress.

The cabin gave every appearance of being left long ago. There were lots like that in the hills and the woods. Stoner sat and watched it just the same. He moved around and set up another OP, watched it some more. As the sun passed its peak and commenced its long slow roll down through the afternoon, he approached the silent cabin from its most blind spot, peeling back the skirting intended to keep unpleasant critters away from the building's underbelly, and drifting himself beneath it.

Another wait and watch. More silence. The crawlspace was dry, uninhabited by anything visibly threatening, and access was clear enough across the width and length of the building. Utilities were boxed away from the main area, and Stoner moved easily over to consider them. He levered away the bug- and rodent-proof panelling to reveal a decently large volume, only part of it taken up by waste disposal pipework. And there was a hatch upward, which yielded to gentle quiet pressure; no locks, just a simple slide catch, operable with a blade, and smooth quiet hinges. The hatch did not fold flat with the floor above. Instead it rested against something inside the main building.

Stoner lifted his head through the open hatch and surveyed the interior. Which was very dark, but entirely unremarkable, as cabins in the woods go. No zombies, screaming banshees or large men with larger weaponry waiting for the chance to harm him. He'd not realised how wound-up his system was, nor that he'd been holding his breath for so long that he needed to release it in a comical sigh and to rush down the replacement air. Stale, but not unpleasant in any way. Nothing major had died in the space above him. Not recently.

He swung himself up, steadily, smoothly, and his slow caution was rewarded when his head made gentle silent contact with the table which stood over the trapdoor and against the legs of which the hatch itself was resting. He'd managed not to concuss himself, and had avoided making more noise than a SWAT assault.

The cabin was empty. Everything in it was old and cold, faintly damp. It had been left tidy. Kitchen utensils put away into their cupboards, hung onto their hooks. No food waste nor dirty clothes. The darkness was because shutters had been closed against the windows, dark to repel the darkness. The whole appearance was that of a cabin closed up for the winter; not the most recent winter, so probably the one before that.

There was no paraffin. Stoner discovered a lean-to containing gas cylinders and a minor mountain of well-seasoned firewood for the swept hearth, several bookshelves stocked with a wide variety of books, all of them well handled and plainly read more than once, all of them fiction of the recreational variety. This had once been a home and could become one again with little effort. There was no sign of rainwater damage. He approved, decided against removing a trophy or any of the small stock of tinned food, and left the way he'd entered, carefully refixing the shuttering around the utility access, and looking in vain for a means to secure it against future burglars. None. An unexpected omission in such a well-maintained property. He set off by another looping and deliberately generalised route, heading home.

Home. That thought again. A thought which should bring with it comfort, not caution, solace instead of solitude – a line of thinking which occupied his recovering mind while the rest of the organism undertook navigation and watchful security while it walked him back to the cabin he tried hard to consider to be his home.

Viking attack comes from the sea, from the water. The boat was heading directly to his cabin, heading steadily with no attempt at concealment. It held its course in the afternoon's damp daylight, the beat of its engine steady. Stoner took the rifle, checked its action, packed his pockets with ammunition clips, shrugged on military camo clothing and a shapeless hat, slipped from the rear of the cabin and into the dripping woodland, positioning himself roughly halfway between the cabin and the shore, maybe a quarter-mile from each. He sank down into the patient watcher's comfortable squat, waited and watched, rifle resting across his lap.

The boat, a small cruiser with a cabin and the capacity to carry maybe a half dozen men, cut its engine and drifted onto the shingle beach. A single man, a black man in a suburban interpretation of a countryman's garb, dropped into the shallow water and splashed ashore. No attempt at concealment. His posture, size and shape were familiar to Stoner, who watched him steadily, with more of his attention on the boat than on the visitor. And he considered; if this visitor had arrived even two weeks earlier would he have been shot without the opportunity to explain himself? Stoner decided this was the more likely option. He was plainly improving within himself.

'Hello!' the man loudly announced his presence with a disingenuous lack of originality. He looked around him, ignoring the cabin in favour of the concealing woodlands surrounding it on all sides but the beach. 'I'm alone. Unarmed.'

Stoner stepped into view, rifle in plain sight. Nodded his recognition.

'Senior Special Agent,' he said, loudly enough to be heard by his visitor but no more than that.

'Deputy Director, now. Well; Associate Deputy Director. I'm glad you still sound like the same pain in the ass Brit, because you sure don't look like Sergeant Stoner, retired.'

'Associate Deputy Director Travis. Almost a pleasure.'

'All yours, Stoner. Can I lower my hands now?'

'Are you really unarmed?'

'Of course not. Do you think I'm stupid? You could have been anyone. Almost anyone.'

'Are you really alone?'

'Yes. And it gets worse.'

'OK.'

'My office and PA think I'm in Texas.'

'Maybe you should be. Better company in Texas. And it's warmer. Drier. Good music. You have a PA? In these days of budget cuts and international austerity?'

'Yeah. Everything you say is true. The rich shall inherit the earth.' Travis dropped his hands, but left them hanging at his sides, still in plain view. 'D'you want to inspect the boat? It's empty, apart from some fresh milk, eggs, decent cheese and a lot of fresh greens. Some… ah… alcoholic relaxation, though I would understand if you'd rather I drank alone. We can unload it in the morning if you prefer. I am staying the night.'

Stoner walked silently towards his visitor. 'It's the meek. You are?'

'I am. Correct me if I'm wrong. You've been sleeping up on the hillside, watching for invaders, and walking recce during the day. Am I right or am I… the other thing? The meek?'

'You're correct. The meek shall inherit the earth.'

'They're welcome to what's left after the rich arrogant guys have gone. It was my view when I left the field office yesterday that by this time you would have worked yourself past shooting me on sight, and that you would be considering moving your bedroom indoors, where only the righteous sleep easily. Am I right?'

'You are.'

'It's good to see you, Stoner.' He held out both hands. 'I have no reason to lie.'

Stoner approached, dropped the rifle's butt against the ground and shook his visitor's hand. 'Yes you do. Everyone can find a reason to lie if they need one. I can't see why you'd need a reason, but my vision has been notably poor – most notably in the time preceding my... vacation in your friendly country. How did you find me?'

'I didn't. Not exactly. I heard stories – grim stories – and set this place up for you. Cleaned and provisioned it.'

'You – what the fuck? – you knew I'd come here?' Stoner's surprise was as genuine as the rifle between them and the death it concealed.

'Mostly. I set up two other hides just in case. You'll remember which and where. No?'

'Yes. I chose this...'

'...because it's closest to the Canadian border. Yes, I thought you would. I set up the Texas house too, because of Mexico, and... you ahead of me yet, Stoner?'

'Lafayette, because of the New Orleans music and the big bayou.'

'Exactly. Now, you may be superheroman who feels no cold and is impervious to damp, but I'm an old, overweight desk pounder who needs to get some warm and some dry outside, while he gets some hot and wet inside. Can we do this please? Soon?'

'Did you bring paraffin?' The two men walked up towards the cabin through the evening's darkening drizzle.

'Paraffin? Travis sounded amused and a little mystified. 'You got... ah... digestive problems?'

'Fool. For the heat and the light. I'm low on paraffin.' Stoner shrugged his shoulders. 'It's not much of a problem for a man on his own, but I'd like to maintain a standard when I entertain a guest. It's a British thing. We all remember empire.'

'Fool yourself. Hold on a second.' Travis looked around him in the gloom. 'OK, it's a while since I stayed here myself, and back then I was preoccupied. Where's the john?'

Stoner shrugged. 'I prefer a more nature-centred approach; bears are not alone in their ability to shit in the woods. And you can never have too much nitrates, so forth, for healthy plants. It's behind that stand of Mountain Ash.'

'Oh Christ; you've gone native. Gone survivalist. I should have thought about that. And your head's fucked up, too.' Travis walked carefully to a clump of trees and opened the door to the small single-roomed structure they concealed, reached and delved inside. He returned. 'You somehow failed to notice the electric light switches? Your skilled observer's superhero vision failed to observe the electric cooker, light bulbs, little things like that? The damage is worse than I thought.' Travis sounded more amused than concerned. Stoner maintained his silence.

As soon as they were inside the cabin, Travis flicked a switch and a dim half-light took the harder edge off the complete darkness. There was a quiet cough and a clatter, followed by a small remote hum. Stoner stood in stationary silence, considering.

'That would be the generator, former sergeant. The generator for the electric lights and the electric heater and the electric stove. We are civilised in America, we know that to return to nature and we know that to live the woodsman dream a guy needs electric light and a decent shitter.'

'It's... noisy,' said Stoner, lamely.

'It drives away bears, vampires and werewolves while at the same time pretending that there's a civilised human being here.' Travis shrugged off his coat, hung it on a hook behind the door. 'You look like shit, Stoner, but it is genuinely good to see you. Can you remember how to make coffee? I left a lot here for you. Beans and a hand-mill, too.'

Stoner hesitated with a moment of motionlessness so intense that even Travis fell silent in sympathy. Then the Brit embraced the American. 'Yeah,' he said. 'You too. Coffee. I can do that. If nothing else... coffee.'

***

'Welcome to America.' Travis raised both his hands in a complicated mock salute. One hand contained steaming hot coffee, the other ice-chilled whiskey. Everything in balance. Stoner nodded in response. His expression wandered loosely between watchful and bewildered.

Travis sipped at the coffee, downed the whiskey. 'You up to telling me about it?' He refilled his glass and gazed into its depths, shifting all focus from reality to somewhere else.

'About what?' Stoner's own focus was upon the coffee. Stimulant to counter his increasing relaxation. He stiffened and straightened. 'About what?' His attention triggered from the safety of his drinks to the disguised danger of his companion. 'About...' he paused. Raised his glass to his lips. Stopped, then put it down untouched. 'I need... A little assistance would be useful. What do you already know? It may be that you know more than I do.' He sputtered to a stop. More coffee, taken slowly to improve the effect and to prolong the experience.

Travis ignored the peculiar performance and spoke anyway.

'The rumours were everywhere.' He nodded to himself. Sank another whiskey and poured again. 'That you'd gone rogue. Gone...' He paused. Considered. 'That you'd taken down your employer and taken up with the operator he'd set you to find and to eliminate. Your employer being the august Mister Hartmann, universally known and disrespected as the Hard Man, with unsubtle soldier wit. A Britgov man. A man from the very bosom of power, the mother of parliaments. A man...'

'For fuck's sake.' Stoner interrupted him. 'I know who he is. Spare me American fucking humour. It's like hot lead on the eyeballs. Interesting but fucking painful.' He stopped and restarted himself.

'Hartmann set me up. There's no way around it. That's what he did. He set me on the trail of a killer he'd set running himself.' He paused, leaned forward and sipped, slowly. 'He set up a sequence of killings, simple covert contracts to remove his own organisation. All the paymasters who funded his operations and who knew what those operations were. Or...' he paused again. 'Or who were in positions to uncover what he'd been doing if they were instructed to look for it.

'He used a fresh set of contractors. He set me to finding the identity of the killer he'd set rolling. Bizarre. Brilliant, too. I reported to him. Every time I made a connection I told him.'

'You found the killer?' Travis was carefully not watching Stoner. He applied no pressure at all. The cabin light was dim, easy on the eyes.

'Yeah. And... It was inevitable. I didn't see it at all. Simply didn't see what was slap-bang in front of me. I was the final target. Me gone, the Hard Man would have been free and clear to move back out of the shadows and back into the political mainstream. Powerland. Simple and clear. Outstanding elegance. I find his team of fresh killers, we have a sort-out and either I take them down or the other thing. They're a team of three – three women – and new, hungry, fast and fit. I was sloppy and wanting out. Killer combination. And he was fucking my woman. I'd not even seen that.'

'I heard that. If it's too painful... no need to go there.' Travis exhaled tangible understanding and calm support. 'Not yet.'

'He... she... Lissa, my woman. A hooker.' Stoner searched for sense. 'She always hated him. Always told me she hated him. Then she... she... was setting up home with him. How? She invited me to visit. I didn't really understand whose was the big house. Didn't understand her game at all. Still don't. She might be dead. I don't know. I think the Hard Man had her killed. On vid. In front of me. Killed by a... by... by a friend. Mine. My friend.'

The two men sipped in silence. Stoner was shaking, steadily, nodding to a frantic beat audible only to himself. Travis looked on, not judging. Then he spoke, softly but with an exaggerated clarity and precision.

'You going to get through this, JJ? Are you? You look bad, and you're not making a lot of sense.'

'Yeah. Tell me. Surprise me.' Stoner threw the contents of his glass into the flames of the fire. Alcohols flared, a pale nothing against the hard crackle of the dry wood.

Travis again. 'You can have this place for as long as it takes. You should know that.'

'It's off the books, right? Some dark ops hideout? And I'm an illegal in an off-books safe house. I can see that lasting well. Not.' Stoner's focus was as flat as the tone of his voice.'

'There is no off-book, JJ. None.' Travis stood, slowly and with caution. Stretched his arms high above his head, lowered them to his hips and swayed, easing internalised tensions. 'The Bureau knows I'm resting an asset here. The cabin's in the inventory. Always was. No one will disturb you, but when you're feeling... rested, you could call in at the sheriff's office. Sound local man. Ex-mil. The Bureau's field office is aware that this place is in use, but not who's here or why. They won't disturb you. They've already told the sheriff we have a resident. So the locals won't disturb you either.'

'I'm an asset?' Stoner's smile appeared genuine enough. 'A bona fide guest of Uncle Sam? Who would've thought it? Who will they think I am? The boys from the Bureau?'

'They've no need to know, and they don't know, don't want to know. We have a lot of badly burned operatives... resting. The wars do that. The guys work too hard, take too-hard knocks and need to rest afterwards. Then they either draw down the pension from a grateful nation or they return to the field.'

'And die there.'

'Usually. Usually they die there. Don't know why. They return to the deserts which broke them and they die in those deserts. Usually under black flags. Which side they're aiming at doesn't seem to matter. They just fight and die.'

'I won't be doing that.' Stoner's voice was steadying all the time. 'No flags; black, stars and bars, union red, white and blue. No causes. There are no causes. Only excuses. And I've run out of those.' He looked up, flapped a hand at Travis, whose attention snapped to him, eyes steady, no trace of the drink in them. 'Is there a way out for me? Would I be useful to the Bureau? Useful enough to justify the cost of the damage I could cause? Because...' He stopped in silence for a while. 'Because I think the only way to balance my brain would be to clear up the fuck-ups around me. Tidy it all.'

'Or die trying.'

'Yeah. That.' Stoner stood again, walked in a random way to the fire, deliberately turning his back on Travis, presenting a clear and vulnerable target. 'Because I would die if I took them on alone. And I can't see how the Bureau could support me. If there's a reason for that support, then fucking hurrah, but tell me what it is. I can't hack any more duplicitous shit right now, Travis. Associate Deputy Director Travis. Is that as senior as it sounds? I was never too clear about the Bureau's seniority tree. Looks more like the Freemasons than a security club.'

'Fucking senior. Too fucking senior to waste my time – my expensive and valuable time – on a burned-out whack-job.'

'I thought we were friends.' Stone turned to face him and smiled.

'There could be that, also. Depends.'

'On what?'

'On whether you're a Brit loyalist or your own best friend, former sergeant Stoner. On whether you'd work with an interested party at your back.'

'An invisible friend?'

'Invisible, even imaginary.' Travis's tone was interrogatory.

Stoner nodded. 'Give me a while, then. Can you

do that? I need to kill the demons and I need to start sleeping again. Can you supply intel?' His curiosity appeared to be both genuine and increasing.

'Oh yes. Intel we have weeping from our satellites' butts. You're welcome to it. But but but. I have to ask. You've always had your own sources; good and reliable. Your own men in black. You know who I mean?'

'I do. Why are you suddenly talking like we're being overheard? Are we? Fuck it anyway. Until I trust someone, I trust no one. No one.'

'You need to trust me, Stoner.'

'Not true. I just need to believe you want something from me that will keep me useful to you. That's enough. That watches my back for me while I've got eyes only forward.'

'That's bleak, man.' Travis leaned back and watched Stoner take a seat again, both of them stretching towards the fire's heat. Stoner threw two hard logs into the flames.

'Not bleak, Associate Deputy Director Travis. Just honest. At least one of us should try to be honest.'

Travis gazed with quiet fascination into the flames. 'You could be very useful. To the Bureau, and to me. You can see that?'

'Yeah.' Stoner nodded. 'It's clear enough. Do these walls have ears?'

'Who knows? None of mine, none I'm aware of, but caution is the mother of survival.'

'Invention? Necessity?'

'Those too. We all need those. How far away from functional are you. Stoner? Be straight about this, please.'

'A month back I was dysfunctional. Entirely. I set up routines, rhythms to find a path. Did that. It's coming back. How functional do you need?'

Travis continued his study of the flames. 'Long term. Decently long term. That's if I'm making an investment rather than rescuing a friend. Do you have a plan?'

'No.'

'That's good.'

'Really?' Stoner's surprise was genuine enough.

'Yes. Plans fail. You always were an improviser. Always admired that. Reckon you'll work through your routines and return as that improv performer?'

'Feels that way.' Stoner paused for consideration. 'Yes. Yes it does. It's...' he paused again, reflecting. 'It's sleeping under the stars again. Sleeping outside, battlefield security. Constructing a hide and working it. No passing trade, none. Taking down a deer to eat. Fundamentalist. The animal organism working as intended. How long's your patience?'

'A year. Take a year, Stoner. Spread out as you need to. Do you need housekeeping? ID? Funding? Ordnance?'

'None of those. But thanks. You'll be watching me? No need to deny it. If I'm active I'll need to recognise your good guys.'

Travis had closed his eyes, but opened one now. 'If you were me, then you'd not trust anyone you saw, unless you had a reason to do otherwise. If... if I were you. I'd only trust me.' He stopped again. 'Remember Father Jean?'

'How could I forget? That was me. You really do think this place is bugged?' Stoner didn't appear concerned by the idea of their being overlooked.

'I was thinking more of his favourite godly sister. And bugged? Like I said before. I don't know. But I also don't know for a fact that it's clean, especially now the power's back up. I'd expect something low level, so recording rather than realtime.'

'My sister? Yeah. What about her?'

'Courier, maybe. Support.'

'She wouldn't do it.'

'Reckon she would.'

'OK.' Stoner's weariness hollowed out his voice. 'Bernadette. I'll talk to her if I need to talk to her. If I don't... I won't. She's done her stuff for me. I want her left alone. She's been hurt enough. Tell her nothing about me. Keep your goons away from her.'

'OK. And why, by the way?' Travis had closed both eyes again.

'Why what?'

'Why didn't you kill Hartmann, the Hard Man?'

'That was a mistake. I... I thought he'd either die, or that he'd be so discouraged that he'd just leave me alone. That's what I actually thought.'

'You said that.'

'What?'

'That you thought he'd leave you alone. Idiot. Didn't you know him better than that? Fuck, Stoner, I know him better than that and I don't think I ever even met the man. How badly did you hurt him? How functional is he now?'

'Compared to what?'

'What? Fuck knows. Compared to you.'

'Better than me. Undamaged apart from... I stuck a blade through his throat. Doubt that he sings like that heavenly chorister these days. Apart from that, he should be OK.'

'You missed the carotid?' Travis sounded incredulous.

'Yup. Accurate, me. I wanted him to get a message. Easier to kill him. Much easier.'

'You should've done.'

'Maybe I was considering my immortal soul.'

'Maybe you were.'

'Maybe I was just sick of the whole squalid business.'

'Maybe so.'

'Maybe... I just made a mistake.'

'That's it. But he's alive and hates you, now and forever amen.'

'Seems like.'

'Spoken to him? Or are you going to let that hot lead do the talking for you?'

'No idea. None.' Stoner reached for his empty glass. Lifted it to his lips, sipped air and set it down again.

'How'd you get into the country?' Travis shifted subjects like drivers shifted gears.

'Canada. You know that.'

'Yeah, surely. But you can walk the border if you want. How'd you get into Canada? That's what I meant.'

'Boat. From the sea. Like a Viking. It's not hard. You guys should take a look at it. Easier to get inside ol' Uncle Sam than into Vlad's Mother Russia. Much easier. Came here from there, in fact.'

'Russia? You did? What were you doing there? You enjoy living dangerously. JJ. You welcome in Russia?'

'Always have been. I was there on holiday. I'd been told that Hartmann was dead. By a friend... by someone else I trusted. Doing badly on that side of things.'

'You reckon?'

'I can see room for improvement. I always did o'erflow with the milk of human kindness, me.'

'You're sounding much more like the Stoner of old, Mister Stoner. I'm sure it's an improvement. Mostly an improvement. Maybe.'

'Yeah. Seriously, it comes and it goes. Sun goes down, so do my spirits. Sun comes up, I feel better. New day, new life. Days getting very shorter very soon. Which is a subtle manly way of saying that I'm glad you showed up. Thanks. And for the cabin, also. I knew you'd find me, somehow.'

'It's easy enough, modern surveillance being what it is...'

'Didn't mean that. I meant...'

'I know what you meant. Just joshin'. Just a little light before the night. Before the dark. Do you really need to clear house back home, JJ?'

'Yeah.'

'Then do it. Just don't rush into it.'

'Yeah.' Stoner walked to another chair, kicked off his boots. 'First night indoors in a while.'

'How's it feel?'

'Strange. Nervous.'

***

Dawn lit, grey and dripping. Travis hauled out of his chair, stretching, aching, yawning. Looked around. No sign of Stoner. The long gun was missing too. He walked to the bathroom, ran water long and hot, drew a deep bath, climbed in and relaxed. Dozed again. Tiredness, bad sleep, booze and fresh air.

Sometime later, his cooling dreams were driven off by the smell of coffee. Strong, black and bitter, and by the bustling of bacon frying.

5

AUGUST THIS YEAR: WE'RE ALL STILL HERE...

The tall man, gaunt too, watched and waited. He watched and he waited for another tall gaunt man. Overlong hair, thick, overgrown windblown beard. He watched and he waited in dark places. A predator. It felt good to be a predator once again. To stand, chewing something, half-in and half-out of shadows, the shady places where the nobodies went in search of becoming somebody, if only for a short time. There was a lot of choice, a lot of potential.

The predator, the tall gaunt animal, selected his quarry. Two men, one of them similar in build to himself, the other unremarkable to the point of invisibility, walked past him, past the mouth of his notional net and into it, into the quiet, unremarkable alleyway. The leading man, the man who superficially resembled the waiting predator, showed something in the palm of his hand to the invisible man at his side. Who nodded, passed something of his own to the leading man in exchange for the package he'd inspected and approved. Both men nodded, the invisible man left the quiet alley, the blind alley. The leading man, the superficially similar man checked the contents of his side of the exchange, nodded and lifted a cell phone to his ear. Telephone light briefly lit the quiet alley, then was extinguished, the phone dropped back into a pocket somewhere.

The predator struck in silence. He came from the darkness and was standing in front of his victim as though from somewhere darker even than the darkness around them. The victim registered surprise, opened his mouth to speak, swung his eyes to his side to seek escape, and the predator snapped the heel of his right hand into the victim's nose, following the crunch with another, harder impact as the stiff fingers of his left hand wrecked the throat of the victim. Who attempted to cough, attempted to draw breath and to swallow and failed at all those simple tasks. He stumbled, threw one arm to his side in an almost unconscious attempt at balance, holding his other arm before him in an equally unconscious attempt at protecting himself. He fell to his knees and rocked forward and back, panicking as he failed to breathe, and as consciousness drifted from him and as his automatic systems took over from his fading volition and its panic, so he began to breathe again. Badly, rattling horribly and beginning to fall, eyes closed, arms dropping to his side, as his lights dimmed and his face accelerated towards the ground.

Stoner caught him, sat him down, leaned him backward so his compressed, bruised airways cleared a little. Reached into his pockets and removed everything he found. A surprising amount of money, scattered around his clothing in pockets, the lining of the hood of his jacket, rolled inside a rolled-up watch cap, itself in an inside zipped pocket. Two cell phones, one of them demanding attention from someone. He ignored that. A wallet. A driving licence with a photo that might pass. He loaded the lot into a shoulder bag, left behind the contents of the drugstore in the victim's pants pockets, dropped him into an approximation of the recovery position, and in the centre of the alley, where he'd be visible... should anyone come looking, looking for adventure, or for theft, more likely.

Nature always provides. Stoner relaxed at the entry to the alley, leaned against a wall and thrust his hands into the pockets of his black jeans; as unremarkable a man as the rest of the other thinly scattered night crawlers who patrolled the dark and who kept themselves as safely far from each other as was possible. He felt good. Maybe it's the gods who provide. Stoner raised his eyes skywards as if seeking answers. There were no answers in the skies. There never are. The skies are just skies, be they ever so romantic, beautiful or packed with miserable clouds, as tonight. Stars look better than clouds, and moonlight shines bright. The gloomy dull dark cloudscapes matched Stoner's purpose for the night. Fundraising. Another spare ID. Nature always provides for its predators, provided they have the smarts to look for this bounty and to recognise it.

So far, so good. Three rolls had produced a few inches of banknotes, a total of five cell phones and three knives, none of them any use at all except maybe for a little ostentatious cleaning of the fingernails. Time to move, to cast a wider net, to prowl a little more into the dark territories which were at once alien and utterly familiar. As he moved further into the street, two black men materialised from the dim sodium-lit murk, one either side of him, both at least his height and both substantially more massive. To their obvious surprise, Stoner steered their company away from the less dim lights and towards deeper, quieter shadow.

'Buddy, can you spare a dime?' His voice was maybe a little rough due to a recent lack of use, but the message was plain. The man to his left managed a chuckle. A deep dark knowing chuckle, intended only to intimidate, not to share any available amusement.

'Don't shit me, white boy.' His dark voice matched his dark chuckle. His companion remained silent, drifted away from the conversationalists as though to maintain a watch on the uninterested streets. 'You looking for something? Pussy? Dreams?'

Stoner continued to walk unhurried into the shadow. 'No,' he said. 'I'm looking for a benefactor.'

'Yeah. They're common here. They roam the hoods looking to give themselves away.' The two men were out of direct sight of the third.

'It's like this. Look!' Stoner shouted and jumped high, startling the man before him, and turned in mid-leap, and brought his two hands down hard, slamming a cell phone into each of the black man's upturned white eyes. One of the phones lit; maybe inspired by the wit of the conversation. The stricken man screamed and clutched his face, flailing through tears and bellowing like a man who's had two phones pushed into his eyes. It's an unmistakeable sound, a sound like no other. Stoner instructed himself to remember it for further study at a later date.

And he ran to face the black man's black companion, who was walking unhurried towards them, extracting a handgun from his belt and taking his time about taking his aim. Stoner took no more time than was necessary to run flat out behind the gun, which roared a shot into the night, killing only every other sound and spawning a sudden tense silence. Stoner's impetus carried both of them backwards, and he twisted his entire body to his left, pushing the black man's gun hand away from them both as he hooked his right foot, heavy with its black

Caterpillar boot, behind the armed man's own right foot and pushed, bracing himself against his left leg and the armed man's body.

The armed man had no such brace, and he fell, awkwardly, thrusting out his gun hand to break his fall. Of course the handgun fell from his hand. Of course Stoner was waiting for it and scooped it up from the ground before it had slid away from them both.

He caught his balance, turned back to the disarmed man, and smacked the pistol – a decently weighty automatic, too heavy and clumsy to be a decent SIG Sauer – against the fallen man's temple, extending his already impressive period of silence into the indeterminate future. Then Stoner stretched his neck against any possible whiplash injury resulting from his high impact speed and relatively sudden stop, and kicked the man in the side of his head. Only once, but once was enough for the heavy black Caterpillar boot. Which was shining where it had no reason to shine, a leprous yellow-black reflection in the vague sodium streetlight. Blood then. No reason for worrying about an early wake-up from his most recent sparring partner. He returned to the original man, the conversationalist.

He was sitting in a wet gutter, holding his hands to his eyes, and heard Stoner's approach.

'You blinded me, man.' Not a scream, not a shout, simply a statement. Stoner warmed to him at once and knelt at his side. Rested the handgun on the fallen man's thigh.

'Recognise what this is?' He tapped the muzzle of the weapon close by the fallen man's groin. A silent nod was the response. Message received. 'Let me take a look. Lower your hands… and be sensible, huh?'

The eyes were a mess, but both were intact, so far

as Stoner could make out in the less than bright light of their street. Stoner rose to his feet again.

'You'll need a medic. They should be able to do something for you. Fuck up your needlework, though. Empty pockets time. Make like I'm a robber and you're the vic here. Make like this sad-ass robber's got one fuck-off great cannon aimed at your nuts, and it will be clear to you that you should co-operate fully.' His voice was a fine impersonation of an Appalachian drawl; he felt proud of it. 'Then I'll call 911 for you. Honest injun.'

The black man did as suggested, in a possibly dignified silence. Stoner dialled the number and smeared any possible prints before handing the phone over. He picked up a second gun, two impressive rolls of banknotes and a pack of Hershey bars, as well as two spare ammunition clips and two bunches of keys. Money and munitions joined his earlier trophies in the shoulder bag. He patted the wearily speaking, maybe blinded man on a shoulder, muttered 'Thanks for the dime, buddy,' and returned to the stationary silent body in the street, wondering how long before the dark protection of the night was ended by blues and twos, by running and shouting, by barriers and scene tape. More ammunition, more rolled notes, several sealed baggies of powder and a further bunch of keys, car keys this time, complete with a remote locking plipper.

He stood, listened for a while to the returning noises of the night, eventually nodding to himself in silent confirmation that sirens were calling him. Then he walked back the way he'd come from, thumbing the car remote until an answering flash and a comic bleat introduced him to his ride home.

***

Town turned through wasteland and into suburbs. The accidental loan car rolled smugly and softly through acres of identikit housing, all made out of ticky-tacky, all looking much the same, until it pulled over, into the shadow beyond the last street lamp. Stoner flicked one of his stolen cell phones into bright life and keyed in a number he could never forget, a long international number. He wondered briefly whether the appropriated service package included international dialling. But his wonder was fleeting; after maybe three rings the called answered the call.

'Hey, Bili.' Stoner's voice caught a little in his throat, stumbled over the sudden breathy silence from the faraway receiver. He cleared his throat. 'How's tricks, babe? Sorry it's been so long. Really sorry. It's... ah... it's JJ. How're you doing?'

And the conversation once begun lasted longer than the stolen cell phone's stolen batteries. When the *son et lumière* died into silence, Stoner stripped SIM card and battery from the phone, dropped them at the roadside, and drove away. The sky was lightening to his right as he headed north.

6

The lone gunwoman wriggled for comfort as the thunderstorm drenched the land. She was alone. The best audience; that audience of one. The solo performance. She was talking again. To herself. Again. 'Where's the fun in this?' Water rattled the roof of her hide. 'Thunderstorms in December. Nearly fucking Christmas. Hideous, shitty country.' She felt a little better for a little light venting. Focused the long sight once again on her target. A cabin. A wooden cabin, nestling into the woods above and to the side of the wide lake. Dim light from shuttered windows, closed despite the morning hour. She was warm, dry, comfortable, calm. And she was in no hurry. The cabin's inhabitant had appeared briefly the previous day, long enough for a definite identification and a photograph, flashed through the ethers to her controller, far, far away. She was sure she had the right man in her sights, but had been instructed to wait until confirmation was forthcoming. As it was, within five minutes.

She glanced at the watch wrapped around the outside of her camo jacket's left sleeve, its face on the inside of her wrist so it presented itself to her as the hand held the stock of the rifle and she took stock of the situation with her target. Ten minutes, she decided. In ten minutes she would take her morning coffee. Strong, hot and black, courtesy of modern survivalist kit. Perfect for the lone gunwoman, the solitary assassin, the lady in camo and shadow. Perfect. The rain was easing. Maybe her target would come out for his swim, or maybe his run or maybe he'd run out naked as a babe in the woods and jack himself off in full view of Mother Nature's privacy before relieving himself into her beautiful lake. Men were like that, generally. Men were pigs. And there were far too many of them.

She really needed coffee.

She really did need that coffee. But she needed to hang onto her discipline more than she needed the comfort of the caffeine. Her face was wet. The understanding almost broke her concentrations, but they held firm. Discipline once again. She was in focus. Focus on the crosshairs and focus on the dimly glowing hands of her wristwatch. Her focus was sharp. She was disciplined. In total control. Total. Her face was wet. She eased her control and glanced up to see where the leak in the roof of her hide was, whether it was likely to worsen, adding to the load on her discipline. She saw no leak, no telltale drops nor drips. A dry inside surface. She aimed her gunny stare back to the target, passing across the wristwatch and noting coolly, efficiently that less than five minutes remained before she could relax a little and bask in the embrace of a caffeine high, As her eyes returned to the gunsight, the wetness on her face, on her cheeks, increased noticeably, and the water was hot water, not cold. Tears, not rain. She blinked her eyes in fury and disbelief.

Three minutes, then coffee.

The cell phone resting on her right hand hummed briefly. She lifted it, keeping its dark side facing the cabin and read the SMS message. 'Sitrep?' it said.

'No visual,' she returned, and closed down the phone. Checked the wristwatch. Coffee time. If the target appeared while she was savouring her morning delight, then he'd live a little longer. Such is the unexpected and unrecognised power of the coffee bean. Humour. A tiny joke. She felt like sharing it. Then she cried a little more and willed the target to appear so she could aim low and injure him, maim him, hurt him, so she could take her time and savour the kill shot. She delayed her caffeine moment for a further five minutes as punishment. The sky lightened and the rains eased, smoke rose from the cabin's chimney. Of her mark there was no sign. She rested the rifle on its stand, and pulled a self-heating mug of coffee from her small, two-day stash. Waited patiently, broke the seal and breathed in the familiar beautiful aroma. Fresh tears. She let them loose. Better out than in. Who said that? A truly stupid comment. Better out than in? In what possible sense? The coffee was delicious.

The door to the cabin opened, a figure appeared, backlit by the glow from inside the building. She watched him with almost no interest. He would be the target, almost certainly, though it was impossible to be accurate at this range without the magnification of the telescopic gunsight. She simply did not care. This was her own time. Down time. Coffee time. She sipped and watched with the power of just her own fine eyes. Her tears dried, forgotten. She sipped, sighed, sipped and sighed again. The figure was walking down from the cabin to the path leading to the lake.

She resealed her coffee mug as best she could, and with a conscious ill-grace leaned into the rifle. Focused.

Confirmed once again that it was the target. Aimed, controlled her breath, took first pressure on the trigger, controlled her breath and fired. The target buckled around the impact. A gut wound. The gut. Exactly where she'd aimed. A bigger target than the head. Easier to hit with a single round. He fell to his knees, clutching at himself, sank back onto his heels and opened his mouth wide. There was a noticeable delay before the echo of his scream reached her ears. She reached for her coffee. Let him live a little longer. In pain. His pain, her gain.

The coffee cooled, she sipped and watched her fallen target, who was occupying his dying moments with an heroic but doomed effort at sliding himself backwards, on his arse, to the perceived shelter of the cabin. The wooden cabin. Not a formidable defence for a fatally wounded warrior, if warrior he was, but dying inside probably felt a little more civilised than dying outdoors, stark bollock naked, sat on your grubby arse, trying to hold your guts together in the pouring rain. She could see the appeal, and maybe her opinion of her victim rose a little. A very little. And he was indeed making slow progress, slipping and sliding steadily reversing towards the closed door.

She finished the coffee, replaced the lid of the mug, and returned the assembly to her kitbag. Considered her instructions. Contract killing was carried out for money. Money was paid only on completion, like buying a house, a car, a business, and the detail was the devil. In this case, the detail advised her that the target was to be taken down outside the cabin by a rifle from a distance. She patted the stock of the heavy and accurate Dragunov. And looked once again through its telescopic sights, almost into the eyes of her victim. He looked right back at her. Spooky. As though he knew where she was. Maybe he did. Maybe in an earlier life he too had been a shooter. That was common enough; taking down redundant operatives was all part of the cheery routine of her profession.

She took the weight of the rifle once more, focusing again and controlling her breathing. The image was blurred, soft, out of focus. She adjusted the focus ring. The blur remained. Something failing with the sight? Her sight, her own sight, not the sights on the rifle. Tears again. She rolled away from the weapon, slid gracefully out of the hide and trekked through the rain and through the soaking woods, approaching the cabin not as a crow might fly, because she would need to swim the lake to manage that, but as a killer with murderous intent might walk.

And finally she stood facing the wounded man. The rain was not easing at all, though the air temperature was falling. The background sting of the rain through the trees was far too loud for her to hear any words which might have been directed her way; his lips were moving and his eyes held her eyes in their glare. The rain washed the tears from her face. She could feel the hot water chilling as it ran onto her cheeks, flowing freely now, washed away by the rainwater, the same rainwater which diluted the steady blood loss. He'd ceased his attempts at gaining shelter, whether from her or from the rain. Or both. They simply held station; woman wearing a soldier's camouflage, man wearing only the rain and his own blood.

He lifted his hand, leaned back so she could see the bruising around the small hole, the pulsing of the blood, the flow rate of which had eased as his efforts at movement had ceased, and when her gaze lifted from the wound to his face, he mouthed a word she needed no sound at all to understand. Why? His lips formed the word and his eyes hammered home the sense of it. Why him? Why not. Why was the small puncture hole killing him? It wasn't; that would be the exit wound round back which had left a trail of bodily ruin behind him as he crawled backwards towards the cabin.

Quite suddenly and completely, she was tired of it all. Sickened by his accusation, she walked behind him, laid the length of the dull black serrated blade against his neck, beneath his beard, and she cut. One slice, applying all of the considerable strength of her arms and pulling his head back against her knees. He didn't struggle. Not at all. Hot blood flowed down his chest, rapidly at first, running between his legs and over his thighs and past the ruined rest of him onto the old and filthy wooden decking of the landing stage. The rate slowed rapidly, and the hand resting to take the pulse from the carotid artery lost that single sign of life with a bland absence of drama.

She replaced the knife's molecule-sharp edge against the neck again, sliced again, steadily pulling the blade as hard towards herself as she felt wise. Coated carbon steel encountered the strong bones of the neck, and she dropped the head to the deck, walked around to face her man, knelt and completed his decapitation. The eyes in the head stared, no longer seeing, expressing nothing at all. No last thoughts, no sign of a departing spirit. Just dead eyes in a dead face, fronting a dead head. She lifted it by the hair and walked to the door of the cabin, her tears still falling, though she was unconscious of them.

The door opened for her. Warmth and a gentle light welcomed her. She accepted both, stepped inside and closed the door behind her. A calm room; with the door closed the rain was silently outside. A fire burned, well-banked to remain lit while awaiting the dead man's return. In the centre of the main room, the only room she could see, stood a stout table. Pine, maybe. She placed the head there, careless of where its eyes were aimed. They were seeing nothing; those lips would never betray her nor her weakness.

A desk. Against the wall. Papers, clutter, she ignored them all, instead collecting the inevitable laptop computer, lifting its lid and booting it into life. It ticked, clicked and displayed a familiar window to the digital world. She ran through the available options, finally opening a browser and connecting the remote cabin with the wider world's web, flickering her fingers with expert ease until the entered a site, a too familiar site; MurderMayhemandMore, a fansite for sickos, a site for eyes so tired of life that they craved images of death, death real or faked, no difference, simply death. And she activated the laptop's own tireless eye, lifting its gaze until the dead, oozing head was the centre of all its attention; single digital eye recording the dulling of a pair of organic eyes, and the bloody weeping from the remains of the neck below them. Then she connected webcam to website and left them to delight each other in the shared mindlessness.

The bathroom was small, but it was comfortable, and contained a decent shower. She stripped, folding her clothes neatly over any and all available surfaces while the water poured with force from the shower head and heated to a decently scalding temperature, rather to her surprise. And as steam steadily condensed around her, she looked at her only truth. Looked at herself, naked in the full-length mirror, fit, sleek and beautiful, wiped the drying damp tears from her eyes and nodded.

'For you, Chas. Always for you. I will forgive you for dying, but not... not yet. Fuck it, Chas, fuck it all.' She ran to the mirror, kissed her own cold lips in hard reflection, stepped under the boiled water and showered away the tears, the weakness, the blood, the rain and the pain of it all. Towelled dry with a terrifying vigour, dressed herself, and piled everything flammable she could find before the open fire, pulled logs and coals from it, setting an unstoppable conflagration into the dry wooden heart of the wet wooden cabin. She discovered two containers of paraffin in the small kitchen and added their contents to her bonfire; dragged a gallon of what smelled like petrol from its place outside the rear door, under the awning protecting the pick-up which rested there, and poured that onto the piled paper, furniture, luggage and rubbish and departed, leaving the dead head's immolation to be transmitted to the wider world until the flames of its pyre consumed the computer.

Even the rain had paused. As the day grew towards noon, she collected her rifle, the signs of her presence, returned to the old all-wheel driver and headed away into the east where even the sun was attempting to rise for her. And at the border of two countries she paused, parked the vehicle, slid down from it and turned around to offer a tired, weary, wasted valediction to the world she'd left in flames.

'*Croeso y Cymry*', read the sign. 'Welcome,' it repeated pointlessly, 'to Wales'. She shook her head and gazed dry-eyed and cold back along the deserted road she'd just driven.

'No fucking welcome here, sister,' she muttered, turning back to the vehicle. 'No fucking welcome at all.' She lifted herself back into the driving seat, her seat, only hers. 'Welcome to a place where total fucking strangers go to get whacked by other total fucking strangers.' She slammed the lever into first gear. 'The welcome home for the totally fucked.' The old engine growled its agreement, heading back to England, home of no friends at all, and only one surviving sister...

7

DECEMBER LAST YEAR: SATURDAY MAYBE

Small town in America. Telegraph poles, supply poles, random parking, snow, ice and the coarse grumble of old engines running forever cold. Steamed windows, steam from breath, steaming exhaust. Stoner walked. It was too cold to stand still, even if he'd wanted to, which he did not. Pedestrians huddled, solitary in their shared stoicism and concentration on the sidewalk surface; grip or no grip, glide or slide, walk, don't walk. Walking was faster than driving, more risk involved. Anonymity guaranteed within layers of insulation and waterproofing. Stoner walked.

Until he found the café. The self-proclaiming internet café, a sign of its times, caffeine to combat the cold, wifi to handle the isolation. He took a small table away from the leaking freeze of the street door, dropped dripping coats over the back of the spare chair, eased himself slowly into the seat facing the main door, his back to the welcome warmth of the kitchen, moving slowly, cautiously, like the invalid he was not, attracting no attention and meeting no gaze until he was set up. Positioned. In place. Then he coughed into the quiet, raised his gaze to catch that of the morning waiter, raised his eyebrows and maintained his quiet until that worthy had arrived and moored up by his table. Standing cool in spite of the welcoming ambient warmth.

'Coffee,' he said.

The waiter rattled off a string of variations on a caffeine theme. Wound down eventually. 'Sir?' he asked. He asked a second time, possibly nervous that his sole customer had fallen to sleep or died as the unwinding litany of beverages available had been revealed to him.

Stoner smiled. A strange facial manoeuvre, unfamiliar somehow. He wondered briefly whether it looked as odd as it felt. 'Hot.' He paused. Shook his head. 'That's no use, is it? I'm sorry. It's early.'

'Jet lag?' suggested the youthful servitor, helpfully.

'Say what?' Stoner's incomprehension was plain to them both.

'You're a Brit, right?' The youth pressed on. 'I wondered if you'd just flown in.'

'Like a goose,' Stoner's smile was drifting a little. 'Brits and geese, flying north for the winter.' The waiter was beginning to appear a little nervous. 'No.' Stoner was more focused. 'I came by ship. May I order some coffee?'

The waiter began to repeat his catechism of caffeine, but fell quiet as his customer flapped a hand and shook his head, the smile vanished and was replaced by a weary resignation.

'One espresso,' Stoner managed. 'Just one.' The waiter nodded and radiated encouragement. 'And a bottle of sparkling water. And then a mug, a beaker, a jug – the biggest bucket, whatever – of filter coffee. White, cream, milk, whatever. You choose. Espresso first.' The smile returned. Stoner resembled a man recently released – or possibly escaped – from an asylum.

'Food?'

'What?'

'Anything to eat?'

'Jesus.'

'What?' The waiter was regretting introducing further variables into an already confused negotiation.

'No. Yes. Bring me a Danish.' Stoner held up both hands in a gesture of surrender. 'You choose. Whatever's best today. That'll be fine.' The waiter left, the street door opened, admitted three more customers, two men and a woman. They stamped their feet and split up, the two men heading for the counter, the woman to a table by the window. The waiter greeted the men as though they'd relieved a siege, but not as friends or as regulars. The woman nodded to Stoner, who nodded back, after a pause. Then he lifted his shoulder bag to the table and removed four cell phones. The woman stared at him. He ignored her, and lifted a small soft case from an inside pocket of his heavy shirt, opened it and spilled an assortment of SIM cards and cell phone batteries onto the table. He looked up then, beamed at the woman. She turned away and studied the menu closely, plainly seeking revelation in recipes, divine intervention in a diner.

By the time the excellent espresso had landed, Stoner had fitted batteries and SIM cards to all four phones, turned them on and lined them up before him. He sipped, then blew hot air onto his fingers. Raised his eyes to the hovering, faintly bewildered waiter and summoned the smile from its lair.

'Good,' he supplied. 'Great coffee. Thanks.' The four screens on the four phones had lit up in their several ways, and Stoner gestured at them. 'Family, friends, the office. They all want something.'

'The wife?'

Stoner shook his head. 'Never had one. Not really sure what they're for. What you're supposed to do with them. Like Christmas trees come summer.' The woman at the table by the window smiled to herself and looked outside while her companions obligingly carried her refreshment to her. Stoner picked up the left-hand phone, tapped its screen and began to read. The other phones dimmed, then lit again, seemingly at random. He replaced the first, lifted and read the second, then the third, then the fourth, then the first again.

'Can you rent me a laptop?' He'd attracted the attention of the increasingly busy waiter. 'Also maybe some breakfast?'

The waiter beamed and accelerated to his table. Paused for a deep breath and launched into a list of figures, specifications which might have meant something to someone, but that someone was not Stoner, who held up surrendering hands and an expression of polite bafflement.

'Fast as you like, decent net access speed. Don't know don't care about anything else. You know more than me and...' he paused and produced a wide attempt at a grin, 'I don't care what it costs. How's that?' Stoner magicked a twenty dollar bill between his fingers. 'Breakfast too, like I said. Something fried. Hash browns.'

'Grits? You want grits?' The youth was encouraged by the sight of the bill.

'Whatever. Whatever you think will keep this old Brit running and active for the rest of the short dark day, huh? That OK? I've a lot of catching up to do. Old friends far away. Missing me. You know what I mean?'

The twenty vanished, connected by cosmic force to the waiter, who rematerialised with a high end laptop.

Ten minutes, maybe a little more, and the waiter

returned, poured a dose of coffee into Stoner's cup. He stood for a moment or two, waiting for thanks or acknowledgement, but neither was forthcoming. He left.

Ten minutes, maybe a little less, and the waiter returned, placed a piled-high plate before his customer. He stood for a moment or two, then snapped his fingers and walked around the table so he could see what Stoner could see. 'Hey, man...' Speech started, then stalled. Both men contemplated a severed head, a head perched upon a plate. This was a video; every so often a background shadow moved, the light changed. The head did neither. There was a tentative flicker, as of a flame, off to one side.

'Man...' the waiter breathed, stared, breathed. 'Is that, like, for real?'

No reply. Although Stoner's face was pointed towards the screen, and although his eyes were open, there was little sign that he was looking at what those eyes were seeing. The waiter pulled his attention away from the screen and back to his customer. He reached a decision, leaned forward and closed the screen of the laptop.

'Thank you.' Stoner had returned. Consciousness had revived in him.

'You OK?'

Stoner considered for a long moment. 'Yeah,' he decided. 'Took me by surprise. That's all. It's a murder fansite, murdermayhem...' Interruption took over.

'Yeah. I know,' revealed the remarkable waiter. 'There's a load of them. Lotsa them based around, y'know, movies. Make like they're for real, like snuff, y'know, where they really kill the actors? But they don't. It's all make up, make believe. You see the same actors – the dead ones, all right? – in other movies, so they're not very dead, are they?' Logic restored, his theme changed. 'Food OK? You want I should heat it some more?'

Stoner shook his head. 'This is cool.' He sank the coffee, winced, and tapped the empty vessel. 'Chance of some more?' He took up his fork and set to work on the piled plate, eating fast at first, then slowing, until maybe halfway down high-calorie hill he was chewing with concentration, with focus and with evident pleasure. 'This,' he remarked to no one; 'this is very good.' The waiter was back behind his counter, his attention taken by customers settling their checks and raising their collars against the white outdoors.

'August,' she said. She reached out a gloved hand. 'You're a Brit, right?' Stoner looked up, chewing steadily. Said nothing. Chewed more. It was the lady from the table by the window. Of her paired companions there was no sign. He swallowed, looked at her hand, then back up to her face.

'December. And yes. Brit.' He ignored the offered hand. His own hand held the fork, poised to slice into a small mess of beans, somehow separated from the larger mess by a sausage of unfamiliar provenance, shape and shade.

'Brits don't shake hands, then? They used to when I was in England.' She smiled at him. He laid the fork down carefully, wiped his hands together on a paper napkin and looked up to her. Placed his unshaking hand palm-down on the table.

'It's an etiquette thing. A performance. Skin to skin. Mano a mano, or some such nonsense.' She removed her gloves, offered her hand again. He took it, folded two fingers into her palm so that his long hard filed fingernails made their impression, and held the grip. 'Hand,' he supplied, 'John Hand.'

'Like Bond, James Bond?' She smiled. 'I'm not the first to say that, am I? May I sit?'

'No, and yes of course. If you like. I'd like to finish this. OK with you?' He'd already resumed his eating. The fate of the unknown sausage was sealed. It drifted, disconsolate in a sea of beans. She sat. Watched as he ate, his attention directed to his food. The waiter reappeared, refilled Stoner's cup once more, held his jug in front of the lady, tapped it in a staccato question. She shook her head and replaced her gloves.

'Aren't your hands cold in here, Mister Hand? Your fingers look white, chilled. You've been outside a while. Takes a time to warm through.' Stoner was mopping at his lips with the paper napkin while she spoke to him. He shook his head.

'That's what the coffee's for. I pour it away as it cools, then laughing boy over there refills it with hot stuff and my digits are reheated.' His expression was bland, flat, largely unwelcoming.

'I'm interrupting something?' She made obvious preparations to assume the vertical position.

Stoner paused, sighed. 'Yes. I have a stack of things to do. I'm sorry. I'm maybe letting down the Englishman's famous reputation for politeness and bonhomie, but I do have a stack to do.'

'A rejection!' She laughed.

Stoner smiled in response. 'That was an approach? August is short for Augusta? Augustine? A gust of cold wind? I'm sorry to disappoint, lady, but I need to press on. It's going to take me all day at this rate. And in any case...' he nodded towards the window. 'Your buddies will freeze out there if you stay in here too long. Great to meet you. We'll do it again someday I'm sure.' He lifted the laptop's screen between them. The image of the severed head was gone, replaced by a stack of overlapping menus and adverts for unimaginable pleasures of the fantasy kind.

She stood, no trace of a smile. 'See you,' she said, and was gone. The waiter watched her leave with patent surprise.

'Pie?' he wondered, directing Stoner's attention to a display cabinet. 'Fresh sometime earlier in the year when fruit was in season.' Both men laughed. Stoner turned back to one of the cell phones, waved away even more coffee. Tapped the phone's screen, held it to his head, to his ear. And then he listened. Tapped the screen and waited. Sipped. Shrugged off another layer of warmth and bulk.

'Stoner,' he announced finally to the phone. 'No, you heard right. It's the real thing. Less frothy, maybe a little bitter, but the real thing.' He listened some more, eyes without focus, expression without warmth. Around him the café trade ebbed and flowed, ignoring him entirely. Lost in plain view. An unremarkable tall, trim, slim man with too much hair in a land of remarkably similar men. Fit men. Not the sleek winter weekend gymnasium Geronimos, who hunted from comfort and luxury, returning to city safety, trophies bagged, boxed and heading for a freezer in an overheated house. Not those. He resembled the men who lived around about. A logger, maybe. A physical worker, almost certainly. Talking into the cell phone at last, after a long time of listening. Nodding too, but with reserve, patent patience and distance, scrolling the screens of the laptop before him as he talked.

The brunch trade gone, a sandbar of calm found the waiter – the same waiter – returned to the table. Interrupted. 'You're running up a tab,' he announced, with neither stress nor distress. Stoner looked up and smiled at him.

'OK. Point taken.' He reached into his bag, extracted a dirty green roll of paper money, unfurled a selection, shook it out a little so the denominations were visible, then folded four fifties together. Handed them over. 'I could be here all day.' He held the waiter's gaze. 'Is that a problem for you? I can't eat and drink endlessly, but like I said already, a table charge...' he paused. 'A table charge is not a problem for me. I just need the signal and the rental.' He tapped the laptop. 'I like this; clear screen. Do you have some earphones? A headset?'

The money did its traditional disappearing act, as did the waiter himself, though he returned a moment later with a tray of savoury snacks, nuts, pretzels and their ilk, and handed over a plastic-bagged headset. He nodded and smiled. 'Stereo,' he said, 'wi-fi hi-fi,' and answered a summons from another table.

Stoner settled the earpieces to his ears, leaned forward over the screen, shifted the mouthpiece to catch his quiet words while obscuring them from neighbouring tables. 'Back again. Yeah. In a café. Cool or what.' Not a question. 'You seeing what I'm seeing on the murdermayhem site?' He listened some more. 'I'm nowhere near you,' he revealed finally. 'Unless unbelievable coincidence finds you somewhere near me somehow.' He paused. 'I do believe I would feel threatened by that.' Another pause, a listening pause. 'OK. Tell me what I'm looking at. Who? Where? When? It can't be live.' Pause again. Nodded. 'In a diner like I said, so you speak louder and listen more carefully. I can hardly start shouting.' His voice was, if anything, quieter than before.

'Don't believe you.' There was no rancour in his voice. 'You're the only person I know who does this kind of shit. So tell me why you're pretending otherwise, why you're involving me, and tell me why I should be involved. There's… there's a lot of things I need to do before I start… being human. If I still know how.' He listened some more.

Eventually. 'OK,' he said, closing the screen he'd been watching and replacing it with a new directory, deleting all the temporary internet files and the search histories he found there. 'I'll call you when I'm ready for your help. And Chas… hold it together til then, huh? It won't be very soon.'

The routine of checking all the cell phones repeated itself. The diner's population changed and shifted, rose and fell, ate, laughed, drank, talked and passed on. In a bubble of his own, noticed only by the waiters, Stoner dialled again on a different phone. Sat back and blew out smoke from a cigarette he was not smoking, sighed, closed his eyes, spoke at last.

'Yeah. You knew? You've been waiting for the call? OK. Of course you have. Where am I? Thought you guys would have known more about where I'm at than I do myself. You must be slipping. Is this a rare attack of humanity? Wish I was there to witness it. You could do humility too, if you're feeling extra playful. Of course you'll trace the call. That's why I'm calling you. It's time I was found.' He paused for a while, listened and considered. Replied slowly. Clearly.

'Of course we'll meet. Of course. Whether you're aware of the time and place before I… ah… catch up with you depends on how well – if at all – I can force myself to believe your answers.' He breathed and listened. 'Well done. You'd worked out I'd be asking questions. Do you know where I am yet? Good. Not entirely losing your famous golden touch, then. Can you fly?

'Oh well done. No tedious jokes about how if the gods had wanted you to fly they'd have provided wings. How tight is your fix on me? Very good. Very impressive indeed.' Stoner flapped a hand at his pet waiter, who arrived, pronto. They spoke a little, and Stoner waved him away again.

'Boston has a large Harley-Davidson dealership. You can find it easily, it's called Boston Harley-Davidson. I just checked. They have a very cool café, serves heavy coffees to encourage punters to part with their cash on a new motorcycle. Forty-eight hours, then. My time. I'll be very early. And...' he paused. 'And although using names on this thing might be a hazard to one of us – that's to say, not to me – coming with any form of malice aforethought would be a poor move. Got that? Great. Fine and dandy. Cool. See you then.'

The routine. Cell phones, their SIM cards and their batteries, separated from each other and stored in their own soft cloth bags, protected from harm and from each other in separate pockets. Bills paid, camaraderie of the internet's secrets acknowledged and shared between Stoner and his waiter, and heavy outdoor clothing fitted, adjusted, hung and tightened against the cold. Anonymity in bulk. A hat to improve the insulation and to disguise the profile.

Stoner slid a discreet final gratuity beneath the last survivor of his coffee onslaught, moved to the main door and left. He walked straight into the afternoon gloom, crossed the filthy street, looked for and found a department store with several entrances, strode to the main of those, entered and immediately left by another minor door, hunched his shoulders against the cold and the onset of evening and walked as rapidly as the slushy sidewalk would permit to the lot where he'd parked his wheels, one indistinguishable pick-up in an ocean of others. Climbed aboard, fired up, dragged a map from its cubby, consulted it, lit lights, switched on wipers, shifted the lever into drive and gunned out into the traffic. Snowflakes swirled and flurried in the lights as he headed for a freeway; road to the big city. Hard to follow in weather like this, and impossible to spot a follower. He didn't even try. Why bother?

***

An airport called Logan; Boston Logan. Two most likely flights, then. Two flights inward from the UK. To meet the deadline he'd imposed, Stoner's inbound guest would need to be aboard one of these two flights. Stoner waited in arrivals. Too warm. Overheated for the weather. The terminal's microclimate suited those who dwelled endlessly in aircon. Anyone who existed in the outside world and ventured into the terminal warmth was in danger of dozing, drifting away from a state of alert.

Stoner walked. Airports are good for walking, vast and flat. He moved endlessly, relentlessly restless. The first flight's arrival was announced. Along with a small army of others, Stoner moved to meet. He mingled; one large man in bulky clothing among a population of large bulked-out men and their smaller, brighter female companions. Like them all, he scanned for the familiar face, the familiar posture, the familiar gait.

Nothing. The crowd cleared after Customs had cleared those the crowd were crowding to meet. No one. Stoner waited. Leaned against a wall, assumed the body talk of the driver, maybe, the driver whose fare had failed to arrive. Eventually he sat. The terminal cleared, and he cleared with the porters, the assistance staff and sundry uniforms, moving back to a general concourse with cafés and seats. A long wait. He sat and scanned an unwanted menu. Chinese, maybe Thai, oriental certainly. An oriental man slipped onto the seat to his left. Stoner looked up, looked to his left.

'Mister Stoner.' The arrival picked up a menu and opened it. 'Is this food?' He shook his head. 'Welcome back to life, Mister Stoner. Welcome.'

Stoner returned his attention to the menu. Waved over a waiter and read off a list of item numbers. 'Eating by numbers, Mr Tran. What is the world coming to?'

'What indeed?' His Asian companion nodded sadly. 'There are many excellent Vietnamese restaurants in Boston. Not as many as on the west coast, but enough. You will feel less uncomfortable eating here, though. So we shall. And I will talk. I will talk and I will answer questions. And then I will leave you so you can meet your friend off his flight.'

'That would be Mallis,' Stoner remarked. Mr Tran nodded. 'Did you... did you delay him?' Mr Tran nodded once more.

'I cannot believe that they understand what tea is, Mister Stoner. So I believe I will drink only water from bottles.' Mr Tran shared his decision with a colossal shining waitress, who glided away, mysteriously light despite her astounding bulk.

Six bottles were delivered to the two men, along with several plates, steaming with a tang of ersatz orient. The oriental of the two diners considered each dish, finally snapping a pair of chopsticks and delivering vegetables, noodles and sauces to his own plate. He considered the characters scrolled onto the handles of the sticks, smiled, gently. 'A sense of humour, Mister Stoner.' Stoner looked up from his own consideration of the food, raised a questioning eyebrow.

Mr Tran smiled some more. 'In case your archaic Mandarin is rusty, the suggestion on the utensils is that the bearer should... ah... live long and prosper.'

'A generous sentiment, Mr Tran, hard to fault in these difficult times. Why are you here?' Stoner picked up a fork and lifted the most obvious meat from the mound of wilted greenery. 'I was expecting someone else, as I said already.'

'To the point, Mister Stoner. Not even a pleasant how do you do for me? A greeting, one friend to another. We are friends, are we not?' He transferred his attentions to his plate, scooped up more vegetables with precision and accuracy despite their slimy coatings, and chewed, slowly at first, then with increased relish. 'Very good,' he announced, pausing. 'Very good. Almost food. Certainly edible. If Burger King made Chinese meals, this is what they'd make. A good impersonation. Fake food in the land of fakery. Mister Stoner. You have questions. One friend to another. Friends, Mister Stoner. As we are, are we not?' He stopped chewing. Looked up and held Stoner's stare with his own. And he answered his own question. 'Of course we are. I would not have travelled halfway across the planet for someone who was not my friend. Would I, Mister Stoner?'

'Depends for whose benefit you've travelled, Mr Tran. You're suggesting that I'm the subject of your goodwill, which may be the case, but equally may not be. How would I know? I hear your words, kind as your words always are, but I doubt my own judgement, never mind the character of others, and interpretation of your motives is way beyond me.'

'You need a friend, Mister Stoner.'

'You reckon, Mr Tran? You reckon? Where is Mallis?'

Mr Tran ostentatiously consulted his wristwatch. 'New York. For another two hours at least, maybe three. It depends upon the weather.'

Stoner stared at his companion. Spread his hands in a gesture of utter bewilderment. 'New York?'

'Mallis.' Mr Tran paused, laid his utensils neatly to the side of his plate and pushed that plate away from him. 'Mallis very occasionally requires reminding that although he and his... sister... the amusingly nicknamed techno prisoners... are highly competent... extremely proficient in their ability to manipulate and sometimes master the world of digital communication they need reminding that they are not alone in that.' He stopped, smiled at Stoner. 'How am I performing in your language, Mister Stoner? I make sense?'

'You do. And your presence here suggests that you speak the truth.' Stoner continued his white man's quest for meat among the oriental vegetation on the remaining dishes. 'You're asking me to believe that you are more than a match for Mallis when it comes to a command of the airwaves and all they contain?'

Mr Tran clapped his hands and laughed softly, suggesting delight of some kind. 'Me? No. But the world is large and covered with people who can do many things. The secret is to know alternatives and to know who are your friends. Professional friends, Mister Stoner, if not personal. Also whose interests collide with your own.'

'Coincide, Mr Tran? Collision suggests conflict.'

'Each in their place, Mister Stoner. Each is as useful as the other. The magic trick is being able to identify which is which. You need to listen to me for a little while, and you need to understand that what I tell you is both accurate and true. Another magic trick – there are very many magic tricks – lies in recognising that what is true for one day may not be true the day before or the day after. I will provide an example. Mallis is in New York. That is true. It is a fact. It is only true for the length of time it is true. Tomorrow that fact will have been replaced by another fact. So if I tell you today – now – that Mallis is in New York then I am telling the truth to you and I am your friend. If I told you tomorrow that Mallis is in New York then I would be lying to you and would probably not be your friend depending on the reason for the lie. A lie could be more useful to you than the truth. Sometimes the action of a friend is to lie to another friend. Do you understand me?'

Stoner smiled, a long, slow and rare gem of a smile. 'Mr Tran, even for a wily oriental you are being particularly inscrutable. Are you telling me that even if you lie to me you are being my friend by doing it?'

Mr Tran clapped his hands together again, beaming his reply. 'Mister Stoner, my friend. I live in your house in the UK and I am your tenant. And I am your friend. Once, some time ago, over a year ago, you described me as being Chinese, and I revealed that I am not. That I am from Vietnam. This is true. I choose my words with care always. Not being a native English speaker is an advantage. I am excused from talking my time with my replies, because you will think that I search for the correct words. That is not always the only reason.' He bowed and opened the last of his bottles of water, drank from it. 'I am from Vietnam.' He bowed again. 'Mr Tran the man from Vietnam.'

Stoner nodded back. 'I remember.'

'Good. I am also from China. Part of me is from

China. In China there are very very many people who are as good at digital data manipulation in all its forms as is your friend Mallis – who is not my own friend – and his partner the woman you call Menace. There are very many people who are better at it and who are employed by the People's Republic to be so good that there are none better. As soon as you spoke with Mallis one of those Chinese informed me of your whereabouts and your arrangements, altered the travel plans of Mallis ensuring that I arrived here before him and that he would arrive in New York where there has been a storm of snow and ice and from where flights to Boston will be delayed.' He paused, drew a breath, and began again.

'Those same Chinese ensured my swift arrival here. I knew you were in the United States, and so was I, but you have hidden your tracks well. The man from China positioned you exactly in a minute, maybe less, and relayed your conversation with Mallis to me. Here am I.' He bowed again.

'So I see. The bigger question is why – why are you here? Is Mallis going to lie to me? Is he my enemy? I have no trouble at all believing that everyone is... not my friend.'

'Everyone in the world we share manoeuvres everyone, Mister Stoner. You are moved around and so am I. You move others around and so do I. Ask me the first question, please. I will need to be elsewhere soon. Already I am supposed to be elsewhere. You should first ask me about Missy, Lissa, your friend – your lover – who was assaulted...' He looked down. 'Who was injured.'

Stoner glared at the world in general. He said nothing.

'She is well, Mister Stoner. She required surgical assistance and she received it. Immediately and effectively. She is no longer working as a hooker – excuse me – and is living under my widest most imaginative protection, and officially in my house. Which is rented from you, of course. She does not know that I am here. I do not know at any single time where she is, physically, so she is as safe as safe can be. But what happened to her was in a way connected to me.'

Stoner's eyes were wide and wild. 'What?' The single word.

'I introduced your friend Harding to the woman you know as Blesses. One consequence of that introduction was the rape and injury of Missy. I am here to apologise for my part in that. My failure was that I had not anticipated it.'

Stoner was a near-perfect model of a man under unbearable tension practising impossible restraint. He spoke slowly, carefully. 'Blesses.' Not a question; a simple statement demanding a thousand answers. 'Blesses.'

'Your kindness returns to hunt you, Mister Stoner.'

'Do you mean haunt? That... woman is devil enough for most men.'

'Hunt, Mister Stoner. I intended to say exactly what I said. She is... confusing. She confuses men. Only men. I think. She is a devil of manipulation, but she confuses only men.'

'She bewitches. She is a witch.' Stoner's tone was acid. Venom. Pain and resignation. Loss and loathing.

Mr Tran watched his companion carefully. 'If it were so simple,' he said, softly. 'If she were a creature of myth then there would be a mythical antidote for her. But she is not. She is a hypnotist. And she has a fine understanding of chemistry and men. Unlike Americans, she has a perfect grasp of the many teas of the world, how to formulate them, brew them and administer them. How to calm, to soothe, to flatter, deceive and completely capture a man's mind. She can do that. She would be a most excellent and valued Vietnamese. Even Chinese, within reason.'

'She's Irish.' Stoner's bald statement fell flat upon the table between them.

'No one is perfect, Mister Stoner. Not even you. Nor me. And certainly not Blesses. The greatest advantage she holds over her targets – the men she manipulates – is their lack of comprehension. Then their fear and their misunderstanding. And what she does is not at all infallible, nor is it particularly reliable. Panic is the problem for the men she can charm. All of them.'

'So when she... compelled? Programmed? Hypnotised? When she did what she did to Shard – Harding – he was unable to resist?' Stoner's disbelief was clear.

'He believed it, so it was true for him, Mister Stoner. Panic. Pure and simple, and he did what he did while he believed that his mind was lost to him. That he held no control over himself.'

'And you expect me to believe that?'

'I expect nothing, Mister Stoner. I'm here to be helpful. To try to be helpful. Lissa – your lover – she is safe. Certainly from Blesses.'

Stoner signalled for more bottled water for them both. 'Shard fucked Lissa in her ass, Mr Tran. Then he practically gutted her. You've seen the movie, no doubt. I'm... what? I'm supposed to find forgiveness? Understanding?'

'I've not seen the video, no. Missy's description of the event is more than enough. I have an Asian imagination; I can see events as described to me as clearly as I may want to. The movie was a message. It was effective. Here we are. You have been... unwell for a half year. That is a long time. That is why I am here with you now, rather than with the companions who are waiting for me.'

'OK. You've come to tell me something. What is it?'

'Stay here, Mister Stoner. Stay in the United States. Were I you, then I would not meet Mallis. He will tell you what he believes to be true, but his knowledge is unreliable because he is being manipulated. It would be... it would not be to your benefit to return to the UK at this time. If you base your judgements on what Mallis will tell you, then your judgements will be unsound. Mallis is excellent at the collection of information. He is not excellent at its interpretation. He may believe – for example – that your enemies are vulnerable or that Missy is in some further danger. Neither is true although Mallis believes otherwise.'

'Blesses is manipulating Mallis?' Stoner's incredulity was plain.

'No. Not to my own knowledge. The information Mallis and his... sister have been collecting is unreliable. His own sister – Menace, as you call her – is less faithful to him, to their joint enterprise than he believes. Missy is very safe. Even you would be unable to find her without more resource than is available to you, and the sequence of cut-outs between her and the outside world is as unbreakable as I believe to be possible. I... even I am uncertain of her exact whereabouts at any single time, as I said, so could not give her up – even to you – if I wanted to do so. Like you...' Mr Tran examined his own fingertips. 'Like you I have several houses, and like your good Jewish god, in my house there are many mansions. She moves between them if she wants to. If she... needs to.

'Two further, final matters. Stay in this country and an ally, a true friend to you, will make contact. Second. It may be – no stronger than that, Mister Stoner – it may be that Blesses and the woman you know as Menace have found a common ground. Consider that, and then I'll need to leave. My companions are plainly becoming restless.' He smiled.

Stoner looked around him. A pair of beautiful Asian ladies waved to him from the far side of the restaurant. He turned back to Mr Tran. 'Them? They're your companions?'

Mr Tran shook his head. 'No. Fans of yours, maybe. You resemble a faded rock star, Mister Stoner, maybe they've mistaken you for one of the dead ones, come back to life. They are Japanese. They are prone to fancies. Which is why they lose wars.'

'Mallis and Menace, then. Are they breaking apart – is their team falling apart? That would be a surprise.' Stoner watched Mr Tran carefully.

'It may be. Everything changes. That is the only permanence. I need to leave.' He unpeeled green dollars from a roll of them, slid them under his plate. 'This is clean money, Mister Stoner. It has not been stolen from criminals nor used to snort cocaine.' He smiled. He stood. As Mr Tran stood, so did a large black man wearing the most vivid shirt Stoner could recall seeing, and who had been asleep across an entire row of seats opposite the restaurant's entrance. He was huge, and unsmiling despite the hilarity of his hideous shirt. His gaze was locked on Stoner, who looked right back. The black giant brought his huge hands together and bowed his forehead into the steeple of his fingers. Mr Tran, rather to Stoner's surprise, performed the same greeting, and turned to face Stoner. 'My driver,' he revealed.

'You didn't fly in, then?' Stoner maintained his watch on the black man, who stood waiting with a deep and immoveable patience. Passengers avoided him and the quiet space around him.

'No.' Mr Tran could do brief.

'So why catch me here? If you'd already deflected Mallis?'

'For the same reason you decided to meet Mallis here, Mister Stoner. It's an airport. You've passed through security – as have I. You carry no metal weapons – same here. But although you are unarmed, I did bring heavy weaponry as a precaution.' Mr Tran smiled again, and bowed again, this time to Stoner. 'The weaponry was in case you were as damaged as some believe – not me, of course – and in case you had brought followers. Which you did not. You are refreshingly functional, Mister Stoner, and I am delighted to be able to produce that observation. If you are unfamiliar with the procedure for leaving a departure lounge without an aircraft – they call it "landing yourself" I believe – then you are most welcome to leave with me. My friend can watch two backs as well as one.'

Stoner paused. 'I've arranged to meet Mallis. He'll land in arrivals, check through security and meet me here.' He smiled. 'The precaution in his case is that I would prefer that he travelled without too much comms tackle. I doubt he carries much in the way of assault rifles and the like.'

'Unlike those who will surely be travelling with him. Two in front and two behind that I know of, plus at least the same who will be unknown to me. In your shoes, Mister Stoner, I would leave a note. Take a rain check. Be elsewhere. As I said already, I doubt he can add any truths to what you've heard already.'

'You'd leave, Mr Tran?'

'I would. I will, in fact. And right now. Coming?'

8

JJ Stoner rolled the pick-up to a halt, reversed it into sensible seclusion behind the derelict attendant's hut in the seasonally deserted car park. He switched off, and waited. Listened and breathed with the pines. The longer he rested, the more the woods returned to their interrupted conversations. Nature, talking with and to herself in as many of her infinite forms as were within earshot. None of those forms appeared to be human, and the peace was profound within a half hour of his arrival. Stoner believed in the universal sanctity of patience, and he relaxed in the cooling vehicle while afternoon faded into the blank black of early evening, while the taint of exhausts lost itself in the oxygen exhalations of the trees.

Relieved of the drone of the drive, his senses drifted, as sniper senses so often do, growing increasingly attuned to the shooter's radius, while the many-layered states of his human brain considered his increasing understanding of the situation. As the darkness outside deepened, relieved only by starlight from above, so he considered that his thinking had become more informed, more illuminated by his too-short conversation with

Mr Tran. Mr Tran, the man from Vietnam. The small man with impressively large and impressively capable friends. Stoner considered Mr Tran's level of knowledge, understanding as he did that the Vietnamese had controlled their entire encounter and, while providing information and food for thought to Stoner, he had also deftly avoided any form of meaningful questioning. Stoner understood that he, Stoner the private soldier, was a long way from being his previously effective team of one.

The darkness was as profound as only a forest can be, the silence loud and busy. Trees whispering, as trees do, birds and small creatures chattering and rustling, larger creatures considering a night of predation or its avoidance, depending on whether they preferred meat or vegetation as dietary mainstays. Stoner swung down from the cab, dragged an ancient and well weathered tarp from its home at the front of the loadbay, and secured it over the vehicle. By morning it would have collected damp and tree litter enough to suggest that it had been standing for a while. He considered easing air from a couple of the tyres to add to the suggestion of dereliction, but decided against it. Locked up, and looked up into the dark, collecting his bearings and setting his route by the pale stain of the pathway. Shrugged out of his comfortable winter city clothes; out of all his clothes. Stoner stood still and sharp and entirely naked in the easy comfort of his solitude. He could feel his skin temperature falling rapidly; could feel the increasing contrast between his body's living organic core heat and the chill of his own dead outer dermis.

In his goose-bumping nudity he pissed against the vehicle's rear wheel; driver's side. His wheels now, stolen though they also were. A possession and an ownership in reinforced balance. A cloth bag from behind the driver's seat gave up clean new underwear and the passenger footwell provided the major clothing he'd worn before changing into his city threads. Military style, Harley-Davidson branded cargo pants in black, matt black studs and zips. Heavy biker's long-sleeve Tee, black with black Harley embroidery. A heavy denim shirt, inevitably black and biker-branded like the rest. He tightened the laces of his familiar Caterpillar boots, kicked each booted foot once against the front tyre and tightened the laces once again, sniffed the breeze with pleasure and set out. A walk. The dark beauty of nature at night. His soldier's directional autopilot would guide his steps. One battlefield is much like another; threats, signals and precautions. Safe passages. Steady steps; the art of the unremarkable. Rhythm and muse, the perfect companions.

The terrain was comfortably familiar to him, even in December's chill darkness, and he walked with a soldier's economy, the rhythm of the relaxed. Arms providing balance and information, feet finding their own levels as they walked, legs absorbing the terrain's inconsistencies. He walked in near-silence, conscious mind mostly detached from the body's locomotion, senses on lifewatch, alert for incongruity but sufficiently relaxed to allow all higher functions to analyse, consider and conclude. Over and over again. Over and again, One more time, every time.

Time passed unnoticed and the terrain grew ever more familiar. As his conscious and subconscious considerations merged and the contradictions between what he'd learned and his interpretations of that learning reduced, so music provided an increasing accompaniment to the beat of his march. His fingers twitched their readiness for a guitar again. Favourite solos played themselves to his inner ear. Tensions eased as he neared the cabin by the lake.

Until he smelled the smoke. Thought it was a simple mistake at first. He continued with his steady walking pace and rhythm. Internal music silent now. As well as walking through the surrounding dark greens, greys and graphite blacks of the shifting night, as well as listening to the very large array of sounds generated by the night and by the creatures that move by night, now he was straining for a repeat of the smoke. And while he consciously tasted every breath he took, he was analysing. Inevitably.

Again. Woodsmoke. Not uncommon in a woods by night. But unexpected in an area devoid of humanity and conspicuously lacking in nocturnal forest fires. Hardly the season for those. Woodsmoke. Pleasant and unthreatening in itself, but intruding where it had no place. He slowed. Stopped. There was almost no wind; the smoke – or its source, at least – was nearby. He moved on. Increased conscious caution. Nasal navigation. Who'd come up with that expression? He couldn't remember. A long time ago, and in a jungle not a relatively civilised woods. If it was important, he'd remember at some inappropriate moment.

Again, the smoke. He was maybe ten minutes from the cabin, maybe fifteen. Without breaking stride again, he shifted from the animal track he'd been following to another, and slowed further. The animals which had created this new thoroughfare were either smaller or less in number than the architects of his original track, and they'd not kept up with their gardening, plainly. He would approach the cabin from above.

THE REDEMPTION OF CHARM

It was lit. Windows bright and warm with invitation. Someone was at home. Travis? No boat visible on the shore; no silhouette black against the star-glimmer of the water. As well as the smoke and the lighting, he could hear music playing. More apparent invitation? Simple carelessness or innocence? He changed direction again, shifting through a series of tiny trails until he was stalking parallel to the only sensible vehicular access route. No tracks, no sign of a vehicle entering or exiting. Even the most skilfully driven 4x4 leaves big trails, and there were none. He kept clear of the road, parallel tracked it to its end; no parked car, 4x4 or otherwise. No boat he could see – though the fact of the night made that an uncertainty. No mechanical smells; no oil nor diesel nor petrol. Smoke. That was all. That and the light. And the music. He could name the song but not the singer. The guitarist was Nile Rogers. It's all a question of priorities.

He stepped off the rudimentary trail he'd been following and sank back into the ground cover. Paused for thought and for consideration. He'd been taken totally by surprise when Mr Tran had appeared at the airport. Classic amateur behaviour. He'd been watching for an arrival from a single direction. He'd intended to be the surprise, not the surprised. That mistake had unbalanced his entire day. A fatal mistake in other circumstances, and an educational experience in these. Dangerous days. In this case the danger lay in simple misinterpretation. His own advice to junior troops when they had been in his care; look and learn. The more you look, the more you learn. Fools rush in, and there are no angels to believe in. He was, he understood with some clarity, out of practice and out of condition. Mental condition. Potentially fatal. The music had faded.

A flurry of sparks drifted over the roof's shadow against the bright sky. A fresh log on the fire, then.

Stoner moved like the predator he could claim to be, up into the hillside above the cabin. He resisted all temptations to approach and peer through a window. A great way to get your head shot off. He recalled more than one occasion when he'd been the one removing the inquisitive head.

And with unconscious and reassuring accuracy, he found himself at one of his bivouac points. In the starlight clarity and increasing quiet of the night, he unfolded the tarp from its waterproof sack, strung it again over his old vantage point, dropped the groundsheet over the cleared space beneath the tarp, reminded by the lack of fresh growth that it had not been a long time since he'd been able to sleep only under the skies and amid the trees, and unrolled the sniper's bivvy bag, complete with hood and with no unwanted animal companions he could discover. He relaxed into the comfort of his paranoia, understanding once again the warmth of it all. He could watch and he could listen. He would sleep, too, lightly and restfully. This is what soldiers do; was what he'd done when he'd been an official soldier, a long time ago.

The cabin was silent. Dark. Stoner watched in comfort, the comfort of his competence keeping him calm. A trap only works if the victim fails to recognise it. He closed his eyes and considered recent events. Relaxed. He also slept.

***

'Not only bears, then.' He spoke softly, his voice too low to travel as far as the cabin, but his diction clear and precise. The figure below him and to his left, between him and the cabin, slammed back against the trunk of the tree whose roots she fertilised. She rose rapidly to her feet, clutching her bright wrap around her and ran from him. Not to the cabin, as he'd anticipated, but in a straight line direct to the lake's chill water. Only when she was waist deep did she turn to face him.

'Bears,' she said. Remarkably untroubled and patently unarmed. Her companion – or companions; Stoner was aware of only one but recognised his own uncertainty – made no appearance. She'd not shouted for help nor had she run to hide. Interesting behaviour.

'I get it,' she announced, and apparently losing interest in dialogue for the moment, lifted her wrap, tied it around her waterline waist and proceeded to wash those parts she'd been exercising when interrupted. 'Hypothermia's a killer,' she remarked, wading back to the shore. 'I'm heading inside to warm up and dry off. You can skulk around playing cowboys, whatever, or you can show yourself and share a coffee.'

Stoner assessed his views of the situation and emerged from around the side of the cabin. Stood still and waited for her by the steps up to the porch. 'Good morning,' he smiled as she crossed towards him. 'Enjoy your dip?'

'Joker.' She approached then passed him, treading the wooden steps lightly until she reached the door and opened it. Turned back to face him. 'You the local headcase, voyeur, vigilante, survivalist fruitcake or latter day saint? Or what? What're you doing here?' Her voice was plainly New York rather than Michigan, and she plainly felt no fear.

'I live here.' Stoner watched her expressions. She simply smiled.

'I doubt that. Coffee? You sound English; prefer

tea? Good joke about the bear, Mister Englishman.' She turned towards the cabin's interior. 'If you're feeling confused, I'll bring the drink to you out here, but I do need to get warm. Which is it to be?'

'Coffee, please. Out here is fine. How many are you?'

'I'm just me. Is that another joke? Oh I see,' she smiled, a pleasant sight. 'There's the two of us; me and Sonny. He's still hiding under blankets wishing his night will never end and flattening the battery on his iPod. Doubt he's heard a thing. Teenagers, huh?' She disappeared into the cabin's interior. Re-emerged maybe five minutes later, carrying two familiar mugs and an equally familiar thermal coffee pot and a small jug of creamer, the whole warming ensemble balanced on a familiar wooden tray. Sat down and poured. 'He's still dead to the world, but the smell of coffee will wake him. Care to share?'

Stoner picked up a mug, breathed the familiar aroma of the coffee brought by his last visitor, and reached for the creamer. Her hand landed on his. 'Speak up,' she suggested.

'I live here,' Stoner repeated. 'Have done for maybe five, six months. Been away for a few days, got back last night and thought I'd enjoy sleeping with nature rather than risk disturbing my most recent uninvited guests. Great coffee. Brought as a welcoming gift by my last guest. Who was also uninvited, but does at least own the cabin.'

She rose to her feet and reached out a hand to him. He took it. 'Pleased to meet you, whoever you are. I'm Mrs Travis. The ex-Mrs Travis to be more exact. Does that help?' She released his hand and sat down once more. Sipped her cooling coffee, drank it down and did refill for them both.

'It does.' Stoner sipped in sympathy. 'He know you're here? So you knew to expect someone?'

She shook her head. 'No. We don't talk about the cabin hardly at all. I usually clean the place up and leave him a note.' She stopped, considering. 'OK,' finally. 'I'm wrong. He suggested it. In a way.' She scratched her memory a little more. 'He sent an SMS, saying I should maybe bring Sonny up here for a break. Damn.' She fell silent, briefly. 'Just one more thing I've forgotten – there'll be lots more.' She smiled at him. 'I get busy. I forget things. Travis did not mention company. That I would certainly have remembered. I would also have remembered if he'd said he'd be coming here himself. Dawn,' she added. 'That's me. Dawn. My name.'

'Hello Dawn,' Stoner raised his coffee in salute. 'To old friends. Jean-Jacques. JJ for short.'

'And for friends? Friends also call you JJ? You Canadian, then? Not English at all. Sorry about that. Can't imagine a Quebecois enjoying being mistaken for an English imperialist.' She was almost laughing. The cabin's door was opened by a giant. A young giant with hair as fair as Dawn's. He groaned, yawned, then regarded Stoner with minimal caution.

'One of dad's?' he wondered aloud. 'One of dad's burn-outs? I'll brew up some more coffee, scare up some breakfast. You here for breakfast, Mister Wild Man?'

'This is JJ,' announced the ex-Mrs Travis. 'He's either English or from a ways north of here. Be polite. JJ; meet Sonny. Sonny can fry an egg all on his own. He is a liberated modern man, and if we're sweet to him maybe he'll fry up something for us also. How you fixed, Sonny? That suit you?'

The young man shook his head at either or both

of them and closed the cabin door behind him as he headed for the stove.

'British, you were right first time.' Stoner stuffed his hands into the pockets of his coat. 'You OK out here? Hot it's not.'

'I prefer to be outside when it's light and the sun's up, JJ. Plenty of time for darkness and confinement. What're we going to do about this? About this unexpected situation? I'd not expected company and intended to spend Christmas up here, civilising Sonny a little, if that's possible. You on vacation, JJ? Or resting?'

'I'd no idea Travis was married.' Stoner shrugged his coat so it rested more comfortably around him. 'We never talked about that – domestic stuff – at all. And you're the ex?'

'Yep. He's up to Mrs Travis the third now. Never learns. One day he'll locate a new Mrs T who's into the up-country living and I'll need to find a new man of property.' She laughed, possibly at herself. It was hard to be sure. 'There's more than the one bedroom, JJ with no surname. Do you need to be on your own? I met quite a few of Travis's business friends and you appear to be at least as civilised as most of them.'

'It's not my own level of civilisation you need to be concerned about, unhappily.' Stoner shrugged.

'You can't be concerned about invasion from the sea, JJ, so what is it? You in hiding? If you're a player in the same great game as Travis I can see that you'd need to hide from it.' A certain weariness, perhaps, in her voice.

'Not so much. More... restoration. A retreat from defeat. I'd rather not talk about it much, but I am no threat to you or Sonny. Not me, personally. And although there may be... there certainly are some who wish me something other than that long and active life,

I doubt they'd come all the way out here looking for me. Although my first thought last night when I saw the place lit up like Times Square was that you were that unwelcome guest. Guess I was wrong.' He smiled again, sadly. 'I've been doing that a lot lately. Being wrong. Do you know how to get hot water in this place other than by boiling an endless kettle?'

She smiled at that. 'It has a sauna and a hot tub, JJ. It's a great place. How come you don't know how it works?'

'I didn't know it had electricity until Travis came out here and revealed the hidden secrets of physics. It's been a tough time at times. Guess I wasn't paying much attention.'

'Guess you weren't. I'll bully Sonny into boiling and heating. You need to shower.'

'I do?'

'You do. There's a...'

'There's a great big clean lake and I need to go swim a mile then run into the sauna? Which is where, by the way?'

Dawn waved towards a tired wooden building. 'That's it. Doesn't look much, but it's great for turning white guys into red men.'

'I thought that was an old boathouse.' Stoner shook his head again. 'Guess I really was not on the ball when I got here. Speaking of; how did you get here? I see no seaplanes or cruise ships.'

'By boat. It's in the boathouse. You go freeze your nuts off and I'll go see where Sonny's fallen asleep. He can sleep like a pensioner.'

'That's one great talent. Encourage him.' Stoner was conscious of his considerably unwashed status. 'If you can sleep well, you can do most everything else, too. Sleep is one of the successful superpowers that Superman never needs. Without supersleep you simply can't do superanythingelse. I stink, don't I?' Dawn nodded and smiled agreement. 'I'll go swim. You're not prudish, Mrs Travis the second?' She smiled again, and shook that smile from side to side along with the rest of her head. Stoner turned his back to her, walked down the edge of the lakeStonerS and stripped, first to his shorts, then shucked those too, walked out into the freezing water, took a series of deep lung-clearing breaths and dived, just below the surface, kicking out into the deeper water with a powerful and comfortable breast stroke.

The cold was outrageous. His eyes believed themselves to be blinded by forming ice, and already his hands and feet had transformed into senseless paddles. Invigoration ruled his soul and the exertion raised his spirits. Cleansing, hard and true. He took a mouthful of water, rolled to his back and held the water in his mouth as it warmed and he back-crawled until it was drinkable. His teeth rebelled at the water, his nose ran and the lake washed away the snot and the tears and he wanted to swim the length of the lake, the savage beauty of the risk in his situation boosting his muscles.

As his eyes lost their finer focus, he turned, sighted himself on the shoreline and mustering every last calorie, burning them in his muscles only maybe twice as rapidly as his inner organism could supply them, locked into a steady crawl back to the shore, counting cadence in his head with every stroke, the rhythm taking control of everything else; a fine way to ignore concerns great and small. If the organism is genuinely concerned for its own survival, higher functions can just go hang. He was in love with life again, he realised, and wanted to laugh, which might well have been fatal. Female company. A miracle all its own.

Knee and hand touched the shallow beach almost simultaneously. Stoner rolled onto his back and allowed his breathing to stabilise, then rolled again to face the shore and raised himself to his feet. Sonny was wading across towards him, water thigh-deep. 'You should have said you were swimming,' he called. 'You OK? You're an amazing colour. Steamer's heating, let's go get some hot into you, old man.' As he strode through the water, Stoner nodded his agreement. The air was warmer than the water, but was chilling him more effectively than the lake had managed. A function of muscle use. He'd start to shiver soon, and would prefer to avoid that – for the sake of his dignity if nothing else.

He nodded towards the younger man's musculature and manhood. 'Quite a weapon you're packing,' the universal common language of men everywhere. When short of anything sensible to say, talk about dicks. And the subject of his compliment was surely impressive.

Sonny roared with laughter, reached down and squeezed his already man-sized tackle. 'Passport to future fame and fortune, huh?' He let go of himself and waded ashore. Stoner followed, running as soon as he was able to do so, pumping his arms to generate some heat. Reached the steam room immediately behind the younger man and followed him up the steps to the big wooden tub, a tub which steamed and dripped heat enough for two chilly swimmers – for several swimmers, in fact. It was almost a pool rather than a tub.

'Built for team sports?' Stoner wondered aloud as he followed Sonny into the water. Then fell silent as the heat shocked both speech and cold from him. Both men sank beneath the surface, still standing upright; a tub for tall folk. Even as tall as Sonny, who had a good two inches over Stoner.

'So what do you do, JJ?' Sonny had hooked his arms over the tub's edge rail and was facing Stoner, polite interest on display.

Stoner paddled his feet like a child in a swimming pool. Closed his eyes, shook his head to clear sudden sweat from his eyelids, then regarded his youthful companion. 'You're what – eighteen? I look for things. People mostly.'

'And you play the guitar? The Fender in the box next to the amp is yours, not a thing of Travis? So you're some kind of bounty hunter? Is that it? You find crooks and turn them in to the Feds. That's how you know Travis, yes? He's some kind of super-Fed. He turned up in a Fed helo once. Picked me up from the school field. Principal went utterly batshit about it, then Travis showed her some kind of ID and she went all coochy-coo. Awesome cool.'

'Impressed all your buddies, I bet.'

'I don't really do buddies, JJ.'

'How's that? You seem almost human... for a teenager.' Stoner smiled over to Sonny, who did not return it.

'I'm difficult, JJ. Real difficult. I have issues. They call them issues. Dawn reckons they'll work themselves out as I... as I mature. But I doubt that.'

'You're what – a fighter? It has its place. The trick is finding that place. Sometimes a long road.' Stoner bobbed below the surface again, surfaced, steaming and streaming the hot water. 'This is hot, not just warm or relatively hot. This is good. I've been here for months and had no notion that this sauna was here. I thought it was an old boathouse like the other old boathouse.

There's a lesson for you, if you want to hide something, put it in plain view. You want people to accept your fighting, fight in a ring or a gym.'

'I just fight and fuck, JJ. Been hard at both since I was twelve. The oldest story. I thought everyone was the same. Thought being on top of the game was always righteous. Isn't true. Not for Travis I'd be in institutions. He did tell me that. Hated him for it, went for him. First time I lost a fight. Hurt so. Made me cry. The last time for that, first time I lost a fight; last time I cried.'

'Growing up, Sonny.'

'Yeah. You fight, JJ? You fight the bad guys you hunt down?'

'They're not always bad guys. And fighting's not fun if you don't know in advance how good the other guys are likely to be. Losing never gets better. You still fight Travis? He's an old man now; you'd take him, no sweat. You've got the reach and the weight. You'll move faster than him. Can't lose.'

'You'd take Travis, you reckon?'

'Yep.'

'You'd take me?'

'You want the truth?' Stoner faced him with seriousness and a straight, quiet face. Man to man, almost. Sonny nodded.

'I'd need to find your limits and I'd need to find them fast. The only way to do that when war's declared is to go hard at it and push your hardest until either you fall or I fall. That's a bloody way of settling anything. Talking is better if you can do it, and if you can't do it, if you're pushed into a fight then the only thing you can do... the only thing I can do is to win at once. No parley when it's started, just winners and losers. Clever guys don't fight. Why d'you do it?'

'Love it. Just... it's what I am. That point arrives and whammo. It's what you're all about too, isn't it? You're here because you lost a fight. That's how it feels. Is it so?'

Stoner nodded. 'Yes. Good try. I won the fight and lost the battle.'

'How's that?' Sonny was fascinated.

Stoner's sigh was a definition of weariness. 'I did the job I'd been asked to do. Gig was over and done. I was running north to meet my lady. Then I found out that two friends had been fucked up. Maybe connected to the job, maybe not. I don't know. And until I do know...'

'You need to find the guys who did that... thing, whatever it was, and you need to fuck them up, only harder. I'll help.' Sincerity. Sonny reached out a large hand. Stoner hesitated a tiny fraction, slapped the open hand.

'Maybe you would. But it's never as easy as that. That's being adult. If I... hey, Sonny, if we went up against the people who I think did the bad thing, then we'd die. Or worse.'

'There's no worse thing than losing and dying; there can't be, but if you die for something that's – y'know – righteous, then you gotta do it, man. That's a man's purpose. That's the point of it.'

'You need to join an army.'

'Oh fuck it, JJ. I'm being with you all the way and you're laughing at me. Fuck you.'

Stoner held out both hands to Sonny, sank below the steaming water, surfaced and said no, no he was not laughing. Everything Sonny said was right. But there's almost never any point to starting a war that's impossible to win. And as the youth regained his good humour, Stoner told him another truth, the truth that his own issues would make him different to everyone else for the whole of his life, and the secret to success lay in making those issues so valuable to others who were too normal, too straight, too weak to have issues of their own that they would pay him to do what came naturally to him. To live a life he wanted to live. That's the reason, Stoner told a surprised Sonny, why his father was supporting him in the way that he was, because issues transform into talents with training.

'My father...' Sonny began, but interruption arrived in the form of Dawn, who hammered her fists against the side of the tub, yelled that she was coming in, ready or not, that they should make room, make room, and then she somehow dived over the rim of the tub and down headfirst into the hot depths, surfacing again facing them and hauling hair from her bright eyes.

'You talking prime shit already, JJ? Telling this thug, this hooligan that being a fighter can be a good thing? When all the while I've been telling him that he needs to read Robert Frost and Emily Dickenson and learn the collected works of Shakespeare if he ever wants to make a real man of himself. Boys,' she cried out. 'You boys are all the same.' Stoner was so surprised that it took him maybe point five of a single second to realise that she'd grabbed hold of his cock and was squeezing it. From Sonny's delighted 'Oh, man. Oh man,' he surmised that her other hand was similarly occupied elsewhere. He leaned back against the tub's wall, his right arm laying along Sonny's left, Dawn bobbing before the two of them, eyes wide and targeting each of them in their turn.

Sonny's moment arrived in a very short time, and he made a lot of noise as he came, shouting through laughter, finally squealing 'Enough!' and hoisting himself clear of the hot water and onto the tub's rim, where he leaned back, legs apart, his family economy-sized cock still that hard purple and still weeping salt white tears from its single eye. 'Yeah,' he announced. Everything can appear to be so simple in a moment like that.

'You OK, JJ?' Dawn was still working him with practised ease, the traditional wanker's grip, thumb and two fingers forming a decent O and sliding over his submerged dick, building a rhythm, then as a climax failed to follow, dropping their pace, changing from a full O grip to individual points of finger pressure, and rebuilding her rhythm until he failed once again to oblige them both with an orgasm or much else in the way of evident arousal.

Sonny looked on with obvious and intense interest. Finally he soft-voiced 'Maybe you'd prefer...' and he dropped back into the heated water and replaced Dawn's fingers with his lips. Then teeth, then tongue, then lips again, then he let go and surfaced. 'You OK, man?' There was plain, simple concern in his voice. Dawn reached out and took his cock into her hand again, but this time mostly simply held it, squeezing gently, relaxing as she caught his gaze and held it.

'There something troubling you, JJ? You're shocked, maybe.'

Stoner lifted his arms from the sides of the tub and submerged before her, reaching plumb bottom of the tub, then surfacing rapidly, his head between her legs, her thighs one on each shoulder, his lips to her lower lips, his tongue parting them, as he propelled the both of them upward and to the side, so she was sitting on the tub's edge with his face burrowed into her and his hands gripping her butt to aid his burrowing and allow a better penetration. She shuddered very quickly indeed, seized her own breasts, forced them together and squeezed them so hard as she came. He dropped away from her, unlatched her legs from his shoulders and backpedalled slowly away until his back was once more against the hot wet wood of the tub and his eyes once again held hers. Sonny reached down, caught Stoner's cock again in his hand, and said, quietly, 'Oh man. You are one unusual guy. No mistake.'

Dawn slid back into the water, paddled over to her two men and turned so they all faced the same wall. She hung an arm around each of them, and said, simply. 'Whoo, my. What just happened?' They hung there together, each thinking thoughts of their own, maybe the same thoughts and maybe not. Then, remarkably and as one, they separated, left the pool and sat together in the steam room.

Sonny broke their quiet after a short time. He lifted his impressive maleness; 'Ready again. What's happened to you, man? Can I... can we make it better?'

Stoner had no words, none at all. So he stood, shook his head, wrapped himself in towels and ran through the light snowfall back to the cabin. While Dawn and Sonny towelled themselves and each other dry and prepared to follow him, the quiet of the woods was disturbed by three loud guitar chords, the amplification shocking in the way it destroyed the silence. The same three chords repeated, this time played in a different way, a fresh inversion, and then again, finally breaking into what sounded like a first verse, a place for words.

'The Wind Cries Mary,' shared Dawn. 'Hendrix. Let's just listen a while. He's playing it for himself. I think.'

9

CHRISTMAS, LAST YEAR: TAKING IT, EASY

'Christmas Day? Are you making fun, reinventing the bad joke or simply taking the piss?' The woman with the blonde Mohican haircut leaned back in her chair at the roadside diner, complete with its strange red livery and obese grinning imbecile all in white as an inspirational logo, and made a stylish performance out of unlacing and kicking free her shin-high combat boots. She scratched her spiked hair. 'In any case, that's tomorrow. Today, sweet sister, is Christmas Eve, everyone is out having a great time and enjoying themselves. Look.' She waved an expansive hand around the completely deserted diner. 'Here they aren't. Unlike us.' She stared into a glass of bottled beer as though it were piss from the very devil herself. Which it might have been, of course.

'We're family, and we're having fun.' Her companion, also female but otherwise as different in appearance as it was probably possible to be, raised an identical bottle to her lips. 'I mean,' she said, 'look at this, antique beer. Bottled while The Beatles were just starting school. A tribute to the preservative powers of alcohol. Be cheery, Chas. You've got to try.'

'I don't. You try if you want to. I miss Chas so much. First Christmas as two sisters, Chas. Chas and Chas, desperate duo instead of unholy trinity.' She lifted the bottle, which provoked the appearance of a scurrying waitress-like creature clutching a small notepad and a worried expression entirely devoid of hope that her customers might place another order, and downed most of her bottle's contents – just poured it down without a swallow. Army style. She stared blankly at the alleged waitress.

'Another of these? Gods no. Even if it was a certified cure for cancer I'd not drink it. Water. Sealed bottles, two off. No need for a glass. Thank you. I think.' She turned back to her sister. 'You've agreed a gig for tomorrow? Who, where and how? More to the point; why? I really was intent on raising a wake for Charity. Loved her, y'know. I'm running out of sisters, sister.'

'Me too, Chas. Me too. You want to turn the job down?'

'Do I get a choice?'

'Course you do. All for one, all that crap etcetera.'

'Not so impressive when the three musketeers turn into the less than dynamic duo.' Chastity nodded agreement with her own sentiment. Charm rested her hand onto her sister's, her soft, chubby and smooth skinned hand contrasting with the blue-veins and hard nails caressed beneath it. 'But I suppose the money would be good. Pensions, pots to piss in, so on.' The water waitress arrived, left bottles, muttered mysteriously and incomprehensibly then moved away again. Christmas carols jingled all the way, ignored by staff and customers alike. The atmosphere was more Maundy Thursday than Christmas Eve. 'How're we doing for money, anyway? What happens to Chas's share?'

'We're fine for money, Chastity. We can stop any time you say.' Charm retrieved her hand, looked at her watch.

'You in a hurry, big sis? Hot date?'

Charm shook her head. 'No, not nearly. You want to grab something edible? Somewhere even more delightfully enticing that this septic pimple on the backside of nowhere?'

'Business before pleasure, sister. Who is it? And where? Sort this, then we can go eat if you like.' Chastity stroked the spikes of her hair. 'If it involves disguises, hats or hoodies, I demand extra pay.'

Charm spread out a selection of photos. 'She's a woman who never changes her appearance, and these are supposedly current.' She laid out some more prints, keyed at her laptop and turned its screen to face her sister. 'She's doing domestics here during the day...' She turned the screen back to herself and tapped data, turning it once again to face her sister. 'Then away from first family joys to her second family – plainly a lady who enjoys domestic bliss so much that she has at least two families. Probably legal wherever she comes from.'

'Which is where?'

'Don't know. Don't want to know. Don't care.'

It was Chastity's turn to reach out, to squeeze her older sister's hand gently. 'Hey. Don't go broody, sis. Christmas cheer, remember? I'm the moody one, remember?'

'Feels more like the end of everything, more like Easter than Christmas. Guys nailed to trees, torture and pain, not bubbly babies and reindeer.' Charm could do gloom, too.

'Hey, it's me has to do the hard work. No Charity to prop me up, no soul out there in the shitstorm to be there when... when I just lose it, when I just need to break everything and kill everyone within range rather than just one mark.' Chastity's cheeks glowed with an anger as honest as it was intense. 'New year. New year we start up fresh. Make our own ground zero and reset all the clocks. Look hard at what we've done this year, learn from it. Where is Target Woman? Tell me that she just served us drinks. Even the bottled water tastes like it's been used to wash nappies.' She sipped cautiously at the bottle with the printed suggestion that its contents were siphoned by angelic virgins from the purest of wells, water which had never been used for anything ever before, and certainly not for cleaning nappies.

Charm slid a thin A4 folder across to her sister. Chastity lifted it, opened it and considered its contents. Address, postcode for the satnav, most likely arrival time of the subject and most probable route. Charm, ever-efficient, had also highlighted three departure routes, and had included a small stack of images of the surrounding area. Chastity looked up. 'And it has to take place as she arrives at her second family? And there's an arrival window for her of, what, a half hour? An hour. So I'll end up sitting like a spent whore in the middle of acres of festive suburban bliss on Christmas Day in the rain for maybe two hours? We seriously do need a bigger team, Chas. And the customer – who is who, by the way? – expects the job to be done at close range, which demands a handgun, and I'm expected to shout this bollocks so that everyone within a mile can hear it? That's loud, really loud. That's also dim, really dim. Also stupid. Who's paying for the job?'

'Thirty large, in cash, and in advance.'

'You already have the dosh?' Chastity looked impressed. Sufficiently so that she downed the last of the apparently health-giving water in her bottle. Charm nodded.

'You can say no, but if you do, I'd need to try to do it myself, or find someone to sub the job to.' Charm appeared unconcerned, composure restored, flicked her thick dark hair back over her ears to stop it falling into her face, wedged it beneath the least appropriate sunglasses on the planet and shoved the assembly higher onto the crown of her head.

'Yeah, yeah. And a sub would want double time because it's a bank holiday, and they'd want time off in lieu, and health insurance, and health and safety, and things like that. Stoner was right, wasn't he? We do need to be bigger than we are. We need more back-up, more infrastructure. He was pretty strong about that when we were in Germany in the summer. Wonder where he is? I'd expected to hear about him before now.'

Charm smiled. 'You mean you'd expected to hear from him by now. He makes an impression, no? Everyone seems to think he's gone off on another big white cruise ship, spending all his money on smart women or playing bass guitar in an Abba tribute band or similar. Except the guys at his club, the Blue Cube. They all think he's retired and gone into hiding. They make up so many damnfool suggestions that they sound like mourners at a wake.'

'Anyone saying that he went the same way as Chas? All lights out?'

'Not in public, but his whore – the black woman – and his oppo, Shard, they've vanished too. Dropped clean off the radar. Funny thing, though. Last time he just cleared off, just before you did the German gig with him, his bestest-everest girlie, the glamour pot who plays bass for him, Bili, she was entirely mental about him not being around. She says hardly anything about him now. Just looks so soulful, so mournful that no one talks about him when she's around. It's just too much grief. Same with Stretch, the big black who rattles the ivories...'

Chastity interrupted: 'I know who they all are, big sis, don't need lectures about them. Bili was great on the ship when they got me out of Israel. Her and Charity got on real well. She can seriously swear, too. Don't talk her down; she's a treasure.'

Charm nodded unwilling agreement, rolled her eyes. 'Whatever. Yeah we do need to have more structure, more support. We also need to have a family meeting to decide whether we're carrying on with it all.' She stopped, utterly suddenly. 'A family meeting without Chas. Oh fuck it all; fuck fuck fuck it all.' Shouting now. Her eyes were emptying a river through the hands that covered them, down her face, dripping onto the greasy red table's greasy surface. Chastity rose to her feet, walked around the table and pulled her sister into her arms, feeling her shuddering sobs and the impossible heat of her tears soaking through all their clothes. The waitress watched in wonder from her kitchen. Scared.

***

'I wish it could be Christmas every day...' Chastity sang tonelessly to herself. She was sitting in a bus shelter as Christmas Day's sodden grey afternoon atmosphere condensed around her. The motorcycle was under shelter too, mostly out of sight in the gloom and by her side. There were no revellers. The suburb was a drowned ghost town. Hardly any road traffic, and absolutely no pedestrians. She was certain that behind every dripping window was warmth and welcome and all the wonder of Christmas, but she was simply damp, faintly chilled and bored senseless.

Her theory was borrowed one hundred percent from a conversation she'd shared with the strangely absent Stoner; maybe the same conversation when he'd expressed his surprise at the three sisters' almost total lack of logistical support. He'd demonstrated to her the way it should work by magicking out of thin air an Irish nun – a Mother Superior in a German convent, no less – who had supplied him with an arsenal when he'd needed one, in return for what seemed to Chastity to be a tiny favour. He'd also talked about the excellence of a motorcycle as a hitter's escape machine. Chastity had absorbed it all, replayed it to herself when her nights were sleepless, and was now applying the wisdom.

The streetlights began to light. Dully at first, as was the modern, allegedly planet-saving way of these things, brightening steadily as the afternoon passed three o'clock, the hour for crucifixions, Chastity mused, if a little late for lunch, even if that lunch, by a semantic twist, was also Christmas dinner. An approaching car, its headlights far brighter than the streetlighting, was slowing and indicating its intention to pull off the road and into a driveway. Countdown time; three more driveways, the car slowed; two, and it moved to the crown of the road, Chastity thumbed the engine of the motorcycle into near-silent life; one more, and yes; this was her target, heading for a brief encounter of the worst kind.

She pulled up the hood of the waterproof jacket – a hiker's jacket over her biker's leather – hunched her shoulders, gripped the pistol in her pocket and ran smoothly across the road towards the parking car. A neat woman stepped from the driver's door. She was very obviously the target. As Chastity neared, she observed the heavy stance of the Mercedes, its unusually thick doors and window glazing. An armoured car. She pulled her free hand – the hand unoccupied by pistol duty – and waved it in the classic manner of someone attracting attention. The woman target paused, confused for a second, then started to return to her car, failing to catch the driver's door before it closed, then fumbling for the keys she'd dropped into her bag a few moments before.

Chastity returned her left hand to its pocket, where it found and squeezed an iPod, one connected to a decently realistic loudspeaker, which in turn shouted out in a young man's powerful voice 'You are the abomination you know you are, and your abomination is ending here!' and Chastity placed a single hollow-point parabellum round into her forehead, and a second then a third directly into her chest, before turning, trotting back to the quietly idling, steaming motorcycle, mounting it and throwing back her hood just enough to allow the crash helmet to sit comfortably and for her to have decent peripheral vision while at the same time keeping her features away from any unwelcome attention. Hopefully. Her gloved hands unscrewed the pistol's suppressor and slipped it into one pocket; the weapon itself relocated to another. Both zipped secure.

All along the road, a great amount of nothing was happening. As Chastity accelerated the motorcycle, she wondered whether her plan had worked completely, that the loud male shouting, as well as disguising her own gender, had produced sufficient noise to effectively mask the three shots.

She switched on the bike's headlight and headed away from comfortable, calm, safe and secure suburbia towards the dangerous heart of the city. 'One life ended, one perfectly good haircut ruined,' she mused. Almost worthwhile, then.

***

Chastity lived in the city. Any city. She prided herself on the very sophistication of the sophisticated requirements she demanded for her homes. A river. She loved to run their banks, drink coffee in their cafés, sail on their boats while wearing only black whenever her moods demanded. Parks, the more of them the more merry she was – although she doubted that anyone if asked would have described her as merry in any sense. She loved parks. She loved to run their pathways and could swim for several hours in their pools. A city without a park was a city without a heart; a park without a pool was a park without a purpose. She believed that, so it was always true, if only for her. She demanded the best and the worst kinds of cinemas, so she could immerse herself in the best and the worst kinds of movies, from spectacular and spectacularly bad mega-macho blockbusters to impenetrable, soul-searching, heart-rending and mind-bending movies from Norway and Japan, Russia and Korea, France and China. She lived for the breathtakingly consistent hypocrisy of Hollywoodland, the desperately grinning grief of Bollywoodland, and could watch nothing made in the UK which had any actors aged over sixty without leaving before she finished her smuggled cookies. That would be all of them.

And Chastity needed bookstores, and the only decent bookstores are found in cities with a university, so she demanded that she lived close to a seat of learning, preferably a seat of learning near to the parts of the city which contained rivers, and parks, and cinemas, and bookstores, and places where she could practise the physical skills which kept her alive as well as people who could act as antidotes to her increasingly frequent periods of emotional instability.

Not too much to ask.

She also preferred not to drive in a city, so it needed to be sufficiently compact for her to walk everywhere – which she preferred, especially at night in her periods of emotional instability, when she would go into any and all no-go districts and hope that some fool would mistake her for a mug, for a tart to be rolled and abused. Driving could be amusing, though she rarely drove for amusement, but driving in a city was hateful. She could have been the original sufferer from road rage, and found intolerable the stupid behaviour of fools who should in her view never have been granted a birth certificate, never mind a driver's license. City streets were filled with potential accidental murderers at the wheels of heavy weapons.

As she rolled down the ramp into the car park which stored the various vehicles of the inhabitants of her apartment block, Chastity reminded herself to remind herself to talk with Stoner some more about the unappreciated and unsung virtues of the motorcycle as a neat means of transport. No wonder they were the wheels of choice in so many third world nations. She looked around her at the brightly festive skyline of the city which was currently her home. She knew all about the third world.

She knew far less about Stoner and was, frankly, fascinated by him. She recognised that, and understood it. In all of her twenty-eight years, she had met only a handful of genuinely interesting people. And rather less for whom she had developed respect, liking, even affection. He was outstandingly competent, she recognised that too, and although she'd met several others with similar levels of ability and the experience to balance it effectively, she'd never actually liked them as individuals. She'd used them and she'd been used by them, but whatever offers they'd suggested, arrangements they'd made had been part of some barter system – everything had a price, be it financial or a future debt, nothing came for free. Except that Stoner had extracted her from a surely desperate situation in Israel for no reason other than that he'd been asked to do so. She would never have accepted a job like that. When she'd been set up in Germany, he had provided support, expertise and startling lessons in the tradecraft she would need if she intended to survive for long in her chosen world – again for no reason she could see.

And in what was probably his most remarkable action in the time they'd been together, he had declined her suggestion, honestly made, that they should make out. Not as any kind of trade, but simply because she wanted it… wanted him in that way. He'd turned her down in a way in which it was impossible for her to take offence, had demonstrated genuine consideration, done far more to assist than he'd been tasked with, and had then simply left. No goodbye kiss, no goodbye at all. He'd simply gone and remained gone.

If she allowed herself to dwell on the man, which she would only permit when she was entirely alone, in a darkened room listening to miserable women singing sadly about the things miserable women sing sadly about, then she would accept that she was probably more than simply fascinated. She hated that. Probably not as much as she hated her certain one hundred percent knowledge that Stoner had screwed her older sister, Charm, and indeed that when he'd last been in the UK they'd spent a lot of time together... probably screwing. She held the suspicion that he'd also screwed her departed sister, Charity, though he'd denied it, with that sickening half-smile men adopt when telling a sickening half-truth. He had no reason to lie about it, either, though that didn't mean much.

Everybody lies; her own sister had even established an entire fake identity to live by, which made for as many complications as it removed – Charm insisted that it simply maintained their own operational security. Too many players in their constipated and enclosed world knew who she was, but Stoner in particular didn't appear to be a seeker of truth, a chaser of facts. Another virtue in Chastity's eyes and in his favour. He simply appeared to lack both curiosity – which was famously fatal to felines – and appeared also to be wondrously capable of detaching himself from everything unimportant to him. Another virtue.

He was also improbably generous in the sack, as she had experienced and enjoyed somewhat, which made his refusal to actually do it, mate, copulate, penetrate and fornicate... all the more strange. Charm had told her in one of their rare moments of shared sisterly intimacy that he loved sex, could do it over and over, and was the only man who'd fucked her while actually playing tunes on a guitar. Chastity had needed to ask for ergonomic details of that one, as bewildered by the geometry of it as much as by the improbability. Charm had revealed that it was a unique way to observe a fellow musician doing two of the things he did best at the same time. Also that the next time he played the song he'd been noodling with while deep inside her and rocking to their shared rhythm he'd dedicated it to her and thanked her for the inspiration behind the solo he played. Somehow this displeased Chastity very much. And she knew too well the reason why. Whenever she considered her sister, Charm, and Stoner together, knowing each other, being intimate, she understood hatred. Not for him. Not for Stoner.

She turned keys, shot bolts, let herself into her apartment. No lights. Time for those later. Stood stock still, listened, breathed in the emptiness. Walked to the wide window and contemplated the shining city spread before her. Turned around, suddenly convinced that he was here. Had let himself in, as he could and would, and was waiting with a half-smile and a questioning eyebrow and a coffee suggestion. Always coffee.

No one was there. Just his picture on the wall. A beautifully composed image shot by someone who could use a camera as its maker intended, a man and a woman, together on a stage, the small woman playing a large bass guitar and singing to a microphone, the man – him – watching her eyes and fingering a beat-up Fender guitar. There was love in his eyes. She would kill for that.

10

CHRISTMAS LAST YEAR: LIFE ON THE OCEAN. WAVE!

'There are times in a man's life when he needs to understand that everything is inconstant, that everything changes. That the only truth is what you can experience for yourself, while you're experiencing it. Doesn't matter what it is or what it feels like. What matters is that you understand that you're experiencing it, that you understand it and that it may continue to work for you or it may not. Happy Christmas, JJ. You may doubt the intent of the sentiment, but that doesn't diminish its honesty nor its validity. This is a well-wishing.'

The voice sounded as though it came from the dark side of the planet, which may have been the case, but its message was undiluted by its tonal qualities sounding as though a legion of devils or the harmonies of the spheres were whispering in conspiracy between the digital bursts which carried the words. Which they may have been, though it was unlikely.

Even less likely to Stoner's empirical view of the ways of the world was that he was hearing it at all. A cell phone sitting on the table where he was assembling his breakfast had rung – a curious ever-ascending scale of tripped-out hippy jingling which he would never allow to disgrace any of his own phones. Any of them. He ignored it while it did its repeated cycling impersonation of an insane atonal acid-head playing with a Stylophone. And then it stopped its chiming, and he ceased his chopping.

Two things: it was not his phone. He knew where all of them were, and none of them was on the table, none of them was the whole deal, they lacked SIM cards and batteries. They were the shells of cell phones. The second thing was that there was no cell signal within dozens of miles of the table, which was a curiosity at the very least. The third – there is always a third party in any legitimate duet – was the way the phone failed to switch to voicemail. Instead its screen flickered several times as it accepted the impossible call. Seriously hands-free operation – operator-free, in fact. Volition-free; no human hand was involved at this end of the remarkable electronic transaction – Stoner stood by the table alone. Woken by the curiously intimate while at the same time all too public sounds of some strenuous and plainly absorbing nearby sex in which he was not a participant, he had run some, swum some, steamed alone in a tub big enough for several, and had retired to prepare breakfast for three.

The very smart phone had switched itself on. How did it do that? The phone had accepted the call. How did it do that? The phone had switched itself to speaker mode. How did it do that? And now a voice he almost recognised despite the revulsion, loathing and fear it generated and some heavyside interference was wishing him a happy Christmas. How the fuck did it do that, by the flaming beard of the outraged prophet?

'When we meet, JJ, as we surely will, we need to

make it a new beginning. If we can't do that, either you'll kill me or I'll have you killed. Neither makes any sense except on an emotional level. And it was unbalanced emotions which got in our way the last time. Think about that. I'll hear you if you speak, but I care not a bit if you'd prefer not to.

'I need to tell you something. It's a true something, although whether you can bring yourself to believe it is up to you. The thing. The video. Her and him. The shame and the pain of it. I didn't do that. I did not permit it. I allowed the access which made it possible because I was comprehensively lied to. Deceived. Worse: I was distracted. The outcome I had agreed was not what you saw.

'I'd prefer to discuss this with the full body-language thing, face to face, no weapons allowed. It would be for the best if you took no unsupported action before that, but you'll do what you want to do. Rightly. Be as unpredictable as you can.

'And, JJ, a goodwill gesture for you to ignore as you please. Take the SIM and the batteries out of this device. It can listen as well as it can talk, and it works as well as a transmitter as it does as a receiver.' The voice grated and sounded tired, old and sick. 'Many agencies can provide remote operation services using airborne eyes and such. My contact details are on your own phones, as you'll see when you power them up.' The voice croaked and its owner coughed. 'I hear you're back on the up, JJ. Hope it's true.'

The disconnect was crackly and faint, accompanied by a descending whine, like a camera flash gun's capacitor charging, but in reverse. Stoner reached over, lifted the phone, looked at its call logs, opened its more intimate cavities and removed both SIM card and battery. Placed the components on the table before him but as far from him as possible. He leaned forward, bracing himself, both legs and both arms spread to balance his weight. His eyes closed.

'You OK?' She sounded as though her concern was genuine. 'Who was that? How did you get a signal out here? Why'd you use my phone? No problem, but how did you know my code for it? Is there any coffee? I can smell coffee.'

Stoner picked up a bowl and poured coffee into it, replacing the pot on the stove, turned and passed the drink to her. 'I did none of those things. I've taken the batteries and the SIM card out of your phone. No number called your number today – or yesterday or the day before that. They can't. There's no signal. Someone – some agency, more like – activated the thing, switched it to loudspeaker and talked at me. Weird, huh? The guy suggested I remove your battery, such like.'

'Who was it? Friend or foe?'

'Dunno. Sorry; I know who it was – someone who should be dead – but whether he's a friend, yours or mine, I… I have no idea. We had a falling out. The worst kind. Good to know that the bad guys – probably – know where I am. I should be moving on.'

'Why? Is someone out to get you?'

'Truth? I don't know. Can't see why they would want to trek here to the arse-end of Nowhere, USA just to… to do what? Set bear traps? I need to think. Coffee good? I also got breakfast… nearly got breakfast. Distracted by digital magic, huh?' He smiled, turned to face her for the first time that day. 'Hello Dawn. You sleep well? You should probably get away from here, in case they do send the bad guys. Those black helos.' His smile had quit.

Dawn leaned into him and kissed him slowly – far

too slowly – on his lips. 'Lovely, JJ. Lovely night. They usually are, if permitted.' Her eyes smiled into his. 'Who are they? And how bad are the bad guys?'

Stoner returned his attention to the breakfast, purposelessly moved some bacon, flipped some hash browns then flipped them back. 'Pancakes?' he wondered. Then: 'Bad as they get. Efficient. The sort of bad who if they want you dead you're dead; they want you damaged you're damaged. Simple as that. The sort of bad guys you can't hide from.' He whipped up a mean pancake batter. Aggression cuisine. 'Coffee's brewing.'

'You're hiding, then?' It was a question. 'Coffee doesn't brew.' A statement. 'That's tea. Coffee filters. So you're hiding?'

'Probably.' Stoner poured pancake batter into crackling butter, inhaled the steam from it. 'Not sure.' He looked up from his cooking, held her eyes. 'It felt like I was hiding before. Now it doesn't. Know what I mean?'

'No.' Dawn laughed, softly. 'You're some spook buddy of Travis. You could be planning a revolution for all I'd know. And you'd lie about it to me. Spooks do that, don't they?' She looked up. 'That's how they're spooks. They tell lies.'

'Never met an honest spook? Apart from Travis of course.'

'Travis isn't honest. That's one reason I'm one of the former Mrs Travises. How can a woman believe any man who tells lies for a living?'

'Like journalists, huh?'

'Not that bad. Sheesh. Nothing could be that bad. Journalists are worse than... oh, I dunno... priests.' They both laughed, softly. Stoner concentrated on an improbably complicated way of producing breakfast, Dawn poured for them both. The dark vapour of the fresh brew eased itself around them.

'He calls all his wives – maybe all his women, I've not met many of those – he calls all his wives Missy.' Dawn smiled at Stoner through the coffee vapour. A shared hideaway.

'Why?'

'Not sure about the truth of it – the honesty thing again – but he told me once it was a relic of Vietnam.'

'He's too young to have served there.' Stoner was definite, thoughtful, began the transfer of food from stove to plate. 'Like me.'

'He worked – no idea whether he served anything – in Vietnam for a time. They called it a trade mission.'

'OK. I get that.' Stoner. 'He's not a military man, then?'

'Oh. Maybe. Depends on your view of what's military. He holds a military rank.'

'He does?'

'He does. He's a colonel of some kind.'

'Army, then.'

'Navy.'

'Holy crap, how do you guys remember anything? You have colonels in the navy?'

'No idea, but he is one. Weird, though.' She paused, sat down, collected cutlery and sliced into a hash brown. 'He never really talked about it. Just sometimes – not often – a letter would arrive, addressed to Colonel Travis.'

'You opened his mail?' Mild incredulity. 'OK, I suppose that's what wives do. Never had one myself, but I understand the theory.'

'No. Never did, never would. He asked me not to and I honoured that. Not too sure why. He was the dishonest one. Read everything that came for me. Played back my voicemail, read my email. Every time I'd open a new account he'd have the password within a day.'

'That's… intrusive. Also seriously paranoid.'

'He always told me it was the only way a marriage to someone like him could work. He had total access to everything I did, read, listened to; he knew all my friends whether or not I introduced them. I met very few of the people he worked with.'

'Sounds like… sounds like no fun at all. You agreed to this? Some kind of super-spook pre-nup or whatever?'

'It was exciting at first. Like a conspiracy. But it gets very old very fast. Great breakfast, Mister French Limey. Tell me about the guy on the phone. Very magic guy if he can make a phone work where there's no signal. How'd he do that?'

Stoner pushed his emptied plate away, stood and brought more coffee for them both. 'No idea,' he said. 'Too geek by far for me.'

'What did he want? Must be something serious to do all that tricky technical stuff. You did say he was supposed to be dead? Travis knew some guys like that. Dead. Not dead. You know what I mean.' A flat statement. She leaned back in her chair and observed her table mate.

'A rapprochement. Maybe a warning. I don't need either, me. Fresh out of vacancies in the Friends Wanted column. Nothing he can warn me about but that shit happens, it continues to happen and it will happen again. Hard to get overwhelmed with excitement about that. Or terror. Whatever. You ever have friends who were exactly the opposite of what they seemed?'

She nodded. 'Oh yes. Lots of those. Women can be bitches. You knew that already? This is, like, news to you?'

He smiled. 'No. Really? Would never have thought it. All angels to me. Every one a blessing.' He paused. Looked up. 'Blesses in disguise.'

'Say what?' There were sounds of life outside their magic circle of two. 'Blessings? You meant to say blessings?'

'Not really. Blesses is a person. A woman. She is... strange.'

'All women are strange to all men, Mister Strange Canadian. JJ. Do you know any women who aren't strange?' She reached what appeared to be a decision. Rose to her feet and passed around their shared table until she was standing next to Stoner, looking over his shoulder at his coffee... at the table... at nothing in particular. 'I'd lay odds that you do not. Long odds at that. All your women are strange.' She rested her forearms on his shoulders, either side of his head. Whispered. 'And what's with the... ah... non-performance? You repressed? You don't seem the type.' She pointed downward, between Stoner's thighs. 'Little guy on vacation?'

Stoner shrugged. Leaned his head back next to hers and whispered; 'He's gone away. Needed a break. Everyone needs a break once in a while. Stops them getting too bored. Boredom's a killer, I've heard.' She nodded, rubbing the side of her head against his, breathing through his long hair, his beard.

'And in any case,' he stepped slowly away from her, apart from her. 'I don't want to spoil a party. A family reunion, whatever you and Sonny've got going.' He raised his eyes, square-on to hers. 'Life is complicated enough. Stressed enough. You and your boy. Should be enough for each other. I don't want to intrude.'

'Don't think you'd be intruding, exactly. More... ah... joining in. You bothered about a troy? A threesome?' She managed to maintain her straight face, her innocent tone.

Stoner shook his head, smiled, turned his eyes

back to the patient breakfast. 'No. Not at all. They're fun, sometimes.' He reached for the warmed plates, set them up, served further food for himself, passed the slice and the long fork to Dawn. 'But they always end up the same way. There's always a loser. They're always competitions.'

'Maybe.' Dawn served herself; a surprisingly piled plate. 'Reckon you'd be the winner, huh? Or you couldn't face losing.' She walked to the table, kicked back a hard chair, sat, placed her plate before her. 'Say grace.'

'Grace.' Stoner parked up opposite. 'Old jokes huh? Don't care about losing, Dawn. Don't care for games. Not now. Not today. You fuck with your boy if that's your way.' He ate steadily, cutting his food neatly, chewing with study and appreciation. Dawn forked eggs, hash brown, no knife, as is the American way, the new order of cutlery.

'Sonny.' She paused in her chewing. 'You think he's my son?'

Stoner nodded, held her eyes. She shook her head, forked in some beans, egg. Chewed.

'He's not. He belongs to Travis. Long story. Born while we were still married – me and Travis – but not to me. A decent reason for a divorce, you reckon?'

Stoner nodded, raised an eyebrow. 'Neat,' he said. 'Neat. You screw your ex-husband's son. Why? For fun? Revenge? I could see that.'

'No. We took to hiking together when he was maybe twelve. Thirteen. Whatever. Then he got real difficult, school trouble, kid trouble, fights, you know?'

Stoner nodded, food forgotten between them. Forks resting a while.

'Then the rest of it. Consolation, understanding, just started and... you know?'

Stoner nodded again. 'Consolation fornication.' He smiled. 'Sounds like a song, a country number with steel guitars and much whining, midnight drives on long dark highways. What does Travis have to say about it?'

'He doesn't care. After the first time, after I told him what happened, he told me I was a disgrace, that I could go to prison for it. Corruption of a minor. Something. Then he said thanks. He kissed me, held me to him – first time in a couple of years – said thanks. And wow, things like that. Strange time.' She shook her head, pushed her plate from her and kicked back in the chair.

'You enjoy it, though? Young man, first love, first fuck at least. Maybe it's flattering?'

'It's like being screwed by a gorilla. You've seen how he's hung? You watch that thing when he gets it really going. Deep. Goes deep, you know?'

'Career in the movies, then. Can't fail. Hung like a horse, built like Rambo, pokes like a great ape. Studios would be crying out for him. I'll stick to kitchen duties.' He cleared their plates, piled things into the sink, made with the suds. 'Where is superboy, anyway? Out wrestling grizzlies, something? Listening from the bedroom?'

'He goes off most days. Runs, walks. Like you do, I expect. Boys being boys, as they usually are.' Stoner didn't reply. Stood, leaned against the sink. Stretched. Joints cracked.

'Think I'll take a shower,' he remarked, vaguely, distracted. 'Could do with one.'

Quicker than any flash, she stood. 'Scrub your back, then. I'll scrub your back.'

Stoner shrugged, walked away. 'Whatever.' He stopped, half turned. 'Sorry. That would be kind. Generous, even.' Carried on, stopped and stripped, then walked through into the wet room, turned on water; steam billowed around him, and he turned his face, eyes closed towards the showerhead. A loud crack announced that his backside had received a well-aimed smack. He leaned forwards, face to the wall, hands on the wall, assuming the position beloved of cops in cop movies. Spread his legs as wide as his spread arms. Was rewarded by scrub, soap, scrub, rinse, repeat and repeat again. He turned, leaned his shoulders back against the wall, Dawn scrubbed, soaped some more.

'You're shivering,' she said. 'You OK?'

He didn't reply, shook a little despite the heat and his obvious perspiration. She washed him, everywhere, all over, cleaned him and scrubbed him pink. His muscles were still, hard but relaxed. She took his cock in her hand, rubbed, squeezed, rubbed some more. He opened his eyes, stared into hers, took her shoulders and pulled her against him. A temporary tableau in a heated waterfall. Dawn turned, walked out into the main room, Stoner turned off the water and walked in silence after her, walked straight into a hot towel, wrapped by her hands around him.

'You're crying.' There was genuine shock and surprise in her voice. 'I'm sorry,' she said, and wiped his eyes. 'Sorry I saw that.' She kissed him then, gently, kindly, with affection, no lust.

'Fucking old folk!' Sonny screamed with humourless laughter. 'Jesus, it's gramps and grandma!' He slapped Dawn hard on her backside. 'Old folks' bathtime!' He laughed again, no kindness in it. Then he was flying, somehow. He'd watched the impact of his strong right hand on the wet skin of Dawn's ass, didn't see the arrival of Stoner, who with no apparent effort and with no sound at all, lifted Sonny from his feet, spun him on some axis or other and propelled him into sudden contact with the sturdy and empty table. Stoner dropped to a squat, caught Sonny's left foot in both his hands, lifted, twisted, pulled and rose, walked backwards pulling that foot.

Sonny flailed his arms and screamed in threat. The wrong response. Stoner squatted once again, lifting Sonny's foot above him as he sank to a crouch, swung his left foot in a fast cutting arc, catching Sonny's right ankle in passing, skidding it along the rumpling rug and bringing the back of Sonny's head cracking hard into the edge of the table. Stoner rose, taking Sonny's left foot, the attached leg and a fair amount of Sonny's torso with him, stopping, standing and watching in silence as the much younger man's head cracked again, this time onto the bare hard floor of the cabin, cracking hard where a second earlier there'd been a rug to ease the impact. No rug.

Stoner dropped the limb, was suddenly smoothly standing next to the fallen youth, who began a groan, a groan cut off long before its prime by an abrupt silence as the tented knuckles of Stoner's right fist contacted Sonny's temple with more precision than force. Silence. A fallen youth. Two naked adults.

'Shit,' said Dawn, quietly. Her attention was entirely on Stoner, standing and breathing easily before her, and watching the fallen Sonny. 'That is some hard-on you've got there. Quite the upright soldier.'

Stoner looked up at her, looked down at Sonny, shifted his gaze once again to Dawn, and nodded. 'That's all it takes,' he said, conversationally. 'Although it has its limits, seduction-wise. And it fades as fast as it shines. There y'go. Actions louder, words betray, things like that.' There was no trace of a tear in either of his eyes. Dark and cold. Resignation.

Dawn took hold of his hand, joined him in quiet contemplation of fallen youth. Shook her head. 'Now what?'

'Depends on what you want. I can apologise and reveal that despite being ancient, old reflexes die hard. Or I can take him outside into the cold and explain that for his own good he needs to learn some manners. Does he fuck around like that with Travis?"

'Dunno. Never see them together.' Dawn paused. 'How long's he down for?'

'How long do you want? Why?'

'Can he hear us?'

Stoner knelt beside Sonny, peeled open an eye and tapped its ball gently with his forefinger. The eyelids squeezed together, but slowly, and there was no other reaction. 'Guess not,' he said. 'Why?'

'Because I've had enough. Of him,' she added for extra clarity.

Stoner nodded. 'Tell him,' he suggested.

'Tried. Failed. Tried again and failed again. That time he was so riled up I was scared, too.'

'Tell Travis.'

'Too steep a climb-down. I don't think I even know how I'd do it.'

'OK. How do you want to handle this?'

Dawn paused. Moved her gaze between the two men, back and forth. From younger to older and back again. 'What would you recommend?'

No hesitation. 'Kill him. Bury him here.'

She waited for more. For maybe a smile to say everything's OK, it's just a joke. But there was nothing. Stoner idled, in neutral, like a machine, a killing machine.

'That was a joke, right?'

'Not really. Easy enough to carry out; quick and

clean. Easy to tidy up. Lost in the woods, eaten by a bear. I've done it before. Traceless. No comebacks. Shared sympathy, much insincere weeping. If his dad – Travis – cared much for him, would he be letting him shack up with... ' he paused, looked away from Sonny, up to catch Dawn's eye. 'Letting his son shack up with his nearly-mother? Legal mother, maybe. I'm uncertain of your American laws.' There should have been an accompanying smile, but there was not.

'You are serious.' A statement at last. An acceptance. Maybe a consideration.

Stoner nodded, watching Sonny.

'Do you hate him?' Dawn was watching Stoner, carefully keeping her attention away from Sonny.

'What?' Stoner shook his head, once, quickly. 'Wrong question. No. No I don't. But I like you. In my own way. He will – most likely – be a pain, a burden. He's just another shit; the world has plenty of those, it can stand to lose a few. More than a few, truth be told. Good guys should look out for one another.'

'Christ.' Dawn shook her head once again. 'I took you seriously.' She attempted a smile. Stoner said nothing. Watched. Idling. The young man stirred, groaned a little.

'There's another way.' Dawn was uncertain, pale.

Stoner was calm, comfortable. 'There are many. There always are. It's between you and him. Not me. You'll be gone from here soon enough. Then I'll be going... sometime later. I'll not see him again, most likely, but you will. Certainly will. He's onto a good thing. He gets laid, he gets great vacations, he gets to do whatever he wants. Best you can hope for is that the lust wears off and he'll get into his teenage buddies' pants and ditch you. That's what the best outcome is, that he just ditches you. You can be his first fuck and his first dump too. A parallel if not entirely pleasing prospective.'

Stoner quite suddenly smiled. 'Did I tell you I have a friend?' He paused again, though the smile held firm. 'Yeah, guess she is a friend – a professional friend at least. She's killed every guy who's fucked her. Every one.' He looked down at the groaning youth. 'I understand her better now. You happy for him to wake up?' He nodded towards Sonny. 'He's surfacing. Not be long now before action hero here starts acting the twat again.'

'She's what? She's killed – killed! – all her lovers? You have some truly strange friends. You one of her lovers? You hiding from her? She the history you don't talk about?'

'Not her lovers. I doubt she's had many – any – of those. No. I'm not hiding. We're sort-of friends, like I said.'

Sonny quite suddenly tipped up onto his knees, onto his feet, lunged at Stoner, trying either to grab him or hit him, his rage the only obvious focus to his attack. Stoner evaded, tripped his attacker, dumped him on the floor again, shaking his head. 'Stay down,' he said. 'We're talking here. Grown-ups, you know?'

'Fuck you!' And Sonny was on the move again, attacking again with all the supercharged idiot optimism and enraged testosterone energy of a wild young male. Stoner caught the approaching fist, rolled around it, twisting and sliding and turning and bending the arm attached to the fist until it was behind the much younger man and rising fast behind him, seemingly independently of its owner until it reached the limits of Sonny's shoulder articulation whereupon its continued upward progress should have halted, but Stoner shifted his grip, rearranged himself until what had been a yell of defiance shifted to a shrill shriek of offended pain and the younger man's shoulder cracked loudly into an unlikely geometry, an unfamiliar profile and quite suddenly Stoner stopped moving and Sonny stopped shrieking. The two men stood, locked.

'Now you've got me.' Stoner's whispered voice was somehow louder than a shout. The two men and Dawn were motionless. 'How do I get out of this? I'm open to suggestions, big boy.' Sonny was silent bar his harsh, fast panting. 'This is called the upper hand for a reason.' Stoner moved Sonny's hand up his back a fraction. Sonny maintained his silence but was quite suddenly sweating more. 'It's like this.' Stoner appeared to be speaking ever more quietly. His audience strained to hear him. 'If I move it much more – and you can't stop me unless you know some excellent martial close combat stuff that I failed to notice so far – if I move it more than a little the sprained shoulder will dislocate completely. Then you've got me in another difficult spot. You follow?'

Sonny shook his head. His lips formed an 'f' but he wisely silenced them.

'A dislocated shoulder is very painful, but you can live with it. A decent field medic or a casualty nurse should be able to pop it back in for you, so long as the head of humerus doesn't damage the rotator cuff when it pops out. I could probably do it myself.' Stoner paused. Nodded. 'Probably could. It would hurt though. Be sore as hell for a little while. But I wouldn't. You know what I'd do?'

Sonny shook his head a tiny amount, and even that made him wince a little. 'No,' he said.

'As soon as your right shoulder dislocated, I would be consumed by fear. You're a spunky young guy, full of piss and vinegar, and I'd be really scared that you'd go for me with your good left hand, which is an unknown quantity for me because you've never landed a punch from it on me so I need to be vigilant. So I'd break the other shoulder. Dislocating it would be less painful for you but harder for me to achieve from this position, without risk of all your great swinging dick super-strength, so forth, so it would be easier to just break the joint. I can do that from here while your eyes are watering a bit from the dislocation. You see my problem.'

Sonny shook his head again, fractionally again. He was growing very pale and was sweating more. 'No,' he said again. 'Not really.'

'OK. Let me ask you a question. It's quite complicated, so you need to listen carefully. It's a compound question, it contains a conditional clause. These are important in English. Your answer, on the other hand, needs to be a single word, a monosyllable in fact. The word you will reply will be yes or it will be no. Silence counts as a no and I do the damage. Got that?'

Sonny nodded. 'Yes,' he said. Quietly.

'If I release you, without dislocating anything or breaking anything, are you going to walk straight to that wall in front of you and sit down on the floor and not try anything stupid or aggressive towards me or Dawn? Sorry that's such a difficult and complicated question, but I'll help you with your reasoning. Hush for a little longer.'

Sonny's eyes were bulging a little, his lips were almost theatrically clenched.

'Good. If you answer yes, but then renege on that in any way, any way at all while the three of us are in this place, then I will either kill you outright – and you must not for one second believe that I either wouldn't or couldn't do that, regardless of what Dawn might ask – or I will break one of your shoulders and one of your knees. Maybe both, depending on how pissed off I am with you. Got that? Good. Now. Answer my question. I'm not going to repeat it.'

Sonny coughed an instant 'Yes.' Followed it with 'Yes I'll go straight to the wall and sit down and stay there.'

Stoner released him and stepped away from him. 'Good,' he said. 'Good boy. Easy with the joint. The tendons are stretched and the bicep may cramp some.'

Sonny walked stiffly to the wall, holding his right shoulder with his left hand. He turned, and slid his back down the wall until he was sitting down on the cabin floor. His expression was a peculiar mix of pain, hate and fear.

Stoner remained where he was, motionless apart from a rhythmic stretch and relax of all the fingers on both hands. His eyes were fixed on Sonny. 'I really dislike throwing punches,' he remarked in a quiet, conversational tone. 'Always bothered that I'll damage my fingers. Screws up my playing – guitar playing. Know what I mean?'

Sonny was silent. Dawn simply stared at Stoner. A matched pair of silences.

Stoner looked over to Dawn. 'You might want to get dressed.'

She nodded, turned back to him and asked 'You?'

'I'm fine.' Stoner walked to the stove. 'I'll do a coffee.' He poured, just the one mug, turned again to face Sonny. 'Good that you didn't move then. Hot coffee in the face can burn the skin quite badly, and the glass from the pot is a shitter to get out of the eyes. You need to remember all these things. They will help you in later life. You need to learn – and fast – that attacking someone you don't know well enough can go badly wrong. You need to believe that you are not invincible. And you need to understand – get your adolescent hormonally fucked up brain to understand – that the only reason I didn't kill you was because it would upset Dawn.' He sipped his coffee, nodded. 'Nice,' he said, probably referring to the coffee. 'I like Dawn. I care no more about you than I would about a dog. Just noisy and irritating and pointless. Got that? Have you got that?' He raised a his voice, but only a little.

'Yes, sir.'

Dawn had returned, dressed for the woods. She held out a shirt, some pants to Stoner, who paused in his appreciation of the coffee to shake his head again. 'I'm not sure that superboy here can be trusted yet. A man's vulnerable while he's pulling on his pants. You can't fight with your arms over your head and tangled in a T-shirt. Superboy might work that out and have a last bash at the action hero crap. Which would be his last act, because I would break bits of him until he was no longer a concern.' He turned to face Sonny, who'd not moved at all. 'Did you get that? *Comprende?*'

'Yes, sir.'

'Cool,' said Stoner. 'Let's hope we're making progress. Can you drive?'

'Yes, sir.'

'Better yet. Are you feeling calm? Comfortable? Have you given up all thoughts of combat?'

'Yes, sir.'

'Well then. You're going to take a walk, then you're going to take a drive, and then I'll never see you again without an appointment. I mean that. You're going to take the keys to Dawn's boat, and you're going to agree with her where she can collect it, and... yes?'

Dawn interrupted. 'It's a rental,' she said. 'I don't need it back.'

'Good. All cool. You get to return the boat to the hire office and you get to borrow her car too...' He looked at Dawn, who nodded. 'You need to go far away, from me and from Dawn. If she ever wants to see you, talk to you, she'll tell you. With me so far? Good.

'You need to learn many things from today's lesson, Sonny. I'm no teacher and I truly don't care whether you survive or no, but it would be useful to your continued existence if you took with you one profound understanding. That understanding would be that you do not – not ever – mess with me. If you do it again the consequences will be very bad, but only for you. And before your little boy brain gets around to thinking about setting your daddy on me, remember that I will already have spoken with him about this, and that he and I will have no argument over you. You need to understand that, which is a lot for a juvenile fuckwit, but there we go. That's it.' He put down the coffee mug and picked up the pants Dawn had offered. 'You still here?'

'Sir?' The voice was quiet, polite, a study in caution.

'Hmm.' Stoner zipped up and belted. A study in unconcern.

'I don't want to go.'

'Say again.'

'I want to stay here.'

'Please do not be stupid.' Stoner rolled the sleeves of his shirt. 'Just go. Now would be best.'

'What about my things? What about... everything?'

'Imagine you have no things. Imagine that your entire future depends on my goodwill and best wishes, both in short supply and dwindling all the time you're not doing as instructed. Imagine that I tell you the simple truth – and truth is always simple – that you are not at this moment in control of your destiny, except in a philosophical and hypothetical sense. The person in control here is me. That's it. What you think is of no importance to me. From a moral perspective I have no concerns for your future at all. It would be easier for me if you simply disappeared into that permanent silence and provided bug food from your hole in the ground than if you do as I've instructed and just go away, very far and very fast. Are you following this? Do I need to draw a diagram or beat up on you a little more for you to understand the permanence of your situation should you actually stay here? If you stay here you will be in a hole in the ground. Were I the kind of melodramatist who takes pleasure from scaring soft lads like you I would make some comment about you digging your own grave in a literal sense, but that's what you're actually doing in a figurative sense.

'You have no choices in this, Sonny-boy. I'm making all the compromises here, only because your death would upset Dawn. My respect for her wishes rests on a balance of your making. Every second you waste tips that balance. It would be easier for me to kill you and offer you as fertiliser to the forest spirits than to let you leave. Don't waste your life.'

'Would you really just kill me? I ain't done nothing to you.'

'If you stay I'll lie awake at night scared you'll knife me in my sleep.'

'No you won't.'

'True. But only because you're going. That simple truth again.'

'You can't make me go. I don't care what you say. You're not my dad and this is my dad's house.' Sonny's voice was rising, as was his colour. Dawn stood, and then sat down again.

Stoner was moving. He moved fast and very quietly, quick bare feet on Indian-pattern rugs. He caught Sonny's left hand, lifted it, separated a finger. Sonny made to rise, Stoner bent back the finger and twisted the arm. Sonny resumed a tense immobility, a stressed stasis.

'You ever had a broken bone?' Stoner's tone of voice was the same conversational tone as before. 'A decent dislocation? A fracture dislocation? Something like?' Sonny said nothing, sweat beading out on his forehead again. 'Here y'go,' said Stoner, and pulled and twisted and bent and pulled again, then released the hand and lifted the arm while Sonny screamed, subsided and screamed again as Stoner stamped his left foot onto Sonny's thigh to provide the necessary geometry for his violence.

'This is your last lesson. Take it or leave it. The finger will set and heal easily, but the important thing right now is that you remember the pain. The pain of a simple single finger dislocation. A shoulder is really bad in comparison, and you'd struggle to drive a vehicle with a stick shift if you can only use one arm. And – had you noticed that we're here again? Again already? You just piss me off despite my kind and reasonable approach. Go now, and I won't hurt you anymore. If you pretend to go and stage some idiot teenage second coming I'll just snuff you out. Pop. Go.' He stood straight, released the younger man, returned to the pot and poured another coffee.

'Dawn...' Sonny rose to his feet and turned to her.

'He's right. Catch.' She threw a set of keys to him. 'Don't come back.'

Stoner hopped up and seated himself on the edge of the wooden worktop. Silent, watching. Sonny collected a wallet, left them in silence. A silence broken by the firing of a boat engine, fading again, slowly.

***

'I'm shaking.' Dawn poured herself a coffee, added water to the pot, collapsed into a chair and stared at Stoner, still perched on the edge of the worktop. 'What now?'

'Now? In what sense?'

'Will he go, do you think? Or will he come back later?'

Stoner dropped from his perch and crossed over to her.

'Truth? I have no idea. I figured that you'd not leave guns in your vehicle, and he's not going to hurt either of us without one. Did I figure correctly?'

'You did.' Dawn relaxed a little. 'Why... why the violence, JJ? He's only a kid. And were you serious? About killing him?'

'Always. Never joke about violence of any kind. I cut him huge slack because he's young. And he means something to you, which I struggle to understand but won't waste much effort trying; women and men are very different. What makes sense to them varies too much.'

'Dawn relaxed a little more. 'OK, I'll try again. Will he come back?'

'I'll try again too.' Stoner sounded more pensive then before. 'I can't see why he would. No point. He needs to believe that I would fuck him up profoundly, which is the case. I guess he'll run back to Travis, or whichever institution kennels him when he's not yomping and bonking with a woman old enough to be his mom. Then when Travis refuses to do anything apart from maybe making sympathetic noises, he'll get obsessed by the sudden lack of sex in his life and focus on fixing that. He'll forget about me. And he'll find solace in the arms of some bendy young girl who's easily swayed by daddy's money and Sonny's dick, and then he'll forget about you too. He'll hate us both and vow revenge, teenage crap like that, but no more. I guess. Maybe he'll get civilised and learn to get on, to stop being difficult, whatever, and maybe he won't. I struggle to care, frankly.'

Dawn's eyes had closed. 'Now what, action hero? What happens now? You've seen off the upstart, rescued the maiden from distress. What do you do now?' Her eyes flicked open, filled with mischief. Maybe relief. Maybe more than either. 'Does action hero reveal to the rescued maiden his innermost thoughts while demonstrating his famous prowess with the pork sword of legend?' She shook her head. 'Hang on, hang on, I'm wrestling with the demure smile of certain innocence. It's not easy.'

'I bet.' Stoner slumped back into a chair. 'This place is remarkably comfortable. Warm. Hot, even. When I first arrived I tried to heat it using wet bits of tree, willpower, so forth. Never occurred to me that it came with central heating. Life is filled with surprises.'

'Do I need to be scared of you, JJ Stoner? I'm stuck here with you. Sonny's got the boat. Should I be scared?'

Stoner shook his head. 'No. Your young boyfriend attacked me, Dawn. I can't handle that, not at the moment. He did it once, he'd do it again. And again. You told me – hell, he told me himself that he'd got issues, whatever issues might be in the minds of youth. I'm not a great one for love and understanding at the moment.'

'Talk about it? In a little detail this time?'

'Maybe. It's not pretty. Sounds like a fairy tale, and it

makes not enough sense. That said...' He trailed notice of his own indecision.

'Obvious that it's going to be screwed up, big man.' Dawn talked softly calmly, thoughtfully. 'You're nearly in tears when I scrub your back in the shower; you demolish a guy way less than half your age and bigger than you, then threaten to kill him if he doesn't jump through the hoops for you. Have I got it so far? Am I missing that essential something which reassures me that I'm not in the care of a schizophrenic psycho whose moods swing unpredictably from gentle to murderous in a second?'

'OK, JJ. Simple self-preservation tells me I should have left with Sonny, but I didn't, and I don't feel threatened. Maybe we're both screw-ups. What do you think of that, huh? So what happened? Can I help, and where do you go from here? Did you spot that I asked about where you go? I didn't include me in that. Mother Theresa I am not, though I enjoy a guy with a little... power in him.'

'I'm going to make a phone call,' Stoner announced, solemnly.

'Say what?'

'But first, let me tell you a story. Let me tell you a tale. There will be questions afterwards, so listen up. I'll brew a fresh pot.' He performed that task, talking while he did so, neatly and deliberately disproving the theory that men cannot multitask.

'I did a job. Don't interrupt. I'm trying to lay it out for you – and for me, because it needs to make sense. Is it hot enough in here for you to strip your clothes off?'

'Say what? I need to strip? You want to check me for hidden microphones and cameras or something?'

'No. I just like looking at naked women. Cheers me up. Always has. I had a partner for a while, few years ago now. Brilliant woman. Irish. Demon intelligence, analysis skills like a supercomputer – a Kray or something. One time I was completely mind-fucked; no real idea of what was happening around us, she told me to talk it through, and she told me that she had a way of helping me concentrate. To avoid all distractions so everything would be clear. She'd do that, she said, by stripping off and fingering herself to her climax while I talked. Her scientific theory was that if my lame male animal brain concentrated on what she was doing, and my sophisticated Hom Sap forebrain concentrated on the story I was telling, then the latter would come up with an answer.'

'Did it work?'

'Yep.'

'And afterwards you screwed like coyotes, yes?'

'Yep.'

'You did it often?'

'Yep.'

'Then what? Why are you in a hut in the hills with me rather than in some other hut in some other hills with her?'

'She went into a convent and took Holy Orders.'

'No kidding?'

'No. That's what she did. You care to apply her scientific reasoning?' Dawn stripped efficiently, lay back in the chair before him. Sat up, drank deeply of her coffee, shook her head, giggled a little, and lay back.

'This is bizarre,' she said. 'No one will believe me when I tell them how I spent Christmas.'

'The short version, then.' Stoner wasn't actually looking at Dawn, but somewhere else entirely. Nowhere in that cabin, in those hills.

'For a long time – dozen years or so – I worked for

a government man. Brit government. Off the books. All sorts of jobs best done by contractors to avoid embarrassment. That was me. I worked for the same guy. We both knew how it worked for each other; he knew what I was likely to be good at and I knew what he would want. After a while it all becomes almost unspoken. You develop a code. Nothing's attributable anyway. Trust is crucial in this, and there was no reason for us not to trust each other. I did a decent job and did well enough out of it, so – presumably – did his other contractors and more formal operators. He did well too, rose as high in government as it's reasonable for a human to get. The guy who knows where the bodies are buried – mainly because he buried them himself – always gets on well.

'But that can only work so far. After a while, to get further up the slippery pole you need to get legit, and that's what he was doing. I think, anyway. I don't know exactly because although we got on very well, we were still somehow remote and separate. His world was not my world. That was part of the success of it, I think. Then he...' Stoner wound down, stopped. Reset. Held up a hand to forestall any interruption.

'Then he set me up to be taken out. To take the big fall. To clear the decks for whatever insanely elevated gig he was after, or just to get me out of the way. The best form of deniability is to be dead. Works every time. Can't fault the logic.

'But I worked it out. He was clever, very clever, and even had me working for one half of him and looking for another half of him, which isn't easy, by setting me to tracking down my own killer... before they'd actually done it, obviously. Which I did, understood that he was the killer he'd set me to locate, and I applied his logic to himself. Extreme prejudice, as you Americans call it. It was… strangely unpleasant. How'm I doing?' He looked up. Dawn appeared to be lost inside herself. Eyes closed. She was shining, beautiful. One eye opened, her hands stopped moving.

'Do go on,' she said with a certain tension. 'I'm enjoying it so far. Looking forward to a happy ending.'

Stoner watched her, smiling so sadly.

'Once he was history, I was plainly unemployed, so I went away for a while. Took a holiday. It was great. It got interrupted by a mission to rescue a damsel in distress – something like that – but that was OK with me. It was, like, a debt repayment. And it worked out well, which was good, so I went back to my holiday, complete with ace holiday romance of the finest kind.'

'Oh fuck,' announced Dawn. 'Oh.' And she shook a little for a little while and then lay still. 'Excuse me,' she said. 'Do go on. I'll be fine in a minute.' Stoner waited, watching in silence until she reached into herself again, moving slowly.

'Someone sent me a vid. A movie. They did it in a remarkable way, a way which would be impossible without heavy access to serious spook stuff that would be way outside anything I could do myself. So he wasn't dead. No one else would or could have sent me the movie. So he's not dead. He called me here on your phone this morning. Which is also impossible without tech I don't even know exists.'

Dawn was sitting upright in her chain facing him. Damp hands by her sides, knees together. 'It was him, then?'

'Oh yes.'

'None of what you said would freak out a spook like you, It was the vid, wasn't it? What was on it?'

'Probably my best friend – professionally; I don't really do personal – hopped up on some chemical super-fuel or something, something seriously mind-bending as well as some sort of hyper-Viagra or the like. My best friend was fucking my... my best girl, I guess.' Stoner closed his eyes, leaned forward. 'She was... crucified. He fucked her every way, screaming something – I couldn't hear what because there was no sound – and then while he was ramming it up her ass he took a blade and sliced her belly open. So her guts just... just fell out. To the floor. Grey,' he said. 'Grey and pink.'

Dawn was kneeling in front of him, not touching him at all. Saying nothing. He shook, rapidly, as though he was doing cold turkey. Eyes shut. Tears leaking.

'I came here to... I came here to run away. I came here to work it out. I've never run away. Ever.' He stood up abruptly, towering over her, shaking as in a hurricane. Stripped off his shirt, pants. Dawn rose, moved to put her soft nakedness next to his hardnesses, but he moved her from his path, walked briskly to the door, passed through it and ran to the lake, waded out, swam out into the dusk.

11

THIS NEW YEAR: A VERY CELLULAR SONG

'And a happy new year to you, too, in case you'd forgotten.'

'I'd not. It's not. I try to avoid frivolous dishonesties. They're less use than serious dishonesties. New year, old year, all the same in the trenches.'

'In that case, this could only be the true romantic in you, as always. You're calling up to arrange a date? A few nights of passion? Wild sex, I think you called it? Or have you forgotten that too? It was... what... a year ago? A little more, a little less. Who cares about the passage of time among friends?'

'I want something.'

'Of course you do. Why else would you ignore me for months and then call me on a phone I never use at an unholy hour of the night? And why on earth did you think I might still use this phone at all, never mind have it switched on while the world is sleeping?'

Stoner sighed, his weariness transmitting perfectly well through all the arcane passages and processes involved in cellular telephony. 'Do you have company?'

'I do not. You?'

'I do, although it might be asleep, dead to the world.

Good morning, Chastity. May you have a joyous new year. Sincerely.'

'Thank you. You too. So you've called up to wish me well and to check up on... what, exactly? You've got company so you're not after a trembling date à *deux*. A threesome? Never mind. It's late, the shining wit has deserted me again. How've you been? Where've you been? Busy?'

'You've heard nothing about me these last several months? That's interesting. I've been living in a log cabin, high in the hills and low beside a long lake.'

'And you can't say where because this is hush-hush clandestine tradecraft supersleuth stuff, huh?'

'Near Moosehead Lake. Any sleuths who want to know where I am... know where I am, I guess. Chastity. I'm well out of it, need to work out how to get into it, and I need to know what's live and what's not, back in Blighty. And I've stupidly assumed that's where you are.' He sighed again.

'Assume away. I am. Been very busy, JJ. You?'

'Less so, I guess. No easy way to say this: I need some little assistance. Need someone to scout the land before I do the back-from-the-dead trick.'

'You died?' Chastity laughed – it sounded genuine to Stoner. 'And I missed it? Dammitall. Such a treat and I missed it. Slept through it, huh? Story of my life. Did no one sell tickets? Sorry. I owe you – we both know that. What can I do?'

'You owe me nothing at all. It would be good to know what's been happening – especially what's been said about me since we last spoke. If we need to set up secure comms, just say and we'll sort it. If it's talkable in the clear, then fine.'

'Nothing to say. Nothing to report. I've not heard

anything about you. Nada. Zip. Nothing. If you were awake, you'd have worked out that's why this phone is live, Mister Tradecraft. I left it active in case you called it. I even monitored your Facebook page, which is a shining study in nothing, too. If you judge a guy by his friends, you are one seriously dull bastard. But I know better, of course.'

'Nobody asking after me? That would be… interesting.'

'Charm asked if I'd heard from you. My sister Charm. You remember?'

'Of course. Out of sight, never out of mind. How is she, chubby Charm? We really should make formal introductions sometime. And how's Charity?'

'She died.'

'Fuck it. I'm sorry, Chastity. Really. When? And how?'

'Not sure, exactly. Not sure this is the time to talk about it. She… said she was going away to die, and… she did.'

'Sorry to hear that. She was… outstanding.'

'Thanks. Enough of that. Tears are for queers, someone said. Do you want me to snoop around for you? Spy out on your buddies, girlies, that sort of thing? Can do that. Between gigs, as you might say. Must be the season of goodwill. No one seems to want to hire contract killers just at the minute. Holly and ivy, rah rah rah, that stuff. Mince pies.'

'Have you run into Shard? My old services guy?'

'I know who he is. Seen him, yes. Dealt with him, no. You want me to go find him, tell him to call his old mate Stoner? I'd need to go look; we don't share space.'

'No. Did he seem OK? Fit?'

'Yeah. Was working security I think. Personal protection crap. Mother Charm will know. You want me to ask her?'

'No.'

'Then what do you want, superspook? That old wild sex thing? Dirty talk down the long phone to liven up a quiet night?'

'Not just now. Thanks, though. It's a cool idea. Keeps me warm at night. So nobody's been talking about me, or asking about me, or... well... anything?'

'You got it. Bad for the ego, but true all the same. Should they be talking? You been a bad boy again? I thought you were sailing the world on a big cruise ship, most likely with that sailor lady you were cuddly with.'

'No. That didn't last.'

'Yeah. Holiday romances. Why bother?'

'You on my side, Chastity? Serious question, then I'm gone.'

'Yes. No hesitation nor conditions. Tell me what you want.'

'Secure comms while I'm on my way home, then somewhere to meet when I'm back. And silence to everyone, even Charm, please. Things have been extremely bad for me.'

'You got it. You want me to go to your club, spy out the land, tell your buddies you're OK?'

'No. Say nothing. Just listen, please. Just listen out. Be a spy – my spy with my little eye, all of that but no more.'

'Noon tomorrow, my time. Got that?'

Stoner paused. 'Yes. Thanks. Have a great new year.' He rang off.

'You too.' Chastity spoke to no one. To static. 'You too.'

***

A rifle in its sack and a guitar in its case, a few clothes in a bag. Little else. Dawn suffered a moment of comprehension.

'We're going somewhere?'

'Pack your bags and travel fan.'

'Say what?'

'It's a song. *C'est chaud*, y'all, *c'est chaud*.'

'Yeah. But it's not. *Chaud*. It's frozen, *froid*, and it's going to snow. Then we'll be stuck here. Romantic. I've been looking forward to it. A hot tub in a blizzard is the only place to be at new year.'

'Sorry. We leave now, dawn's early light, such as it is, and get to my truck and onto a highway before the big snow arrives. It's coming from the north, so we're heading south.'

'Airport? Boston Logan? Detroit? The Tunnel of Light?'

'We'll see. Just lock and leave. Big outdoors clothes.'

'You reckon. Mister Brit Hero? You reckon the dim American lady would be going for the spandex and stilettos?' She threw a cushion at him, vanished into the bedroom, then the bathroom, then she was pulling on big boots, jacket and hat. 'Ready,' she announced. Stoner bowed.

'Excellent,' he said. 'We travel light. Like bandits.'

***

'Who was that on the phone? Sounded like someone you know well. Woman, too, huh?' Dawn matched Stoner's steady tread along the ice-crisp tracks which led to bigger tracks which led to trails and finally to a nearly-driveable path. They walked easily, relaxed. Naturally quietly through the faintly creaking near-silence of the frozen woods.

'She's a sister,' Stoner appeared reluctant to interrupt the rhythm of his walking with conversation.

'So am I. That's not unusual for us women. Harder for you guys.'

'There are three of them. Charity, Chastity and Charm.'

'They sound like a bad joke.'

'Nightmare. And one of them – Charity – has died. That was Chastity on the wire.'

'Nightmare? How d'you mean; nightmare?'

'They have a nice little family business. They kill people for money. Tough work, needs doing, so they say. Bad laundry bills.' He shifted the guitar case from one hand to the other. The rifle was slung across his back. 'There was some confusion last year. I told you my boss – ex-boss – put out a contract – quite a complicated contract – on me? Yeah, the contract was with the sisters. Chastity would have taken the hit, most likely.'

'She missed?'

'Too long a tale. We reached an accommodation. It was seriously edgy for a while. The last job I did – last year – was with Chastity. We get on well enough. I need someone to trust. She's it. She's very good.'

'You trust some woman who took a contract on your life? That's nuts, even for an Englishman with a French name and a bad boy beard.'

'Yes. Can we be silent now? I'd like to think a little. You can listen to the radio.'

'I don't have a radio.'

'No one's perfect.'

***

They had retrieved Stoner's truck. It appeared undisturbed, still had a shrouded motorcycle in the load bed, fired up easily and needed only a little fresh air into its tyres. Two of them pumped by Stoner himself by foot power, while Dawn connected up an electric device and while the big engine warmed itself and its oils, ready for the trip, so it supplied the power to Dawn's electric foot. Snow fairies danced down from the hills, swirled out of the tree heights, advance scouts for the forecast winter wonderland. The season's short day would end soon, shrouded in its passing by the deadly beauty of blizzard. They piled into the warming cabin, belted in, and eased into the trails, heading for the harder, more civilised route to town.

'Call Travis.' Stoner adjusted his seat. 'You should talk to him about Sonny.'

'You mean I should get him on the phone so you can talk to him about spook stuff, huh?' Dawn smiled with her voice, her attention on the gathering winter's evening.

'I mean what I say. He needs to hear from you. I don't want to talk to him particularly, but I would like you to pass on a message.'

'You reckon there's a signal out here? We're a little remote.'

'Bet there is. Bet any property that's Travis's responsibility will have signals all around – just not always at the gaff itself unless you know how. Try it. Easier than arguing about theory. The empirical approach – always worked for me.'

'Hey,' she said, not to Stoner. 'It's me.' Then, 'Happy new year to you. Yes. Certainly interesting so far. Can we talk about Sonny a little bit?' And they did.

Finally, as the lights of the first town appeared through the dark, Dawn offered the phone to Stoner, who shook his head. 'Take a message, Miss Jones,' he suggested in a very English voice.

'Fuck you too, mister,' she laughed and switched on the device's speaker. 'Speak to Mr Travis. Remember to be polite at all times. Remember that I have just revealed to him that you threatened to kill his son and heir.'

'Is that true, Stoner?' Travis sounded more amused than enraged. 'Did you really threaten to top off the little shit?'

'It was the closest I could get to true parental affection. Not a skillset I've been trained in, exactly. I felt I should motivate him in the ways of the world while at the same time restoring my struggling self-confidence and self-worth. I did a course on the importance of self-belief when all around you are either failing you or falling about laughing at you. It was a good course.'

'I bet you were top student.'

'I taught the course. Everybody failed. They were all too nice.'

'I've no problem with you doing a little parenting, Stoner. None. Maybe I should slap him about a bit. What did he do to force you to that brink of unwilling violence? You being a justly famous exponent of the healing powers of peace and love, as I've just explained to Dawn.'

'Oh yeah? Good. I was about to get seriously down and dirty with the former Mrs Travis, and had polished up my grammar and social skills appropriately, washed behind my ears and so on, and the young fuck came unannounced and interrupting, and slapped that same former Mrs Travis on her wet ass and laughed at my johnson. Which is unforgiveable. In my day I'd have minced him into home on the range hamburger, but as I now follow the one true path of peaceful enlightenment I only threatened to kill him. May also have knocked a few teeth loose. It did me good. I enjoyed it. Being a teacher is an under-rated pleasure. Please thank him when next you talk. Appreciate that.'

Travis hooted with laughter. 'I wish I'd seen that. He slapped you on your ass, Dawnie? Oh hell. That'll teach you to make hay with teenagers.'

'Like you don't do that, huh?' Dawn's contribution was possibly pointed.

'Girls don't count. Boys are delicate flowers. You know that. Hey, Stoner, you finished with the cabin? I can get it housekept and back into service?'

'Housekept? You rewriting the English language now?'

'I speak the pure American, white boy. Like espresso, *comprende*?'

'Great White Mother, there is no hope. If I said that you should stretch out for me, would you get my meaning, o linguistic maestro?'

'Gotcha. Easy to do. You heading back to the farm?'

'I am. But in no great hurry. No rush. Better eaten cold, so they say. Next stop is this town here, can't remember its name...' Dawn supplied the name. 'Thanks for that. I'll find a motel, hotel, something, then reach out for that tunnel of light tomorrow, maybe the next day, assuming that the weatherman didn't lie. Would aim to be there in forty-eight hours tops. You colonials do know how to keep snow off the roads, I imagine? Thank-you again, Travis. My debt to you grows.'

'Never a concern. I just look to the future, JJ. You make sure we both have one, you hear me? Dawn, take the phone away from this English madman so I can whisper sweet somethings in private.'

While Dawn talked theatre, music and mutual friends, Stoner swung the pick-up into a slot outside a well-illuminated structure which proclaimed itself to be a hotel, almost in the centre of the town, close to a couple of busy restaurants. Switched off, swung down into the chill but still mostly snow-free air, collected his guitar and headed into the lobby. Dawn followed, as night follows day.

***

Stoner leaned on the counter, guitar in its sack at his feet, every inch the rangy, skinny, wild-eyed has-been musician you thought you recognised but couldn't actually approach to say; 'Hi. Aren't you...', leaving the victim of your curiosity to fill in your gaps for you. The girl on desk duty approached, eyes widening as the distance between them shrank.

'Hello sir,' she began. 'Aren't you...'

'Looking for a room,' said Stoner. 'Yes I am. Room for two.' He looked into her eyes and smiled. She looked down, suddenly flushed. 'And one guitar, of course.' His smile widened. If desk girl had noticed Dawn, who'd seated herself at a coffee table and picked up an old magazine, she showed neither sign nor shame. She was, very obviously and with commendable honesty, interested.

'Here's the thing,' he said, every inch the lost limey traveller. 'I've been away from home for a while, so have – you know – failed to check on my balances like I should.' He extracted a card from a pocket, laid it carefully, as though it were fragile somehow, on the desk between them. 'I'd prefer to pay for the room using this, but might have hit the limit.' He beamed. 'You know how it goes!'

She knew. She certainly did. 'No problem, sir. I'll check it now.' And before she'd even lifted it from the desk, Stoner produced a fold of dollars so impressively fat that it stopped her in her tracks.

'Don't want you to worry none.' He spread his hands wide. 'If the card's died I'll pay cash, but card would be better. Better to keep the cash for the bandit country.' She beamed her agreement and slid the card into a wireless reader of some kind.

'How long you planning on staying, Mister Hand? And which grade of room would you prefer, sir?' Quite plainly the card was a lively, healthy and vigorous card, as cards go.

Stoner disappeared the fold of bills somehow, though his wide smile still spoke of confidence and resource. 'Quiet, comfort, a little space to stretch out. Whatever. If you have an especially favourite room, then that would be my favourite too.'

Dawn was at his side. 'I'm just going to step outside and shop a little. OK, honey?' Stoner nodded with distraction, his attention on the transaction being enacted before him, involving the hotel's receptionist, its computer and a process of registration and validation, identification and confirmation.

'The lady here has everything in hand, I think.' But Dawn was gone, into the sharp dusk, the lobby's outside door closing itself behind her. Stoner turned back to the receptionist. 'Is there wi-fi? Do you have a device I can rent? I've been in the mountains for a while; be good to reconnect.' Stoner signed a card receipt, the register, declined to sign for Dawn, explaining that the lady was not his wife and may in fact prefer her own room – up to her of course. He beamed at the last statement, as did the receptionist, familiar as she was with the ways of others.

He took the stairs to his room, on his own, no luggage other than the guitar case, waving away the suggestion that the hotel could provide assistance, and bounced around for a little while, opening doors and drawers, opening then closing windows, finally heading back down to the lobby to collect an access code for the hotel's own computers, one of which was his to use for as long as he liked, free – of course – of charge.

Which is where Dawn found him. She appeared above his shoulder, watching. 'Facebook? Never really had you down as a Facebook freak, JJ.'

He nodded. 'Yeah. Can't beat it. The truth is in here. Every word in here is true. Did you know that? I know this because I read it on Facebook, where no one ever lies. Especially not me, and even more especially not my friends. Righteous, one and all.'

Dawn pulled up a chair and stared around his shoulder. 'You're telling your friends... what? This is surreal, JJ. You feeling the pressure a little? Need something to calm the nerves?'

'Nah. Never calmer. Feeling a focus is all. Welcome, too. I like this social networking thing. Look here; I just posted a beautiful pic of this very hotel in this very town.' He waved at the big flat screen, which showed a sunny scene indeed, majoring on healthy hearty holidaymakers enjoying all the legal pastimes associated with the great American outdoors; canoes, kayaks, killing things various, hiking, biking, sliding and gliding. He'd posted several others, all of a similar vein, all sharing with his alleged friends that he was having a great time.

'Forgive me,' said Dawn. 'I thought you were, y'know, clandestine? Hiding?'

'No more. John Hand never hid from anyone, not even when he was alive. Popular guy, too. Look.' Stoner displayed a surprising familiarity with the ways the social site worked, adding several comments and one-click approvals of the activities going on in the lively online world he apparently shared with a variety of others. He rated a couple of books he'd never read, also a couple of movies he'd not watch unless the only alternative was death by slow strangulation, and commented several times on a long thread about global conspiracies and black helicopters. He checked the exact time, then sent a personal message to 'Challenger', simply saying 'Bingo,' then 'Here I am.' He closed the message window and switched to Google images displaying an intimidating array of photos of their area, clipped and copied, then pasted another portrayal of nature's almighty beauty onto John Hand's Facebook page, commenting on how exceptionally sunny it was at this time of year. Eleven of his friends immediately liked the image, gifting their tiny digital thumbs of approval in realtime.

The personal message window opened itself; a reply from Challenger, containing a number, a ten-digit number broken up into pairs. Stoner wrote it onto the hotel's free notepad, using the hotel's free pen, then replied, simply 'stsp', then shut down the connections. He turned to Dawn. 'Dinner?' he wondered.

***

'Tell me this.' Dawn and Stoner presided over the wreckage of a meal well-consumed. Nothing fancy, but plenty of taste and fibre. Although the hotel was light on residents, its restaurant was apparently popular, and there was a decent gathering; quiet, well-mannered, and respectful of their privacy.

'Anything.' Stoner raised his half-drunk coffee cup

to acknowledge a similar salutation from another man with another woman sitting at another table. 'But in just one moment.' He parked the cup, after draining it, rose and walked over to the other couple, gesturing to Dawn that she should stay where she was, which she did. The other guy rose to his feet, smiling, but with a little caution.

'Mister Stoner,' he performed the greeting with casual ease. 'Good to see you in town. Wondered if that was your Harley-D Ford pick-up out there. You're looking... well.'

'Sheriff. You too. Yes, indeed it is.' He nodded to the neatly dressed woman. 'Ma'am. Don't let me disturb your evening. I just wanted to say hi to Joshua here.' He nodded generally. 'Great restaurant. Very good food. Ma'am, Joshua. See you both.' And he returned to his table, where Dawn waved prettily to the sheriff and his companion.

'Who's that?' she asked. 'There's a definite touch of Tommy Lee Jones there, no doubt about it.'

'More Woody Harrelson, I'd say.' Stoner settled back into his chair, relaxed enough. 'You had a question?'

'Mr Hand?'

'Don't worry about that. He's just paying for the trip. He won't object.' He smiled and accepted another coffee. Dawn shook her head to the same question.

'An alias?'

'Yep. And a little testing of the waters.'

'Like the Facebook performance? I was married to Travis for a long time – it felt like a long time anyway – and I think I'm seeing an operation. Am I?'

'You are, yes. You OK with that for a while? There's no risk to you – none I can see, at any rate. The sheriff seems entirely relaxed, and if there was shit going down around here, he would know, I reckon. He knows something of who I am and why I'm here. Travis's office spoke to him, I think. I was in a bad place when I landed here, no doubt about that.'

'No risk? How so? You Brits play Queensbury Rules or something? I find that hard to believe.'

Stoner looked at his watch. 'You happy to share a room, Dawn? No pressure on you. I'd just like to know your feelings on the subject.'

'Me too. Yeah. Not a problem for me. You sure you'd not prefer to take that young piece of ass from reception to your bed, though?'

'All options should be kept open.' Stoner signed the check, pulled a green twenty from his pocket and tucked it under his empty coffee cup. 'Let's go pay our respects to Mr and Mrs Sheriff. He knows me as Stoner, by the way, such is the confusion of existence.'

'Do I tell him who I am?'

'You've been here before, so he knows who you are. And he's a gentlemen. He won't ask any questions.'

He didn't.

***

Stoner dropped into one of the four easy chairs in the wide room. Kicked off his boots, lifted his right foot onto his left knee and massaged it. 'Tell me,' he said, 'how Sonny isn't your son but Travis is his father.'

'I was intending to ask a few questions.' Dawn kicked off her own shoes and dropped her jacket to the floor.

'Later. We've got all night.'

'You reckon? You reckon that despite whatever your Mr Hand and Facebook performances produce, you reckon we're safe?'

'Yep.'

'You're talking about the colour thing, huh? Skin colour?'

'Yep. You're a paleskin, Sonny's just about blonde and Travis is a black man, black as a man can be and stay visible. It's not easy to figure that out.'

'No figuring. Sonny has all his mommy's Nordic beauty.'

'She was a Nordic beauty? How so?'

'Ask Travis. He introduced the lady to his genes for her kind attention, not me. I never was actually introduced. Maybe if I had been, I could have asked her your question – which, to be honest, has also occurred to me and doubtless to others too – and satisfied your curiosity. In any case, white boy, I may not be entirely paleskin. How would you know? Sonny does have at least one of his father's better features.'

'I can guess. I was mainly wondering...' She interrupted.

'Whether Sonny's some other guy's son and if so why Travis took the heat? Again, you're not the first to consider this. Does it actually have anything whatsoever to do with you?'

Stoner held up his hands, palm-out, in a gesture of peace.

'Meanwhile, Mister Brit, how do we actually get you in the mood to provide a little honky comedy for a lady who's been deprived – by your Britannic majesty – of her source of satisfaction?'

'I thought you said it was all too much?'

'I may have been trying to make you feel better.'

'You were?"

'No. I have this great idea. Why don't we undress each other, nice and slow so we get the idea, and then heave into this convenient bed and cement the special relationship in that most traditional of ways?'

'You mean, let's just do it?'

'That works.'

'There's a difficulty.' Stoner removed his outer garments, quick and efficient.

'OK.' Dawn caught up in the undressing stakes.

Stoner peeled out of his underwear, stood before her.

Dawn stripped and sat on the edge of the bed. 'That is not the terrible weapon which created the empire on which the sun never set, now is it?' Her tone was light. 'Hey,' she reached across the tiny distance and held him, squeezed a little, rubbed a little. 'Hey,' she said again, 'let's show him the lure. Show him up close.' And she pulled Stoner to her until they touched, then released him and lay back on her elbows. Looked at him. Reached for him again and rubbed a little, squeezed a little, rubbed a little more. Released him again. A thin string of glistening clear liquid fell from the tip of his cock and landed, pooling slowly, directly onto her spread lips.

'Hmmm. How does that feel?' She looked up to his face. 'You just... you just don't find me a turn-on? Pussy doesn't do it for you?' She lowered her eyes. 'Since the video you described... you've not been turned on at all? Except when you kicked the shit out of Sonny, that is. You looked good and motivated then.'

Stoner dropped to his knees, peered at her across her pussy, her belly and between her breasts to her face – a long slow stare. He ran the unusually long fingernails of his right hand down the lips, tidying the hair neatly aside as though he were styling it.

'Hey, hey,' she caught her lower lip between her teeth. 'This is seriously strange, JJ. It feels... scary. I feel like I'm... wide open.'

'You are. You're deliciously attractive.' He shifted position a little, raised his left hand to her, ran the knuckles one after the other from her clit to the limit of her lips, lifted his hand away. Held it up for her to share his pleasure in the gleaming wet of his hand. Lifted his hand to his face and licked it clean. Reached to her again and inserted both thumbs into her as far as they would reach, one above the other, following them with both forefingers and moving fingers and thumbs apart until both middle fingers grounded on each side of her clit. He moved his hands, attention shifting from her face to her pussy and back again. 'This OK for you, Dawn?'

She released a loud gasp, and a sudden gush, not from her mouth but into his hands. 'Sorry,' she squeaked between the fingers she held over her mouth.

'Shush, shush...' he replied. 'Just let go.' And as he instructed and he encouraged, she accepted the instruction, seeing it for the invitation it actually was and let go, a truly unusual, remarkable display of vaginal vocals and shudders which began between her cunt lips but extended to meet the spreading deep red flush of her belly and the valley between her breasts.

As soon as her climaxes calmed and she opened her eyes again, he removed his thumbs from her, replacing them with all four fingers of his left hand; once inside her, he left them stilled. He used the long, hard guitar-player's fingernails of his other hand to scrape the wet from between her inner and outer lips, until her eyes closed again, she started to move again, and her pussy spat and sobbed again, squeezing and soaking his left hand – all of it.

Finally, they lay together, side by side, in a very damp place. Dawn reached for him, found him, held him, squeezed, and rubbed. Finally, 'On your stomach,

Mister Stoner.' He rolled over as instructed, and Dawn sat on his bony buttocks and massaged his shoulders, the tight muscles of his back, eased his long, hard arms out from his side and rotated the shoulder joints, one after the other, folded the arms back against their sides.

'You play guitar good, huh?' she asked. He grunted, rolled once more onto his back. Dawn sat on his chest, legs wide apart before him. 'A woman can tell these things. It's all in the hands, isn't it? Dexterity, a little pressure when needed, and a lot of gentleness too. You play lots, I'd guess. Bet you have plenty of lady fans, too. So what happened to Johnson, huh? Care to talk about it? I'm not shy, I'm not shockable, and any guy who can bring me off like that is a good guy in my world. And… ah… thanks for not being put off by the squirts and the fanny farts. Lots of men… most of them, in fact… really find it a turn off. You don't, though?'

'No.' Stoner rolled over, lay spread-eagled on his back, butterflied, arms and legs splayed, eyes closed. 'It's rare enough to be a true turn on for me. Not the other thing at all. Fine by me. Let go, have a good time. It's a hotel; they can handle the laundry. They're used to it. And they charge for it.'

'You're… how can I put this?… you're well experienced. You play pussy like an expert – hey, you even know when to stop. How is that, by the way? How can you tell? I didn't shout "Pax!" or something? Really. How?'

'You just go slack. Loose. Flappy. I'll think of a better word.' She hit him, playfully.

'That is enough. Jeez. Flappy, he says.'

'Yeah. Like you had a dozen babies in the last year or two. Big ones. Quins maybe.'

'Shut up! So you're all tuned in and turned on and Johnson just swings around, just hanging around, dripping a bit, but ignoring the proceedings. This is unusual. Unique, I'd say. Would you care to explain, my *gaucho amigo?*'

'Can't.' Stoner reached around her and squeezed and stroked and rubbed her backside, working his fingers into the crease between her buttocks.

'See. If I didn't know better, mister Brit, I'd say you were horny again. Huh?' She slid down his body, away from the attentions of his hands and rubbed herself against him, grinding her sex into his. He groaned, placed his hands behind his head, lifted it, the better to observe the proceedings. Dawn slid further down him, collected his cock in her hand, peeled back the foreskin as far as it would go and abraded the vee beneath his glans with her thumb and its nail. He groaned, shuddered a little.

'Feels good, though?' She carried on, rolling and rubbing using both hands. Stoner shuddered some more. 'Well this is cool,' Dawn carried on, with some skill. 'Give me a clue about when you've had enough... oh. Oh my.' He came, slowly and stickily in her hands. 'That's a thing,' she said, and squeezed gently and steadily until he stopped. 'Let's have a bath,' she said. 'Baths are so romantic. Maybe there'll be a candle'

***

Dawn rose some while after Stoner, who she discovered sitting in the lobby, fully dressed and applying himself once again to the hotel's complimentary computer. She kissed him on the head. 'Do they serve coffee here, or do we need to find the dining room all over again?'

'No idea.' Stoner's attention was on the screen. 'You ask, they deliver, I guess.' He tapped the cold empty coffee mug nearby. 'It worked for me. Although I didn't in fact ask. It just arrived. America is great like that.'

'I feel great, too,' Dawn shared. 'Thanks for a truly special night.'

'Yeah. Good. Thanks. Great. Why don't you grab breakfast or something? I won't be long. The connection isn't the fastest on the planet, and it keeps speeding up then slowing down again. Irritating.'

'OK babe. What do you want?' Dawn scooped up a pile of hotel lit, some of which may have contained clues to a menu.

'I'm booking some flights. The excellently affluent John Hand – fine fellow; you'd like him; great sense of humour for a dead guy – is looking at buying a few airplane tickets. Not sure where I fancy, though.'

'I meant breakfast.'

'I ate already.'

'OK.' Dawn wandered off in search of food. Stoner left off his unsatisfying assault on the world's airlines and opened up a Facebook account. Lots of messages, lots of friends doing whatever it is that friends do, especially friends who either don't actually exist or who are as false as only Facebook friends can be. Cascades of varying dishonesties, amusing and imaginative, or more often the exact opposite; misunderstood quotations, ersatz outrage at falsehoods and obvious provocations. It was all there, a deep sea of misinformation – the misinformation superhighway at its most entertaining. Stoner greeted several friends, almost all fictional or unknown to him, and shared with anyone interested to read about it that he planned a trip home to catch up with long-lost buddies, maybe do a little sightseeing on the way, and did anyone have any suggestions concerning the route he should take.

Several did. They varied from the almost-intelligent, via the plainly insane – alien abduction is rarely reliable as a means of transport – to the interesting. He chatted with steadily increasing irony about several of them, pondering all the while on the way so many people lived lives parallel with their own realities. At least, he hoped that they did more than skulk about the ethers, waiting for someone interesting to happen by. Toothless tigers of their own wide plains; lords of nothing, captains of self-importance. Today, Stoner loved them all. His friends provided details of airlines he'd never heard of and certainly would never use, but which offered routes from wherever he was to wherever he might prefer to be via all manner of obscure locations, all of which were guaranteed to be remarkably relaxed in the security department. A couple recommended renting a car, driving to Mexico, selling the car and paying for a return trip by tramp steamer. They'd read that in a book, apparently. His favourite was a suggestion that he work his passage on a cruise ship by playing guitar in one of the house bands. Creative nonsense, all of it. The collective crap of the pathetically inept. Amusing, always.

Stoner returned to the less relaxed business of purchasing flights from the USA to the UK. Compared several alternatives, finally selecting a lazy overnight flight from Detroit to London, a high-grade sleeper costing a comfortably large amount of money. John Hand's card provider accepted the transaction, the airline invited him to share their joint delight for the benefit of any Facebook friends he might have, so he obliged. It is impossible to be too friendly in this modern age.

Dawn crashlanded in the seat opposite. 'Where're we going, lover man?'

'Home. How's that sound?' Stoner looked up from the screen and smiled while Dawn ate something white, fruity, crunchy and packed with synthetic goodness.

'Yours? Mine? We start a new one?' Dawn chewed cheerfully, while Stoner raised a querying eyebrow.

'We spend a couple of days together and you're counting bathrooms?' He looked back at the screen. 'I'll be heading back to the UK. You to... well, wherever you live. Which is where, actually? I don't remember covering that, although I may have been distracted.'

'I work in New York, live in an apartment. It's very urban, hence the need for trees. I can feel a time for change in my life, JJ. Is there space in England for an American attorney?'

'Is that what you do? Does that mean you're very rich?' Stoner sat back in his chair and surveyed the room and its occupiers. 'I always understood NY city attorneys to be rich beyond dreams. What could be better than that?' He saw no one he recognised, several parties looked at them from time to time – his clean but dishevelled appearance plainly raising an etiquette issue or two – but nobody appeared overly interested.

'In any case, I need to get back to the UK. A lot to do. Like I said.'

'And you don't want baggage? Is that it?'

'It wouldn't be fun, and it wouldn't be helpful, is the truth of it.'

'I'm taking a deep breath now, just so you know.' Dawn took that breath and held it, pointing at her puffed cheeks. Stoner nodded. 'So, I've taken a deep breath; here comes the question, the difficult one. When you've done your business in England, will you want to see me again?' She paused, holding up a hand to preserve his silence. 'There's more. When you've done whatever things you need to do, sorted things out and done all that male revenge crap, which you plainly need to do – and I can't fault you for that – do you think that your dick will start working again? Like a man's dick should?' Her voice was fairly loud, she was providing morning amusement to the nearest table.

Stoner smiled. 'Who can tell? I'm less bothered than you seem to be. Do you need to make a scene? You don't seem the sort, but I'm usually wrong.' He shrugged. Reached into a pocket, extracted a set of keys. 'These are for the truck. Subtle it's not, but it should get you home or to wherever Sonny's left your own vehicle. Just tell Travis where it is and he'll get it collected.'

She stared at him, open-mouthed. 'What? Just like that? You really don't care, do you?'

'About what? I care about lots of things. So many things that there's no room at all for... relationships. That's all she wrote, Dawn. Take the truck or take the coach. Whichever works best for you. I'm booked out of Boston Logan. Need to be getting along, winter being winter and weather being weather. If being angry helps, then go ahead. Vent a little.'

'How're you going to get to Boston? This isn't little England.'

'Train. Bus. Motorcycle. Steal a car, hitch a lift. Whatever.'

Her voice softened, quietened. 'What's changed so suddenly, JJ? You had news, something like that? I... we did appear to be getting along OK, know what I mean?'

'You could call it news. Provision of focus, objective definition, maybe yes. Dawn. I know how to reach you. You can always find me – friend John Hand on Facebook if you don't want to go through Travis – and we can see where things stand after... y'know. After it's all done.'

'If you're still standing.'

'Yeah. That. If I'm not, best to avoid the collateral. There's bound to be some of that. It's the way of things.' He closed down the terminal he'd been using, logging out as he did so.

'JJ?'

'Yeah.'

'Keep the truck. It's easier for me to catch trains, a bus or two, than it is for you. Unless...' she smiled a sad smile. 'Unless you're using the truck and me as a decoy or something. Hunter's lure.'

'I did think of that. You get the class prize for clever, but I'd not do it. That collateral is too much of a risk. The truck's clean, so far as I know. And... ah... yeah. Thanks. It would be easier if I could use it. I was thinking of you, y'know?'

She slid the bunch of keys back across the table. 'One more cup of coffee for the road?'

'Yeah. Please. If I keep the truck, I guess there's time for a cup of coffee.' He reached across to her and took her hand. 'Thank you. I will be in touch. Honest.'

'You want to... go to the room?'

'Love to, babe, but best not. That way I'd never leave.'

'Smooth talking limey shitster.' She flagged a waiter.

12

THIS NEW YEAR: SIX STRING SVENGALI

All that lingered was the fading zizz from the cymbals and snares. Then came the applause. Drummers are too often ignored behind the ramparts of their kit, and with this in mind, maybe, Stretch the mountainous keyboardist reached out a long strong hand to the man behind the mountain. 'And let's hear it for Styx,' he yelled, conscious that no microphone was likely to pick up his acknowledgement. Styx the drummer shambled around to stage front, holding his hands over his head and clapping in appreciation of the applause, nodding and offering baby bows.

'And we all thought the solo would never end!' Bili the bass grabbed a mic and laughed with the audience. 'Let's hear it for no more drum solos!' The audience loved it, loved her and loved the tight quartet's eclectic show. Of course the problem with the audience loving the show is that the audience feels a need to share that love, so they applaud, they cheer and they clap, which means the band feels a need to share their own love of the appreciation, and the traditional way of doing this is to play another number, commonly called an encore, which is a French word meaning again. Some bands mischievously perform a literal encore, in that they repeat the last number, which isn't a real concern if the band is as eclectic and as improvisational as this particular tribe, but others sometimes suggest that it short-changes the audience.

'Aw shucks,' laughed Stretch the impressively large pianist, doing his big best to appear abashed. 'We only know the one song. We got to play it again?' The audience made it plain that they approved. Styx padded back to his stool, slipped his knees either side of the snare, tapped toes onto bass drum and hi-hat pedals and looked up expectantly. Bili swung her big red Rickenbacker bass into what might have been a comfortable playing position, and all three looked to far stage left, where Amanda rolled her eyes, took a deep breath and surprised them all by blasting from her shining tenor saxophone the opening stanza to 'Baker Street', one of the most recognisable lumps of sax music of all time. She stopped, looked up with an air of innocence. 'What?' she wondered. The audience whooped; they all knew the tune.

'Oh.' The mic picked up every word perfectly and shared them all with the audience. 'Just because we've never played it doesn't mean we can't play it, does it now?' And she turned to the audience, who shouted encouragement and clapped some more, more loudly.

'Two, three...' yelled out Styx, rapping sticks together in time, and off they set into maybe uncharted waters, although you never can tell with a tight band. Maybe they rehearsed the tune every afternoon in secret, and maybe they genuinely never had played it before together, the key word being that last one; together. But they all knew it, that much was clear. And after the opening sax expo, Bili stepped to her mic and sang the lyric, and Stretch's keys and Styx's skins merged with Amanda's quiet sax utterances to back her up, and then there were solos to be played, firstly by Amanda again, which she did, and where there should have been a weeping, charismatic piece of bent-string guitar break, there was a tiny pause while Stretch dreamed up a keyboard equivalent, keeping everybody happy. The only guitar on the stage, an elderly and road-weary Fender, leaned on its stand by its amplifier, unplayed that night, as many nights before. A half a year of silent nights.

Set complete, the players wandered off into their own social whirls, each boasting fans, friends of their own. Stretch made a stately progress to the bar, where a figure he recognised raised a glass in salute, and when the two seriously substantial men cleared a space between them, their clasped hands and shining eyes spoke louder than any amplifier.

'Stretch!'

'Buddy! What on the planet are you doing here, big guy? What the heck, man, it has been too long. Much too long. Great to see you. Really great. You... what... you gigging over here in the old UK? Texas not cold and wet and friendly enough for you? Damn, Bud. Damn fine to see you. Damn fine.' Shoulders were slapped, beers poured and glasses raised. 'Come sit,' offered Stretch, and a too-small for two large men table cleared as its original tribal inhabitants made their understanding excuses and left the two men to it.

'You look good, big man,' managed the white American, once they'd seated themselves around the pygmy-proportions of the table and parked their glasses without spilling from them. 'I'm winding down the tour tonight, just up town a little from here. Heard about this place, heard who played here, thought you might like to play a little dirty blues, a little dirty Texas blues before I head back home. And yeah, hell, Stretch, it is good to see you, looking so well. Can you slip out for a little? Can they manage without you? I'd sure like to hear you rattle the ivories with me again. Huh?' He sank some beer, shook his head a little, smiled, very, very broadly.

'Yeah. Buddy Whiteman asks, Buddy Whiteman gets. I cannot refuse the call. But you need to come on back here, maybe stretch a string, sing a song for us, too. What-say, big man?'

'I say...' Buddy checked the time. 'I say we better catch a cab.' He rose, as a mountain, to his feet. Stretch caught the glance from behind the bar, nodded, grinned.

'Cab's here,' he said. 'Ready and waiting. Let us rock.'

***

A little past eleven that evening, they returned. A little further past eleven, Stretch, a black man with the whitest smile in the whole of the UK, introduced the man he was proud to call his friend to the audience he was proud to call his friends too. There was some shuffling; Buddy was a very large man, broad as well as tall, and more brilliant than either. He dominated the small stage, thanked the crowd with a Texan ease, and looked over at the elderly Fender guitar leaning near its amplifier.

'Do I play this one?' He looked to Stretch, who shrugged, and looked in turn to Bili, who somehow appeared to be lost; a tiny blonde woman behind a big red bass. She nodded, said something no one heard.

'Hideaway, then. Just to warm up,' called out Stretch. All agreed, measured their instruments, Styx called time and play they did. And then more. And more yet, until the two in the morning curfew, door close and talking time arrived.

'Fine guitar. Thank you, miss.' Buddy had somehow divined that Bili and the elderly Fender were connected. 'Great set. Thank you all. May I return next time I'm over here?' Immediate and unanimous agreement, approval, and with the sensitivity which is rare but shared when it's there, everyone left Buddy and Stretch alone. Two mighty American musicians, one white, one black, chatting together in a small English jazz bar, space provided free, as were coffee, nuts and nibbles demanded by the hour and by their exertions.

'No accident, then?' Stretch sipped alternately at bottled chilled water and steaming coffee. The buzz of the background provided any privacy they needed. 'Is everything OK at home, Buddy? Cathy and the kids – all good?'

'Yeah. All fine. No accident, Stretch. I'd no idea where you'd disappeared to, man. I wondered whether you'd failed to return from some SEAL event of which we the people know nothing. Never occurred to me that you'd be playing the blues in a backstreet somewhere in minor Britland.' He took a breath. 'I need to ask you to return to the US with me.'

Stretch smiled, sipped and shook his head slightly. 'I doubt I can. I left... uncomfortably. Under an overcast and darkening sky, Buddy. I don't...' he smiled that slight smile again. 'I don't think my passport would let me see more of America than a small locked room in a big locked building. I'm not in hiding, not exactly, but it was plain that I was unwelcome – permanently unwelcome – in the eyes of Uncle Sam.' He looked up. 'But if there's a way I can help you, bluesman bro, I surely will.'

'Times change, so they say.' Buddy rubbed his eyes. 'I was approached by a man called Travis. Snappy dresser, city type, black guy, could be you know him?' He looked up, questioning.

'Could be I do.'

'This Travis – Uncle Sam – upgraded my flights; no money involved, if that's important in any way.'

'Travis is a Feeb. You know that?'

'Know he's government of some kind. Very polite. Talks like Morgan Freeman.'

'You know Morgan Freeman?' Stretch's eyebrows headed north.

'Cat has a fine understanding of the black man's music, even when it's played by ol' whitey here!' They both laughed.

'But yeah,' Stretch nodded. 'That does sound like Travis. He was OK, last I saw him. What's he want? And you reckon he can make me welcome, from what he said?'

'He said to tell you "Stoner." Said you'd understand what that means. I never was one myself, but respect the needs of others. You or him being a stoner...'

'Stoner's the guy whose Strat you've been playing. Cool Brit guy whose club this is also. He's... ah .. he's been away for some time. He's... ah... he's an agency dude too, if you see where this is going. Bili – the beauty on the bass – carries his torch, and is burned bad by it, but won't say zip to me. What's Travis had to say about Stoner, huh?'

Buddy hefted to his feet, towered over the table. 'He just said what I said. And here's your tickets – same flight as me – leaves...' he checked the time again. 'It leaves in maybe five hours from London Heathrow, so if you need to pack, you'd need to be packing... well hey... right about now! You coming?'

Stretch nodded. 'Oh yeah.' He rose to his feet, paused. 'Did Travis say anything about secrecy, need to know, crap like that?'

'Not to me.'

'Then I'll tell Bili who I'm going to see. Ease her worried mind a little.' He shifted tables, hunched down next to the small mountain of blonde curls resting face-down on the wood. Tapped the table top next to her. She raised her face.

'Good music, big man,' she slurred. 'Your mate, Baddy, he's very good, good as JJ. Maybe better, even.' She appeared to be on the edge of a steep precipice of sleep or tears, hard to say.

'Buddy, not Baddy, crazy lady.' Stretch used both of his big hands to open a wider window in her hair, so he could see her eyes. They blinked at him, sleepily. 'I'm leaving with Buddy tonight, Bili. He's taking me to JJ.'

'What for?' There was more attention, more focus in her eyes.

'Don't know. Won't know until I get there.'

'He's called a couple of times. He's in the USA.'

Stretch sat down at once. 'You've spoken to him? Oh, that's good. How was he?' He waved a holding hand to Buddy, who had collected his coat and was plainly ready to leave.

'Sounded... just... tired. Spoke just about nothing. Told me not to worry, that he'd be away for a long time, months, and that he'd moved a pile of money into my bank account in case I needed it. I told him that I love him and he told me he knew and that it was the same for him and then I felt so shit that I started to cry and then I hung up.' She raised her eyes to a level with his. 'Now go fuck off out to Americaland, find that fucker and bring him back. Stay safe, Stretch. Be safe.'

Stretch took both of her small hands, hands with their long hard fingers, into his own huge black paws, kissed her on the forehead. 'Yeah,' he said.

Amanda sat down at the table. 'You guys OK? Like a funeral here. Great set, Stretch; that Buddy, boy can he play. He here tomorrow? We should announce it if so. Get the club a real boost.'

'Manda?' Bili rested her chin in her hands. 'Fuck off with the business crap, OK? Stretch and Boddy are off to fetch JJ home. Isn't that so, Mr Stretch?'

'Sure is, Miz Bili. It sure is.' And he walked to the door, catching it before it slammed behind the departure of Buddy himself.

'JJ?' Amanda leaned back and watched as Bili's head sank back to the table. 'That's cool. Come on Bili, let's get you upstairs for a nap. You'll feel just as lousy in the morning as you always do.' She heaved the tousled woman upright, and steered her towards to doorway to the upstairs apartment.

***

Airport lounges; worlds of their own, worlds apart from anything sane. Multilingual, yet culturally arid. Exotic and compellingly bland. Stoner sat, one big man in a land of very many big men, a single soft bag by his feet, a Kindle reader in his hands, reading. Theoretically reading, at any rate. A bigger man sat down opposite him, separated by four legs, four feet and maybe two metres.

'The Tunnel Of Light. Gets me every time. Reminds me of music I never played but my girlfriends did. Psycho disco. Hallucinogens. Easier times. How you doing, JJ?'

'Hello to you too. Welcome to America.'

'I thank you. Speaking as an American, I'm unsure how I feel about being welcomed to my own country by a mostly Brit Brit.'

'Immigration OK? Homeland Security sounded no alarms when you performed the prodigal son routine?'

'Nope. They were fine. Didn't even crack any wiseass jokes. No cavity search, either, more's the pity. I always get constipated on over-ocean flights; could've done with loosening things up a little.'

Stoner folded away his reader, dropped it into his bag. 'So I worked out the tunnel from your seriously silly message. We're off to... ah... "hang with the good doctor"? That would be Doctor Wu?'

'I never understood the appeal of crosswords, JJ, until very recently. That would indeed be the good Dr Wu, no less.'

'Hoped so. Doctor Who is a Brit TV show, and I struggled to figure out what that might mean.'

'We see it in the US also. Seriously bad. Unfathomably popular.'

'The revenge of a fallen empire. We inflict terrible TV on our former colonies. It's a tradition. You send us desperate tit shit like Game Of Thrones and we retaliate with silly shit of our own. How's things at home, Stretch? You guys been keeping the club ticking along? Earning a shilling for the landlord?'

'What you mean to say – I'm getting the hang of this cryptic crap – is how's Bili? She's coping. She's not... right. Not cussing enough and swilling too much. Needs you around, I guess. She did tell me you'd been in touch, though, which displayed impressive confidence on your part, she being a lush and you being a fugitive.'

'Half-right, black man. Fugitive, though? Not so much a fugitive, more a penitent.'

'You do look like an escapee from a penitentiary, JJ. What gives with the hair and the beard? And the thin – huh? You given up eating for Lent?'

'Lent's Easter. We just made it past Christmas, Christ-sake. Stretch, I need to listen, not tell; hear, not speak. What's been going on while I've been away? Anything might be important. Won't know till I hear it.'

'Whole lotta nothing, mostly. Club's doing fine. Your pal Amanda's sort-of acting like the manager. Books acts, counts cash, keeps the chimp behind the bar in funds so he can keep the willing waters flowing, and she plays a seriously mean saxophone most nights. Bili seems to live upstairs, mostly. No real trouble. Plenty people, talking mostly music. Employed a drummer, some buddy of Amanda's, very good, styles himself Styx, as in the river and what he beats the skins with, very clever for a twelve year-old drummer...'

'He's twelve?'

'Figure of speech, man; he's in his twenties at a guess. Doesn't even do speed, so he's doing well for a drummer, and he can speak, too. Whole sentences sometimes. And he can keep a beat, which does assist on the musical front.'

'Shard been around?'

'Your old soldier pal? Not a lot recently. Like, he lived at the club after the business with the Hard Man – did you really stick it to your boss, as the scuttlebutt has it? – anyway he got very odd, like he was working that horse, or worse, if you know what I mean? All pinprick eyeballs and always on the very ragged edge, asking after you every damn day. Then those weirdo blondie sisters were there, scheming with Bili and Amanda, then with the tech-geeks too, then Bili and – is it the Chastity sister? – they went away and Shard just got more and more remote and strung out. And then I was away a little – need to make a dishonest dollar every now and again, as you know – and then Bili was back, seemed cheery enough, said you were off playing the sailor and enjoying the navy life or something. Said you'd be back soon, she reckoned, but you didn't come back, and after a month – maybe two – she went back to switching your amp onto standby every night and off at the close, and tuning your guitar every day. And drinking. Maybe more than drinking, man, not for me to say.'

Stoner nodded quietly. 'I miss it, man. Miss it more than I even dreamed I'd ever miss anything.'

'Yeah. That shows in how you don't come back but live in Detroit or some similar shitsville looking like a hobo, lost man. Bili – I'm just being honest, man – she'd be dead I reckon if not for Amanda. Amanda – don't be calling her Mandy; she likes that not – has just, like, taken over as big sister or the like. Makes her eat. They write songs together sometimes. Very bad songs, JJ. Very bad indeed.' He smiled.

'And then Buddy turned up, couple nights back, told me that Travis – you remember Travis? Feeb guy? – had arranged for me to be once again welcome in my own country, at least for a while, and that you needed my help. That is the story of my life. What's been the haps with you, my long-lost friend? Why you wasting your life in the ruins of the former Motown?'

Stoner told him at some length and in some dirty detail. They shared maybe an hour of understanding. And then the two men, one stringy, tall and white, the other huge and taller and black, stood up and embraced like brothers. Stretch shook his head. 'I'd made Shard for some kind of commando, certainly a knife man, but butchering your blonde ho' on camera? Man. Man, that is serious sick shit.'

'Yeah. Agreed. Screwed me over royally.' Stoner sat down again. 'Finally, then. I made it plain that I was heading home to reclaim the farm, and booked hotels and flights using the Hard Man's – Hartmann's – card and workname, John Hand, and I'm booked on a flight from Boston Logan to London...' he looked up at one of the many clocks in the hall, 'about now.'

'Man. We are in Detroit. Have you suffered some cranial catastrophe and lost all sense of geography? Or are you hiding in plain sight, once removed? Laying false trails for the Indian scouts... or whatever they are these days? Dr Wu is most likely in Texas, unless I seriously mislaid my intelligence.'

'Reckon your hidden smartness is safe with me, old buddy, and speaking of Buddy, where is he? Didn't you fly together?'

Stretch nodded. 'Yeah. Flew into Detroit together, he took an internal down to Fort Worth or Dallas, Austin, somewhere.'

'Houston. Think Bud lives in Houston. Thereabouts.'

'All right. Whatever. You booked flights, or is we walkin', white guy?'

'We's drivin'.'

'Say what? The lone star state is some few miles from Detroit, and the US of A is a little larger than the UK, geographically speaking, my man.'

Stoner stood again and stretched. 'We drive. We disappear. We pay cash, I have lots of cash, and while we take turns driving we talk through the long hours of shared wake-time and we produce a plan. Every so often I'll go online and reveal that I'm in Turkey, or maybe Thailand, maybe Guatemala...'

'You don't want to go there. They sell whiteys like you into slavery or boil them for soup. I read it on the internet. Like the sound of Thailand better. Buddhist piety and seriously beauteous hookers, chicks with dicks; unbeatable combination. Also it is hot. I need hot after too long in British fogs.' The men hefted their bags and walked back into the cold, wet night.

***

'Choose a small city. We're looking for crime, grime and cash motels.' Stretch was playing driver, Stoner stretched out on the back bench as best he could.

'You've got the road map, Stretch. Care to pass it back here?'

'Nope. Just make a choice. Choose from any signs, and I'll steer us there. I know we thought we'd do the trip in one long haul, but I need a bed and a bath if I'm going to survive the week. And I don't like to talk about life's little necessities, but I would feel better tooled up, and I'd feel better with a layer of banknotes insulating me from life's trials.'

'Stretch has gone soft. Who would have believed that?' Stoner's jibe had a smile inbuilt.

'Yeah. Too long easy soft living, man. How come you're capable of making like The Rock? You been pulling a lot of action in my old country?'

Stoner exercised the muscles of his neck. 'Some. Slept in a woods – in a forest if you like – for some weeks. Maybe months. Don't remember a lot of it. Spent a lot of time hunting. Two-legged targets. Great thing about the general lawlessness of the great out-there is that it's never too hard to find an armourer and a banker. Some especially useful guys can do both. Pimps, mostly, several narcos.'

'Gotcha. Uncle Sam's free ATMs.'

'As you say. Best country I know of for such excellent social provisions. Help for the homeless.' Stoner read a name from a passing roadsign. 'Sound good?'

'Sure does. A night of R&R, a little cashing-up for me and we'll be on our way again. Two more days with nights spent in beds. I'm too old for this macho superhero gig anyway. You in a rush, noble man? You ready to share the great plan?'

'OK. Here's how it all feels to me. First; you don't need money, cash money. The guitar flight case in the back has no guitar in it. Just cash. But I'm light on handguns. Have a rifle in the loadbed along with the motorcycle, but no handguns.

'By now, the opposition – if they're looking as I think they are – will have observed that I wasn't on that plane from Boston. It's not entirely easy to hop off a transatlantic flight at an early stop, so they'll have worked out that I never got on.'

'They'll know that you didn't check in.'

'They may know you're here with me.'

'They will. Bili and Amanda know, and neither chick is so stupid as to attempt futile resistance.'

'Check. So as soon as we land in Texas, I'll do a little Facebook, reveal in some pointless semi-coded way that I'm planning on Mexico by road, then by airplane to... that's as far as I got.'

'Fly under our own names,' Stretch began.

'You're planning on coming with me, big guy? I'd thought you'd stay here, get rehabilitated, draw your navy pension, the like. You're really OK with heading back to the UK?'

'Unless you deny me, then yeah. Fly under our own names to Eastern Europe. They still let you into Russia? Russia would be good. Maybe Ukraine, Beloruss, Latvia.

Somewhere. Make a seriously obscure approach to the killing zone. That is your purpose, yes? Killing? Seeking, destroying, and the like. Talk straight now, I prefer to know what I'm doing before I do it. If the opposition is smaller than the CIA, FSB or MI6 then you'll exhaust them by endlessly trailing false scents. No one has enough freelances to follow as many false trails as we can make. How'm I doing?'

Stoner laughed aloud. 'Better than me. I'll just sit back and let you handle all of it, master chief.'

'Chief,' corrected Stretch. 'Chief will do just fine. Oh my, look here. A motel of the seedy and broken kind; the perfect spot for a couple tired guys to have a break. Bet they know where the pimps hang out, too, huh?'

***

Stoner was standing by the curtained window to their shared motel room. 'We appear to have company.'

Stretch yawned. A deep, wide expanse of a yawn, accompanied by a general cracking of joints as he flexed an assortment of large muscles. 'Quality company? Quantity?'

'Low grade low-life. Either connected us to your little exercise in the vigilante approach to cleaning vice from the streets, or they've developed an unhealthy interest in the truck or the bike in the back of it. Or both. Hard to say in the dark.'

'Not Feds or police?'

'If they are, they're both rubbish and undercover, not a common combination.'

'How many, and what colour?'

Stoner paused a while, considering. 'Three, which means four with the other in their own vehicle. Hispanic.

Am I allowed to say that? Hispanic? Mexicans, getting retaliation in early on account, maybe.'

'Retaliation for what?'

'Not sure yet. Depends on the level of violence when I intervene or remonstrate with them.'

'Big words, big man. Hispanics will be confused by such high class linguistic skills. Actions always speak louder.'

'From the mouths of babes, and big black badasses, I hear only wisdom.'

'Amen. You want help with the garbage disposal, then? Or can the white colonial oppressor manage it all on his own?'

'Teamwork is best. Practice maketh man, as they say.'

'They do? They say that?'

'Not sure. Don't think so. I like to be ahead of the trend. Here we go then. A simple pincer movement? Can we do this in complete silence so that your beauty sleep is undisturbed by constabulary intervention?'

'You always talk like a dictionary when you're nervous?'

'I'm not nervous.'

'Then you have no excuse. But you are correct about the beauty sleep thing. I surely do need my beauty sleep.'

'Doubt it'll help much – can only be so much sleep in a single night. Won't make much difference to the beauty.'

'Yeah. Let's go. Can you open and close a door without it sounding like a declaration of war, great white oppressor? Give me the keys to the truck.'

'Why? Just curious.'

'Pissed American citizen is less memorable than

some irate limey. Only I speak, but you can join in with the violence.'

Stoner tossed over the keys. 'Everyone needs a purpose, an incentive.' He opened the door, slipped out, followed by Stretch, who closed the door behind him, then melted into the dim neon night, materialising at the side of the young man who was working on the truck's door lock.

'These help?' Stretch enquired with innocence, quietly, almost a whisper. Keys rattled. The youth froze.

Then, 'You going to hand over those keys, man?'

'Nope.'

A knife flicked open in the younger man's hand. 'You should,' he said.

'You're right,' said Stretch, landing a huge left fist in the young man's gut. 'You should watch the hands, not the shiny shiny thing,' he remarked, landing a heavy right onto the youth's left ear. The would-be thief fell to his knees, coughing and dribbling puke. Stretch collected the knife, whispered some more. 'You should go now, and quietly. Don't make me sleep in the cab, and don't make enough noise to wake everybody up.' The youth wobbled upright. 'Oh yes,' said Stretch, very quietly. 'Don't mess with the military; we travel in teams. Got that?'

The youth coughed, but into his hands to muffle the sound. He nodded. His eyes flicked to left then right of Stretch, then left again.

'No need to look for the help. My buddies will have suggested their departure. You dig?' The young man nodded, holding a hand to his bleeding ear. 'You gone yet?' The young man walked unsteadily back to the road, looked both ways, twice, then began walking slowly back towards the town.

'That went well,' Stretch remarked to the night. Stoner appeared at his side, nodding. 'Yeah,' they said together, and returned to their room.

13

HERE AND NOW: SWEET SOUL SISTERS

Two sisters. One blonde, the other not. One tall, slim, athletic to a point of near-severity, the other not. One talking, the other listening. Side by side on a bench, gazing in parallel, not at each other, opinions as parallel as their view of the shared scene before them. Not an argument, they very rarely argued, but certainly a disagreement.

Chastity continued to speak. Hard staring at an unseen horizon. 'He asked me to help. I don't know how many times I need to repeat this, sister, but I can see no reason why I'd refuse. I didn't refuse. I agreed. I can see no reason why I'd change my opinion of him, nor my willingness to help if I can. He helped me. I treasure that.'

'Can I join in yet? Chas, he's a dead man. He's not going to survive this – I like the guy a lot, but I can't see how it's survivable without divine intervention. You're many things, but divine isn't one of them. We – you too – need to think of ourselves here. There's opportunities.'

'There always are. Come on, the game's changed. The older order is going away – off to golf clubs or watering holes in the ground or wherever old gunners go. If we want to stay in the game, then...

'Do we even want to stay in it? Do we? Both of us? And if we do, do we really need to be affiliated to some bigger group? I prefer to contract. Damn it, Charm, I want to stop at some point. I miss Charity. Stoner was right about killing screwing up your head, the inside of it. We're not soldiers, sister. We're not – I'm not capable of just endlessly repeating the sheer squalor of murder. I can't hate everyone. It reached a point last year when I thought if I did, y'know, hate, real, live, angry hate then I could carry on with the blankness of it, being remote through hate. But that was awful. I thought I was a butcher. Thought I could be if I tried. A butcher. Chop chop. I'm not. I thought I had no morality, but I do. Anyone can point a rifle, Charm, anyone. Reckon I'll always be up for that, but our speciality? Getting in close, messing the scene, creating mucky dirty fictions to lose the realities in... I just hate that. I hate that as much as I should hate the johns, the marks. But I don't hate them enough. Not without Chas. Charity... balanced me somehow.' The slim blonde fell silent. Her older, darker sister spoke.

'Which has what exactly to do with helping him? Helping Stoner? You're picturing some domestic dream involving him? That won't happen.'

'Really? Suppose you think he'd rather settle down with you in some semi-detached suburban shit hole, huh? He doesn't even know who you are, sister. You're just recreational sex to him. One of his fuck bunnies. There's a load of those. He called me, remember. Not you.'

'I'll definitely remember that. How could I forget? But trust me. He's not going to survive this. If he did, he'd just run away again. I can't see him remaining a player. Not without the Hard Man – Hartmann – behind him, pulling his strings. He's too soft, too easy.'

'You think Hartmann is out of it? No longer a player?'

'Not sure. Truth for you, sis, I'm not sure. He's much more... separated from the cosy politicals than he was, but politics is a much dirtier game than contract killing. He could come back. Not sure how, but he could. I think he'll be replaced.'

'If Stoner made it back, he'd be the obvious candidate.' Chastity continued to survey the distant hills.

'He could be.' Her sister mused. 'But I don't see it. Here's a thing, though. Mallis sees it your way.'

'That freak?' Chastity smiled for the first time in a while. 'I wondered when he and that bizarre sister – is she really his sister? – would turn up in your considerations. Calculations!' She smiled more. 'Mallis and Menace – whoever did name them the techno prisoners, huh? – they wouldn't last a single round against Stoner. And here's another thing, when we were in Germany, he warned me about Mallis. Told me that the guy was honest – which was a tiny surprise – but only to trust the honesty as far as it goes. That I should be aware that truth for Mallis is always a commodity. Something like that. Said it's like that for everyone.'

'Not so. Come on; don't be naïve. Do you,' Charm hesitated. 'Do you – here's a question – do you trust Stoner?'

'Yes.' Chastity's answer, instant, said without pause.

'Why?'

'I think the guy's very straight.'

'He's a killer. Stop it with these romantic notions, Chastity, the guy was thrown out of the army for killing defenceless ragheads in the desert.'

'We kill people for a living. And for fun. You and me. So what? Oh I forgot. You don't like doing the dirty any more. You're management – maternal fucking management. You need to stop mothering me, Charm. I don't need you to tell me what I should do, what I should think, what I should feel. You had a sister who did need you. I don't remember you being around much at the time.' The statement fell flatly between them. Charm declined to pick it up.

'The men he killed were unarmed prisoners.'

'Says who?'

'Mallis. And Shard – Harding.'

'Ooh. And they're reliable? Trustworthy? I'd ask Stoner himself.'

'Do it. Next time you snuggle up in some faraway hotel, just before you start choosing names for the babies, huh?' Charm laughed suddenly, unexpectedly. 'Did you really not get it on with him in Germany?'

Chastity shrugged. 'No. Not exactly.'

'Why not? The guy has the morals of a stray cat.'

'You should know.'

'I do know. It's almost refreshing in its way. Anyway.' Charm's smile had faded back to neutrality. 'What does he want to know?'

'You're going to help him? You're OK if I do?'

'Why not? If it's really important to you; if it makes you happy. And... and... if you really do believe he can survive the shitstorm if he comes back to the UK, then... he would be a good guy to be on the right side of.'

'That would be you on top, as usual, huh?'

'Don't be coarse, sister. You're only jealous.' They both laughed, neither sounding particularly happy, neither sure why they laughed at something they did not share. Charm reached out a manicured, soft hand, tapped her fingers against her sister's hard thigh. Chastity ignored her hand, focused instead on the question which accompanied it. 'What did Stoner want when he called, anyway?' Charm removed her fingers, rebuffed and plainly offended.

Chastity thought for a moment. 'Hardly anything. He just asked about the lay of the land, who's said what, who's around. But only as far as it relates to him. No background, no real heads-up or intel as you'd recognise it.'

'He's in the States. At least, that's what I was told. I was also told he's on his way back.' Charm sounded bored, irritated.

'Cool.'

'I was also told that Stretch – y'know, the piano player from the Blue Cube – has gone over there to assist. And that they should both be back now, but they didn't turn up as expected.'

'Interesting.'

'As you say, sister.' Charm sat back, scratched herself in a particularly unladylike way and groaned as she followed the scratch with a set of long muscle stretching exercises. 'You'd better look at this, then.' She unfolded a laptop, flicked it into reluctant life. Chastity slid closer beside her.

'Look at what?'

Charm tapped keys, waited, tapped some more. Performed a couple of multi-key wrist shuffles, sat back. 'Knock yourself out. I'm going to brew. Want something hot, ferocious killer woman?' Chastity nodded, grunted, lost in reading.

'So,' she said while Charm bustled around doing kitchen domesticity like a normal human, 'Stoner is using the Hard Man's worknames – at least two of them – to buy tickets, pay hotels. This is all from Mallis, right?' She waved a hand at the screenload of figures, dates, location references. Charm nodded, made like mother with the tea bags.

'Menace, to be accurate, but I'd imagine they're the same figures.'

'You deal with her, rather than him? How come?'

'It happens sometimes. Menace places the contracts for a lot of what we do. It's odd with them. They both sign off with a cap M, but their ways of presenting are very different. Menace isn't a natural Anglo speaker.'

'She's not?'

'No. She's never ever direct. It's like dealing with a Chinese; lots of shouting and emphasis on nothing. The opposite of Mallis, who'd tell you about your own sudden death in that flat monotone of his.'

'I don't think I've ever really met Menace.' Chastity pondered.

Charm laughed, a strangely awkward, almost embarrassed performance. 'Stoner tells everyone he's never met me.'

'Yeah. He did say that.'

'It's great to make an impression, huh?'

'What are you trying to say, sis? You use fake names more than anyone. We should call you Legend.' She held up both hands in surrender. 'A joke, hey! Come on. You do better tea than almost anyone.' She turned back to the screen, sipping and breathing in the vapours. Almost smiling, not a friendly smile…

'According to this, then, he's in at least three places. He was on a flight from Newark arriving yesterday…'

'Didn't arrive.'

'And on a flight from Boston Logan…'

'Wasn't.'

'And in a truly grand sounding hotel in the deepest middle of nowhere, USA last night. Huge suite I hope, going by the billing.'

'Yeah.' Charm was almost sullen. 'He's having fun. But he shouldn't be.'

Chastity sat back, sipped at her fragrant infusion a little more. 'Question,' she said.

'Go ahead. Nah. Fuck it. You're going to ask me why the worknames and accounts are active and why the Hard Man is letting Stoner spend money on them like it's throwaway day in the OK Casino? Right?'

'Right. Also, if it's just one huge smoke and mirrors trick, where is Stoner and why is he pretending to be everywhere else?'

'That's easy. He's old school. Hide in plain sight. He does it well. When he was a contractor he'd roll up on some huge, really loud motorcycle, dressed all over in the sort of biker grunge kit that has grown men running away, take the hit, sometimes in plain view, fire up the bike and clear off. No one ever issued an accurate description. The Hereford boys all loved it. D'you remember that Hereford shooter? What was his name? Mincer or something like that.' Charm giggled, almost girlishly. Chastity fidgeted. 'He always reckoned that his buddies in the regiment would take bets that when one of those "gangland killings", those "sectarian attacks" took place, that they were all Stoner if there was a motorcycle involved. And every time they'd ask him, he could always – bloody always – prove beyond doubt that he was somewhere else, doing something else and that someone else was doing all that biker leather crap. And he'd make like he knew who it was, too, but couldn't say.'

'Mallis would know.'

'Says he doesn't. Says one reason he trusts Stoner is that Stoner's the only operator who has more on Mallis than Mallis has on him. Scary if so, huh?' She shrugged, parked her teacup, and leaned back again.

'Hereford shooter boy also reckoned that Stoner gave professionals a bad name, just riding up, popping some guy with a pistol, then riding off again. Him and his sniper buddies spent years training and technical stuff, and Stoner got paid more for behaving like a bandit.'

'Didn't he snipe as well?'

'They say so. You know him better than me, Chastity dearest; ask him. He talks sense to you. He just fucks me occasionally and talks about guitars. At the same time sometimes. Makes a lady feel loved. Appreciated. Not.'

'Ooh; bitchy!' There was a sharp edge to Chastity's voice.

'Believe it. Why the Hard Man's letting Stoner spend like this I have no idea. When I see him, I'll ask him.'

'You think you'll be seeing Stoner soon, sister?' The younger sister suddenly intent; Charm blithely oblivious.

'Reckon so. Menace thinks that Stoner's doing some huge headjob here, but I'm not sure of that at all. Feels to me like he's running round in circles. Like... he's done the lying in the dark gig, the licking wounds and that, and the vanishing completely for months trick – Menace reckons he was completely off the radar until around Christmas – and now he's laying scent everywhere, confusing the hounds. She thinks he's here. Here in the UK. That one day soon they'll start finding the bodies. That there'll be lots of bodies. That it's all a simple question of what order he converts the living into the recently deceased, and how long and who – if anyone – can stop him.' Charm paused. Cleared her throat. Stood and performed an encore with the teapot before continuing, slowly, reflectively.

'I think that so long as he's laying trails no one's going to feel his pain. That as soon as the games stop, the killing starts. Hey, Chaslady. You know his mind – I only know his body, after all. What do you think? He's asked you for help. Not me.' A bitter smile.

Chastity folded the screen of the laptop flat again, reducing their shared light. There was now a darkening evening where previously there had been an almost sunny afternoon. Both sisters shivered. Charm rose to her feet and slid shut the curtains over the windows.

'Feeling the cold, Charm?' Chastity wasn't smiling. They sat together in the near dark. 'It's like a storm, isn't it? Electricity somewhere.'

Charm hugged her arms around herself. 'We've done nothing against him. Nothing. You haven't. I haven't.'

'You're worried that once he starts clearing out the dirty linen, he'll clear it all out and start again? He won't just take out those he knows have wronged him, hurt him? And he'll come for us because he doesn't know we've not hurt him?'

'You put a bomb in his club, Chas. You shot out the lights of his car.'

'True. I think he saved my life in Germany.'

'Did he talk about Blesses?'

Chastity sat up straight. 'Yes.'

'What did he say?'

'That she was out of prison, that she was free, and that he wished he'd killed her. Who is she? Do you know her?'

'Blesses will kill him.' Charm started to sob. Suddenly. Shockingly. Gently shaking, the tears rolling like warm rain on leaves. 'She'll kill him if he's lucky. If he's not, he'll wish she'd killed him. And if she tries and fails first time, then he'll kill everyone he sees nearby in case they're being worked by Blesses.'

'Charm! Sister! Hey. Hey...' Chastity held her sister's face between her hands, calming, soothing, with only a faint air of distaste. 'What is this crap? Who is Blesses?'

'She's a fucking witch. An Irish witch. A fucking devil. The devil. You want to know the devil; that's her.' Charm was crying openly, no dignity nor restraint. Shaking, hard.

Chastity pulled her sister to her and squeezed her in a harsh impression of support. A dry-eyed demand: 'You know this woman? You've met? Have I met her?'

Charm subsided, pulled herself away from the chill of the embrace, and stood up, alone, lost, shivering. 'She was at the club last year, Stoner's club, with Lissa, Stoner's girl; the black girl he preferred to me... to us both, in case you forgot that. Blesses and Lissa were acting like friends, like just the girls, y'know?

'Shard was there, too. He was – I think; it wasn't, like, yesterday, it was while you were away being international action woman of the year – he was pissed that Charity had gone with Bili the bass player to talk Stoner into getting you out of Israel. Shard really was pissed, too, at himself, and at Chas and at Mallis for deciding to send Bili instead of him, and he was pissed most of all at Stoner.

'That was some weird boy shit; that Stoner had vanished after thinking he'd killed the Hard Man and saved the world, like guys always think they're doing, knobbers that they are, and he'd done all that without saying anything to his best mate, Shard. Only Stoner doesn't do best mates, does he? He doesn't do mates. He doesn't even do lovers. Not really.' Charm sat down and started to sob again, head in hands, the teapot standing like a silent witness.

'Jeez, sis, have you got this so bad? You got something for Stoner I should know about?' Chastity pulled her smaller, darker sister to her. 'Hey, babe. He is just some guy, right? Right?' She tilted her sister's face and peered into her drowned eyes. 'Oh for fuck's sake.' She stepped back. 'Fucking fucking fuck.' She leaned on the wall. Opened a door. Slammed it shut. And again. Repeat.

'He's not, though. Is he?' Charm's voice had drifted into something alien, gentle, almost dreaming. 'Not just some guy. Some other guy like all the other guys.'

Her sister leaned against the wall, shaking her head slowly, her eyes rolling so that Charm was steadily in their focus, their aim. 'He is. Just. Some guy. When all is boiled down, JJ is just a guy. He walks, talks like a guy, he does guy things and he takes a piss standing up. Just like they all do. Christ, Charm. He does not walk on water. He beats up on people because he's paid to do it and enjoys it, and he'll fuck anything with a hole in it.'

'Except you.'

Chastity levered herself from the wall and took a single step towards her sister. Stopped. Backed up. Resumed her slouch against the wall.

'Yeah,' she said, quietly. 'Except me. Remind me, why don't you?'

Charm stood, suddenly, went to her sister. 'His loss,' she whispered, and took her sister's hand. 'His loss. Not yours. You're right. Just a guy. I love...' her voice trailed. Chastity stared at her. 'I love his music. Stupid, stupid. I love it. Some nights...'

Chastity leaned against her sister, her eyes quieter. 'Yeah. OK. I've heard you play together. Listened to it. I see what you're saying. Nah – I hear what you're saying. He is a bluesman. He does say that.'

Charm smiled, held onto her sister's hand. 'Yes he

does. He always says he's the bluesman; he knows when to leave.'

'Blesses. Talk. We can do the romantic crap any time.' Chastity stepped back.

'Why? Why her?'

'Stoner... talked about her a little while we were in Germany. And his completely fucking weirdo religious nun buddy... ah... Bernadette, a nun who runs guns, would you believe it, she spooked him completely when she mentioned that Blesses was out. Like I said. I never saw him spooked like that about anything else. I did tell you about Bernadette, yes?'

'Yes. OK.' Charm took herself to a bottle, opened and poured two drinks from it, passed one to her sister, who nodded. 'Teatime done for the day? Drinktime now?'

Charm nodded right back, sipped slowly. Tears gone; calculation returning almost visibly. 'Blesses does things to men.'

'Golly!' Chastity almost smiled. 'Really? That's not entirely unique, sister dear.'

'Fuck off.' Charm smiled, distracted by what she was attempting to say. 'Blesses... oh tits... it's like witchcraft. You know?'

'No.'

'She... like... puts a spell on men. Know what I mean?'

'No.'

'It is completely weird. She... and I know what this sounds like, but I've watched her do it... she puts them under a spell. They do anything she wants them to.'

'Woo-hoo; get me some of that, lady.' Chastity was sneering now. 'I can't believe you're spouting this crap, sis. There are no witches. You know that. There are no werewolves and no vampires and no little grey aliens with musical spaceships. Come on. Talk sense. Stoner's spooked by an Irish witchy woman who can put a spell on him because he's a guy? Get outta here, as the Yanks tell us.' She wound down when she understood the expression on her sister's face. 'You're serious?'

Charm nodded, sipped, spoke slowly. 'I watched it happen a couple of times at the Blue Cube. Once with Shard and the other time with some guy I didn't know but she did. The same both times. Drinking a little and chatting a little, and suddenly she was staring them in the eyes, real close, and then they were just silent and doing exactly – exactly, to the letter – what she told them to do. Incredible.'

Chastity watched her sister. Placed her untouched drink on a table. 'Serious?'

'Exact.'

'And... you think she could do this to Stoner? Big nasty man that he is?'

'Don't know. Truth. Stretch is a big man, and he just stayed well away when Blesses was in the club. Not like he was avoiding her, exactly, more like he just wasn't around her at all. I saw him look at her a couple of times, then just look away.'

'Why don't you have a thing for Stretch?' Chastity produced an interested tone, changed the subject a little. 'He plays that piano as well as I've ever heard a piano being played. And he's a big guy, and American and black, which is at least a couple of good points.'

Charm smiled. 'Yeah,' she said. 'Never seen him with a woman. Maybe he plays for our side, huh? What're you going to tell Stoner? He going to call you, or what?'

'Facebook. Or the murdermayhem&more website, I think.'

'You could post more movies of severed heads to attract his attention. You were good at those.' Charm raised an eyebrow at her sister. 'I was almost worried that you'd really lost it with those.'

'Yeah, me too. Charity... I really miss her, Chas my sister... she thought so too. I think I was. Then somehow I wasn't.' She shook her head, looked down at her drink, left it where it was. 'You seriously think that this Blesses bitch has some kind of weird witchy shit? That would be... well. I don't know. It would be like suddenly believing in fairies, or something.'

'Ask Stoner.' Charm was all at once efficiency and cool. 'Call him now.'

Chastity sat down at the laptop, shaking her head as she rattled keys. 'Facebook. I'll message him.' She did, several times to and from several names, none of them hers or his own. She sat back. 'I hate waiting for boys to call,' she announced. 'Give me a job to do. Anything. I want to pull the wings off something... someone. Anything available in the Big Girl's Book Of Contract Hits?'

Charm took over the laptop. 'Well,' she mused, hitting multiple keys in complex ways and launching the browser into the deceitful world of the dark web; 'There's always someone somewhere...'

14

WILD ROVER

'I just wanted to hear your voice.' Stoner purred into the handset. 'How are you doing?'

No answer. No hang-up and no dial tone.

'Hey. How's it going? Do you miss me? It's been a while – too long. And we parted so hard, really. Unfinished. There were things we should have done... y'know... together.' His accent had drifted from mainland UK across the Irish Sea and picked up a Belfast brogue on the way. A harsh voice, speaking harsh words softly. 'Why so silent, sweet lassie? Why so... quiet? I can hear you breathe... hear your breath. So soft. So few of them left now. Enjoy them. Share them with a loved one. Count them. Soon... soon.'

A voice answered from the hiss of the ethers. 'Man up, soldier boy, man up for me. You'll not take me down, man across the sea.'

'You remember.'

'I do. I remember everything. I recall it all. Do you?'

'I do.'

'Good. Coming for me now, are you? After all this time? And you... you so very far away.'

'Not so far now. Not nearly so far.'

'I'll make sacrifice for you, Jean-Jacques. Maybe kill a chicken, or a goat, or maybe an Englishman with ashes for a soul.'

'Kill what you want to kill, sweet lassie; do what you want to do. Don't worry. Take your time, don't hurry.'

'You'll be coming to lend me a hand, huh, Jean-Jacques?' Her smile was suddenly perfectly clear through the vague voice in the handset. 'Business to finish. Always best to finish what you shouldn't have started.'

'Beautiful day to you. Enjoy them all. We'll be together soon.'

'Jean-Jacques?'

'Hmmm?'

'Missing you already. Kiss kiss.'

Stoner tapped the phone to end the call, flipped it onto its front, slid plastics, removed the battery and the SIM card. Laid them either side of the dead phone. The large black man seated opposite paused in his study of the menu.

'Romance always spurs the appetite, huh?' He grinned over the colourful display of dead meat he held before him, a vegetarian's very own horror show. Neither of them was a vegetarian. 'This would be your girlie, the one gone rogue? Blesses, huh?'

Stoner nodded, picked up his own illustrated guide to the range of dead cow off-cuts on offer. 'Hmmm.' He suddenly smiled. 'Believe me or no,' his Irish accent was with him still; 'it is good – very good – to have a plan again. At last.'

'You have a plan? I thought we were just careering around the States, heading nowhere and doing it fast, while posting insanely inaccurate locations on whichever websites appeal to you. Or is that the plan?' A waiter approached. They both ordered. The hypothetical vegetarian would have run away screaming.

'Do you want to hear it?' Stoner ran his fingers through his long hair, scratched his thick beard. 'And I think I should get a haircut. I feel a little out of place in the gentle world that is middle America.'

'No need. You look like an aging rock star or an escaped convict, maybe a midlife acid casualty. Tell me the plan if you like. I don't... I don't really mind. I'll be with you anyway.'

'And looking like an aging fuck-up is good somehow?' Stoner was scanning the beer adverts.

'Yep. You look a little threatening and seedy and certainly avoidable. All that is good. You don't look like anyone on the run or a gun for hire.'

'And I've got you with me to add a distraction.'

'Yo humble servant, massah. Anyone scoping the two of us would take me for the threat.'

'Even before they heard you playing with a piano? Impressive.'

'Just so, white trash. Exactly so. Now make with the plan – after the food's strolled over to join us, huh?' He flagged down an improbably beautiful film starlet-alike and ordered beers, light American beers, and lots of them. The food arrived, with a fanfare and a flourish. Both men sat back in approval while the servers performed a serving ritual which would have been the envy of many religious ceremonies, and then they backed away, confident that decent gratuities would soon be theirs.

'The plan.' Stoner opened his left hand, slicing potato with his fork in the American way. 'Head home – that would be the UK – and take out everyone I don't like. Sound good?' He transferred potato to mouth, and chewed steadily, with every appearance of happiness.

Stretch laid down both fork and knife, took a deep, deep draught from his glass, poured more for the both of them from the half-gallon jug on their table. 'In any particular order? Y'know; alphabetical or by regions, height, body mass, something even more logical and possibly even partially sane? Or will you prioritise in order of perceived offence? I say perceived there because it's almost impossible to get the truth out of someone with a large calibre handgun held to their head or a totally sharp knife at their ear.' He drank some more. Slowly.

'You speak from experience here, o mighty black warrior?'

'Indeed I do.' Stretch belched in a comfortable, quiet and almost civilised manner. 'I do indeed. Do you have a number in mind here? An approximation would be fine. To the nearest round figure, y'know; the nearest dozen or so – hundreds if you're feeling really cranky about this.'

'I am.' Stoner was eating his dead and well-burned steer with every outward appearance of relish and delight. There was in fact no sign at all that he was contemplating vegetarianism as a new lifestyle. He drank some more of the beer, nodded his appreciation of both food and drink to a waitress, who hovered, beamed radiantly, and then departed.

'Glad to hear it.' Stretch had completed the skilful transfer of deceased bovine to stomach, and was mopping up the vegetables, sauces, relishes and dips. He waved the empty bread basket vaguely in the air. Almost by magic and almost instantly it was replaced with a filled basket. 'It never pays to be half-hearted about this kind of thing. Many future troubles are set in motion by inadequate carnage at the earlier opportunity.'

'You're still speaking from experience?'

'Still. Yes. Yes I am. If a limb is seriously diseased it needs removing. Being right-on and humane and praying for the gangrene to depart whence it came rarely works. As it is with rats, also, and similar vermin. Eradication is the only answer. It's easier in the long run.' He paused. Considered the fact that Stoner was only halfway through his meal, poured some more beer and shook his dark head at the enthusiastic waiting team. 'There would have been no Gulf War Two if we'd all stomped our way up to the Mediterranean killing anything mobile the first time.'

Stoner smiled. 'And if the Allies had marched on Moscow instead of stopping at Berlin...'

'Exactly. We are as one.'

'And the problems in Palestine?'

'Easily fixed. Two nukes and – poof! – no more problem.'

'Nukes delivered onto who, exactly?'

Stretch grinned while Stoner mopped his plate. 'That is the key question, my friend, the key question. Now that we've solved the world's many ills – in principle at least – could you go for cheesecake?'

Stoner nodded. Stretch ordered. Staff scurried.

'The plan?' Stretch still sounded amused.

'Half-formed,' revealed Stoner, speaking softly in a mock conspiratorial way. 'First, we take Manhattan...'

Stretch interrupted. 'That's a song. You cannot conquer the world with music. Many tried, all failed. Consider Michael Jackson.'

'Are you drunk? OK, I was joking about Manhattan. We're almost in Texas...'

'Is that a song also?'

'No. You're interrupting. This brief but masterful plan will take all night if you carry on interrupting. Eat another steer or whatever Americans do when they need to focus.'

Stretch demolished his dessert, then ate Stoner's and flagged for a replacement. 'Continue while I consume, Mr Stoner.'

'We're heading for Texas...'

'To meet up with Buddy and play brilliant blues with Dr Wu, yeah?' Stretch sounded almost excited, in a booming, black mountainous kind of way. 'I like this plan. It involves loud and energetic music and loud and energetic women. Hopefully.'

'It does. While we head for Texas – which should be a lyric if it isn't already – I shall bombard any and all online social sites with photos of my journeys to... hell, pretty much anywhere that is not entirely Texas. Then, confusion sown among anyone interested in our whereabouts, I will permit someone other than me – you would do – to post excited tales of our conquering the rebellious South in musical and mayhem terms, complete with vids and soundstuff and lots of pics to identify us beyond all doubt even among the blind, by which time we will of course be in Mexico, which is conveniently proximal to Texas, by lucky coincidence, whence we will commence our departure for shores even more foreign than these.'

'You're drunk.'

Stoner nodded his head. 'Maybe so. How does it show?'

'No one sober could say "conveniently proximal" without laughing at the pomposity.'

'Agreed. This weak piss you Americans refer to

erroneously as beer is plainly stronger than it looks. And tastes. And I've not drunk much recently. And I have been worried about... well, pretty much everything, really.'

'You doubted yourself?'

'I did.'

'That's bad.'

'Thank you. Apart from the doubtful wisdom of playing black man's music with a bunch of black men and white men who want to sound like black men, I have rarely doubted myself.'

'Amen. Who're you going to kill? Anyone I know?'

'Oh yes.'

Stoner leaned back in his chair, ran his fingers back through his hair, gathering it behind his head. 'What d'you think? A man-bun, high up on the top of my head, Chinese topknot style?'

Stretch scratched his own military flat top. 'You want to look like a decadent, substance abusing, self-abusing hipster accountant or wannabee middle-aged schoolmaster intent on the seduction of American teenage virgins?'

'There are such critters? American teenage virgins? Really? It's easier to believe in unicorns and the healing power of prayer.'

'Your cynicism will be your undoing. I can't say that I ever met such, although possibly a unicorn just the once, but I am a believer.'

'Great song, wasted on monkeys.'

'Monkees, like trainee monks or whatever, but yes.'

'Yes what?'

'I have forgotten. There is a god and she is most merciful. Praise the lady.'

'Stretch. Petty Officer Stretch.'

'It's Chief Petty Officer McCann to you, white boy.

That's who I was. Before. Not plain dishonest Stretch. A refugee in his own country.'

'Refugee? From who? I've been wondering how you regained these shores. I thought there was a bounty on your head, or something.'

'That's just bad hair, limey.'

'Say what?'

'Never mind. The exile was precautionary. It was strongly suggested, not quite imposed. The military – so I believe – apparently have no interest in me right now. Although...'

'Although what?' Stoner appeared decreasingly drunk as the drinking continued.

'Although the military still pays me... or it did, last I checked.'

Stoner was sitting upright and fully focused. 'They do? How so?'

'I retired. Semi. Inactive service. You know that.'

'I did not. Now I do. I thought you were kicked out after...' He paused, shrugged. 'After Rose and...' He paused again.

Stretch shook his head slowly. 'No. There was no evidence against me. Adultery is not a court-martial offence, not a military matter, not in wartime.'

'This is peace. We are at peace.'

'You post-imperialist running dogs may believe that the sun has set on your empire and that you exist in a quiet world of subtle manipulation and powerplaying, but the US military believes different. In any case, that don't matter none. After Rose passed over and I was found to have a cast-iron alibi – thanks to you, my man – and no provable motive, seen from any perspective that might stand in a court, I was advised that any bad blood between Davey – that would be Davey Santos,

Rose Santos's husband, an army man – and me would be viewed by the authorities as being very bad form and undesirable. Undesirable in a custodial sense.'

'You killed Rose, Stretch.' Stoner held his gaze, steady, like soldiers in a movie. 'He must have known that – Davey.'

'You might think that. You might indeed think that. For so it was, my friend.'

'Did it end there?'

'It did not.'

'OK.' Stoner nodded.' No need to say more.'

'Some little time later, I saw action again. Two kinds of action. The kind of action where when you observe a bad motherfucker you attack that motherfucker to his extreme prejudice. And the other kind of action whereby you are rendered powerless by the fact that although a motherfucker is a motherfucker, if the motherfucker wears the same stars and bars on his jacket that I do I cannot reduce the world's tally of motherfuckers by one more. Such is the unnatural injustice of the world. And Davey Santos was still army, well respected and white.'

'Hispanic.'

'Hispanic is more white than hard-on black like me, man. Not that it helped Santos much in the long run."

'OK.'

'Yeah. Well. After that tour I was up for a promotion and another medal, a medal with a purple ribbon.'

'Respect.' Stoner raised his glass and sipped.

'My third. I have a collection. Which put the Navy into a hard place. A senior white officer suggested that I accept an honourable discharge in the light of my injuries. The much more senior black officer in the room at the time but not officially so suggested that favoured reserve status would be a truly honourable thing.'

'Favoured what? Never heard of it.'

'Me either. I took it. The condition was a simple one. I needed to vacate the USA for an undefined period of time. And add Davey Santos to the long list of subjects not to be discussed. Period.'

'Where are we now, Stretch? Why're you here in the US and why are you drinking us both all the way to sobriety?'

'Because I am a fucking man of honour, JJ Stoner, the never-retired endless sergeant. And I honour you. When you need me, here I am. And you surely do need me. Blesses will kill you, sure as shit is shit, shinola is shinola. That is the only important fact.'

'You reckon she will?' Stoner did not sound distressed by the thought. Not at all.

'I do. I watched what she did to your man Shard, and it was hideous to behold. No need at this point to construct poor jokes about his appearance. Many of us appreciate the art of the tattoo. Any case, Shard was a warrior, and he was your man. That witch twisted his soul, and I would believe her capable of doing the same to you.'

'But not to you.'

'Of course to me. Me more easily than you, because I believe in all that voodoo shit, man. And you are plainly an unbeliever. It won't help you. Hideous, as I said, to behold.'

'So tell me.' Stoner sipped some more.

'It was a Tuesday. It was raining.' Stretch looked at his companion expectantly.

'What is this? Some kind of spot the song contest? It's OK. You've won.'

'You don't know the joke.' Stretch performed crestfallen, a decent enough impression of that under-used expression, too.

'No. I don't do jokes. I do wit. Right now I'm witless. That's my kind of joke, Stretch. Can we get along now?'

Stretch shrugged. 'A question. How and how well do you know the scary critter that is Blesses?'

Stoner shrugged right back. Two grown men in a shrugging contest. 'I met her in Ireland while on a job.'

'For the Hard Man?'

'As you say. The first time she messed with my head she simply sent me after the wrong guy, somewhat to his eternal regret. Then the Hard Man pointed out my innocent error, was relaxed about it, everyone makes mistakes, and suggested that in future I wait for his own agent in place to make all the correct introductions and do the targeting. Thing is... Blesses... I had mistaken her for the Hard Man's agent... did make those intros. Or... and this is where it's spooky... I thought she had. Afterwards, I honestly couldn't remember whether she had or she hadn't. She'd known who I was – how? She'd know why I was there – how? And she'd sent me after the wrong man.

'But get this. When – finally – I made contact with the right agent I remembered seeing Blesses in the bar that night, remembered what she was wearing, shit like that. Basic tradecraft.' He stopped. 'You know what I mean?'

'Indeed I do, noble man, I do know tradecraft. When all Uncle Sam's sophisticated hardware has run down its batteries and the satellites have gone for a doze in whatever passes for a quiet evening with satellites, the Mark One Eyeball and a decent bit of a memory for faces is still the best way of doing shit.'

'Right. The agent – the real agent – asked me to describe Blesses and I could not. All I could remember were her voice and her eyes. And I couldn't even remember what colour her eyes were, just that I'd looked at them a lot, somehow. So we – the agent and me – put on a repeat performance and Blesses… fuck me if she didn't appear again. Forewarned, forearmed, so forth, so I took the correct hit and faded quietly away. Puzzled, but not too bothered. Put it down to just one of those things.'

'You run into her again?' Stretch was watching his friend closely.

'Yeah. Never went well. The same agent – a woman cop in fact – put her down some time later, and Blesses got sent down. I thought she was locked away for ever and a day, maybe a couple of complete lifetimes. But no. She's out, they tell me.'

'Was it her you were insulting on the phone a little earlier?'

Stoner spread his hands wide. 'What can I say?'

'Why d'you do that?'

'I'm going to kill her. Dead. Completely dead.'

'I entirely get your intent, my noble friend, but I do not get your method. Seems the lady has a way with us weak guy types, you know?'

'Long gun. Long gun.' Stoner appeared to be drifting somehow.

'I wonder…' Stretch was watching him closely.

'You wonder what?'

'Whether she does still have a hold on you. Whether you'll be unable to pull a trigger with her head in the sights.'

'Not possible. Simply not possible. And you know it.'

'I sat with your man Shard after she'd been at him. You've told me what he did to your black blonde. Sliced her with a blade, didn't you say? Guts on the carpet, hers, didn't you say? And you think I think she can't get into your head at least as much as she got into Shard's head? How could that be, huh?

'So set up a shot and get a girl to take her down. One of those killy sisters; your favourite blonde bombshells. The one you fetched out of Germany. Chastity. I liked those guys. Chas and Chas. Loved that. They were around the club a lot when you did your second disappearing act. Then just the one of them; Chastity. Charity disappeared. I did wonder whether you'd disappeared to the same place. Y'know, quality time together?' His lifted eyes asked the question.

Stoner shook his head. 'No. I think Charity's dead. Chastity said something like that.'

'Something like? Either someone's dead or they're not.'

'You reckon?' Stoner stared at the tabletop between them.

'Point taken.' Stretch was watching the crowd surrounding them. Out of habit, mostly. He ordered a second dessert, something with an improbable name and considerable chocolate. Ordered nothing for Stoner, who sat devoured by his own thoughts.

When he'd finished eating, again, Stretch had a question.

'A question,' he announced. 'I have a question.'

'Sugar gives you brains,' Stoner revealed.

'Say what?'

'You have a question?'

'Yeah. How d'you have a phone number for Blesses? You've been out of the game – mostly – for most of a year and you have your insane voodoo killer demon witch at the end of your cell phone address book? Spooky stuff, noble friend.'

'You don't trust me? You don't think I'm telling you everything?'

'Of course I think that, and yeah, I do trust you. I am

curious. Sounds like we got allies. I should know about them.'

Stoner bowed his head. 'You knew how to find me because..?'

'Travis the Feeb.' Stretch; quick as a flash. 'OK, so Travis gave you Blesses' number?'

'No.' Stoner dredged a phone from a pocket, dug its SIM card and battery from another, stitched them together, stabbed at the device for a while, slid it across the greasy table.

'Wondrous stuff. So C2 suggested that redemption lies at this cell number? You Brits are masters of the cryptic. This a crossword clue? A Brian Of Britain question?'

'Brain, you oaf. Brain. Nothing so subtle. C2 is Chastity.'

'This is Chastity's cell number? No security in this, brother.'

'All true.'

'She an ally, then?'

'Let us hope so.'

'You have more?'

'Allies?'

'No, ice cream. Course, allies. You need to drink more. Maybe play some bad jazz. On a guitar, please.'

Stoner looked away. 'Allies,' he said, quietly. 'I don't know. How long to Texas?'

'Depends how we travel.'

'I have a motorcycle in the back of the pick-up.'

'Yeah. I noticed that, trained military specialist that I am. I even had a conjecture, trained military analyst that I am. I theorised that as the truck is a Ford but is badged as a Harley-Davidson, that you have contracted that peculiar American infection and have indeed got a

Harley hidden – none too well at that – in the back there. You're also wearing Harley branded clothing. Suits you, fits like a secondhand shroud, but the colours are funereal enough for the gig in hand. So you have some obese porker of a motorcycle in back. You're telling me in subtle cryptic Limey lingo that you're gonna ride that old chopper down to those Texan mean streets and shit like that. Do I get to call you bro, bro?'

'Yes.'

'Yes what? It's OK to call you bro? Can't call you bubba because you ain't black enough, bub.'

'More than anything. I dream of being called bro by a six and a half foot black guy who looks like he chews railway lines for jaw exercise. And yeah. I fancy the ride.' He held up his hands in a sign of peace. 'Don't take offence. I've been mostly alone for a long time and I'm having trouble with having company – fine company though that is. No offence, my friend – my good friend.'

'None taken. I was always the same before a mission. And after it. That's how I got into trouble with other men's wives. It's just easy to be alone in company when all you gotta do is screw the company, not talk to it.'

'That didn't work so well with Rose Santos.'

'As you say, smart man. As you say. How d'you want to play this? Let's stay off the wires, huh?.' Stretch picked up the cell phone – Stoner's phone – which lay between them. Skipped it across the table to its owner. 'It's been buzzing. Maybe it needs a lie-down? Maybe it's also bored with the company.' He smiled. Stoner collected the phone, flicked its screens.

'Interesting stuff here,' he said, quietly.

'Blesses?' Stretch leaned across the table.

'Not so's you'd notice.' Stoner dismantled the device

once again. 'Chastity would like to meet up. Wants to bring her sister, too.'

'Thought she was dead, the sister. We dealing with zombies now? That's fine by me, by the way, just being curious. I worked with zombies before. Secret Service is full of them. Quiet guys.'

'Shut up. Her other sister. Charm. Who I don't know, despite everyone telling me I do know her. So another mystery woman I've met but don't recall. That's two. That's too many.'

'What did you say to her? About meeting?'

'Nothing. Nothing. Didn't reply. Like I said, I need time to think. Can you remember how to drive on the right, big American sailor boy?' He grinned at Stretch.

'Hell man, I can drive anything anywhere. I drove most of a Humvee most of the way through most of Iraq, most of another one through most of Yemen and the whole of Egypt. Also Somalia. Nice place, Somalia. Hot and dry. Not like the UK, which is the only country where I prefer not to drive. To drive in the UK you need to be blind as well as insensitive to the honest feelings of others.'

'I surrender. You got the gig. Bubba, you can drive my car.'

'Fuck off, Stoner.' Stretch grinned widely. 'The truck is faster than the bike, so I'll just park it up at Super 8 motels when I get bored with driving and if you see it and fancy a beer, just stop.'

Stoner hauled to his feet. 'Yeah,' he said, looking around. 'Super 8. You always did have class.'

'Need a hand getting that motor scooter down from the load bed? Heavy things, Harleys, and you're half the man you used to be.'

'Thanks and no thanks. It's easy enough. Besides, I

need to change from my suave sophisticated man about town persona into lean mean bikin' machine guy. This takes some time. I'll order you something to keep you smiling while I run out on you. Got all the kit in the cab. Just need to change into it.'

Stretch flagged a waitress, ordered whiskeys and coffees for one. 'You'll get soaked and frozen, get run down and killed by rednecks and then die of solitude and hypothermia, man. And you'll be forced to eat Froot Loops and grits, lettuce, maybe spinach; killer carbs all of them. That's the biker gig, huh?' He was watching ever more fatty food passing through its own rites and rituals in the kitchen.

'That's why I do it, big black man. Compensating for white man's inadequacies and guilt. Slavery left its mark, you know. The white man's burden, things like that. I'll leave the truck keys on the tyre. And I'll ride around the carpark of every Super 8 I see in case you're parked up with some luxury hooker inside.'

'All else fails, big mon?'

'Then I'll make loud music with Dr Wu and the Texas Whatevertheycallthemselves. You could sort me a guitar. A good one. How come I've never played a decent Fender in the USA, where they make the things?'

'Because they make good Fenders only in Japan and they sell them cheap to Englishmen. Fenders made in the USA are for display purposes only. Works of art. That's why they're so expensive, man.'

'Gotcha. I'm gone. Enjoy the trip. See you at the right time.'

15

GIRLS' SCHOOL

'Ladies' night tonight. Mostly!' Bili was relaxed as ever as she chatted with the microphone, on stage at the Blue Cube, like she was chatting with a single friend rather than an audience of maybe a hundred friends. 'Amanda and me, and Styx makes three.' She grinned, and the audience grinned right back. 'OK, so Styx is a guy, so he says, but we'll not hold that against him... will we?' The audience applauded, like she was a top class comedienne who'd just cracked the world's best joke for the first time. The Blue Cube's audience was the very definition of the friendly audience. And they'd loved Bili for a long time.

A subdued set. Bili sang and played trademark beautiful bass, Styx played the drums, and chimes and even handbells in a hippy lapse or two, while Amanda multitasked like a modern woman, offering spells on piano and even guitar as well as bursts of brilliance on her own saxophone. But it was subdued. Applause was warm, friendly, comfortable and relaxed.

'There's no edge,' Bili remarked as the resident house band did intros and standards from the world of jazz competence. 'We're no better than these guys.' She waved a hand towards the stage. 'Weird.'

Amanda looked tired, out of breath, though that could have been the result of working too hard on the sax. 'It's just...' she shook her head, heavy black hair rose from her shoulders then fell again. 'Without JJ, and without Stretch, too. It's just... lame. We're all great players, Bili, but we are not stars. Hard to admit it.'

'Yeah. Agree.' Bili asked an attentive fan for a bottle of Perrier water – a big bottle, please. The fan stared at her, asked whether she was serious. She convinced him with a nod. 'I've been thinking of taking a break from the stage until we... until they get back, you know?' The water appeared, she chugged from the bottle and pulled a pained face. 'It's like this apology for a drink.' She waved the bottle at the fan, the bar, at anyone who cared, making bring-me-a-glass gesture. 'It's excellent and it's really really good at being what it is, but what it is not what I want. What we want. So Stoner's band without Stoner is like G&T without the G.'

'And without the T too, if Stretch isn't around to make his noise.' Amanda appeared to be deflating. 'I'm brilliant on the sax, you know,' she remarked for no one.

'Hey.' Bili took her hand. 'Don't wilt, Amanda. You are brilliant. So's Styx and so'm I. We're just... less.' She pulled a cell phone from somewhere, fumbled a little as she activated it. Amanda shook her head.

'I don't know why you bother, Bili. He doesn't call.'

Bili grinned, surprised smile lighting her face like a firework display. 'You reckon?' She waved the device. 'Here you go.' She squinted at the display. 'He's on his way to play some – ha! "bad blues" he says – with Stretch down in Texas. Be heading back...' she paused to breathe again. 'Be heading back in a week, ten days max. Oh fucky fuck. "Call any midnight," he says; "your time". She looked at her watch. 'Oh that's cool, in about an hour. Blues in Texas, huh? Sound good?'

Amanda smiled quietly. Then; 'Pleased for you Bili. Really pleased. Say hi from me, yeah?' Bili's thumbs flickered over the phone's screen. She was smiling, fiercely.

'I told him. Told him you said hi. Told him...' she watched the screen. 'Told him that I'd not chase him, that he could just call if he wants. No stress.' She read the screen again. 'Woop woop, the old goat's actually live right now. He says hi to you too. And...' she laughed. It was a shower of rain after weeks of drought for her. 'He wants to know why we're not performing. Says we should get off our joint fat arse and make some noise.' She stabbed the screen again. 'I just told him to fuck off.' She tapped the phone closed. 'Let's go wake up this dozy bunch of amateurs, hey, Amanda? Let's do some noise.

They did that, and it was good, and for the first time in a while the Blue Cube bounced to the power of a great rage of jazz unleashed, the two women playing at their best, maybe for the benefit of an entirely absent listener, a remote audience of one, maybe two.

***

'Thanks for this.' JJ Stoner was gazing through a one-way window down onto a parking lot, rain, sleet maybe, was sluicing down the pane.

'It's fine. Welcome to your new life.' Travis slid a sheaf of paperwork, several envelopes and a lit-up laptop across the desk which separated them. 'You are officially an employee, an asset. How does that feel?'

'Impossible, frankly. What exactly does it mean?'

Stoner reached for the papers, frowned, looked up into the grim smile of his companion.

'We will never know. The job surely has a salary, which will surely be paid to someone whose name may or may not be either your own given name or the one in that small hillock of crap. There may also be benefits and paternal leave, and annual leave, and a pension and even time off for good behaviour or premature death... who knows? I don't.' A smile cracked away the frown. 'Thank you, JJ. No thanks for me required. When you sit down one night, unable to sleep and desperate for a cure to that insomnia, you can read that crap. You will learn several things. Firstly that Uncle Sam will support you in every way in your actions on behalf of said kindly – if sartorially challenged – uncle. Impressed?'

Stoner nodded. Grinned. Shrugged. Grinned some more.

Travis retained his sombre lawyer look. 'There's lots more. Contradictions abound. For example, on that hypothetical sleepless night, you will only be able to read this pile of crap if you are sitting in this room and have the combination to that safe – or me here to open it for you. Otherwise, although your contract exists and is binding and legal in every sense, neither you nor anyone apart from me and my fellow bureau directors will ever be able to read it.'

'This is standard for you guys?'

'Oh my yes. Or then again, probably not. It's probably not entirely legal for me to recruit a known agent of a foreign power – which is being generous, by the way – to work alongside me in Uncle Sam's great crusade against... ah... whatever said uncle is crusading against. Like every one of my colleagues I can think of, I have actually no idea what the great crusade is all about.

Mainly it seems to involve getting up the noses of every nation on the planet where the dollar buys lots more than it does in the US and where the food involves either fish or goats.'

'And you get to kill lots of people in strange and interesting places, and then get outraged when they throw stones at your drones or spit on your tanks... things like that.'

'You've got it. My, but you're smart for a Brit. Care to naturalise and become Secretary of State?'

'Is that possible?'

'No.'

Stoner looked around, spotted the water cooler and operated it. Offered a recyclable container to his companion, who shrugged, nodded and accepted the drink.

'Welcome,' said Travis, 'to the convoluted legal nightmare that is Homeland Security. Where the only laws that apply are our laws and nobody else's, and we make them up as we go along. Ignore the legality of what you're doing for a grateful nation of slobs who do not give a damn and do what you want to do.' He sipped. 'Do you reckon there's enough water coolers in the USA to require the entire output of a power station to keep them chilled? And if so, would that power station be a nuke or a coal burner? Makes you proud that we can – but we do not – recycle the little cup. This is a lesson, JJ. This is US foreign policy. You'll enjoy it. We're a post-imperial nation which avoided all the tedious crap involved in actually having and running an empire. You Brits could learn from us.'

Stoner smiled. 'Yeah,' he said. 'You're correct.' He rocked himself back in his chair and stared at the ceiling. As ceilings go, it had nothing to recommend it.

'And so we drift, like a coupla swells with all the time in the world, to the reason for your generosity. It's that gardening moment, isn't it?'

'Excuse me? Gardening?'

'A tiny but somehow always funny joke I shared with Hartmann before taking a gig. I'd always remind him that I don't do gardening. So if he wanted something from me, it surely didn't involve pruning plants.'

'He laugh at that? Hartmann?'

'Not once.'

'Good. I like him more.' Travis smiled gently, then sobered. 'The price for Uncle Sam's generosity is what we used to call a sanction, then called wet work, and now I think we prefer to consider it as assisted demise, theory in Washington being that as we believe in endless love, and peace, and forgiveness, and the purity of everyone's immortal souls, we are helping unhappy people ascend to glory. His will be done, you might say.'

'I doubt I'd say that.'

'Suit yourself.'

'Who, where, when and how? Is it desperately dangerous? Is it survivable by an ancient, under-fed Brit like me?'

'Couldn't say, but you are supposed to be good at that kind of thing. Any case, you're also supposed to not give a shit, so... why you bothered, Stoner man?'

'Don't suppose I am bothered, not really. Just seems that you – that's you, Travis, not the legendarily slippery Uncle Sam – you are being remarkably helpful to me. Ignoring our obvious mutual admiration, brotherly love, multi-ethnic and sound approach to sex with a shared woman – there must be some more to it?' He paused. The question hung between them. Travis smiled, said nothing. Stoner shrugged. 'If it's a one-way ticket then

I'll need to take down Blesses before I do whatever guy, guys or entire national populations you're after. I don't care much about dying... but Blesses slides down before me into that long darkness, Travis. Anyone I know?'

'Can't see why you would. It's some banker, but I won't say more, you don't need to... what's the matter with you, man?'

Stoner was laughing; genuine out-loud laughing. 'A banker? That's where the whole performance with Hartmann started out. Killing bankers. Paymasters and the like. Great and small, little and large. OK if I subcontract?'

'Not really. Although we will of course deny you and everything to do with you, we prefer to know exactly what it is we're denying.'

'Gotcha. Details in this lot, or do I just choose a bank at random and pop off a few of their tellers?'

'Sounds ideal. Except this is no ideal world. She'll be on the same plane as you tomorrow.' He looked ostentatiously at the clock on his cell phone. 'Today.'

'She's a woman?'

'You have a problem with that?'

Stoner shook his head. 'Everybody dies. I'm heading to the UK to kill a woman.'

'Yes. Your she-devil. Your very own angel of death, huh?'

'The world is filled with them. A question, as we're now blood brothers or something. Blesses?'

'Shoot.' Travis was commendably deadpan.

'Let's hope so – preferably from a considerable distance. One of your MQ-9 Reapers would be my weapon of choice. How're we fixed for that?'

'I believe they're fully booked for about the next forty years, but I will enquire upwardly if you wish.' Travis looked entirely serious.

'You serious? You could actually call in a drone?'

'For you? For this? No. Not really. Not in the US or UK. But I have done the next best thing.'

'You have? Pray tell, boss.'

'You're getting a ride in a bureau helo to the airport to catch your internal.' He gestured towards his cell phone. 'According to unknown forces and mighty mechanisms beyond the wit of normal man – or of you and me – that flight is already being held for you. As will your international. Your new uncle is a persuasive uncle. You'll be at London Gatwick in time for brunch. Unless you'd prefer to chew fat here for longer? I'm easy, me, either way. Airlines may become disgruntled, though.'

Stoner shook his head slowly from side to side. 'Impressed. How did you get Brutish Airways to accommodate your wishes on my behalf?'

'Not them. Blocked Airways is the joke here at the moment. You're flying with the virgin.'

'Just the one? Virgin?'

'There's a lady banker on board. They probably named the plane in her honour, something like that. Virginity being rare among Brits even at birth, so we're told.'

'Let's get going, then.' Stoner finished his no longer chilled water, balanced the cup at an angle on the edge of the desk, and stood. Travis tapped his cell phone. A very young man appeared and placed a suitcase on floor by Stoner's feet. Left again in silence.

'Clothing suitable for one Limey travelling top class. Whatever that means. In any case, you might like to gel that retro hair of yours, maybe trim the facial foliage a little.'

'The woman? The mark? The target? A clue?'

'She's sitting across the aisle from you. She has the

window couchette; yours is in the middle. You can study her all night. You can follow her when you land if you like. You cannot murder her in her seat or in the john on the plane. Airlines get very sniffy about that kind of thing. Short answers; the helo awaits. Do you need a weapon or weapons?'

'No. A rental car would be nice.'

'It will be waiting for you. Even now it's getting a wax'n'shine. You're planning on running her over? Neat. Original. Especially on a plane.'

Stoner reached for the suitcase. Paused. Smiled faintly. 'Time frame? Preferred method?'

'Within twenty-four hours of landing, please. She has a meet after that which she needs to not attend.'

'Do I need to take anything from her?'

'No. We'll do that.'

'So I'll have a tail? Back up?'

'Clear-up only. And you'll be clean; no tail. Use the phone in the case to call uncle and then leave it with the vic. That's all. Then do what you gotta do, and get in touch. If you survive it, of course.'

'That your motivational speech?'

'Yep.'

'Used it much?'

'Yep.'

'Final query. Blesses. She one of yours, now or at some other time?'

'Yes. Tying off that particular loose end will see you lauded and rewarded by a grateful nation. She has been a headache.' Stoner rose to his feet. Travis held up a hand. 'Blesses,' he said, holding eye contact. 'She knows too much for us, that's your uncle, to want her walking free. Got it?'

'Got it. That bit about laud and reward. That true?'

'Not a word of it. Now go away. The helo's costing more waiting for you than you or I will earn in our illustrious lifetimes.'

***

The delayed Virgin flight was taxiing into the sodden east coast evening; Stoner tapped a final text, a note for Bili.

'Leaving for Texas, in the driving rain. Play that for me. Play well, Bili.'

He shut off the device before any reply or abuse could arrive from the cabin staff. Nodded to the woman in the seat across the aisle. 'Let's hope for a quiet night,' he said. 'Busy day tomorrow.' She nodded, no obvious interest in him, plugged in headphones and pulled curtains. Stoner took stock of his surroundings. Men to the right of him, in front and behind, the only woman to his left, as Travis had told him she would be, so it was.

16

HOW WOULD I KNOW, WHY WOULD I CARE?

The unfolding unwinding stresses and strains inevitable after a long flight, a long night flight. Stoner had slept well enough, had listened to a savage selection of alleged music, talk and radio on the headset provided, and surfaced as the Airbus shifted altitude and attitude as it began the long approach to its destination. As ever, he was amused at his fleeting mental preparation for jump. An old habit. This was the new age; he now waited for his planes to land rather than jumping out of them at altitude. At least it bounced him awake. He converted his pretence at a bed into an equally unconvincing pretence at a chair, then slid his curtains apart, finding himself gazing at the midriff of a cabin steward pouring coffee and water for the lady across the aisle. Who smiled at him. Stoner returned the smile and accepted coffee for himself.

'I hate flying,' she remarked. 'Not sure why. Always want each flight to be my last, know what I mean?' Her accent was heavily New York.

'Need to be careful what you wish for.' Stoner smiled in a vague way. 'I'd cross the pond by ship – every time – but it takes too long, really. At least ships are comfortable. And excuse me.' He untangled himself from the clutches of the nearly-bed and barefooted it to the restroom, washed and freshened in preparation for onslaught by airline breakfast. After which he unwrapped a soothing eye pad, tapped it into place over his eyes, effectively cutting off conversation, and dozed through the routines and rigmaroles of landing. And the scrummage to leave the plane. And the lemming rush to clog the exits. By the time Stoner left his seat, there were maybe three other passengers in business class; entirely civilised. The adjacent woman was one of them.

'You've done this before?' She smiled.

'Too often,' he confirmed. 'Definitely a ship next time. And now for the great Gatwick experience. Better than Heathrow, though that's not saying very much.' They left the plane together, she remarking on how little luggage he had, he shrugging it off. 'I have a house here, so I travel light.' She nodded. Customs, then, and slow immigration, both of them traveling on US passports. She had luggage to find, he did not, and waved to her as she circled the carousel.

Car rental formalities next, his new identity working as well to collect the hired vehicle as it had to board an airplane, and as he crossed the concourse heading for the renter's parking lots, he saw his flight friend once again, this time fully armoured with a business suit and formidable luggage. He waved. She stopped, waited while he approached.

'Give you a ride?'

'You have a car here?' Stoner waved the keys.

'The best sort,' he smiled. 'Someone else's. They can worry about dings and dents. You going far?'

'You not in a hurry?' She looked around at the queue for taxis. 'I'm heading south to the coast. You?'

'Only to Crawley, cultural centre of... well, nowhere.' He smiled, they started walking together, a transaction mutually agreed in the undiscussed ways of these things.

'Is Hove on the way to Crawley? I'm light on UK geography, good with figures, less so with navigation. And I'm called Ellen.'

Stoner reached out a hand, shook hers and took the handle to her larger suitcase. 'Steve.'

She laughed then. 'You had to think about that!'

He smiled back. 'Yeah. I'm supposed to be Stephen, you know how it is with names, abbreviations are so working class. I'm in no rush, so Hove is easy. Don't know that I've ever been there. What happens in Hove?'

'Business. Only business. I'm in banking.'

'You are? We got lady bankers now? The world is saved. I shall take my savings out of the old sock under the mattress and invest them now. What sort of banking...'

***

Dinner was a peculiarly pleasant affair. Stoner and Ellen laughed and chatted and ate and drank, as people do, and at the crucial moment in the evening, when Stoner remarked that he really should be checking in at home and Ellen was enquiring about his family, while he reassured her that he was single and she reached across the table, rested her hand on his and assured him that he had no reason to leave. Not if he might prefer to stay.

'Hotel breakfasts, huh?' He squeezed her hand gently. 'My favourites.'

They talked more. She talked about her work while Stoner listened. She talked about her marriages and her children while Stoner listened. She talked about how hemmed in by career and domesticity she was, how trapped and constrained. Stoner listened and agreed, sympathised and commiserated.

'Do you think it's wrong of me?' Ellen had assumed the sincerely fake expression of an honest soul wrestling with her conscience.

'What?' Stoner rested his elbows on the table and leaned across. 'Deciding that you'd rather spend a night in company rather than on your own? Would I be here if I thought that was wrong? Hey, I'll even spring for supper, so your company won't see it on your exes.' He laughed softly. 'Unless your bank is a particularly understanding bank and understands that its executives need a little R&R the night before some high-powered banking performance.'

He flagged for the bill, paid it, rose and pulled back Ellen's seat for her. She giggled, unexpectedly. 'I should have drunk some more.'

'Why?'

'I feel like a schoolgirl.'

'Yeah, me too.' They both laughed; she at his weak joke, he at the idiocy of their situation. In the elevator, she leaned against him, giggled some more and offered her lips to him.

At the door to her room, she giggled some more, wondered whether she should have ordered a bottle of something, champagne maybe, unlocked, walked inside and performed a dumpy twirl in the middle of the room. 'Home,' she said. 'Home for a little while.'

Stoner walked around her, dropped his jacket onto the bed, nuzzled her neck, savouring the rare delight of cheap scent and sweat. 'I need a shower,' he whispered. 'You any good at back scrubbing?' She giggled some more, not unappealingly, not really. He stripped, fast and efficient, then performed the same duty for Ellen. Stepped back to admire her uncovered form. Diplomacy is not entirely a lost art.

Ellen stared at Stoner. 'Where did you get the scars?' She was fascinated, ran her fingers over a couple of the seams in question.

'Here and there. I was a soldier once.' She wasn't listening. Her hands had reached his groin and were fumbling, inexpertly but with growing enthusiasm. For no reason he could willingly understand, Stoner's private soldier stood to immediate attention, seemed genuinely enthused by the prospect of activity. 'That,' he murmured to her, 'feels fine.'

The hotel's better rooms boasted a decent bathroom facility, including a large walk-in wet room, subtle lighting and soft smells. Plainly romance was not entirely dead in the world of the international banker. Stoner pulled Ellen to him, into the warm clouds and the promising scents of the room. Ellen pulled right back, grasping his buttocks with a mighty grip. 'Let's do it here first,' she asked, eyes suddenly wide and eager.

The hiss of the shower drowned the dull crack as her head impacted with as much force as Stoner could muster against the unyielding tiles of the wet room wall. He followed through and cracked her head against the equally unyielding if slightly more abrasive ceramics – the better to provide a decent level of grip – of the floor. Stoner checked her pulse; slow, weak. He gripped her nostrils between thumb and forefinger of his left hand, while holding her mouth shut tight with his right. Her passing was rapid and calm. An unconscious descent into death. The shower poured on, promising much but delivering only water.

He dressed and left, quietly as a gentleman should. His last act was to send a message from the cell phone with but a single number in its address book, and to leave the print-free device where it could not be missed.

17

THE WAY SHE LIED

Night drives have a charm all their own, and Stoner usually enjoyed them. The rental Ford was not a vehicle he would have chosen for himself, but it was anonymous, smooth enough and efficient. He ran north from the southern coastlands, looping northwest around the nation's capital, then heading west along a too-familiar and spookily silent highway until he reached a service area. He deserved servicing, he decided, as well as maybe a litre of strong coffee.

After which he felt seriously unwell. A surprise. Coffee – even British motorway coffee – is not famous for inducing a lethargy so profound that driving a single further mile would be simply silly. His world spun before him. He rose unsteadily to his feet, bought and consumed a litre of sparkling and frighteningly priced water, and understood that he was driving no further that night. His body was simply falling asleep where it stood. The motorway motel, then.

'Wise call, Mister Strong.' The receptionist appeared to be at least as dozy as Stoner felt, and he wondered briefly why that functionary was calling him by a new name, then he remembered, embarrassment averted.

The receptionist had more wise words to brighten his night. 'Never makes sense to keep on driving when you're this tired. We get a lot of guys who land after a long haul, reckon they can drive home and then just flake out.'

Stoner nodded, accepting the wisdom with a docile grace. Took the room key, declined to order breakfast and filled in the registration form. 'No idea what the car's number is,' he confessed. 'It's a rental. I just picked it up today.' His world was dark at the edges. He believed that falling down on the spot and snoring uncontrollably was a serious probability.

The receptionist just nodded. 'Got the keys?' Stoner dropped them onto the counter. 'I'll fill in the numbers and leave the keys behind the desk for you. You collect them when you hand in your room key. This happens a lot.' He was friendly, too, and plainly waking up. Unlike Stoner, who felt neither awake nor friendly. He felt drugged, and he felt resentful of that increasing conviction. Nothing to be done. He waved acknowledgement at the smiling receptionist and wandered to the elevator, which ascended a single floor as instructed, leaving him a short walk to his new room. Where he parked himself on the end of the bed, stared at the face in the mirror. Which looked back with anger in its exhausted eyes.

'This is how it ends, then,' he remarked to himself. 'Fuck it.' He kicked off his shoes, dropped clothes to the floor and lay back, swearing steadily for almost no time at all.

***

The morning shone around him. He felt good. Stared incredulously at the time. Showered, dressed in his business-class business clothes and performed morning duties, faintly surprised both at being alive and feeling as fit and healthy as he did. Eight hours deep unconsciousness had left him with an almost nervous liveliness.

He recalled his exhaustion of the night, as well as his conviction that he'd been drugged somehow and had been primed to meet his maker. That was OK. Maybe his imagination and sunny disposition had got the better of him. Whatever, his case, with clothing a lot more to his taste and a lot more comfortable than the outfit he'd been wearing for the flight and much else, was still in the car. Check-out wasn't for another hour, so he headed out to collect a change of clothes.

Paused at the reception desk. A smart young woman greeted him.

'You have my car keys,' he told her, smiling back at her, passing over the room key. 'But I'd appreciate dodging back to the room to change once I've got my case from the motor. I was a little pooped last night.'

The woman looked around the desk, crashed a couple of drawers open and closed, finally coming up with a bunch of keys. 'These yours? A rental?' He agreed that they were, she agreed that his returning to change clothes was not a problem at all, and he joked merrily that he hoped he could find the thing, as all Fords look the same the morning after.

It took a while. He truly did have no memory of where he'd parked it, and resorted to wandering the rows, pressing the security plipper until a vehicle responded. He did however have a certain memory that the car had been a Ford and not a VW, such as the vehicle which answered his call. He approached with caution, feeling a growing sense of resignation. Working for Travis was full of surprises.

His case was in the passenger footwell. Of course it was. It did not explode nor emit poison gas when he lifted it up. And, opening it when back in the room, he found a strikingly different new cell phone, enough UK currency to buy a terraced house in the north of that country and an anonymous note. 'Job well done. Walking around money enclosed. No need to roll the drunks today.'

Breakfast was predictably hideous and desultory, but it failed to diminish the odd feeling of wellbeing which persisted despite his best efforts. He drove the stout German car to the nearest railway station and parked it, kept the cash, left case and cell phone in the passenger footwell, locked up and caught a train, leaving the car's keys on a table in the station café. No one had followed him. Maybe Travis used satellites instead. Drones, maybe. Venusian spaceships, even. The reach and resource of his latest best friends was remarkable. Also intimidating, at least a little.

Although, out of long habit, Stoner had bought a ticket for the train's distant destination, he left it at the first decent-sized town it encountered on its slow rattling journey. At the taxi rank he squeezed into the first of the short dull row of dirty, sweating cabs and asked for the nearest Harley-Davidson dealership. Was unsurprised to learn that the nearest was a long way away, in UK terms if not in US, and in his turn surprised the driver by agreeing that it was a way but he still wanted to go there. So they did, bemused driver and amused passenger both. Stoner enquired of the driver whether his aged Japanese saloon could make it so far – maybe thirty miles – was assured that it would, and thereby unleashed a torrent of a taxi driver's view of the state of British football. Ideal for a doze, which Stoner enjoyed. He rather hoped that his

American issue clothing was wired for sound and that someone somewhere, connected somehow by tenuous but frighteningly expensive digital satellite technology, was being paid to listen to the ensuing nonsensical monologue.

Things could not have improved much for the hypothetical eavesdropper when they finally reached the H-D dealership, that remote cultural outpost of profound American historic iconography. Stoner flexed the plastic which accompanied his brave new identity and replaced his entire wardrobe with branded clothing, revealed his shock and disappointment that they could supply him with no branded underwear – because he was a boy and not a girl – but compromised with a full set of everything else, including Kevlar-armoured heavy denim jeans, jacket and gloves, boots which appeared to be as sturdy as his own Caterpillar preference although branded by motorcycle rather than earth mover, and a holdall to hold all the duplicates. The bill was impressive, and the card showed a gratifying resilience.

The saleslady was petite, tattooed, polite and tremendously impressed. She wondered whether Mister Strong would like to buy a motorcycle to accompany his excellent understated choice of apparel, and even appeared to understand when Stoner explained that to him it was all a fashion statement. To reinforce the point, he bought a pair of inevitably branded black textile watch caps and wondered in his turn whether a cup of coffee was a possibility, and whether he could change into his smart new clothes in the men's room? Both answers were positive. It was a good day for both parties. Stoner began to approach an understanding of the popularity of retail therapy. The saleslady was delighted to arrange a fresh cab while Stoner changed, and exchanged her business card, with her private cell phone number hand-written and sealed with a juicy X, for a handsome tip. She looked completely bewildered by that, and Stoner felt obliged to remark that it was common in the USA to reward fine service with a gratuity. The saleslady's expression revealed her doubts about this, but she accepted the gift graciously enough.

Stoner changed into his new entirely branded clothing, left the originals – all the originals as supplied by his new American employers – in the changing room, neatly folded and with their high-grade labels prominent, then sipped coffee with his new best lady friend until the cab arrived. She would certainly remember him, should whoever swapped his vehicles and supplied his discarded clothing turn up to collect it.

She might also remember the destination he requested from the cab. Were there, he'd wondered, any nearby dealerships specialising in camper vans? Particularly VW camper vans? Turned out there were two, and one of them had in stock a perfectly converted VW Transporter at an almost sensible price, which after a short period of adult discussion Stoner paid in cash. He made jokes with the happy used car dealer, too, remarking as they filled in the paperwork that some days he struggled to remember his name, never mind where he actually lived. They had both laughed at the comedy of this, and Stoner decided that he should at least pay a courtesy call to his home... but maybe later.

Before then, he had a little more shopping and a lot of catching up to do.

***

'Christ, man. It's the middle of the night. Where are you and what do you want?' Travis did not sound unhappy to hear from his recruit. Not unhappy at all.

'I am where I am. A good thing in a fellow of my age. Thanks for the largesse. You found your car? I prefer to be off the radar, just a little, just for a little while. You know that.'

'Sure. The guys picked up the car. No problem with that. Just trying to be helpful.' Travis laughed in a half-asleep way. 'How long do you need to be disappeared?'

'Is it important?'

'In a way. The big chief and I have another gig for you, Stateside this time, but it's not urgent and it can certainly wait until you feel a little bored with renewing old acquaintance, maybe making music and things like that. Speaking of that, your other black man buddy is growing anxious about your whereabouts. Anxious enough to be asking around.'

'You guys have ears and eyes everywhere, seems like.' Stoner sounded as unconcerned by this as he actually was.

'Pretty much.' Travis was plainly not into any recognisable forms of denial. 'We're shit hot at tracking innocents, non-combatants and solid citizens – of almost any country – less good at finding criminals and terrorists, but we have made a start. If we eliminate all the good guys we keep track of then whoever's left is surely guilty.'

'That make sense to you guys?'

'Nope. None at all, but statistics reveal that the more we rush around prying into the private lives of Joe Citizen the less Mr Bad Guy bombs us and kills the good guys.'

'Really?'

'Nope. I made that up. More US citizens are killed by other US citizens than by foreign aggressors, so it would make more sense for us to simply lock ourselves up than it does to gallop around the globe being frantic, but that would not extract votes from the populace. Or those sanctified tax dollars.'

Stoner smiled into the cell phone. 'The power of democracy.'

'As you say. Now, assuming you did not actually drag me from my private time to discuss nonsense, is there a reason for the call, other than to confirm that you have yet another cell phone and are somewhere in what I believe is called middle England?'

'You're tracking this call?' Incredulity tinted Stoner's tones.

'As long as you're talking to me, my colleagues, my office, anyone we consider to be important – which would be me, my colleagues and my office – we're tracking you. Pretty much real-time. Cool, huh? It's what NASA's for these days, never mind that journey to Mars crap. If you call up bad guys who use burners we don't have access to – which is what crims do, bastards all – then we can't track you. We can track most innocent citizens, like I said. It's confusing, I know. Soldier on. And ditch the burner you're calling me on... but you'll do that anyway. Crims do that. If you were Joe Innocent you'd keep the phone and we'd track you. The relentless power of righteousness, and shit. Makes no sense. I love it. Dawn says hi.'

'She does?' Stoner's incredulity was drifting to new levels.

'She does indeed. We shared a relatively civilised dinner, your name came up, and she said to say hi. Hi. You made a hit there I think. If you married her I could cease with the alimony. She's a great attorney.'

'I'll bear that in mind, should I ever need one.'

'You will.'

'Really?'

'Yep.'

Stoner shook his head, leaned back in the VW's comfortable seat. 'I give up. Travis, I...' His voice trailed off. 'Try again. I've spent the thick end of a year working out how I want to sort out the little problem which lost me most of that year. Now I'm here, it's very different. The more I face it, the more different it appears. I've always had a support structure and clear goals. I'm a soldier, and there has always been back-up and data. You hearing what I'm saying?'

No hesitation. 'You have the back-up. Certainly the data. This number, any time.' Travis was completely serious. 'Your paranoia will insist that we're just using you as a tool, which we are, but we – I, if you prefer personal service – see a longer future than that. Sort out what you need to sort out. When that's done, we'll get together and consider the future. If you fall, I will be sorry, JJ. Genuinely. We both know that failure will be fatal, most likely. Don't tell me anything of your purpose or locations; these calls will always be monitored and recorded and then discussed by strangers. Ask for anything we can deliver and it's yours. Make sense?'

'It does. My old base, you know it?'

'Musical, domestics or industrial?'

'The latter. Is it safe to use?'

'Call back. One hour.' Travis hung up. Stoner stared at the silent cell phone, then removed its innards, dropped them into a pocket and drove into the dark, wet, cold evening.

One hour later, parked up and paid up in an otherwise deserted holiday park, he reassembled his cell phone and called back.

'Good security.' Travis wasted no time on polite handshaking, pleasantries or the like. 'Looks exactly as it did last time we looked at it, which would be a little over a year ago, they tell me. Fine system, currently transmitting a consistent signal on a consistent frequency. The frequency will be to your security service provider and the signal will be to confirm non-tampering or non-entry or both. We've no way of telling which without triggering it.'

'Can you do that?'

'Only by sending someone around to kick in the door, and you're nearer than I am. And you must have the key. So would there be any purpose to that?'

'No. I was just checking. How long have you been watching my place?' Stoner displayed no rancour at the observation, merely interest.

'We've known you for a long time, have we not? So we've held a watching brief for... oh... several years. Is there anything in there you actually need?'

'No. It's a strange sensation, being unable... unwilling to drop by my own place. A chap could get... homesick.'

Travis emitted a noise which could have been a laugh. 'Yeah. As if. Is there anything else? You've things to do, people to see, things to do to people, so on, and so have I. Is there anything we can do before you take time out and then call back?'

'You can tell me how come there's nearly no delay in this conversation. It is a little spooky.'

'NASA again. You call my number and the mighty electronic birds switch the signal until your phone is talking direct to the satellite that's talking direct to my phone. Takes about a minute. Why? You after a merit badge or something?'

'Just curious. I'll call if I'm in a deep pit and need digging out.'

'Can't wait, JJ. Good hunting. Find your problems, fix your concerns and get in touch when you're done. Fairy Godfather out.' And Travis was gone.

Stoner surveyed the interior of his camper van. It was anonymous, it drove well, and its bed looked more comfortable than a forest floor. Food, sleep of sorts, then.

18

MERRY GO ROUND

A bright morning, early city street scenes all around. Early-day damp with a promise of further damp to follow. The Blue Cube's modest, unassuming and single sign was unilluminated, all appeared calm and dark, both inside and out. Stoner had been watching both of the usual entrances since the last of the straggling small crowd had quit the premises in the small hours. Few of them, quiet, too. The Blue Cube; his own, his very own jazz bar, blues club, business premises and occasional home from home. His long absence appeared to have reduced the audience – by more than half, his best estimate.

He doubted that anyone seriously interested in his reappearance, and who didn't expect him to pop up playing rockabilly or dirty country or the like in deepest Texas, would expect him to return to his old haunts in the UK. But any theoretically interested person or persons more likely known than unknown would be unlikely to have limitless resources to watch everywhere. And of course although he left the keys to the club with the Cube's small staff, he maintained a private entrance or two. More usually they were useful as exits, but doors work both ways. He used the most private, which showed no sign whatsoever of being used for... well, a very long time. His own markers were intact, hinges still silent but stiffening through a lack of recent use and fresh lubricant.

Inside the club felt strange to him. Entirely familiar but somehow alien. His own but not his own. The security systems responded to the same old codes and shut themselves down as instructed. The place was eerily quiet, strangely clean. He walked in near-darkness behind the bar and cracked open a bottle of water, drank from the bottle. Walked, still in the same calm near-darkness, to the stage, swinging the bottle lightly from his fingers, and ascended the steps to the small stage, turned and surveyed the empty club. He felt seriously conflicted by the entire experience. Everything was the same as it should be while at the same time entirely different to the way he remembered it. His seriously work-worn guitar case stood at the back of the stage. The stand where he had always rested the instrument between sessions was nowhere obvious. His tired Marshall amplifier was standing behind a much more modern device, plainly replaced in the affections of whoever needed amplification.

His old Fender guitar sat easily in his lap as he tuned, fingered a few chords, tuned again, hummed a few verses, tuned some more, strangely restless. The guitar felt odd... polished maybe. The strings were certainly new enough, although of the correct weight for his taste. He replaced it in its case, wandered around and discovered another case, standing by the closed piano, this one containing an acoustic guitar, a fine blonde Gibson model unfamiliar to him. He carried it to the stool behind the piano – the stool he preferred to play from being absent – and strummed a little.

Melancholy sat hard with him. He wondered – quite suddenly and with no welcome at all – what he was doing. Why he was in the UK. Why he was in the club. What he actually intended to do. Stoner felt the departure of his self-confidence like a physical thing. Water draining from a broken bottle. Here he sat in the centre of his own personally constructed universe, and he felt alone. A stranger. Worse; he felt himself to be an intruder. He pined for the pinewoods around the Moosehead Lake. Suddenly and inexplicably, he wished he was there and far from home... far from here.

He played a finger-picked instrumental tune he half remembered from the days before his playing focused entirely on electric solid-bodied guitars. A famous tune by Davey Graham dedicated to some woman called Anji. Unbidden and unwelcome somehow, his memory unearthed a series of images of women to whom he'd dedicated the song down the years. Music to watch the girls go by. Back when things were simple. Back when he wore a uniform with stripes on its sleeves and followed easily understood orders. And then somehow he found himself playing – and worse, humming – the tune and the clever chord sequence of *Girl From Ipanema*. At least that made him smile.

But the blues hung around him like a damp cloud, the stale atmosphere and the subterranean chill grinding his fingers to a clumsy halt. He leaned into the near-darkness, quite powerfully and quite completely wishing he'd stayed in the USA, had maybe journeyed with Stretch down to Texas after all, where he would even now be kicking the shit with bigger men than he and trying desperately to keep up with the way those guys could play.

'Coffee, I suppose?' A small light lit behind the bar.

Water chuckled as it heated. Simple stuff, water. Easily pleased.

Stoner pulled the acoustic guitar back onto his lap, picked a verse of intro from its bright strings and sang gently.

'I know my baby, she's bound to love me soon

'I know my baby, she's bound to love me soon

'She throws her arms around me like a circle round the moon.'

After two more random verses and a final attempt at a solo instrumental break, he wound down, hauled himself to his feet, replaced the beautiful blonde guitar in its case, latched it shut to keep it safe, stood it behind the protective piano and hopped down from the stage to the table with the lit candle and the aromatic morning coffee.

'Hello Charm,' he said, quietly. 'Your instrument?'

'Yeah. One of several.'

'Like... names, too. One is never enough for some people.'

The woman smiled through the flickering candle shadows. 'You worked it out, though. My secret laid bare. Was it difficult?' The candlelight produced deep pools of shadow around her eyes, shallows of darkness across her cheeks, and occasional flickers of silver reflecting in the dark curtain of her hair.

'I think I always knew. I think...' Stoner laid a hand flat upon the tabletop, then rolled it palm upward. Charm rested her own hand in it, briefly. 'I think it was... easier not to think about it. Even if I had needed to think about it, which I didn't think I did.' He laughed, suddenly. 'Good to see you.'

Her dark eyebrows raised over her dark eyes. 'You sure?'

'Yep. Could have been a whole lot worse. Everyone

kept on telling me that I knew you, including your own sisters, and I always agree with everyone as you know, so I knew I must know you, and the options were pretty limited when I actually thought about it, and I ended up deciding that if an alias was important to you then it was fine with me. Didn't really connect it all until just now, though. Was the deception – small though it was – malicious?'

Charm sipped her own drink, leaned away from him, the flame in her eyes receding into the daytime darkness of the club. 'No. There was a need, because that earlier... situation called for it, and then...' she paused. 'Then it just got too difficult, and pointlessly... involved. Seems stupid now.'

'What should I call you, then?'

'Whatever you want. Silly bitch would do, I reckon. I'm Amanda to everyone here, and Charm to the rest of the world I deal with, mostly.'

'Other IDs too? Is there more coffee?'

'Of course. Like you, huh? Who are you today?' She rose smoothly and collected the jug and creamer from the bar, pouring for them both.

'Point delicately made. Thanks.' He sipped.

Charm stirred her own brew, slowly. 'JJ Stoner is in or nearly in Texas,' she said.

'Odd, isn't it?' A smile drifted across Stoner's features. 'I'm well used to ID changes, but this time it feels completely insane. I feel... a little unsure of myself. Bizarre.'

'Know what you mean, man of stone. In here, in the club, it's like a separate existence with real life somehow held away. I know it's a fantasy, that it's simply silly, but somehow it felt important to keep it that way. Chastity's gone to catch up with you.' Charm opened a cell phone, checked the time. 'She'll be landing around now. Should I call her?'

Stoner shook his head. 'Best not. Unless you want to. We have business, you and me, so I'd say. Need to do some talking.'

'Today not the day to shoot first, questions later?'

'Too late for that, Charm.' Stoner rolled her name as he pronounced it, as though experimenting with the sound and the combination of that sound with the vision before him. 'In any case, I am unarmed. Disarmed. I stand before you a weak and feeble guy, a guy of whom history will say... "Who? Who cares?" How much coffee did you brew, and have you kept the fridge well stocked with water, maybe a beer for later?'

Charm watched him steadily, the pointless sunglasses swivelled to the top of her head and resting there reflecting the club's dim and scattered lighting as though she had her own personalised halo. A very, very small halo. 'It's much as you left it, JJ. Takings are well down, the crowd dwindled. It is painfully obvious who they come to see – to listen to. It was a steady decline when you'd not returned after a couple of months, then it all fell to bits when Stretch was infected by your big boy wanderlust, whatever. Galling. Bili and me, not the main attractions. Got us a new drummer boy though. Goes by the name of Styx, would you believe. No effect on the falling crowd. Humbling. That's not what you asked, is it?' Her smile was a small smile, but at least it was a decent attempt.

Stoner sighed, long and deep. 'It takes time. People get used to a thing. Then that thing gets taken away and the people follow – or they would if they could. They can't do that, like in this case, then they find another thing, either where the first thing was – that would be

Stretch, maybe – or somewhere else. In time, the crowd starts to grow again when different people start to appreciate the new thing, maybe a twin-girl lead with sax instead of axe. It takes time.'

'You're being kind. You've always had an audience. Chas told me about the time you were on that cruise ship – last year. Said the ship was crawling with musicians, perfectly competent musicians too, then you roll into a bar late at night, borrow a guitar, jam a couple of songs and the audience is alive, the joint is packed and swinging, and you're getting heavyweight admiration from all and sundry.'

'She's very kind, your sister. For a murderous killer bitch from hell, of course. How's she doing?'

'Hard to say.' Charm rose to her feet, headed towards the bar, taking the emptied coffee jug with her. 'I'll brew some more. Do you want more light in here?'

'Prefer the half-dark. Bright lights make me judgemental. Shadow's less unflattering. Some things are better unseen.'

'Also unsaid?'

'Probably not. Probably not at this juncture. Probably better if we did a little straight talking. Just you and me.' Stoner's eyes never left her. His voice was light, but his body endlessly tensed, then relaxed as he remembered to relax it. Then it would tense once more. Repeat.

'You reckon to kill me, JJ?' The idea did not appear to terrify her. Not at all in fact, as she watched the coffee drip through the machine's filter, the whole contraption hissing and issuing an occasional contended bubble. They all burst. That is what bubbles all too often do. It is the way of bubbles. All life in a coffee pot. Still life. Mostly.

'Not immediately, sweets. It might come to that. I

hope not. You add colour, and colour is good. You do not however add clarity. If your sainted parents had wished to make life a little simpler, they could have called you Clarity rather than Charm, although charm you certainly do possess, and it is a rare thing. Clarity, Chastity and Charity. Did all three of you sisters – a bizarre notion, even now; the three of you – understand that I was the Hard Man's target? That you would need to kill me, back then? Tell the truth. Just as it was. Unless I fall – and I will not fall – any lies now will come back to harm you.' His tone was mild and controlled, the words falling soft into the candlelight and the aroma of the relentless coffee. But his face was set, bleak, angry maybe, unhappy certainly. Edged.

Charm was standing up, standing by their table. 'Oh, fuck,' she said, sadly. 'Can I distract you from this? I don't feel prepared somehow. Can't I just suck your brains out through your dick or something? Take your mind off the whole honesty crap? It always worked before.' She smiled a tiny, sad and damp smile. Stoner entirely failed to respond. He poured coffee for the both of them, stood, walked to the bar and returned with a bottle of dark red wine, uncorked it.

'Let it breathe,' he suggested. 'Then when your throat needs lubrication from all the talking, try that. It's a decent enough drink.'

'You?'

'Sober so far. Best that way. React in haste, as they say, repentance always comes too late. I'll offer you a little prompt. A while back, last year, my... boss, my... professional friend of ten... twelve years, Hartmann, the one and only Hard Man contacted you and contracted you and your sisters. Charity, Chastity and Charm, all of you set on a course which would remove every one of the Hard Man's professional... friends. It would have left him free and clear to be respectable. No murky unhelpful back catalogue to titillate the media. Government. High office, that kind of crap – that's what he wanted. That's where to start, not with the silly names or your entertaining exploits before we met. Fun though I'm sure they are.'

Charm sipped at her coffee. Placed the mug carefully on the table. 'OK,' she said, finally. 'The contract came through Menace. The person, not the sentiment.' She looked up, caught Stoner's eye, tried to smile. Shrugged.

'Her client – I'd no idea who that was, it's the best way – wanted a short series of hits, hits taken in a specific manner and presented in a specific way. I...' she shrugged again. 'I tried to turn it down. Charity was in chemo with her cancer, was trying to kill it by killing herself. Me? I didn't – don't want to ever kill anyone again. Chastity insisted that we took the contract. The fee was outrageous, would pay for the best of everything for Charity and set us up for a straight life. I couldn't argue with that, so the final call was for Charity. So I folded, and it started. You want the whole history?'

Stoner shook his head. 'No. Save that for your kids. Menace, you say? Not Mallis? Of the two, I know Mallis a little less badly. OK. It makes sense so far. Where did Amanda – that's you, in case you're having a moment of denial – aka Handy Mandy, for fuck's sake, aka Amanda Hanwell if memory serves – fit into all this? I ran into a brace of bozos who were demanding – demanding, fuck's sake – that I knew who you were and where you were. Which I did not. Ignorance was certainly bliss at that point, if not for the bozos. They turned up here, isn't that right? Looking for you? Little girl lost, all that. You span me some tale...'

Charm held Stoner's gaze, unflinching, even while pouring herself a glass of wine with complete non-spilling accuracy. A neat trick. 'That was an echo,' she said, finally.

'A what?'

'The last job before the job from Menace was a non-lethal infiltration of some hood in the big city.'

'That also come from Menace?'

'No. From a rival hood. Worked for her before. I'd used the alias recently so knew it was active. Loads of folk know me as Mandy Hanwell. I always liked Mandy – down to earth. Easy to deal with.'

'And kind to dumb animals – male animals. So the whole thing was an accident? A coincidence? Doesn't seem very likely.'

'It's worse than that.' Charm had lost interest in holding Stoner's gaze and was instead evidently fascinated by the table between them, her eyes occasionally flicking to the walls as if seeking invisible answers written there. 'When we met I'd no real idea who you were apart from being JJ Stoner, bluesman and club player – and a person on Mallis's make-contact list. I didn't know you as Stoner the stone killer until later, when Menace explained who you were, how it needed to be, that your name had been added to the contract, the last one on the list. She looked genuinely baffled when she explained – for the first time I think – who you worked for and who our contract came from.'

'You still up for that blow job? I need something. This is painful.' Stoner's day was not improving.

'Not really. Call up a fangirl or something. I have no appetite at all. Even the wine tastes like cabbage. I hate cabbage.' She stopped. 'OK. The damnation part. If you kill me... do it quick. I mean that.'

Stoner said nothing, moved nothing. Entirely motionless. Sniper once more.

Charm drew a loud breath, closed her eyes. 'I set up the whole thing with the two thugs. Set up their accosting you on the street – even warned them how tough you were. Then...'

Stoner interrupted, voice like flint. 'And you set up the scene here with the same guys, knowing that I am soft with women, protective, weak. Stupid too.' He just stared at her. Her closed eyes were her mute reply.

'When did the contract for me appear? At what point in this sick history were you told I was it?' Stoner steepled his fingers before his face, stared at them.

Charm looked up at last. 'This isn't easy,' she said.

'I bet. Just tell me how it is. How it was.'

'After that. Too long after that. After we'd got... for fuck's sake... friendly. Menace told me what the final hit was. Who it was. She...'

Stoner interrupted suddenly. 'You deal with Mallis much in this? The other half of Menace and Mallis, the badly punned techno prisoners dynamic duo?'

She shook her head. 'No. Not at all. I knew who he was, heard about him, seen him around, but part of the contract was a stipulation that I didn't deal with him at all. Not at all. He was never there whenever we talked... not until Chastity got herself stuck in Israel and you did the extraction. She has a real thing for you, you know.' A single tear rolled unexpected and unwelcome down her cheek. 'So did Charity. Charity refused to complete the contract. Said she'd rather kill Menace – then herself – than you.' A second tear followed the first. She shook her head savagely. Glared at him. Ignored the tears. The weakness. Stoner didn't seem to notice the tears, the imminent collapse, the totality of the surrender.

'You would have carried it out... would have completed the contract? Think carefully before you answer.'

'Yes.' No hesitation. 'Yes. Wouldn't you, situations reversed?'

The same absence of hesitation. 'Yes of course.' Stoner leaned back in the chair, then reached forward for the bottle, swilled some wine around his mouth. Spat it onto the traditionally sticky carpet. 'If I drink any more coffee I'll be sick. I feel sick.'

Charm nodded. 'Yeah. Whoever said the truth will set you free was a dickhead. The truth is fucking horrid here. Chas... Charity told us – both of us – about your playing a song for her here. She came to see you because Chastity was going to take you out with the device here in the club. You should be flattered. Chas thought you'd take her down if she used the blade or the gun. And even if she put you down and your buddies knew who'd taken the shot she reckoned that you'd reach out from the grave and gut her. But anyway Chas... Charity claimed you, said you were untouchable. Chastity immediately respected that. Contract void.' She forced herself, to focus, to ask a question of her inquisitor.

'And then you sliced the Hard Man. How did you work it all out?'

'Didn't. Don't know. While you three were working the head on me, I was looking in the other direction. Choose any answer that suits you. I'm considerably angry, Amand... Charm. Considerably. Need to think.' He stood up, stood still.

'I can...' Charm stood up suddenly, strangely clumsy. Awkward. Reached for the waist of the pale jeans she was wearing, began to remove them.

Stoner was quite suddenly beside her, pulled her to him, all the way to him, hugged her and held her tight.

Then he leaned down, tilted her head back, removed the sunglasses from the top of her head and kissed her once where they'd rested.

'If you pretend affection, humanity, lady, I will drop you where you stand. I will break off little pieces until you feel the filth you've done to me. Can we just make a little music?'

She stared, open-mouth, wide eyes. Then looked down and away from him. 'Yeah,' she said. 'We could always make some music.'

***

'So what's been going on while I was away?' Maybe a half hour of a serious musical workout appeared to have calmed Stoner, to have pressed some reset button. Charm was subdued, hung her head, said nothing but played some very good, very proficient piano for Stoner to solo against. Neither of them had sung a note. Neither of them had said a word while they played. The music was non-peaceful, not cool at all, and the aggression in it would have had any audience bouncing for more. Shouting, calling, drinking and paying.

'JJ?' Charm's voice was quiet, barely audible over the decaying hiss of the unplayed cymbals and fizzing snares of the drum kit. She left the piano stool, walked to the edge of the low stage, lowered herself and sat down again, kicking her heels against the front of the stage. 'Can we...' she looked up at last. Then looked away. 'Can we go upstairs for a while? I need something. Just... physical. I'm not trying a stunt. There's no one else here, you won't be compromised if you've other... y'know... other guys... girls you don't want to offend. Feels like begging, but... fuck.' Her voice failed. 'Just you and me. Can... ah, crap. I feel... I don't know what I feel.'

'Would you really have completed the hit? On me?' Stoner's voice was level. Then he laughed, shockingly somehow. He was nowhere in sight, the dim auditorium had swallowed him into its darkness. 'I thought you were sweet on me.'

Charm laid back, flat onto the stage, her legs hanging over the edge. 'Yes,' she said. 'You need it in writing?'

'No,' he replied, suddenly standing beside her. 'Not really.' He looked out towards the far shadows, in the direction of the main door. Spoke to someone else. 'How did she do? Was that the truth, however much of it you heard?' Charm sat upright, bolt upright, stared around her into the gloom.

Shadow shifted. Dark moved against dark. A pale patch gained resolution against the dark. Took form.

'A curious tale, well told. Not too much drama, little tugging of the heartstrings, very uncomfortable to hear. Not least for me. But... the tale fits the facts, or could be bent a little to fit the facts.' A figure walked entirely silently from the club's inner darkness. 'I even bolted the stable door behind me. Stoner. Charm.' The figure stopped by their table; a shapeless man dressed in seriously unfashionable black, black hair. Black fingernails, also long. White, white face. Make-up. Black around the eyes, on the lips. Mallis.

Charm stared, Stoner appeared to be considering a smile of greeting. He coughed quietly, moved a little closer to Charm, protectively, maybe.

'Sorry I missed you in the States, Mallis.'

'A kind lie, well intentioned. It was nothing. Should we sit?'

'Are you a threat?' Stoner again, Charm was still

staring at the newcomer. Plainly an unexpected intruder as far as she was concerned.

'To you, no. To Charm here?' A pause. 'No.'

'Those conditional negatives, Mallis? Charm's neg sounded less than permanent, frankly.'

'Stop with the pedantry, Stoner. I came here to meet you, to talk, to discuss, to educate ourselves to – hopefully – our mutual benefit. I'd not expected a third party. Generally speaking I do not like the unexpected, be they ever so charming.' He nodded to Charm, who had retaken her seat.

'You flirting, Mallis?' There was a definite hint of humour, humanity to Stoner's voice.

'For a clever man you can be desperately crass sometimes, Stoner.'

'Suit yourself.' Stoner looked at Charm, who appeared to be trying to disappear, to dematerialise somehow. He looked back to Mallis; they sat down in unison. 'How – I need to ask this – did you know I was here? I'm supposed to be elsewhere.'

'In Texas, yes. A good screen.'

'For an amateur. I hear your sneer, Goth-boy.'

'You're imagining things. You're no amateur, so don't even think about pretending in this company. I'll answer, but then I will have questions which are... are burning at me a little. Thorns. Unwelcome.' He paused. 'I set up the security for the club, all the exits carry alarms, in and out. They log and store patterns for later use if ever needed. The hidden exit – or entrance in this case – calls me when it's unlocked. Calls me in real time if I ask it to. I asked. It called. Here we are.'

'Anyone other than me used that entrance while I've been away on vacation?'

'Not with your personal codes. Can I ask a few

questions? I have, as I said, thorns. Irritating and unwelcome.'

'And I too want answers from you, Goth-boy. So play patient with me.' The lightness had left Stoner's voice. He sounded – for the first time – dangerous.

Mallis was a study in don't-care. 'Your answers will come in both my questions to Charm and in her replies. One of us is an analyst, Stoner, and one of us is a man of action. Try to remember that.'

'And me?' Charm sounded steady.

Stoner nodded. 'You're the star turn. Time for that unforgettable live or die solo, sax or no sax.' He turned to Mallis. 'Fire away, Goth-boy.'

Mallis regarded Stoner without any visible emotion. 'How are you? Really? You don't look... your normal self. Are you fighting fit? How damaged? That was why I tried to catch you in the US, before you returned – returned invisibly. Very, very, very clever. Too clever for you to achieve. Care to explain how you did that? Or is it too private for Miss Charm here? Or too... sensitive for me?'

'Coffee, Mallis?' Stoner asked, Mallis shook his head, Charm shook her own in a very small way. 'Just me, then.' He stood and prowled the bar, clattering things more than was usual. 'I flew in, using a shiny new ID, some little while ago. All very legal.' He poured. More creamer, less coffee than usual.

'I'm sound, and thanks for asking. Damaged? Yes. Fighting fit? Won't know until I need to know. Could do with some gym time, could do with a run. The beard is growing on me. What's been happening while I was away? That's what I wanted to ask you in the States.'

Mallis appeared to be entirely relaxed. Earlier

signs of stress had been replaced by his customary dead expression, eyes flat as the pancake make-up he appeared to be wearing. 'The order of things has been changing,' he said at last. 'No one was looking for you. No one seemed to care – with a few notable exceptions of course.' He nodded almost imperceptibly towards Charm. 'You were simply gone.'

Stoner watched him carefully. 'You saw the video?'

Mallis shook his head, again only slightly. 'No. Heard about it, but it sounded so ridiculous and – frankly – pointless that I didn't give it a lot of thought. I assumed that you had simply gone to ground in the US and had retired – in a sense – from your working life. We had talked about that before, as your memory may confirm, assuming it's still working at your age.'

'It comes and it goes. As with so many other things.'

'Indeed.' Mallis radiated politeness. 'May I ask a few questions of Charm, here?'

Stoner shrugged, sat back. Then quite suddenly rose to his feet, climbed onto the stage and removed his old Fender guitar from its case, sat down on the edge of stage, and with every appearance of disinterest in whatever happened in front of him, began practising unamplified scales. There are many scales. Stoner began his scales in the key of E major, shifted to F major, followed by G major, and seemed set for the long haul.

As though synchronised, Charm and Mallis looked first at the unlikely instrumentalist, then at each other. Mallis spoke first.

'You told this man' – he nodded in Stoner's approximate direction – 'that your contract with the Hard Man came to you from Menace. A long, complex contract to kill, among other people, Stoner himself. It came from my partner. Was that correct? And was it the whole truth?'

'Yes. And yes to the second.'

'All the information you needed to carry out that contract also came from Menace? From my partner?'

'Yes.'

Mallis looked up and stared flatly into her eyes. 'You need to be gone,' he said. 'Now.'

'Mine.' Stoner spoke softly, the guitar silent now, resting innocent in his lap.

Mallis's gaze remained on Charm, though his words were directed elsewhere. 'You cannot be serious,' is what he said.

'Too easy to react too soon, to compound a failure in such a way that it can't be corrected. Charm should leave – we have words to say, thee'n'me – but it would distress me greatly if she fell foul of some creature of yours before she and I have the longer, larger conversation due to us. Anger more than distress, to be honest. Mallis?'

Charm rose to her feet, staring at Stoner, eyes fit to burst from her head, face whiter than the Goth's make-up. Mallis nodded. 'I'll send a message,' he suggested, thumbing a device held out of their view. 'You should leave now.' He looked up at her. 'Safe from me. Saved by Stoner. By the stone killer. Wonders will never cease.'

'See you at opening time. Maybe you should bring your sax.' Stoner was calmly replacing his guitar in its case. 'But leaving would be good. This guy can get nasty when angered, and I believe he is quite seriously cross right now.'

Charm departed, leaving no more words in the emptiness she left behind her. Dignity and pride retained in the calm of her exit. Mallis rose and slid the deadbolt behind her. 'You understood what she told you?' He walked behind the bar, unzipped a bottle of cheap vodka and lifted it to his lips, then returned to his original seat, stood the bottle on the table in silence, dropped his heavy black overcoat to the ground beside the table, and sat down. Picked up the bottle. Drank a little more.

'Fuck,' he remarked, conversationally.

'Steady now,' Stoner remained where he was, on the edge of the stage. 'Such language in one so cool. Someone stole my stool. Can't trust anyone.'

'You do understand? Still you make with the jokes?'

'When there's nothing left, you just need to laugh. Anything else could be fatal. Far too easily fatal.'

'You're correct, Stoner. I was entirely surprised that you were so comprehensively fooled by the Hard Man, but you were clearly not alone in your blindness.' He stopped, sipped, coughed, and continued. 'Do you believe her? Charm?'

'Yes. As in, I can see no reason for her to lie. What she told me could have killed her right here, and I was almost concerned that you might pull her head off right in front of me. Thanks for the self-restraint. Blood can be so... sticky. Really messes up the furniture.'

'Thank you for applying the restraint, Stoner. It wasn't mine. So Menace has been moving behind my back.' He might have been talking to himself, but it was difficult to tell.

'For a long time, I think. Only you'll know the damage that might have caused.'

Mallis nodded. 'Incalculable from where I am. Tell me, as a man rather more experienced in the ways of women than I, what's the probability of Charm being in contact with Menace at this moment – this very moment, right now – advising her of what is going down here, with you and with me?'

'My view? No odds. I think... no, I feel that she's made a choice, that if she's talking to anyone it will be her lethal sister.'

'Chastity.'

'Just so. Chastity who as we speak is in Texas waiting for me to show up and sing her a song.'

'She's not.' Mallis sipped more from his bottle. Looked up to Stoner; 'This really is a very poor spirit. Is it all right to replace it with something a little less obviously an industrial solvent?'

'Knock yourself out. Where, pray, is the athletic and always entertaining Chastity, if she's not where her sister says she is?'

'She's at Parkside.' Mallis had opened a bottle of Stolichnaya Elit, and was using a glass from the bar as an intermediary as he interrogated the bottle. The conversation between Goth and vodka appeared to be amicable. 'She's waiting for you.'

'Would you care to explain?' Stoner's teeth were audibly gritted. Mallis sighed, sipped a little, then poured himself a decent dose, toasted in Russian and threw it down his throat. Poured. Sounded desperately weary.

'You called Bili the bassist and told her you were off to some shitkicker paradise. With Stretch the SEAL and part-time pianist. Kicking ass or kicking shit; such was your implication. Chastity's view – not mine, as it happened – was that this was rank poor tradecraft and that you were setting a false trail, like a cowboy with a dead goat.'

'Excuse me?'

'Whatever. I rarely drink alcohol. It ruins my syntax. So I am sounding like a foreigner.'

'You are a foreigner.'

'Incorrect. I am English. British at the least of things. It says so in all my best passports.'

'Chastity.' Stoner was smiling, despite himself.

'She told Charm that she was off to make music with you in the desert, and...'

Stoner interrupted. 'Bili told Chastity what I'd said to her, to Bili? I'd like to understand the dynamic of this.'

'Yes. No. Yes I would too like the understanding. No, Bili told Charm, who was with her when she caught your cold. Call. Caught your call. Charm told Chastity, Chastity told me and asked me for access to Parkside where she decided you would turn up. Like bad penis. She instructed me to say nothing to anyone else.'

'And?'

'I have said nothing to anyone else.'

'Not even to Menace?'

'No. I am stupid, is obvious now, but not totally stupid. And I have not seen Menace to talk with in several days.' Mallis appeared to be in some pain, and drank a little more. Then a little more. Stoner added to his pain.

'Menace is in America.' He poured himself a shot of the excellent vodka and threw it back, toasting the both of them in Russian.

'You are correct, I think.' Mallis considered the emptying bottle. 'The day itself has taken itself away from us,' he announced, remarkably. 'You have a safe with a numeric combination lock.' It was a statement. Stoner nodded confirmation. 'Please put my coat into that safe. I shall go sleep upstairs with the bottle. Is that OK with you? Thank you. The terrible noise you describe as music will give me nightmares, but it is better that I stay here, and as your safe is steel shield signals from the devices in my coat will be undetectable. Probably.'

He rose, and walked slowly, majestically towards to doorway to the stairs. Stoner shook his head, smiled sadly, distractedly, and carted the heavy coat to the shielded safe.

19

NO PLACE LIKE IT

Stoner ran. He ran in silence, more or less. The Volkswagen camper van was parked up like a shining invader from another planet in an apparently forgotten scrapyard near the entrance of the worn out industrial estate he might previously have called home. Parkside. A place of very many memories indeed, almost all of them memories for other people, almost all of those deceased a long time ago, in a world war far removed from the current colder conflicts. He ran, cheap service station trainers performing unexpectedly competent service as running shoes, cheap service station beachwear masquerading as sports kit. He ran.

All old military bases boast perimeter roads, Parkside included, although as it was over a half century since the place had held any formal military credentials that road was lost in several places, and was a road to nowhere in several others. Stoner ran. No one appeared to have the slightest interest in him. Few other examples of the living were obvious, the whole place performing a decent impersonation of the set of a zombie movie. Decay everywhere, a subdued hum, a background of deliberate disinterest. All good signs. Nothing out of the ordinary, nothing untoward.

He returned to his beached camper van, checked the rudimentary telltales and trips, found nothing. Unlocked, climbed inside and luxuriated in the carpeted floor and the almost comfortable seating as he changed from tasteless cheap imitation clothing into more expensive and motorcycle-branded biker gear. Mostly black. Climbed up front into the captain's seat. Fired up, and rolled the heavy Transporter around the dozing not very industrial estate until he reached another nondescript and overgrown track down to another set of ancient ex-military buildings. A sign outside. Transportation Station, it announced, dimly, and green lights glowed inside all three examples of the letter 'o'. Encouraging.

Overgrowth and an air of dereliction are both good signs when considering the quiet approach into a building. Stoner considered the soaking wet paddling pool which had formed over the entrance to the tunnel at the rear of his own Transportation Station, a route which, once opened from the outside, surfaced again in a vehicle inspection pit within the building. He contemplated it. Nothing about it appealed. Apart from the considerable volume of water, the flooded pool stank of decay and rotting vegetation. More zombie movie props. Also undisturbed for quite a long time. Algae takes a while to blossom into weed, which then lives for another while before dying, and it then takes another while before it rots... as was the case before him. There's no doubt a branch of forensic science which has considered the rates of plant growth, death and decay. Stoner was solid in his belief that he would rather pierce his own eyes with blunt needles than study plants and the details of their dying. For him, the signs and smells of rot were sufficient. He was aware of his sadly superficial approach to many things, this was merely another example.

He walked around to the front of the building, extracted a cell phone from a pocket. Keyed in a signal and instructed the device to send its code. The green indicator lights switched smoothly and in sequence, left to right, to red. He took a key from another pocket and approached the door. No key needed. The door was unlocked. He swung the handle, slid the door sideways on silent steel runners and entered.

Quiet. Near-dark. Silent VW Transporter vans, three of them, confronted him. A massed accusing Teutonic glare. Four eyes – one Transporter had two smashed headlights. Stoner's memory tickled a smile to his lips. To his right, the building opened out into an almost civilised space. Comfy chairs. A sullen black motorcycle standing on a bright red workbench. A spotlight pooling brightness onto an opened bottle of red wine, two glasses, empty and waiting.

'You spoke to Charm, then?' Stoner talked into the silence. A chair... a something... scraped on concrete.

'I did. Welcome home, Mister Stoner. The wine's a decent specimen, it's been open for a while. It's breathed enough. We should – maybe – drink it. Resurrections are always worth some sort of celebration.' Chastity appeared in the light. A blonde short-hair today, hard and fit in tight-fitting black. No smile to match the friendliness of the words.

'Nobody died.' Stoner stood his ground. He was on his own turf, in his own home, maybe, but felt threatened, intruding. Lost, somehow. Estranged.

Chastity laughed, once, quietly and entirely without humour. 'Everybody needs to. Anyone who's not dead yet will be soon enough. Not soon enough for me. Mostly.'

Stoner walked, slowly, steadily, as though he was watching for traps, trips and trials. He reached the strong, silent woman in black. Held out both hands, palms up and open. She held his gaze, then reached out her own hands into the field of his vision. Her left hand held a stubby black pistol, her right a longer black bladed knife. She maintained her grip on his gaze, and lowered the weapons into his hands. 'I can relax,' she said, quietly into the stillness. It was almost a question. Stoner held her hands, his and hers, sharing their grip on the weapons.

'Hey.' Finally.

She relaxed, a very little. 'Hey,' she replied, the neutral pitch and timbre of her voice matching his own almost perfectly. 'Pax?'

'*Pax... vobiscum.*' Stoner cooled before her. '*Et cum spiritu tuo.*'

They moved forward together, weapons forgotten somehow.

'Someone told me you were dead.' Chastity was making conversation.

'Happens a lot. Too often. Not been true so far, but one day...'

'Yeah. One day it will be. I almost believed you'd... y'know...'

'Topped myself? Nah. You?'

'Not yet. Don't want to go on my own. Know what I mean?'

'Oh yes.' Stoner moved them, holding together like some bizarre four-legged animal, a beast with two backs, two heads and a single purpose, towards the bottle and the attendant glasses. 'No point in the very big bang, the only true dramatic exit, if you can't share it with others.'

'Exactly. As one. As always, Mister Stoner.' She tilted

her face upwards – only slightly upwards – to his. 'A kiss before dying?'

'You've poisoned the wine? Seems like a waste. I've come a long way. Have a thirst, me.'

She kissed him on his cheek. He turned his head to catch her lips with his own. Missed. Noses rubbed instead. Both mouths smiled involuntarily. He released himself from her and her armoury, a slow Thai martial artist's unconscious detachment, and poured. Gestured towards an easy chair, soft and low, high arms and a high back to match. Leather upholstery, all in black. Took himself to a chrome and black leather wheeled stool, sat, and scooted the thing until it faced the easy chair. Chastity parked herself, weapons sheathed. Raised her glass to his own.

'Absent friends,' she shared.

Stoner nodded. 'Whoever they were.' They sipped, focused on each other, totally. 'These walls have ears, m'dear. But you know that.'

A small smile wandered across her features. 'Don't they all? Don't they fucking all. Cheers.' She drank, rested her glass on the floor by her chair. 'You're going to give me the third degree about what's been happening while you've been... away.' She gestured vaguely at the walls around them, walls near and far. 'There's no point. I don't think I can answer anything, not really, not sensibly.'

'And not here?'

'As you say. Not a great vintage, this?' She raised her glass, held it against a light, a dim light. 'You got wheels?' She waved at the brooding row of VW Transporters. 'These look... tired. Neglected.'

'I'm on foot.' Stoner smiled at her. Wandered over to one of the vehicle work bays, rummaged in a red steel drawer. Extracted a sheaf of stick-on numbers, and reached behind the workbench to retrieve a pair of blank vehicle registration plates. The press tool to affix numbers to plates did not look to be new. He prowled back to the bottle of wine. Poured for them both, raised another toast and drank. 'Let's go running, huh? Just you and me? How's that sound? Cosy? Lovey-dove-dovey?'

'Fuck off. Just fuck off.' Chastity swallowed, wiped her lips with the back of a hand and stood. 'Let's go run, before it gets dark, and before you've got to be somewhere else, mister busy-boy.'

'Nowhere to run, nowhere to hide, that's me.' Stoner sprinted to the door, keyed something into a pad. 'Gonna kill everything, gonna burn everybody, gonna be king of the night for a day.'

'That a song?'

'Not yet. Could be if you want.'

They left the building. The single spotlight lit the half-emptied bottle as the door rolled shut and locked and the brooding silence of sleeping machinery returned.

***

'A camper van? Are you deranged?' Chastity stopped, stood and stared. She shook her head, turned to him and shared the widest smile he'd ever seen her wear. 'A camper. Love it. Let's go to the seaside, hey hey!'

'Got a date with Charm tonight.'

'Yeah. Sweet sister, sweet soul sister of mine.' Chastity's tone suggested a certain ironic interpretation of her words. 'You never break a date, man of stone?'

'Always. Which bit of the seaside do you suggest? This is England, plenty to choose from.'

'Don't know, don't care, head west.'

'Why west?'

'Because it's away from here, it's probably Wales, and the last time I was in that strange and unfriendly place I hardly killed anyone. Hardly at all.'

Stoner grinned at her as he keyed the ignition. 'We could drive all night, like lovers do.'

'We're not lovers. Unique among my surviving family, I am not your lover.'

'A sad situation.'

'You say.'

'I mean it.' Stoner piloted the VW from rotten concrete roads onto less rotten concrete, then onto a real, genuine road surface. The loaded springs settled into the rolling rhythms they'd been built for, the curious camper van body rolling a lot less as the surface smoothed and their speed rose. 'I have few regrets. This is one.'

'I bet you say that to all the girls.'

'True. You'd win.' The Transporter bounced, effectively deflecting Chastity's poison glare.

'Does it often work?'

'Define that word?'

'Get them into bed.'

'Dunno. No idea. Let's pretend we're being serious. Just for a minute. I find that being honest scares people off, especially women who fancy a night of no frills bouncy-bouncy.'

'How so?'

Stoner manoeuvred the camper off the Parkside trading estate, wondering as always what it traded, where and why, and headed west, towards the sea.

'The UK's an island,' he remarked, surprising the both of them.

'Well done. You get a G for Geography. Why d'you say so?'

'Didn't intend to, Chastity. It just slipped out. And no no no, I don't say that to all the girls either. I was thinking of heading to the sea – as you said – and it dawned on me that I'm on an island. You too.'

'Kind of you to include me, even if you didn't intend to.'

'I was thinking of a showdown. On a beach. Nowhere to hide and no point to running.'

'Get Carter.' Chastity spoke softly.

'Don't know him.' Stoner headed them relentlessly onto decreasingly minor roads. 'Should I?'

'It's a movie, mister culture vulture. Michael Caine.'

'They pass me by, mostly. Any good? Any relevance? You got an active cell phone with you?'

'Last scene of Get Carter's on a beach. Everybody dies.'

'Gotcha. Uplifting. Life lessons for losers. Phone?'

She produced a cell phone. 'Look,' she shared. 'It's a phone. You've got several of your own. I know this because I've seen you use them.'

'How common's the number on that one?'

'How d'you mean? Is this magic tradecraft and spook stuff?'

'Yes. How many folk know that number's yours?'

'Charm, probably. Why? We're not as paranoid as you with phones. Use Facebook for comms, mostly.'

'Call Charm, then. Text is better yet. Tell her – from me – that I can't make it tonight. Just that. That you're heading... oh, I don't know... anywhere that she'd be unlikely to go meet you.'

'You want whoever else knows the number to know we've been together, maybe still are, and you want Charm to know that you're standing her – your lover sometimes, huh? – standing her up to be with me. To probably be with me. Have I got all that?'

'So far as it goes. There's more of course, but if I told you the rest of it you'd either kill me, I'd kill you or we'd need to sign a suicide pact.'

'I'm confused.' Chastity thumbed a message into her phone.

'Yeah, me too.' Stoner just drove.

'Done. Do I, like, throw it out the window now?'

'Nope. Anyone who wants to trace you by following the phone won't necessarily expect me, and if they're following me...'

'I get it. Cunning. Pointlessly complicated, but you got to feed your paranoia something, huh? Are these things always so slow?'

'Sorry? Oh. OK. No. It can go fast, for a camper van, but we're in character and we're in no hurry.'

'In character?'

'Middle aged dawdlers with no particular place to go.'

'Speak for yourself.'

'I was. At least, I was speaking for the kindly inhabitants of a very similar camper van who... ah... generously donated their registration number. They certainly looked middle aged. The type of people to have their insurance and road tax all paid up, and unlikely to have any speeding offences. So we can travel incognito, undisturbed.'

'Where are we going?'

'The seaside. Catch some rays. Play at being Michael Caine. I'll do a lot of running on a beach, you make with the bins and watch over me. Also make tea. Not too sure whether middle aged camper van drivers dare drink coffee. It's a courage thing, I reckon.'

'You talk shit. Seriously.'

'It's a talent. A rare talent. You should try it. Eases

the soul and makes for immortality.' Stoner stamped on the brakes as a black European luxury car carved its own space in front of them and braked. He flashed his lights. Muttered appropriately. The vehicle in front of them accelerated away, as though they weren't there.

'Despite the endless paranoid nonsense – OK, OK, tradecraft – despite the seeming complete absence of a plan, you do in fact have one?'

'Always. Improv is the mother of invention.'

'You sure about that?'

'I just made it up. You don't like?'

'Have you been in the States for a long time? Too long?'

'Why d'you ask?'

'You're talking shit in the way Yanks talk shit. Not Brit shit.'

'I'm unsure whether that's observant of you or perceptive. Grammar's often a problem. Yeah. Been in the colonies until very recently. Peaceful there. Hardly anyone tried to kill me. Did quite well for myself. Made friends. Fit in like a teaspoon of salt into a sugar bowl. Great place. Hope to return. Come with me.'

'That an invite?'

'If you like.'

Time passed, slowly and companionably. The companionable van navigated effortlessly through several series of road junctions.

'Stoner?'

'Yeah.'

'We're not heading for Wales, are we?'

'How can you tell? Impress me with your Girl Scout observation woggle – whatever.'

'Asshole. Wales is in the other direction.' She waved. 'This is heading south west. Somerset, Devon.'

'Cornwall. The ocean. The end of all things. Finisterre – finished with terra. Romantic, huh? Catches the poet in your soul.'

'I don't have a poet.'

'But you do have a soul?'

'You tell me, Father Jean.'

'That nickname will be on my tombstone, I reckon.'

'I'll carve it. And then I'll dance on it.'

'Cool. I'll watch and enjoy. Didn't know you danced. Many talents. Sharp shooting, cookery, serial killing and dancing. My girl, things like that.'

'I'm going to sleep, dim boy. Shut up and drive. No radio, and do not sing.'

***

Dawn. Cold and watery light. An unenthusiastic morning. Stoner had switched off the engine some time before. Chastity slept, curled into the big seat beside him, her breathing quiet, almost controlled, her limbs unmoving, disciplined, still. He watched her breathe. Listened to the calm smoothness of it all. Wondered how someone like her – no, someone exactly her – could sleep so well. Killers, generally, do not. Acts of violence breed internal violences of their own. To a point. After a point, so legend has it, the senses become numb, comfortable with the nihilism of it. Stoner had watched this grim process in others, studied it growing slowly in himself. And the last time he'd been alone with this woman, with Chastity herself, he had asked her how far gone she was. How far from the last killing. Killing herself. Her sleep had been less calm, more damaged than now. He wondered whether this was a good sign, a bad sign or no sign at all. Simply something to be aware of.

She was looking at him. No change to the rhythms, to her own personal vibration, but she was looking at him, steadily. She was so otherwise unchanged that Stoner wondered for a second or two whether she was in fact still asleep with her eyes open. She spoke, fixing that idea.

'Here, then. Which is where?' She rolled upright in her seat, assuming the vertically seated position.

Stoner released the yawn he'd been denying. It is difficult to yawn effectively in silence, and he'd been enjoying her sleep.

'Devon.' He released his seat from its conventional driving position, and swung it around until it faced into the body of the van. 'Coffee?'

'Tea. The spook who has everything presumably has tea?' She sounded entirely awake, not at all like someone who had been awake for only a moment.

'Been awake long?' Stoner stooped from the big seat, the formerly driver's seat, and released the several mechanisms which raised the van's roof, allowing him to stand upright.

'Wow. That's cool, camper man.' Chastity had figured out the rotation operation of her own seat and had swung it around to match Stoner's introspection. 'A little while. I was listening to you breathing. How come it took us so long to get here? Devon's not far... not far from anywhere else in the UK.'

'We travelled a road less followed. I wanted anyone who might be behind us to appear. They didn't. Either no one was following or they have a novel method of doing it. All phones are dismembered – without power cells – and only I know about the van. That narrows the odds.'

'You are one paranoid bastard, JJ. Still OK to call you JJ, JJ?' She smiled. He poured boiling water into a teapot, swirled it around. Reboiled the kettle, added tea leaves to the pot and poured the freshly boiling water on top of them.

'Seems a little obsessive for builder's tea, JJ.' Her smile was in her voice.

'It's impossible to be too obsessive. I obsess over forgetting things to be obsessed about. Obsession keeps me alive. Did all through last year, mostly. A bad year. A very bad year. Thanks for keeping in touch.'

'*De nada.*' Chastity stood at last, stretched herself, arms raising until they made contact with the elevated roof. 'Cool van.'

'You said that.'

'I did?'

'Not sure. You know how it is.'

'Not really. You telling?'

'Need a scrubbing.'

'You? Me? Should I be mum?' She reached for the teapot.

'As you wish. Me certainly, you probably, although I'd not say, being a gentleman and you being a bloomin' blonde. No milk. Sorry.'

'Yeah. A gentleman,' she paused. 'A gentleman would offer a lady milk for her infusion. So...'

'Would you like some milk?'

'No. Thank you for asking. That's me being a lady.'

'Terrifying.' Stoner pointed to the far end of the van. It was not very far away. 'That's a shower of sorts. I would like a shower. I need a shower. You... you may like to have one. Would milady care to go first?'

'Fuck. Serious gentleman speak. Yeah. Me first. Does this thing recycle its dirty water? I'd rather you bathed in my delicate feminine ladylike effluvia than I in your male grunt filth.'

'Pervert. No. It gets rid of dirty water through a hook-up to the campsite's services.'

'We in a campsite?' Chastity put her tea to one side, stripped with practiced efficiency and a complete absence of provocation, picked up the drink again and smoothed her naked way to the tiny shower. 'No curtain?'

'You grown modesty as well as ladylikeness?'

'Yeah, right. I was thinking only of your furniture, such as it is.' She turned to face him, struck a pose with her right hand on her hip while drinking the last of her tea from her left. 'Still like to look, Pervo-boy? Like to watch?'

'Yep. Some things improve with absence. Abstinence makes the heart grow fonder. Some crap like that.'

She laughed, Turned on the water, just enough water to wet her skin, shivered until it heated, and washed herself with maximum studied provocation. 'Towel me down, sailor boy?'

Stoner threw a towel at her. 'Sailor. Yeah. That's me. Sailor on the seas of fate.' He shook his head slowly. 'You're a feast, Chas. Simply a feast. Looking more muscled than I remember.'

She towelled with determination and vigour. 'Yeah. Your turn. You got two towels? Or are just such a hot guy that you evaporate the water? Like a radiator man?'

Stoner, stripped with a military efficiency to match her own, parked up on what may have been a couch, maybe a bed, maybe something else in the curious world of camper vans, and smiled.

'I should have brought a book. You going to talk all day or can a grimy guy get a shower?'

Chastity stepped aside. Her eyes broke contact with his in a theatrical way, drifted south, focused, paused, returned to catch his attention again. She raised a single querying eyebrow. 'Holy orders or a system malfunction?' She nodded at his lack of arousal.

'Probably. Time and place. The unusual thing. You need to call home?'

'No need. Maybe want. Should. How d'you suggest, paranoid spook guy?'

Stoner stood and relocated to the small shower. He was wider than it was and pretty much as tall. He shrugged. 'Next stop a hotel. There's a laptop under the sink. You using Facebook, something like?'

'That is the plan. That OK? Do you still have that handy phone gadget with the app for bug spotting?'

Stoner nodded. A trickle of warm water ran from the shower head, ran with no obvious enthusiasm down his body. He opened his mouth to catch a taste. 'The van's clean,' he said. 'But.'

'But what?'

'The guy who supplied the app wouldn't set it to catch a bug he'd planted to download with the app, would he? No. No he'd not. So using a laptop and Facebook should be more secure than using a traceable phone.' The water, for no evident reason, rose suddenly in both volume and temperature. Stoner grabbed soap and scrubbed. Chastity located the laptop, dialled in and checked up on her several Facebook friends, commenting here and there, finally leaving a message for her mother. As always, the conflict that her mother was long ago deceased yet still active on social media worried her not at all. She shut down the laptop, attacked Stoner from behind... grabbed the sponge from his hands and scrubbed his back, vigorously, violently. Then she pulled him around and addressed his front with similar application and force, finally washing away the last of the suds with her bare hands. Held him in one of them. Stared down. Squeezed.

'You've had a bad time, huh? Care to share?'

'Not yet. How's your mother?' He collected the damp towel and applied it to himself.

'Charm? Don't know. She'll reply when she's ready. Talk to me? Explain your thinking.' She parked herself in the reversed driver's seat, entirely relaxed in her nakedness – and his. 'You've surely not dragged us off to Devon for the surf.'

'You can hear it?'

'I'm not deaf. I can smell it and hear the gulls. Don't distract yourself. Think. Talk. D'you need some proper caffeine? Tea's civilised and stylish, but... y'know.'

Stoner sat on the maybe bed, maybe couch, rolled his towel into a pillow and stretched himself out. Chastity gestured towards his groin.

'That tackle should be doing something, Stoner. At least pretend a little attraction, cheer me up a bit. You're making me feel adult... old, even.'

Stoner snorted a little, rubbed himself, producing an instant erection which appeared to surprise them both. 'Better?'

'You betcha.' She bounced and wriggled in a fine pastiche of a teenager with the hots. 'Now talk. Any guy who finds his right hand more of a turn-on than this...' she spread her legs wide before him and squeezed a breast in each hand... 'deserves a dose of heavyweight listening to. Huh?' She closed her legs again, sat back, demure and mostly modest. 'We should agree terms and conditions, going forward.'

'Excuse me?'

'Y'know, management speak. Let's agree the blindingly obvious. Point one; we are on the same side here.'

'We are?'

'Yes. No hesitation, deviation. I'll repeat it until you believe it. We are. Tell me what happened, tell me what you want to do and what you want me to do.'

Stoner's physical enthusiasm subsided. He stood, applied water to the silly little kettle, placed it on the silly little stove, rinsed their cups in the silly little sink, brewed instant coffee – black – passed a half of it to Chastity, sat down. 'How much do you know?'

Chastity sipped, considering. 'I know... I heard lots of things. If they were all true, then your dick's frankly piss poor performance is some way towards excusable.'

Stoner waved a hand, suggesting she continue.

'You were on your big white cruise ship, no doubt porking the eyeballs out of that officer with the great tits and smart hats, when someone sent you some pics of Shard, your right hand man, screwing the tart you call Lissa, who everyone else refers to either as the Dirty Blonde or Stoner's whore, depending. The pics were explicit to the point of violence. You went completely and inexplicably batshit – she's a whore, for Christ's sake – and cleared off to the land of drone strikes and random mall murders for R&R. How'm I doing?'

'Good. So far as you go.'

'Care to add a detail or two? Aid my weak feeble girlie understanding of your rough tough boyland struggles?' She smiled, her words defused.

'It was a vid, not pics. Real movie, silent. Contents as you describe at first. And don't go heavy with the sarcasm, sweet Chastity, I know Lissa better than you and I know how and why she whores – I knew that before we hooked up in the thing, whatever the thing we had was. I'm a whore in my own way. I can't judge her. It was good.'

Chastity nodded once, then again, slowly, thoughtfully. 'A lot worse then? The video? You should tell me.'

'Why?'

'I want to know. What fucks you up, y'know? What takes big bad JJ Stoner, scourge of the unlamented, and sends him running all the way across the world, tail between his legs, then brings him back with firm resolution but a limp dick to... to do what? Masked avenger shit? I need to know what hurt you.' She stopped, leaned forward in her seat. 'I have a care for you. I could lie and tell you it's professional, that I owe you for... before... but you should know. I... care. I want to look out for you.'

'Going maternal, huh?'

'Don't mock. Don't even think about...'

He interrupted her. 'I wasn't mocking, Chas. Not one bit.'

'Tell me it's mutual, then. That way I feel less stupid.'

'Respect, Chas. For now that needs to be enough.'

'For now?'

'For now.'

'OK. Talk, soldier boy.'

'In the vid. Shard's fucking Lissa, who's tied to a cross, an X not a T, spread out so she can't resist.

'What?' Chastity was waving a hand at him. 'Why would she resist? She's a whore, right? Fucking holds no fears, right? And he's been there before, Shard, right? So there's no way she's gonna be uptight and no way that's gonna make you uptight, bad man.'

Stoner had ceased all movement. Snake like. The silence hung, and closed tightly around them.

'What?' Chastity broke it.

'They'd been together – fucked together before?'

Stoner's tone was a study in calm neutrality, contradicted by his body language.

Chastity shrugged. 'So they say. I wasn't – y'know – actually there, but Charm told me and... you didn't know?'

Stoner should his head. 'No.'

'Does it matter? Is it important?'

'Don't know. It's another piece of information I didn't have before. Let's get the story over and done. That OK?'

Chastity held out a hand, apologising. Stoner shook his head.

'All the time, all the time he's doing it to her, Shard's yelling, screaming maybe. Silent movie, remember, but he's yelling all the time. Like a madman. Lissa's just hating. Following the cameraman and hating. She does hate very well. She remembers her Africa. Then Shard gets into her again from behind. I'm not into hot phone sex chat, so I'll leave out the details – it was heavy. Trust me.

'Then he guts her. With a knife. I didn't see that coming...'

Chastity was on her feet, leaning over him, grabbed his face with both her hands. 'He killed her? That can't be right. She's not dead, your whore, Stoner. She's around.'

'No. He reached around her, sliced open her belly. Blood and guts. Nasty. Real wet work.' Stoner's voice was dry, matter of fact. 'Her guts just fell out of her. Loops of it. Hard focus. Bright colours. Bands of grey and pink.' He paused, thinking. 'Then Shard just fell down. Strings cut. And Lissa hung there, bleeding, wide awake, cut open, losing blood, guts. Hating.'

A silence hung between them. Chastity broke the

pause by rising, dressing smoothly and in silence. Threw Stoner's clothes to him. They landed on him, and lay there like a discarded skin. Ignored.

'Get dressed,' she told him. 'Get dressed, and we'll go for a walk. Maybe a run. You need air, and so do I.'

Stoner looked up. Focus and calm sat heavily on him. 'I don't care about the thing, y'know? The fucking, the gore, that crap. Don't care. I'm too old.'

'Crap. The fuck you don't care. How can you not care? Fool. What spooked you, spook boy?'

Stoner pulled on socks, a shirt, jeans, all of them black. 'Blesses. The only way Shard could have done that was because Blesses made him. She... she controls. Only men. It's impossible but she does it.'

'You make her sound like she does magic, JJ, and there is no magic. None.'

'Keep on believing that, Chas. Hang onto it when all else falls around you. She is poison. Pure. She...' He took what felt like a year to lace a boot. 'I spoke to Hartmann – the Hard Man. He speaks badly now, very rough voice. He denies that he made the vid happen.'

'Maybe he lies.'

'He surely does do that. And only he could have pulled the strings that got the vid into the captain's computer on a cruise ship, fuck's sake. The Hard Man and Blesses? Working together? Against me? That makes me a dead man. That makes anyone close to me dead meat. I got all that in about a second. Just a flash. Clear as the video I'd just watched. Destroying. Destroying shit.'

'She's had a claw into you, too, then? Blesses?'

Stoner shook his head, slowly, then rose, flexed his fingers. 'Not now. Let's walk. Run some, maybe. Eat. Make merry.'

'For tomorrow we...'

'Yeah. You got it, soulful sister. You surely do.'

***

'This paranoia of yours.' Chastity spoke as though she was making polite conversation over tea and a biscuit, maybe in a church hall in a genteel suburb with arranged flowers. Stoner was sitting at the wheel of the parked camper van. Mostly listening, so far as was obvious.

'Why do you think anyone would be following you? Why would anyone be interested? I don't really believe anyone's interested in what you're doing any more. Don't think you're on anyone's radar. Not really. But... here you are. Sitting in a shitty camper van, parked in a shitty car park somewhere close to the arse end of absolute nowhere, with not another interesting soul in sight, believing that the bogey woman is hot on your heels, ready to consign you to a fate worse than death. That said bogey woman cares enough to... anything. She spooked you so bad last year that you ran away and hid. Job done. Game over. Set and shooting match all to her. Advantage Blesses. And you're still running. Still paranoid.' She sighed and stretched. 'I want out of this sitting room on wheels, and you need to break something. Kill someone. Stop acting like some pathetic adolescent who's scared of his shadow.'

'You done?' Stoner did not look concerned.

'Yeah. Mostly.'

'You don't need to be here. You can check out any time you like.'

'But you can never leave.' She laughed. 'Very clever. All life in a song lyric.'

'You got it. You can take the van with you.'

'I need a bath.'

'Agreed.'

'Stoner, you dull fuckwit, will you stop making out that I smell?'

'Yeah. It's my only self defence against your endless complaining. Mad axe women are supposed to be above constant moaning.'

'Says who?'

'There's a bistro over there across the road. Bistro is modern English for coffee shop. We could get decent coffee.'

'One minute you're complaining that I smell, the next you're after another caffeine fix. You truly are that international man of mystery.'

'In the bistro, I bet they have ads for holiday cottages.'

'Now you want a holiday? Wow.'

'I want a cottage.'

'Yeah? Why?'

'I want to live here for a while.'

'You want to rent a holiday cottage? That is so insecure, Mr Paranoid. Even the dimmest of bad boy spooks could trace that.'

'I'm going to find one and break into it and live in silent fucking seclusion for a while. It's off season. There'll be loads of empty cottages.'

'You're going to break into a holiday cottage? You call that a plan?'

'Call it what you like. Doreen. That's a good name. Call it the Doreen plan.'

'You're losing it, Stoner.'

'Let's hope so. Come along now. Find a cottage. Break in, and you can have a power shower, sweaty girl.'

'Fuck off.'

'OK.'

***

'Now we change the door locks.' Chastity walked through every room in the shuttered cottage, found the main fusebox and switched on the main switch. 'Nothing's exploded, no alarms. Owner's not a spook, then.'

Stoner entered the room behind her, treading silently in her footsteps. She walked backwards into him, stopped rigid when he caught her in his arms and pulled her off-balance and against him. 'No jokes about guns in my pockets, please,' he said, softly.

'No jokes needed.' Her reply was as soft as his own comment. She did not pull away. Stoner whispered into her ear.

'There's nothing in the garage. Plenty of room in there to park a motorcycle and keep the camper van clear of snoops.'

'There are no snoops. We're miles from anywhere. This is Devon. Everybody's dead or retired. Or both. Why are we whispering, given that there's no living ear within ten miles?'

'Romance. Pure and simple. Romance. It's romantic to whisper.'

Chastity lifted herself away from him, turned to face him. Stoner stepped back a pace, raised his empty hands as if to confirm their innocence. She smiled weakly and whispered still. 'The age of romance is long dead, along with the last romantics.'

'You think?' Stoner lowered his hands.

'I know. I should get a shower now? The water will be warming, this being a modern fake cottage and not some purgatorial stonebuilt slum. You think I smell?' She shook her head. 'I mean. Really smell?'

'You smell great. It's just a ruse to get your kit off again. I believe you should do that at every opportunity. It makes an old man very happy.'

'Just not your old man, huh?' She smiled, defusing any hurt in her words.

Stoner shrugged. 'Some things are worth working on, huh?'

'You say.'

'I do. How's my stratagem working? You in danger of showering? Take a long bath. I'll book a ringside seat.'

Chastity laughed. It was sudden as it was shocking, and sounded totally genuine. Unforced. Young. Simple. A laugh. No more. 'And then what? We do wild sex? You talked about nothing else at one point. Germany.' Her smile replaced her laugh. The lines in her face faded as she relaxed. She reached out a hand. Held it maybe halfway between them. Stoner reached a little and took it.

'Wild sex? Yeah. Even if it's only between me and myself, huh? Things being what things are.' He maintained his hold on her hand. The grip was mutual. Equal. 'You offering not to kill me? Wish you'd never told me that. That you've killed every guy you've fucked. That does detune a chap.'

She breathed steadily, silently for several seconds. 'Every man who's fucked me, JJ. It's not the same thing. Not... exactly.' She towed him to a wetroom, a large downstairs bathroom, well outfitted with a vast bath, a shower with space for several fat people, basins and bidets and plumbing and quality. Quality everywhere and outstanding. Let go his hand, turned and undressed, entirely without her usual efficiency. Slowly. Her back to him but entirely conscious of his attention. Then she turned to face him. A moment shared.

'Tell me about Charm.' Stoner collected Chastity's clothes, added his own and threw them all outside the room, pulled its door to, seated himself on a hollow throne, relaxed, relieving himself. His eyes returned to her body, hers to his.

She scratched herself, slowly, rasping her fingernails through the short hard hair around her sex. 'Would you like to shave me?' She turned on the shower and tested its temperature. 'Are your hands steady enough to do that? Would that wake him up?'

Stoner stood, took a single step. Stopped, took back the step and sat down again. Smiled, a wan smile. 'Yes,' he said. 'I'll do that. I'd enjoy that. There's time yet. But today, now, this moment, it's a distraction. Tell me about Charm. The way she lies. That in particular.' He paused. 'Don't shave. Save that for me. I'd like that. I'll dream of it.'

'I bet.' Chastity soaked herself, soaped herself. 'I bet you'll dream of me.' She snorted. 'Is Charm so good a fuck, JJ?'

'No. She is what she is. Dislikes herself, I think, and that never makes for intimacy. Self-obsession is difficult to share. Tell me about her, huh? And the dream? I'm serious. I need a future to believe in, just at the moment. Just now. I've not seen a future since the ship. Just a whole lot of death. Endings, several endings, all of them just... deaths.'

'Yours included.'

'Every time.'

'You're more interested in her than in me?' Chastity stood beneath the shower, her movements slowed and stilled. Water, steaming, ran from her, sluiced over her breasts. Her eyes held his.

Stoner shrugged, accepting a defeat. 'No. Not as a person. Not as anything special. She's your sister, Chas.

Every second word she says is a lie. Why? Why lie so much, all the time? She's your sister.'

'You said that. It's the truth. Why the repetition?' The water ran over her. She scratched her pubis again, absent-mindedly.

'You work together, you're close, so far as I know. Maybe I'm reluctant to badmouth your sister to you. It would make no sense for there to be a conflict of loyalties at a point where focus and a single track would be what's needed. Fatal. Could be that. Even.'

'Arse. Say what you mean. Respect me, Stoner Boy.'

'Respect. She's a decent fuck. Another. One of many. There's lots of those. Recreation not procreation. Getting it on. Everyone can do it. And they do. The world is populated by the result. Charm – Amanda, whatever – she's one of those. Relax. It's the best way I know to relax. Willing, able, takes her time, enjoys herself. No intensity at all. No stress. Rock and roll. Lie back, slide it in and consider the world and its wicked ways. Dope for a junkie.

'She used her sex as a direct line to me, got my attention, blew me like I was a saxophone, revealed that she plays the sax – which she does, and very well – and bingo! There she is, running my club, being best friend to all my best friends. Always there. And if there was any single moment when the thought that maybe she was more or less than she seemed, it was Do It To Me Big Boy time again, and puff-pant memory fade and my, my, can that lady blow. The curious world of the Hanwell sisters. Handy Mandy Hanwell. That's it.'

'Hanwell?' Chastity turned the water off, shook herself, gestured to a pile of folded towels. Stoner threw one to her. Then changed his mind and took it back, towelled her down gently. Like a friend, almost.

'Your family name. Amanda Hanwell.'

'She tell you that?'

'Yeah. It's not? It's another lie?'

'Yep. We're the Weise sisters, we three. Two now.' She paused. 'Hanwell was a joke once, a long time ago when we were girls. It's a lunatic asylum.'

Stoner laughed, draped the towel over her shoulders and rubbed the base of her spine with his knuckles. 'Thanks for that. She made that up too?'

'Sounds like it.'

'Why?'

'Can only guess. Backing both horses in a two horse race? She'd do that. We're different. I take sides and stick to it. Charm always wants to keep her options open. She used to say that there were no losers until someone lost, and then there was always a winner. She'd have backed the winner. And the loser, but we could all ignore that and forget about it. Easy when you know how. So she'd say.'

'So she'd accept a contract against me as the long end game but hedge her bets in case I survived and thrived?'

'You got it. You don't keep all your brains in your dick.' She grinned. 'Luckily, given...'

20

LIQUID ACROBAT

'No one sees them. They're invisible.' Stoner was poring over a stack of online adverts for motorcycles. Harley-Davidsons of course. Plainly he was immune to the lure of modernity. Chastity pointed at one of the potentials, one of the candidates.

'They'd see that, all right. More bling than a cheap jeweller's on bargain day. That's up there with the Indian wedding level of bling. It's impressive... in a seriously crass kind of way.'

'You're missing the deal.' Stoner's attention was on another of the machines, paused and captured as it scrolled by. 'Everyone sees the motorcycle. No one sees the motorcyclist. The more hard core, the more we're ignored. Even if I didn't seriously enjoy riding a motorcycle, I'd ride one to avoid attention. By letting the bike grab the eyes and letting me become scenery. Furniture. You should try it. You'd like it. Girls look good on motorcycles. Legions of sweaty youths would dream creamy dreams of you at all points.'

'I know that. I have a bike. I use it for jobs sometimes. No big deal. It's easy in traffic. I get wet. And in any case I look like a bloke when I ride it.' She paused. 'Surely you're contradicting yourself? They'd only see the bike, not me. That's what you just said. Is this the famed Stoner confusion theory in action?'

'Nah. Spot the difference between sweet young blonde thing aboard a blingy throbbing beast and a dull middle-aged guy aboard some middle-aged guy's wank fantasy? Got that? If you were nearby and in biker chick chic on a bike, I'd be invisible to any other males in the vicinity anyway. Law of nature. It's the rules. It is what it is. Clichés like that. I can seriously do cliché, me.'

Chastity slapped him across the back of his head. 'You were on a bike the first time we met, as I recall. I also recall that I was undistracted. It was a green bike. Dull. Very quiet. Not your sort of thing at all. Very very slow. Couldn't keep up with a Ford sedan... a decent sedan chair would have dragged it away from the lights. Thought you only went for Harleys, anyway, tough guy?'

'It was a Harley.'

'No. Denied. It was some flat as a fart trail bike. I remember it well. I drove especially slowly so you had some chance – a small chance – of keeping me in sight. Then you gave up and went home. See? I do remember.'

Stoner caught her hand before it slapped him again. 'Bikes are like guns. There's lots of kinds. Lots of specialist types. Like soldiers. Trick's choosing the right kind for the right gig. That's a surveillance motorcycle. Slow and quiet and unobtrusive. Equally invisible where it counts. And it is a Harley. I have several of them, here and there. Couple of them seriously stealthy. One of them's proof against EMP, don't you know.' He mimed excitement and pride. Unconvincingly.

'OK, JJ, I surrender. EMP? Some kind of social disease?'

'Yep. Electromagnetic pulse. What you get after a thermonuclear explosion. Big electrical flash that fries

electrics. Little bike's hardened against it. NATO bike.'
He performed some more pride. She smiled.

'Rider nuked and toasted but his bike still works?'

'You got it, smart girl.' He leaned back and stabbed at
the laptop's screen with a hard finger. 'That's the one.'

'How can you tell? Not very blingy. Looks dull.'

'Boys know these things. It's a boy thing. Like girls
and dollies, you know.'

'Fuck off, Stoner.'

'Yeah.' Stoner tapped a message into the machine.
'Bet he'll take cash, too. Biker rebel guy. They always
do. Right-on guy, plainly. Look, the bike's got skull
pattern handlebar grips, and skulls painted on the
gas tank. No one would take a guy riding a bike like
this seriously. He'll take cash from a bad-ass bro like
me, that's a betcha.' He sounded almost pleased.

'Dodging taxes, somehow?' Chastity's interest in
the subtle art of acquiring a motorcycle was plainly
reaching a new low point.

'eBay charges. Paypal charges. Whatever. Real rowdy
rebels revolt against such violations of their inalienable
right to behave like an asshole and be stupid. Gosh.
Look.' He gestured to a message on-screen. 'Told you.
Cash best. My kinda guy.'

'You have enough cash?'

'Yep. And all of it belongs to someone else, so it's not
even wasting my own savings on a piece of silly shit.
Everybody wins. Even losers win. Let's go buy a bike.'

'Stop and get me a helmet, decent gloves. I have the
boots already.'

'You make no sense, Bat Woman.'

'I'll buy it and ride it to wherever your current paranoia
level wants it. Another cut-out in case it gets traced.'

***

'It's kinda amusing, in a go-slow agritech kinda way.' Chastity greeted Stoner's return to their holiday home from home with the irresistible welcome of fresh coffee and a tray of fresh rolls. The keys to the motorcycle she'd bought with Stoner's cash lay on a worktop. The keyring was a model death's head, inevitably, and the coffee aroma fought with another, less appealing smell.

'You smell of gas.' Stoner dropped the keys to the camper van onto a kitchen worktop. 'It makes a change from the usual. Does the mighty American secret weapon leak fuel?'

'Its filler leaks.'

'You over-filled it? That is not a fault. Better too much fuel than too little. Fools rush in when fuel runs out. Things like that.'

'I over-filled it. Do you make up shit like that all the time?'

'Creative genius. Some are born to be grating, things like that.'

'If I find you a guitar, will you cease to be an irritating attempt at a smartarse?'

'Nope. My only talent.'

'Preserve us all, then.'

'As you say. Could you kill your sister?'

'Tell me again what you just said.' She shook her head and held up a hand. 'You just asked if I'd kill my sister?'

Stoner nodded. Chastity leaned back, hopped onto the kitchen counter. Stared. 'You asking me to do that?'

'No.' Stoner poured for them both, topped up the coffee maker's water, ready for the inevitable refills.

'Curious, mostly.'

'How so, soldier boy. Remember what curiosity did to cats.'

'Who could forget. You killed Charity, right?'

'Who told you that?' Chastity was stationary. Static as a cobra and her attention as focused, tight as any reptile could achieve. She dropped silently from the counter, seated herself at the table, opposite Stoner. Who lifted his coffee, looked at the table top.

'No one. It's what I'd have done in your situation. She'd only need to ask you once. She did, didn't she?' He sipped and pulled a face, the drink was still too hot for comfort. He looked up, raised an eyebrow to repeat the question.

Chastity nodded. 'Good call. Yeah. Clever boy.'

'How'd you do it?'

'Hot bath, candles, scents, lots of booze, laughter, release, the black blade, both femorals. Clean. The end to all suffering.' She laid the same black blade on the counter top, between them. It absorbed the dim light in the room, somehow. Drew all attention into itself.

Stoner nodded, laid his hands on the counter top, one each side of the black blade, palms up. No threat. Chastity spoke, softly.

'Three weeks ago. Roughly. I'm not counting. And neither is Chas. Not anymore.'

'OK. That recently? Sorry. That's... bad timing. She... left messages. Texts. For me. I didn't pick them up. Until I called you. A fortnight ago, maybe.'

Chastity spun the blade, a slow movement, deliberate. Its point, flat black and focused, pointed directly at her. Stoner repeated her gesture, spun the black knife. The blade pointed at him.

'I would have done it if she'd asked me. She was

noble. I'm... I'm glad it was you. It's time to change horses. I'm done with the running and the hiding. I've run and I'm hidden. Time to bring it all back home. Quickly. Two would be quicker than one. Suit you, Chastity Weise?'

She nodded. Rose, poured her coffee into a sink, and undressed in silence, dropping her new biker gear where it fell. Skinned. Standing stilled, beauty and a black hard blade.

***

'The key to all of it – certainly all the unpleasantness – is Blesses. Everything else is human, mostly, so negotiable, mostly.' Stoner was talking. Chastity was walking at his side, around a canal basin towards a sea lock, a mildly interesting relic of an earlier industrial age. The sun was hanging low in its sky, just above the ocean. Stoner pointed at it. 'America,' he announced, mysteriously.

Chastity followed his gaze as she matched his pace, step by step. 'That's mysterious,' she concluded.

'It's where I want to be.' Stoner's pace was steady as they approached a choice of three destinations; a track to a surfer beach, the end of the sea wall, the bridge over the stout wooden lock gates. He led them over the gates, retracing their steps along the opposite side of the canal basin, this time around heading away from the sea. 'England,' he said, without any need to point. 'History.'

'Gotcha.' Chastity could also be brief. 'Future. Past. Your Bonnie lies over the ocean.' She could do mysterious, also.

Stoner sighed. 'Leave the song quotes to me. That way I can understand them. That would be one of us with the understanding, rather than none of us. A result.'

'So you say. How're you going to find Blesses? And then what? Let me guess? OK. I did the guess. I am correct. Do I get a prize?'

'Finding her won't be a problem. It's the then what which won't be easy. Did you know I tried to kill her already? Before before?'

Chastity was scanning the opposite side of the canal basin, alert, vigilant. 'No. Do tell, master sniper. You are a decent shot, so you tell me.'

'Nothing to tell. There's a café over there. Coffee, cake and confessions. I shot. I missed. I shot again. I missed again.'

'Drunk? Stoned? No visibility? You hit all the alleged humans she was using as shields? Intercession of angels? Do tell. Gun jam?'

'Nope.' They swung left again, over a road bridge and headed for the café. 'It's weird just talking about it, trying to remember how it happened. I can remember how...' he paused, 'exactly how it went down, but I can't remember how.'

'You make no sense.' Chastity was unflustered, her pace steady, controlled as they walked in step past the café. 'You either remember how or you do not. You can't both remember it and not remember it. Say more, then tell me why you're struggling with this, and why you react so badly every time the name Blesses turns up. It's like watching a haunting.'

They paced towards the noisy ocean once again, the sun was lower in the sky. All around them fun families were enjoying family fun. It was unnerving to observe.

Stoner shrugged, transformed the shrug into a rolling of his shoulders as they walked. Their pace picked up, though neither commented on it nor appeared to be leading the other. 'I fired. Easy range, good clean weapon. SIG Sauer. Single handed shot. Missed. Ran on – something of an emergency – took a second shot and missed again... and then again. Caught up to her... What?' Chastity was waving an interrogatory pair of hands at him. He paused, though their pace continued, relentless, synchronised.

'Why were you shooting at her?'

'Too long to explain now. And irrelevant. I'm working towards something you need to know.' No irritation in his words, maybe a little loss of tone to his voice, a hint of distraction maybe.

Chastity nodded, once. 'OK.'

'I reached her, she spoke at me – I have no memory at all of what she said – and I aimed, point-blank, and...' His voice trailed, uncertain.

'You missed again? Point-blank with a SIG, your own dream handgun, JJ?'

'No. Not clear to...' He stopped in his tracks, eyes aimed over the ocean. 'This is so freaked out. The foresight is one hundred percent between her eyes. Five rounds left. Grip perfect, balance intact. Finger is outside the trigger guard and... and... I cannot take the shot.'

'Fuck.' Chastity had turned to face him. 'You're still here, so the angels intervened?'

'Bernadette shot her. Both knees. Precision. Blesses fell – like you do with slugs through your knees – daylight came back to me, and when she started talking again I kicked her in the head. Lights out.'

Chastity was watching him carefully. 'Let me get this straight, then I'll drag you to the café, set up a caffeine IV and let you overdose. Bernadette – the nun I met in Germany, the fat one who does big guns and who you

315

told me was a priest – she was there and tooled but you still needed to do the conquering macho hero thing, why? To save little old her in her fancy black habit? But you screwed up and she took the shot anyway? Makes no sense.'

'Bernadette was gut-shot and unwell with that.'

'Gotcha. Sense made. So the purpose of the history lesson is to tell me that you doubt your own ability to take down Blesses from close up, right? Which leaves two immediately practical options. First, you do it with a long gun. Second, I do it for you. And you're also telling me something else. When I met Bernadette that time, last year, and she told you that Blesses was released, from a secure prison or some such, you went all stressed. And Bernadette went all quiet and you did subdued together. So there's a lot more history? I don't need to know it, but thanks for the heads-up. I'll take your shot for you.

'There's more.' She held up a finger for silence. 'My keen female intuition suggests you reckon that Blesses – who sounds dead cool, by the way – had the same magic fluence on Shard, which is why he did all the strenuous nice'n'slice with your whore for the cameras. Have I got this straight? Blesses does things to guys that turn them to wobbly jellies, then she does voodoo mind tricks and they're powerless to resist? Sorry, JJ. Sorry, but it sounds like so much BS to me. Sounds like a bad plot in a bad novel. You'll be doing zombies next. But your enemy is my enemy, like I said. You want her taken down, it's a done deal. Easy job. You point, I shoot. Wam bam, no more ma'am. Cake?'

They had arrived, somehow, at the café. Parked up on benches in the early evening light, ordered. Watched the sun's dying display in a short, shared silence.

'Yeah.' Stoner broke their truce. 'It does sound stupid. But it's true.'

Chastity smiled at the waitress, who served them, smiled and left. 'Truth is what's real. What's real is what happens. No matter how stupid it sounds. You have a problem with this person, you either need to avoid her or deal with the difficulty. And if you're correct, and she's hunting you, then you either run and keep on running, which surely gets tiresome after a while, or you turn and bite back. Are we sharing the cake or are you dieting?'

'I think that what she does, she can do only to men.' The light in the sky was spectacular, and fading fast. 'I suspect that she and the Hard Man go way back. Way, way back. It all began in Ireland.'

'Don't go all whimsical, JJ. Find her – you know how to do that – point me at her, watch from a safe distance through your voodoo-proof X-ray specs, and problem solved.' She lifted cake crumbs from the plate using the tips of her fingers. 'And then what? Or is there no future plan here?'

Stoner watched her. 'Just like that?'

She nodded her agreement. 'Exactly like that. Cake was stale. Someone needs to pay for that.'

***

'I'll take the motorcycle. You can dream up some breakfast.' Chastity appeared fresh and alert and well-slept. Stoner felt as he imagined he looked; like he'd spent the entire night walking and watching over their borrowed home, interspersed with attempts at sleep. He was nervous, agitated, unhappy maybe. He shrugged.

'Whatever you want. It's your life. Anywhere in particular? When do you want breakfast?'

Chastity was collecting kit suitable for a motorcycle ride. The morning was not warm, although it was dry enough so far. Skies clear, mostly. No serious threat of rain nor promise of serious sunshine. Quiet. Uninteresting.

'Couple of things I want, and data requests best made from somewhere other than where you already can't sleep.' She looked across the room to him. 'You should have let me sort you out, ease your tension. That's what your whore would have done, so why did I know without asking that you would have declined my generous – nay, selfless – suggestion? Had I made it. Which of course I did not, because I knew you'd reject me, and no girl needs that. Especially not a blonde girl.'

Stoner paused in his impersonation of a man who has no idea what to do next.

'You shaved your pussy yet?'

'Nope.'

'Good. Something to look forward to.'

'You betcha. Quite a show. An event. Anticipation can be an inspiration.' Chastity collected the keys. 'Be about three hours. No more than four.'

Stoner bowed, slowly, carefully, like an old man with the ache. 'Brunch, then. Ride well.'

Chastity dropped the keys into her crash helmet, dropped the helmet into a soft chair, walked across the room to her companion. Tilted her head to one side, looked up at him and raised the quizzical eyebrow. 'You OK, big guy? Demons? Your own she-devil?'

'You got it.' Stoner saw no point in lying to her. 'Hauntings, like.'

Chastity took his hand, pulled it to her. He did not resist, instead he held her fingers with his own, and looked at the far wall while doing so. She tried to catch his eyes only once. 'JJ. You've run and you've hidden. The only person who knows where you are is me. I can think of no situation in which I'd rat you out. I'm mostly out of loyalties. Apart from to you.'

'And Charm. Your sister.' Stoner's focus had returned, though he looked exhausted.

'I think that's a longer story. Best told in calmer times, big man. Every book has its last page.'

He nodded, slowly, as a man with a head filled with fragilities. Drew breath to say more, but Chastity beat him.

'You want to ask what happens when I'm forced to choose. Right?'

He nodded.

She said: 'Let's cross that bridge when it blows up under us, huh?'

'No,' he said. 'This is that bridge.'

'All right. I'll lay it out as it is. There's no way I can see that happening – me being forced into making that choice, that call. No way I can see that Chas... Charm and my interests would be so divergent. If she works against you, she's working against me. I will point that out to her – the next time, the very next time we're in signals. She's no soul-free killer bitch, she's far too straight, serious and sensible for that nowadays. Dirty work – some dirty work – is best left to others, to the troops. She'd screw for Britain, Olympic effort, but would delegate wet work. Wet pussy work, fine and sometimes fun.' She laughed, once, dry. 'Slice'n'dice, not so much.'

She wound down. Looked at him again. Met his eyes. 'Go lie down. Take a bath. Take a nap. Anyone sneaks in and kills you, I'll do the vengeful angel routine. You can watch from above.' She smiled. 'Below. Whatever.'

'Yeah. The return of the Angel of Death, huh?'

Chastity mimed ferocity. 'That was a while back, no? But yeah. Angelic. That's me. Go sleep, Tarzan, stop… just for once cease with the paranoia. Exhaustion will kill you. Blesses – fuck – no one knows where you are. Even if they cared, which… mostly… they do not.'

She walked to the door, collecting her helmet, gloves on the way. Turned to face him again with her hand on the handle, blew him a kiss, and left.

***

'That was quiet.' Stoner appeared in the kitchen as Chastity stripped off her riding gear. 'You fitted new silencers?'

She nodded her agreement. 'Bloody awful racket. I felt really ridiculous, conspicuous, exposed. Hated it. Shop loved me, though. New exhausts, complete set of new riding kit, blonde girl using their wi-fi to surf a little.' She held up a cautionary hand, waggled a finger. 'I even borrowed their PC to do the surfing, and a very nice Harley-powered customer loaned me his cell phone to do other stuff. Is that paranoid enough for you?' She paused again. 'You look like you slept all morning. Food?'

'Waiting for you. I ran into town. On foot. My own feet. Bought food, brought it back, piled it high then fell asleep. Feeling good.' He grinned, briefly. 'Did you get what you wanted?'

Chastity nodded again, creaking a little in her new leathers. 'These too tight, huh?' She gestured at the pants. Stoner shook his head, held up a pair of approving thumbs.

'Ten out of ten,' he offered. 'You win the beauty contest.'

Chastity shrugged. Pulled a large smartphone from a pocket, slid and prodded it to life, parked it on the worktop, pointed to the image she'd summoned. 'Beauty contest? No contest. She wins. Every time. Have I got the correct bitch? The demon psycho bitch from all those dismal Catholic hells of yours?' She looked up, interested in Stoner's silence. 'I see I did. Now close your mouth, get cooking and listen up, super-soldier.

'She's in the States. Last seen within the last twenty-four and in Dallas, Texas. In the company of... wait for it, wait for it... d'you wanna guess?' She mimed a decent Texas accent, rolled her eyes and threw a pout.

'Menace.' Stoner broke eggs, whipped them, did things with a very hot pan and butter.

'Yeah. You score the high ball. Mallis sends his best.' She paused. 'But only to me.'

'Really.' Single word, like a single shot. Flat.

'Yeah. Somehow your name didn't figure in any of the jolly chat. Interesting, huh? Charm didn't mention you either. Remarkable, I thought. My big sister, mother Charm, better known to the male populace as Randy Mandy, your Number Two lover – is that right? It's hard to work out the rankings – didn't mention you once. Analyse the ass out of that, super-sleuth. Oh my. Bacon too. Marry me. Who needs sex when there's bacon?'

'Handy Mandy.' Stoner was grilling bacon, frying eggs, toasting bread, slicing onions and cheese and potatoes, while a pot – a genuine pot – noisily perked fresh coffee. 'I considered kedgeree,' he remarked with careful disinterest, 'but doubt I could kiss a girl who'd been eating fish for breakfast.'

'You have a girl in mind?'

'Not really. Here comes brunch.' He loaded a plate, slid it over to her. It stopped with perfect precision beside the cutlery in front of her.

She thanked him, nodded, started to eat. Slowly. 'You not eating?'

'Not yet. Maybe later. Need some thinking time.'

'You'll think better with a filled belly. This is good.'

'I'd just go back to sleep.' He poured coffee for them both, pulled a litre of water from a refrigerator and downed maybe a quarter of it. 'Mallis, then. Give me more? Please?'

'Sounded about as lively as I've ever heard him. I don't know him, not really. Charm usually deals with the other one. Only seen Mallis in passing before now.'

'How d'you identify yourself to him? How d'you contact him?'

Chastity looked up at him, shook her head a little. 'Facebook message. Same as Charm. How do you contact him, then? Psychic energy?'

'Text, usually. SMS. He calls back.'

'Each to their own. This really is good eating. Thanks.'

'You're welcome. We aim to please. How did you avoid mentioning me, how do you have a picture of Blesses and what happens next?' Stoner suddenly laughed. Genuine humour, it appeared. 'Like your arrangement with Charm, the Hard Man would normally do the pointing and planning and prep, and would wind me up and set me running. This is quite strange. Think I've been losing myself in a freedom.' He shook his head. 'I am one fuck-off excellent soldier, and like all the extremely best soldiers I work to a chain of command. It is – I guess this has been the problem all down this line – impossible not knowing who is the boss. Acceptance, then. The boss is me. Fucking puzzling, Chastity.'

'Hard to picture you as a little tin soldier, Stoner. But an amusing image. So I shall say this only once: until this is done, you – that's you – are the boss. Just trust me.' Chastity laid cutlery aside, sipped coffee. Heaved a deep sigh of contentment. 'Mallis provided a half dozen images of your own private nemesis, several angles and consistent age-wise, so probably recent. I have probable flight times for her return to the UK – he'll leave a message when departure is confirmed. How does he do that? Hack into airline mainframes, something like that?'

'No idea, not really. His data's usually accurate. Except where Menace is concerned, so it appears. Which is also a bit of a puzzle. You know where Shard is?'

'Mallis does. I asked after Shard, aka infantry sergeant Harding, also Stretch, aka SEAL McCann, your black whore, and Bili the bass player from your club. He'll have worked out that you'n'me are in signals from that list, but like I said, your name didn't come up once.'

Stoner nodded again. Rose and poured for them both. 'The problem with perked coffee is that it stews if you don't drink it quickly.'

'Yeah, like beer goes flat. Old excuses die hard, huh? Soldiers are all soldiers. Your whore... sorry, JJ, I will try harder... Lissa and Shard appear to be sharing an address. They both appear to be working, the man said. As what, I have no idea.' She held up a hand. 'Questions later, not that I can answer them. This was mostly a Facebook message performance, not a face-to-face over supper with a voice recorder concealed in my drawers. OK? OK.

'Bass Bili isn't on his radar. Not at all. Mallis was specific about that. Stretch is back in the UK, though Mallis told me he wasn't at home. Do you know where home is for him?'

Stoner nodded. Then shrugged. 'You think I'm paranoid, try Stretch. He's my paranoia guru. For such a truly massive guy, he can be very hard to find.'

'You want to locate him?'

'He'll find me if he wants me. Same way's I'd find him if I wanted him. I'm not interested in having a party. Well. Not... yet. Lissa? Shard? What's that story?'

Chastity waved her empty coffee mug. Stoner refilled it. Rinsed the percolator, parked it to drain. 'No more free refills, huh?' She smiled a dim smile. 'You didn't know about them, did you?'

Stoner shook his head. Drew a long breath, released it as a sigh. 'Never... never really thought about it. They at it while Lissa and me, were... you know?'

'Don't know. Don't think so. No one ever said. All I'd heard was that they'd been an item before you hitched up with her. Story... one story was that she only did him for money, that you got it all for free. But that may have been just crap. How would I know? All I thought was that she was a weakness. Your weakness. I could never see how a paranoid fuck like you would maintain a vulnerability like that. She went off to live with Hartmann – your boss, the Hard Man as you'd call him – didn't she? How come you didn't see that coming? How come you don't hate her? How come you do hate Blesses but not some fucking tart who betrayed you at every fucking last step? And you so full of tradecraft, and shit like that.'

'You're getting hysterical.'

'Fuck off, Stoner.'

'Yeah. Roger. Willco. I don't know. Just... do not know.' For a moment, not a long moment but a noticeable moment, Stoner looked lost. Vulnerable. Weary. 'You can't distrust everyone. That's the road to madness. So you choose – somehow – what not to look at. There can be only so much focus. There needs to be comfort somewhere. Belief. So.' He stopped. 'Do you know much about Lissa, my Dirty Blonde?'

Chastity shook her head, a study in silence.

'Refugee from somewhere hideous in Africa. The cliché, guns, murder, torture, rape, the old post-colonial cocktail. You seen the tears tattooed on her cheek? Blue tears?'

Chastity nodded, studying silence some more.

'Kills. Hers. Refused to talk about them. All heart of darkness stuff. Revenge. She didn't want to go there, so I didn't. A respect thing. That's the thing I don't understand. It was all about respect. Shard? Guy's got his brains in his balls, that's all. Can't blame him for that.' He trailed a quiet moment. 'I'll go see him at some point. Later.' He looked at Chastity, directly. 'There's more, isn't there?'

She nodded her agreement. 'Charm reminded me that we have commitments. Two outstanding and arrangements made. Soon.'

'Hmmm. Soon?'

'Tomorrow.'

'Location? Logistics?'

Chastity smiled at him. 'We escape into what we do. Comfort zone. How did murder become more relaxing than facing the truth? No need to answer.'

'Soldiers. That's all it is. Do you need help? I'll rephrase that. Would you like help? You surely don't need any.' He smiled, spread his hands in apology.

'I'd like to borrow the bike. One-fifty, one-sixty miles, each way. Get there, do the dirty, come home. Come back here.' She corrected herself with a small smile. 'I'm sure you can occupy yourself. Hang around that café down by the canal and chat up the waitresses.'

Stoner smiled back. 'I'm sure I can. Show me how your comms work?'

'The site. Murder, Mayhem and More. Details are all on there. I'll read them later, delete once the job's done. Easy, simple, invisible. Site gets a load of traffic, so even if some mighty techno-guru was monitoring it they'd not be able to tell one from another in anything like an effective time. So they say. I just use it.'

'Show me?'

'Café with a decent wi-fi signal is all we need... And then I'll be needing a shave. A close one. Care to oblige, or are you in voyeur-only mode today, super soldier boy?'

Stoner grinned, patted her on the arse. 'Lead on. Where you go, I shall surely follow.'

21

SAME OLD STORY

Busy bar. Busy street. Black bike badly parked on the pavement. Back wheel backed against a wall, sharp end aimed at the city centre, poised for a rapid exit. Black-clad rider, mostly in leather and entirely female and vividly blonde, crossed the street, leaving the bike to interrupt the pedestrian ebb and flow while she entered the bar.

'Reservation?' A harassed man looked up from the screen he'd been considering. 'We're busy, full, no single tables tonight. Sorry.'

'Meeting someone.' Flat delivery, disinterested tone. No smiles, chaste or otherwise.

'Sorry. Who? I have the table list.' The harassed man was joined by a beaming waiter. Then by a third man, older, overweight and red around the cheeks, who pushed his way to the centre of the tiny drama.

'Ms Hanwell,' he announced, extending a pudgy hand at the end of a pudgy arm. 'Good to see you.'

The black rider nodded. 'To see you too.' She unzipped the black hard leather of her jacket, sliding the smooth zipper down to her waist, revealing to all interested parties that she was wearing nothing between jacket and skin. Decency was maintained, but the message was clear. The pudgy third man appeared to be on the verge of a faint. The improbable couple moved together into the bar, through the drinking, shouting section and on into the less hectic restaurant. The harassed man at the desk waved his arms in dismissal.

'It takes all sorts,' he remarked to the retreating backs of his colleagues. Another small group of optimistic diners appeared before him, and the rituals of refusal began all over again

***

The hotel room door sighed closed behind the couple, sealing them in sudden silence from the corridor ambience. The pudgy man ushered his companion into the room, his nervousness and his anticipation, terror and lust fighting a visible battle as the woman in black leather walked into the centre of the large, well outfitted room, and turned in a complete circle. Her survey complete, she carefully placed her motorcycle helmet onto a soft chair, and a Harley-Davidson badged shoulder bag onto the desk.

The pudgy man was controlling his fears well. 'Welcome to my own small world.' He spoke softly. 'What's that for?'

Chastity lifted the lid of the laptop computer she'd extracted from her bag, and smiled. A curious smile. She connected a lead to the nearby socket, placed there by considerate hotel designers for that exact purpose. 'I'll record tonight's delight,' she said, her soft tones matching those of the man before her.

'I think not,' the words fell between them. 'I didn't buy a scam, and you'll not be blackmailing this fool.'

Chastity smiled up at him. She released the jacket's zipper, it in turn released her breasts, which swung into view with every appearance of enthusiasm. 'Don't be silly,' she smiled some more. 'Do you know your way around computers? I expect you do... you did say earlier that you do, at any rate.' She smiled, shrugged her breasts inside her jacket again, away from his gaze. He nodded, his caution maintained only by an heroic act of will, plainly.

'The laptop records to this device.' She produced a bright blue memory stick from the bag, plugged it into a port in the side of the laptop, which confirmed its arrival in the smug way of laptops everywhere. 'You've already paid for the device. All it will contain will be your own blue movie. You can keep the laptop too, for what it cost... if you'd prefer that. I don't think it was expensive, but I'll check with the office.'

He shrugged himself out of his suit jacket, hung it carefully on a hanger, brushed its lapels down with the backs of his hands. 'OK, OK. But... ah... why?'

She smiled again, wider than a smile, maybe. 'Two things. I get off on being on camera. OK?' Her audience of one nodded, stared at the image on the screen before him. 'Second, we can watch it together when we're done, when you're... complete. And if it turns you on as much as it'll turn me on, then we can have an encore. How does that sound, huh?' She worked the zipper of her leather pants, running it all the way down, as far as it could travel, which was all the way around from the front to the waistband above her backside, revealing both that she was wearing nothing beneath them, and that she was entirely pinkly blushingly bald between her legs.

She sat down on the chair before the desk. Adjusted the laptop so its screen showed both of them, preparing

for the oldest game they could play together. Lifted
a leg towards him and wondered 'Help me off with
these, sir? Please?' Before he could assist a lady with
her footwear, she lifted what appeared to be a small
roll of dark blue cloth from a jacket pocket, and slid it
over her head. A balaclava in blue, white rings around
the holes for her eyes, a bright red ring around the
hole for her mouth, which smiled at her companion's
confusion.

'Freaky, huh?' She rocked her head back and laughed,
a deep-throated and theatrical sneer of a laugh. 'You
specified something interesting, and that's exactly what
you get. It goes with the recording. You keep that, and
as I must remain anonymous – for obvious reasons – I
can't be identifiable. You, I'm sure, have seen my face
before.'

'I... did wonder. You're... in the... movies? Wow. You
get your kicks... Wow.' The limit of his imagination and
vocabulary reached, he subsided, staring at the booted
foot in front of him as though he'd never seen its like
before. Which may well have been the case.

'One second.' Chastity leaned across to the laptop,
tapped a couple of keys, a red light lit in the top right
corner. 'Lights,' she said. 'Action.' Then, 'Boots.' And she
leaned back into the chair, hooked her arms around its
back, and lifted both of her legs, presenting her man
with both booted feet.

'Which?' He spluttered, vividly red around his face
and neck.

'Left, fool.' He unzipped the boot, carefully, and
slowly, and with total concentration. As he loosened it,
a black handle appeared. He pulled it clear, stared at
the sheathed blade attached to the black handle, then
looked up at her. 'Put that to one side,' she instructed.

'We'll judge later whether you get to use it.' He was beyond focus, performed as instructed, and moved to the right foot. Unzipped, pulled, removed a second black blade and placed it with reverence beside the first. Sat back on his heels. 'The calf zips,' she nodded her masked head at the legs she held, completely steadily, before him. He unzipped them both. She placed one foot on each of his thighs. Pressed down with her heels. Drew her feet together so they met in his lap, rested briefly, pressed, caressed, then withdrew. He watched them, silent. 'Strip,' she instructed him. 'All the way. Slowly. I want to see what's coming over me.'

He did, eventually and clumsily standing naked before her. Chastity sat upright in the chair, ran her eyes over him, slowly. He shivered. 'You cold?' she wondered. He shook his head, possibly judging himself incapable of coherent speech at that exact moment. His was a once-fit body gone to seed. His arousal was plain if not exactly an inspiration, his cock hanging heavy and fat between them. Leaking slightly.

Chastity nodded, reached for the two knives, placed the broader of the two on the desk, right at the edge of the laptop lens's field of view, and stroked the cock before her with the sheathed blade of the other. It strove, it bulged, it purpled to a deeper shade than before, and a shining lubricant string drained from it to the carpet below. She caught the gleaming string with the sheathed blade and inspected it with every appearance of enjoyment.

'Hmm,' she said. 'OK. You deserve a little encouragement. A small reward for your custom.' She smiled again, her lips pale inside the rude red rim of the face mask. 'Knees,' she said. 'On yours. Watch closely.'

And she leaned back again in her chair, lifted her

ass from its seat, braced her legs and spread them wide. 'Look,' she said. 'Something you don't see every day.' Her cunt lips parted, audibly, sighing in the almost silence between them. He stared. Then he stared with wide-eyed fascination as a blue plastic circle appeared between the vivid pink of her inner lips. The circle grew into a shining, glistening blue cylinder which eased slowly – so very slowly – from her.

'No hands. It's yours. Take it. No hands.' She watched as he lowered his face to her sex, grasped the blue cylinder with his lips. He pulled, but his lips slid on the gleaming shining plastic. He let go, wiped his lips on the back of his hand and tried again. She chuckled, and pulled the blue cylinder part of the way back inside her. 'Work for your reward, man. It's worth it.'

Her client caught the plastic with his teeth, angling his already wet face and taking considerable care to avoid biting her lips. He pulled. The blue cylinder came free, and he sat back, every inch the dog with the bone. Looked up. 'Open it,' she suggested, settling back onto her chair and closing her legs once more, folding her hands demurely enough in her lap, her oddly masked face ambiguous.

The cylinder came apart. It revealed a set of three small tablets resting in a soft fabric cocoon. One green, one yellow, one red tablet. Once again, he looked up.

'How many times?' She cocked her head to one side. 'Green for... just the once, maybe. Amber for maybe more than once. All three, and you'll not believe you had it in you. Your call. Make some meat for a lady, huh? A performance for the movie. Your movie.'

He threw the tablets back as one. Coughed. Choked, heaved himself upright and ran to the bathroom for water. Returned and apologised. 'No need. Just watch,' she said. 'Face the camera and smile as soon as you have something special to smile about.' He did, standing by her side, he upright, she seated, he overweight, middle-aging and blushing through the dark body hair. He shook his head a little, staring at his images, on the screen and in the mirror behind it. His cock was growing. He stared some more. A smile planted itself across his face, widening as his tumescence increased.

Chastity lifted the lighter of the two knives, reached across and under her breasts with her right arm and ran the sheathed blade beneath his balls, sliding it in a gentle sawing motion. His hardness continued to increase, the dribbling likewise. His breathing was audible, and a deep red flush had laid itself around his neck and across his chest. She looked up to his eyes, facing her in the mirror. 'Do you trust me?' she wondered, smiling.

He nodded, struggled to speak. Cleared his throat like a politician about to tell a particularly large lie and squeaked out an affirmative. She smiled. Showed her teeth. Gently withdrew the knife from below his balls. Removed the sheath, revealing a flat black and very thin blade. She ran the blade across the back of her own left hand. It hissed in the room's heated silence. Drew no blood. Not a single drop. Again she reached across, beneath her breasts, which shone with a tension of their own, her nipples tiny and very hard, and she drew the blade steadily through the hair above his groin. Clearing a path, a pale line in the dark hair, a line from his navel to his prick. Which stood like a teenager's, upright, fat and stretched, curved to his right, pointing with a tremor at her image in the mirror and on the screen.

She slid the blade from the base of his cock to the rim of his glans, drawing no blood and watching the tableau in the mirror. He shook, shouted suddenly, throbbed hard, the single eye at the tip of his sex opened, closed, opened again and he came hard, his body doubling over with the intensity of it. He leaned, panting hard against seated Chastity, who smiled steadily at his reflection.

'One,' she said. Then, 'Oh look,' she turned and gestured with her eyes at his cock, which had eased a little from its tension, but was still staring at the screen and at its own reflection. 'There's more to come,' she said. 'A lot more.'

'I need... can I lie down? That was... incredible.' He stared at himself in the mirror and on screen. 'You... the camera recorded that?' He sounded almost confused, his voice out of focus. 'Wow,' he said again. 'Look at this,' and he squeezed himself, drooling a little more into the pale puddle on the carpet. 'I feel giddy. Christ.'

He tottered to the bed and fell backwards onto it, his arms hanging limp at his side as he panted, hard, as though he'd run a race, not been jacked off with a knife blade. Chastity rose and walked to his side, being careful not to block the lens. She raised his sweating head, propped it with pillows, and gestured towards the mirror and the screen. 'Look,' she said, as he panted and gasped for air. 'Watch.' And she reached for him, clasped him in her hand, restored his hard-on to its former glory with precision and practised vigour and worked him until he came again, his seed pooling in the hair of his stomach, his erection hardly diminishing even after its second mighty effort.

He groaned. Mumbled something incoherent. Reached with his own right hand for his cock, grasped it, squeezed and groaned again. Hand and its contents fell against his stomach, as his gasping grew more desperate and his breathing grew more shallow. 'Hang on to that,' whispered Chastity. She turned towards the lens, performed a neat curtsey, and walked out of the picture and into the bathroom. Hot water showered, and she sang as she scrubbed, emerging some time later, towelling with enthusiasm.

She glanced at the laptop, checking that the red recording light was still lit, and felt for a pulse in the neck of the man who lay inert before her, holding his last thoughts in the palm of his hand. She removed the blue memory stick from its port on the laptop, vanished it into her bag. Then she dressed, packed away the laptop and the tools of her trade, collected her motorcycle helmet, surveyed the scene and left, throwing the two towels she'd used into the open laundry basket as she passed it in the corridor. She walked across the city street, back to her motorcycle, checked the skies, covered her sex-goddess leathers with a well-padded practical one-piece riding suit, loaded up and left, rumbling with menace through the night lights, heading south.

22

NIGHT AND DAY

The tail became obvious as soon as she hit the motorway, heading hard for the South West. Traffic was light and the vehicle following Chastity aboard her motorcycle made no efforts to evade her attentions. It made no effort to overtake, but sat at the same easy distance behind her. She was cold by now. The night air easily defeated the insulating properties of her leathers, and the lack of underwear didn't help at all. Her mood was as bleak as the temperature of the skin on her face, chilly behind the visor of her helmet. She'd carried a vague plan to return all the way to the borrowed property in Cornwall, but was more than a little attracted by the sundry cheap motels along the way. The tail persuaded her that she should pull off sooner rather than later. Which she did.

With her faithful follower in attendance, conscientiously maintaining a sensible distance between them, she swung the Harley onto the first of the southbound service areas, riding off the tarmac and onto the grass of a deserted picnic area, pulling up and switching off by an unwelcoming bench set, basically an assortment of rough planks nailed together to form an uncomfortable place for an undiscriminating family to share their own hideous interpretation of a good time. How that time might in any be good was a mystery to her, although fans of horror movies might have enjoyed the bleak moonlit monochrome misery of the place after midnight.

Her tail rolled to its own halt on the hardstanding of the car park. She glanced at it as she removed helmet and gloves. A single figure dropped out of a door, kicked it shut and walked towards her. There was neither caution nor urgency in his step.

'You been following me all day?' Chastity was concerned that chattering teeth would be interpreted as a sign of weakness. 'Can't a lady go about her business without a chaperone?'

Stoner threw a heavy coat to her. 'Picked you up on the slip road. Wasn't really looking. Not as such. Had a little business of my own in the city, thought you might head this way after closing your own deal. How'd it go? OK?'

She'd enveloped herself in the coat while he spoke. 'That crappy van has a stove, right? Why are we standing out here? I'd kill for a coffee, kill twice with added sprinkles for a hot chocolate. Added sprinkles and a flake if there was a brandy, whisky, rum, whatever as well.'

'Everything comes to she who waits. So they say. Gig OK, though?'

'Yep. Exactly as foretold, foreseen... fuck's sake it's chilly, JJ. You might not feel it, but I do.'

'You need more meat on your bones. Better yet, wear better kit. You look like a soft porn version of Batwoman. Ultimate cool. Not to say deadly cold. Really. Go brew and change if you like. I've got my riding kit with me and can bring the bike back if you'd prefer to drive.'

'You're not joining me?' She threw the question back over her shoulder, already heading for the warmth of the camper van.

'I'll watch the roads for a little while. See if we've earned attention. Either of us. Easy to see from here. Snuggle up for a little while. Warm yourself up.'

Stoner sat for a while. Rose, walked the perimeters of all the car parks, finally walking the wrong way down the sliproad as far as the main carriageway, which was quiet, mainly empty, clean and glowing yellow in the night. He shrugged, returned to the van, maybe he shivered a little.

***

'So you were following me? Why?' Chastity sounded more curious than concerned. She placed a mug of coffee in front of Stoner. The van's interior was a lot warmer that the roads outside.

He lifted and sipped. 'Had a little business of my own to pursue, so when you told me where your gig was, it seemed sensible to pursue profit while you pursued pleasure... in your own unique way. This is almost pleasant.' He nodded some appreciation.

'Profit?'

Stoner nodded, slid open a drawer, invited inspection. Two old handguns and an impressive bundle of banknotes packed it. Chastity smiled, waved the drawer closed and leaned back. 'Your own private drive to get crime off the streets?'

'My civic duty,' he confirmed with a modest shrug. 'Pimping, hooking, dealing, and worst of all, serious tax evasion. Every citizen has duties. Not enough take them seriously.' He leaned over table. 'And how was your evening, madam?'

'Cosy,' she replied, opening her shoulder bag and removing the laptop. 'Care to see?'

Stoner stopped, became still. 'Thought you were done with the chopping off heads things, Chastity. Thought that contract was complete.'

'I bet you believe in angels, magic and the total honesty of all politicians, too. And that your trains always run on time.' She booted the computer, waved the power lead around in an impressively blonde kind of way. Stoner gestured to a panel by the table, Chastity plugged the lead into the socket behind it. 'Thanks. You'll make a great boy scout. Sit back and try to ignore the dodgy lighting and lack of cunning camerawork. Consider this as art noir, cinema *verite*, dodgy home porn, whatever you prefer. Shove up.' She forced some space at his side, wrapped herself more tightly in the bulky coat, and they watched in silence.

Stoner broke the silence which followed the movie's climax. 'You should use a better camera. Maybe two or three. And you look truly stunning in that hat. It surely is the secret you. How dead was he? Or was the gig getting the footage and now you'll blackmail the family fortunes from him? He didn't look very rich. But then... the quality of rich people is in decline. He didn't look like much of a footballer or a rock star. Politician?'

'No idea. The vid goes to the customer. And he's dead. Good riddance. No loss. Should look like a coronary if Charm's pharmacist is up to snuff. Watching myself makes me horny.'

'You told the truth!'

'Say what?'

Stoner mimed utter incredulity. 'You told the mark that watching your own vids makes you horny. And it was true. I reel before such honesty. Honestly, I am in awe.'

'Horseshit.' Chastity swivelled to face him. 'Though it is true. I'm soaked as a sponge. Do you want to check?'

'I believe you. Really. Do you need something for it? For the honesty, not the leakage. Honesty is rare and should be preserved.'

Chastity glowered at him. 'For the sake of all that's godly, Stoner, I have a cavity. A vacancy. A hole that needs filling. You have the tool for the job. Spare a lady's blushes, fuck's sake.'

He stood. 'It will happen. It will. It's what comes afterwards which is a concern. Really, lady. Can we leave it at that? Just for a little while.'

'Which is how long, approximately?'

'A week. Two at the utter outside.' He sat down. Then stood again, anger on his face, unguarded, unexpected and unwelcome. 'Right now? Right here? Nothing , absofuckinglutely nothing would make me happier. There is – believe me or not – nothing, no thing, that I want to do more. Apart from live until after I've sorted… stuff. After that, both of us still in the same mind, then let's just do it. Go away, somewhere legit, stay there and out of sight, just do it. See if there is the real thing. See if we both survive it.'

'Bili.' The single word was as tangible an object as a cartoon speech bubble. It hung between them, glowing.

'What? What on earth does she have to do with it?'

Chastity held his gaze, her tension obvious. 'She is the one. The one for you. Isn't she? So don't come all "It's all about intensity" with me. I'd just be another notch for you, another lay for us both. Needn't be more than that. Neither of us should expect it. It just needs to be gotten out of the way so we can... y'know .. get on with... things. Life.'

Stoner backed away from her, reached into a cupboard beneath the alleged bed and began to haul out heavyweight motorcycle gear. He spoke as he toiled, not meeting her eye at all. 'Bili,' he said. 'Let me tell you about Bili.' The pile of clothing extracted, the drawer closed, Stoner rummaged, hesitated. Sat down facing Chastity, his expression even more opaque than his usual stone face. 'Bili in brief.' He reached for coffee, found the jug dry, began to fix more.

'She and me, we have been the best of friends. We love each other.' He stopped and looked at her, hard. She said nothing, nor did she even smile. 'Have done for years. We go back years. Anyone – anyone and everyone – anyone lay a hand against Bili and I will destroy them. My guarantee. No hesitation.'

Chastity spoke, but gently. 'Yeah. I get that. I think everyone near the two of you gets that. So why pretend there's a hole in your soul I could fill?'

'I don't. Pretend. Bili... Bili doesn't do boys, men, dicks. Bili does tits and ass, pussy, everything you have and I do not.'

'Oh.' Chastity held up her hands. 'Umm. She doesn't come across like that. And Charm told me that you and Bili and her and you had, y'know...' her words tailed away.

He laughed, quietly, but with some humour. 'Yeah, we did. Several times, all of them considerably excellent. Bili – just like your sweet sister – can swing it both ways. I would think that maybe Bili is receiving attention to relieve her tension from sweet Charm, were I of a dirty mind. They do appear to spend a lot of time together.'

Chastity held out a hand. 'Give me coffee. This is a day of revelations. You think that Chas and Bili are an item? Chas... Charm does boys, lots of boys, always has. I don't... don't think I've known her go one on one with a fem. Weird image, JJ. Like you screwing a guy. Nope. Actually, I could see that. More like you getting screwed by a guy. That ever happen?'

'Yeah, but not too recently.' He stopped himself. 'That's a lie. In the States, while I was... away. While I was... unhappy. There may have been...' He faded out.

'You would know. You would have been there, hopefully. A transcendent experience? Out of body and out of mind? Seems unlikely.'

Stoner drank, tabled the mug and pulled off his Caterpillar boots, stood and reached for the heavy rider's pants in the biker kit pile. 'I was not myself.' He stared into her eyes. 'I was lost. We spoke at the time, you and me.' He busied himself with the heavy pants, dragged the heavy Caterpillar boots back onto his feet and commenced with the lacing. 'The being lost was close to being permanent.'

Stoner wound a scarf around his neck and heaved on a heavy, armoured jacket, settled the gear into a comfortable position. 'Got the keys?' he asked. She threw them onto the table, they slid to within a half inch of his hand, maybe less.

He tapped the keys with a fingernail. Looked at his feet, then raised his eyes to hers, his filled with something close to fury. Chastity was very quiet. Very still.

'I've had it, Chas. Had it. All the way. There's things I need to do, and they're becoming less obscure. I can see what's happening, what's happened. I can see a path through it which would... clear things up for me. I need a friend or two with me on the ride – professional and personal. I have plenty of the former, vanishingly few of the latter. You're one. Very rare. I'd not want to break that by screwing it up by screwing. Pussy's pussy, Chas. Half of the world has one and gets screwed by the other half. Nothing great. Nothing lasts. Breeds as many lies as it reveals truth and understanding. We do the deed... We've had this conversation before. This is the last time. You need to agree, right now, out loud and up front.'

His expression was one of expectation struggling with the anticipation of disappointment.

She reached out over the table to him. 'Deal, JJ. The big deal. I'm up for that. Then what?' She took her hands back. 'Then what, JJ?'

'No terms and no conditions. Anything wants to happen can happen. Until then I'll just jack off, you do what suits you.'

She smiled, slid open the camper van's side door for him. 'See you at the ranch, then. I'll play security guard when I land – I'll be there first, you choose to ride seriously slow motorcycles, Mister Stoner. No offence.'

'None taken, Ms Weise.' He stepped down into the chill, the air hung with a haze, fresh sparkles lit edges, some surfaces. 'Great night for a ride. Clears the head.'

Chastity unzipped the heavy coat, her leather biker jacket, rested her breasts in her hands and in his view. Her nipples hardened like a rapid-action magic trick in the frost. 'I'll keep these safe, safe and warm,' she said.

Stoner pulled a hand from its glove, reached out and traced around her left nipple. 'Yeah,' he said. 'That's a good sight for the long night. Babe...' And he loped like a bulky great ape across to the bike, which fired at once, and they left, heading south together.

23

HERE I GO AGAIN

'Pax. JJ. A truce. Please. We should talk. Call me when you get this. Any time.' The voice rasped harsh and surprisingly loud around the spartan lounge of the borrowed Cornish holiday house. Stoner sat and considered his cell phone. Replayed the message, picked up the phone and removed its battery and SIM card. Chastity gazed at her feet. Wiggled her toes. Said nothing. Stoner spread his hands wide.

'Well? he asked.

'Taking a risk? Using your phone here?'

'Not really.' Stoner was plainly untroubled. 'Active for less than a minute, even if anyone in the game was looking, which I doubt. In any case, there are so few cell towers around here that triangulation would be vague at best. Useless, most likely.'

Chastity nodded. 'OK. Was that... I'll rephrase that. That was the voice of a dead man, yes? Hartmann. Your old master, best buddy and things like that, yes? You left him for dead, bleeding out through his throat. Messy and painful. He still sounds messy and painful. How come he's still alive?'

'Your sister – the decently departed sister, not the

sax-pumping Charm – told me she'd finished him off. She even posted a vid of his severed head on your Murder, Mayhem site. Convincing stuff. Convinced me, at any rate. But the Hard Man – Hartmann to you – was the only person I could think of who could get Blesses released and who could subvert maritime comms to post video to the exact ship I was on. So he didn't die. Charity did die, which makes it impossible to get an honest answer. A lesser man would be violently unhappy about this.'

'And you're not?'

'No. Past all caring, is the truth. Really? I just want to resolve the whole thing and go live somewhere quiet. Maybe get a job. Something useful. Teacher, maybe. Art teacher. Maybe music teacher. Something socially crucial. Y'know. Media Studies. The History of Art. Global importance, obviously. Y'know.'

'No. I don't know. You talk a lot of rubbish for a smart guy. You wanted the quiet life, you'd have stayed in the States. You going to call him back?'

'Not from here. Thought I'd take a stroll up-country when you go do your next gig, and call him from near Parkside, the Transportation Station. Not the actual place, because who knows how wired for sound and vision that is, but very nearby, just to sow a little confusion. When and where, for you?'

'Not too far from yours at Parkside. Nearly Wales, nearly England, near to Hereford. Long gun gig, which is dull but probably safe enough.'

Stoner nodded, thoughtfully. 'Fifty, sixty miles or so from Parkside, then. OK. When?'

'Day after tomorrow. Weather dependant. Job's on a golf course.'

'Hard to hide on a golf course.'

'Yeah. Nothing is easy. Then you die.'

'Positivity is its own reward. You got the details from Charm?'

Chastity nodded. 'Can I use the camper van? I could most likely take the shot from the roof.'

Stoner nodded. 'Sounds dreadful. Suicidal. Perfect for you.'

She smiled, vaguely. 'The weapon will be left in a vehicle in the golf club car park. Very simple. Foolproof. Typical Charm clarity of thought. You want to ask me about Hartmann? About Chas – Charity?'

Stoner nodded. 'Suppose so. I can understand her not killing him, but not why she told me she had, and why she set up one of those dead heads for the video camera. Looked like him. Fooled me. Though I didn't exactly examine it.'

Chastity stared at the ceiling, seeking inspiration, understanding, maybe. 'Video's low-res. Head could have been anyone's, or just a fake, even. She told me he was dead. Charm knew otherwise, it seems, but the subject didn't really come up. We've been busy, and times have been stressy, too. It's all too… complicated. Fancy lunch at the café by the canal basin? Don't think there's much to be gained by endless reruns and I'd like their wi-fi.'

'You girls need to keep up with the social media. I can understand that. Game on, then…'

***

Stoner arrived early. Cotwolds café, beloved of American and Japanese tourists, serving over-priced under-cooked greasy coronary fodder and claiming a genuine Shakespearean legitimacy for it. There's no evidence that Shakespeare ever visited pre-tourist hells in Oxfordshire, and if he had it's doubtful he ordered English Rarebit, but gullibility and a need to believe – in anything, apparently – runs deep in the arteries of global tourism. Stoner stared glumly at the menu, drummed the hard guitarist's fingernails of his right hand rhythmically on the tabletop while contemplating caffeine and homicide, maybe one, maybe the other, maybe both. Life has many uncertainties. An apparently elderly gent sat down opposite him, undid his overcoat, but left his scarf securely wrapped around his neck.

'I'd go for the fish,' suggested the Hard Man, sounding exhausted and cautious.

'There's none on the menu. You look terrible. Other suggestions?'

'No. I've never seen the menu. What do you expect? Clairvoyance? Accuracy, good humour and a healthy approach to eating? You look very well. Youthful. Fit.'

'Thank you. Only one of us is a liar, then.' Stoner waved to a waitress. Who ignored him in the quaint English way so admired by foreign tourists, and continued to gaze wistful and romantically out of the window at the unattractive fake old buildings across the street. It's possible that had there been any other customers they would have distracted her, but there weren't, so her concentration was entirely focused on anything apart from her customers. Two of them. Maintaining an impressive level of civility, considering.

Stoner looked up, met his companion's bleak gaze. Rose to his feet, walked behind the counter, took two cups and their saucers from the shelves, stood them with a clatter on the counter, and poured coffee for two. The waitress stared at him, speechless. He took four plastic containers of some chemical concoction which made coffee less brown and which was claimed to be indistinguishable from milk, despite never having seen a cow, and the lids of which displayed a vague misrepresentation of a Cotswolds village despite having been printed in China, placed two in each saucer and walked briskly back to his table.

The waitress recovered a little. 'Hey,' she said, dully. 'Who do you think you are?'

'Food standards,' announced Stoner, producing an official-looking but impressively out of context business card and flapping it at her. 'And my colleague here is from the English Tourist Board. This is a snap inspection. You're doing well so far. Is there a lot of work for the mentally subnormal around here?' He sat down, cracked creamer into coffee, stirred and sipped. 'This,' he said, more loudly and gesturing with his cup, 'This is disgusting. The coffee is older than you are. The creamer is a month past its sell-by.'

She stared at him, removed her frilly waitress apron, draped it over the back of a chair and left the building without saying another word.

'You have a way with women, JJ. Always told you that and it was always true. Unsubtle, but they love you for it.' The Hard Man sipped carefully at his own drink. 'Your verdict was harsh, fair of course, but harsh. It often pays to talk first, act later.'

'How alone are we?' Stoner was considering the doorway at the rear of the café; presumably it led to a kitchen.

'In here? Completely. There may be a chef, though it seems unlikely. Out there?' He shrugged. 'Only you know how many troops you brought with you.'

'One. You?' Stoner placed his coffee cup carefully on its saucer, rose to his feet and walked to the rear of the room, opening the door and scanning the kitchen beyond. 'Any chance of a cheese toasty or two? We're near death out here. You do serve refugees from England?' He returned to the room, closely pursued by a worried looking Asian woman wiping her hands on a traditionally filthy Olde England apron.

'Yes. Of course.' Her English would be perfectly comprehensible to anyone born east of Singapore, less so the further west you moved from there.

Stoner turned to face the Hard Man, who appeared to be bewildered, but mostly exhausted. Pale, grey-faced and worried. The Asian woman retreated to her kitchen, cooking sounds followed. A radio was switched on, presumably to disguise the urgent if quiet telephone conversation which also followed. In preparation for any supernormal events, all things being possible in the English shire counties, Stoner walked quietly to the door of the café and turned its 'Open' sign around, so that it presented the word 'Closed' to any potentially starving punter who was feeling adventurous. Deterrence is preferable to retaliation after alien invasion. Many movies have revealed this, so it must be true.

He returned to his companion. 'You're looking well for a dead man.'

'You too, JJ. You're looking a lot better on it than I, I'm afraid. You're mean with a blade.'

'I left you alive. It was a mistake, I think. Not one worth repeating, to be honest.'

'That a threat? Few threats work these days, sad to say.'

'Not really. Depends on many things, like the size of your army outside.'

'There's no one. I said I'd come alone, and I did. You said you would and you didn't. Wise move, probably. I don't care. It's not important.' His voice was a mangled mess, quiet and harsh. As though he was permanently on the edge of a bout of coughing, but without the cough to clear the throat. 'Like I tried to say when I called you in the States, I want to apologise. What's done is done, it's behind us now, and we either move forward or the other thing.

'I brought no support for several reasons. First, because I said I'd be alone. In a brave new world I will try to avoid lying to you. Second – more truth – I am almost but not completely disconnected from the old world. Third – more truth – I am here to apologise. Genuinely. To remind you that I have always respected what you are and who you are. Right from our first conversation, way back, out in Afghanistan, Pakistan, Somewhereistan – I've forgotten. Finally, and my voice will give out if someone somewhere doesn't make with another drink soon, I'm offering to help. Only if you want it or I can supply it. I am very... disconnected, like I said.' He sat back, his shoulders drooped and he looked remarkably like an old man. Pale. Grey. Tired.

Stoner gazed across the table. The clattering from the kitchen had subsided. Either the Asian woman had also departed or something at least notionally edible was on its way. He stood, walked once more behind the counter, collected two bottles of apparently local and unnaturally aerated water, and returned. Placed both bottles in front of the Hard Man. Gestured. Sat back and observed the tremor in his companion's hands as he uncapped the first glass soldier. Considered his own next words, aware that they would be important.

'Forgiveness is easy.' He stopped again. 'Forgetting takes longer. Trust lost is trust lost. Lost in an instant, takes years to rebuild. So thanks... thank you for this. Your betrayal bothered me much more than it should have. We work in the betrayal game, no? What's one more in a lifetime of lies? You surprised me by deciding to retire me terminally, rather than simply telling me it was time to stop. I'd have accepted that. From you, if from no one else. That's the trust thing. I wanted out anyway, and you knew that. So why? Why call a contract on me?'

The Hard Man's eyes flicked past Stoner to the kitchen door. He shrugged. Sipped a little. Sat back. The door opened, quietly but hardly silently. Stoner tensed, arms and legs braced, eyes narrowed. The Asian woman delivered beautifully prepared and presented toasts, from a variety of breads and with a variety of cheeses. 'On the house,' she said, approximately, bowed, refused to meet their eyes and backed carefully out of range, finally heading back to her kitchen.

'Lissa.' The one word fell between them. Stoner said nothing further, reached for a slice of thick toasted bread, some butter, spread the one on the other. The Hard Man ignored the food, sipped from his bottle of water. 'I knew you'd never accept that. When I understood that... late on... I changed the contract to include you. I... I suppose I should say that I thought you'd take down the Hanwell sisters, Menace's sub-contractors, which might have tied up a loose end or two, but it wouldn't be true. I thought the woman with the blade – whatever she was called, stupid names – I thought she would take you out.

'JJ. You'll never understand this, but Lissa changed everything for me. Obsessed me completely. She told me you'd never cared, that she was just your whore. I believed that. She might have been telling the truth. I don't know. I wanted to buy all her time so she didn't need to whore. That's called marriage in these Christian lands.'

Stoner held up his hands. 'Stop there. She was your whore. You paid her money so you could do your thing – whatever thing that is. Whatever that is, it's not any sign of respect and true affection familiar to me. You treated her as a whore – not me.'

The Hard man nodded, tried to cough – an ugly sound. 'It...' his voice faded, restored by a sip of water. 'Damn it all, this isn't easy.' He coughed, sipped, both gently. 'First time I saw her I thought she was beauty on legs. First time I saw her was after an operation – she was a collateral arrest, if you like. Whoring... making some money by doing the same old same old with some very bad boys. You were involved, but only briefly in the action. You and Harding. Long gun. Christ...' He sipped some more, breathed noisily through his nose for a while, mouth closed.

'OK. Sorry for the amdram. Speaking is really grim. Thank you for your sympathy and understanding. I debriefed Lissa, got a little back story. She was bright, very bright – as you know. Did a deal to get out and for me to lose the records. Do you really want all this? Now?'

Stoner nodded. 'Confession is good for the soul, so they say.'

'Maybe. Maybe so. She did what we'd agreed and walked free – clean. I had her details – and followed her up. She got into a thing with Harding, as you'll know, and I flipped. Hit her. Hard. Just the once. She just laughed at me. I hit her again. She laughed, called me names... and named a price. She just didn't care. She was music for me. Everything. Everything I'd never known I'd wanted.

'It was just amusing. She moved in with you, carried on with our arrangement. Refused to talk about you – apart from insulting me by telling me how... good you were at everything you did together. I'd beat up on her, she'd just mock me and I paid and paid and... felt better than I can recall. Just wanted everything. To possess her. Absolutely possess her. Totally.

'And then, right out of nowhere, she told me she was leaving, heading back to Africa – back to home. Her own home. So I offered to make her a home here. She told me you'd long-ago made the same offer, and she'd turned you down.'

'That's true.' Stoner was silent, eyes closed.

'So I talked divorce and marriage. It was ill-reasoned and very sudden, and I didn't think for one moment that she'd accept. But she did. That's it.'

'You should have talked to me. Finding it out for myself – in pretty much the most insulting way possible – just freaked me out. In a weird way, simply setting a contract on me was... oh, I don't know... almost acceptable, rules of engagement kind of thing, but setting up a home with her? As well as your home with Mrs Hartmann? What was that about? Don't answer. It makes no sense and I don't want to think about it. That's it.' Stoner wasn't finished, although he was notably angry. 'Do you want a funny? Do you want a laugh? I left you alive for Lissa. If you were what she wanted, then fine. Fine. Got that?'

'You should eat, JJ. The cheese is very good.' The Hard Man had cut transparently thin slices from one of the less mouldy cheeses and was chewing it, over and over. He rolled it into a cheek, like a hamster might. 'Swallowing is very difficult. There's going to be another operation which will make it easier, they say. Being cut like this was an experience beyond anything I'd expected. I'd expected...' He paused to sip at his water, washing the chewed cheese down with it. 'I'd expected that once they'd stopped the bleeding, then it would heal up. It doesn't. Who knew?'

Stoner constructed a sandwich of his own. 'Thought you'd been a soldier? Battlefield troops – and medics more than anyone – know all too much about what are supposed to be minor injuries. You deserved it. You always told me I was a good guy to have on your side. The reverse is also true. Where do we go from here?'

'Where do you want to go? What do you want to do? Why – a big question which has been making me think – why did you come back?'

Stoner shook his head, slowly, once, twice, three times. 'Are you crackers? Did the blood get cut off from your brain?' He appeared utterly exasperated. 'Tell me something useful about Blesses. She's yours, yes? Another asset?'

The Hard Man sipped more water. 'Do they have any vodka, gin? Booze numbs the pain, eases the chat.' Stoner obliged, finding a bottle of dull red wine already open, tapped on the door to the kitchen and called out thanks for the food. Settled back into the uncomfy chair and waited.

'Blesses was an asset, as you say. Irish lass whose family enjoyed the very close and permanently fatal attention of the Provos. So she had no family remaining, saw no way out, survived only because her man was something in the politics on the Republican side. Saved her, but not her family. Are you bored yet?'

'No.'

'She brought seriously excellent intel to a colleague. She wanted revenge, being a God-fearing Catholic girl and a firm believer in an Old Testament way of getting what she wanted. My colleague was a man of limited imagination and a wearyingly poor view of our task in that beautiful country, and he refused to sanction any form of direct retribution. He merely rattled on about seeing justice was done, utter meaningless nonsense like that. Happily, he'd asked me to sit with him while they talked, witnesses being valued more then than now.'

'The relentless march of progress.' Stoner sipped his own drink. Folded bread and cheese together and chewed them steadily. The Hard Man crumbled some cheese and chewed it less steadily. Sipped wine and swallowed carefully.

'I caught up with her before she left the building. Suggested – in a charming manner – that I employed a less conventional approach to intelligence matters, and that she might prefer to work with me a little. See how it worked out. She was suspicious, rightly, but when I offered to arrange a fatal beating if she supplied a target whose enmity and guilt she could prove – only to me – then she did develop a little enthusiasm. It worked very well.

'She has a way with her eyes. I can't tell you how it works – because I don't understand it – but it was brilliant as a way of getting useful intel from reluctant Provos. She didn't need to screw them, thus revealing to us how crap was the UK's honey-trap technique, but somehow made them want to talk to her about... well... everything. I mean that, everything. Anything.

'So I sent her on a psych course. Several of them, in the UK, US and the old GDR, where they were very, very good at that kind of thing. Really heavy spook stuff. Spooky, too. They trained her in the use of chemical encouragements, psychotropics mostly, which she could manipulate to great effect. Quite considerable effect, in fact. Very, very scary to observe. She was very different when she returned. Very. She… it's hard to describe. You've seen her in action, JJ. She… It's like she controls men, they want to do what she wants. It's like some massively exaggerated suggestion system. Works through the eyes. She looks at you and… you want to do what she wants to do. I used it lots, and to very great effect. She, more than any other single thing, got me into the position I was in before you popped all the bubbles with your knife.'

Stoner watched and waited. But the Hard Man appeared to have wound down, at least for the moment. 'She was in prison.' Stoner spoke quietly, considering his words. 'I helped put her there, as you know. A long time ago. When you debriefed me after that, you told me that she would stay away forever. Too dangerous to have around, you said. I wanted to kill her. I should have.' He paused, then laughed with a total absence of humour. 'Seems I should be better at killing people, huh?'

The Hard Man nodded. 'I'd not argue. After you won our own private war…'

Stoner interrupted him. 'Fuck it, matey. That was no war. Only you knew it for what it was. I believed we were on the same side. That's deceit. Shit at its most shitty.'

'We all make mistakes. That was one of my worst.' The Hard Man grimaced, sipped at more of the wine. 'The actual worst was deciding after you sliced me that I wanted to win our war anyway, and then deciding it was smart to free Blesses. Not an easy task for a dead man, as you'll appreciate, but I carry a lot of markers in the halls of Westminster. Carried. It's done now, pretty much. Retirement beckons, one way or the other.'

'Stop feeling sorry for yourself. This world-class up-fuck is down to you. Do you know where I can find Blesses?'

'You sure you want to, JJ? The stunt she pulled with

Lissa and Harding was nothing to do with me. Nothing. It was... Heartbreaking.'

'My heart weeps for you. I've heard conflicting stories about where Lissa went after her snuff film stardom. But I can't even think about that. Nothing else matters while Blesses is walking. How do I find her? I half expected her to walk in here. Does she know you're here? With me?'

The Hard Man shrugged. 'Not that I'm aware. We're not in touch. She didn't visit me in hospital. No flowers. Not even a card. Loyalty's not what it was.'

Stoner smiled a wry smile. 'The great betrayer betrayed in his own hour of need, huh?'

'Probably. She was supposed to go after you when she left the big house. Instead...' his words trailed off as he tried to avoid coughing, mostly successfully. He pulled a handkerchief from somewhere and dabbed at his lips. The blood was red, fresh. 'Ah, fuck this. If I set up Blesses for you, will that be the end? Can we have a stand-down? If not, and if you're going to come for me anyway, JJ, I'd rather end myself my own way.'

'Can you set her up?' Stoner mused aloud. 'If you point me at her, chances are that she'd know and then she'd know where I was and what I want, and... Far too stupid and complicated.' He reached a decision of sorts.

'Tell me nothing. Walk away from me. Give me a hint of a suggestion of a reason and I'll just take you down. You know that. You can trust me. You know that, too. I don't feel much... don't care much, as you know, but I am truly pissed with all this. If I paused for thought I'd end you here. So just fuck off and leave me alone. Go now.' Stoner laid a familiar blade on the table between them. Long, triangular in section, three-edged, dull and black. 'Just... go.'

'OK. This for free. Separate Menace from Mallis. Mallis refused to handle any contract which even looked a tiny bit like it might head your way. The man has a loyalty to you. Menace... the sister... is the opposite. You've come between them at some point. Mallis refuses to believe Menace would harm you or work against him.'

The doorbell chimed to announce an arrival. Stoner looked over to the door, the Hard Man sipped the flat red wine with no appearance of interest nor enjoyment. Probably not a great vintage. Chastity, her bright blonde hair concealed inside a headscarf, and her body bulked up by a heavy and considerably shapeless overcoat – a coat certainly large enough to conceal one of the smaller howitzers – walked past their static tableau and rang the service bell on the counter. No response. She rang it again with the same effect. She turned to the two men, no acknowledgement from either party, no sign of recognition.

'Service is well up to the usual standard,' she announced in a conversational way, her voice suggesting that she was a native of the American deep south. 'Long may it remain that way. We need to be on our way.'

The Hard Man looked up at her, eyes narrowed. 'Do I know you?' There was at least an echo of his voice's former strength in the question.

Chastity looked straight between his eyes. 'Not yet,' she replied. 'But he does. Come along, soldier. Sup up and saddle up. We're moving out.' Her deeply southern accent was excellent in its authenticity, anyone but a Mississippi native would have been convinced.

Stoner stood.

'So this is how it ends, JJ?' The Hard Man appeared to be unmoved by whatever was happening around him. 'Can you make it quick?' Stoner reached inside his clothing to a pocket, pulled out a roll of banknotes. Uncurled a couple of them, much more money than their meal had cost, folded them together and placed them under a saucer in the English way.

He followed Chastity towards the door, pausing to rest a hand on the Hard Man's shoulder. 'Another day. Maybe. Be good. Live long and prosper, as we used to say. If I decide to take you down, you'll feel nothing, know nothing about it. A promise.' As he held open the door for Chastity, he returned its sign so that it once again read 'Open'. There was no queue outside. The dull street was as empty of life as it was devoid of interest. A damp wind was the only activity.

24

OVER THE HILLS AND

Chastity was at the wheel of the fat camper van, anonymous among several thousands of its breed in the scenic heart of England. 'Look,' she said, suddenly. 'I know you old guys need to have a nap in the afternoon, and I respect that, but I need help with the directions.'

Stoner grunted alert. 'Sorry,' he said. 'I was thinking.'

'The snoring helps, does it? I'll try that one day. In the meantime, we're heading west. Remember?'

'Satnav.' Stoner rubbed his eyes and yawned, stretched, rolled his shoulders.

'Great idea. Just one flaw.' Chastity gestured at the dashboard. Stoner mimicked her gesture, transforming it at the last moment into a pointed finger, a finger he tapped onto the screen in the centre of the dashboard.

'Satnav,' he revealed, smugly.

'Reversing camera,' she replied, returning his smugness with added female superiority.

'You sure?'

'Sure. Try working it.'

'I've never... It doesn't light up when you reverse,' he countered, uncertainly and with added defensiveness.

'Try turning it on.' There is no defence against an

unkindly logical approach. Stoner reached for a map.

'Where are we going?' He ruffled the pages helpfully.

Chastity sighed, a deep and profound sound, almost like a whale. 'Put a battery into my cell phone. Add the SIM card. Read the instructions in the saved calls folder. Can you find that OK, or should we swap seats, you steer this barge while I operate the single brain we have between us?'

Stoner reassembled her phone, compared its instructions with the lines on the map, disassembled the phone, and issued directions. The camper van rolled onwards into the afternoon, heading west, gradually, as is the way with camper vans.

***

They were maybe a mile from the golf club, where Chastity's target was scheduled to meet his sticky end. Stoner suggested that they pull over, so he could adjust his clothing. Chastity obliged. 'We don't really have time for tea,' she remarked. 'One of us has a deadline to meet. Ho ho.'

'Change of plan. This is Plan P for Paranoia. OK with you?'

'So far. Your cosy brunch with Hartmann has reawakened all your warm cuddly feelings towards humanity in general?'

'Of course it has. Do you have a laser sight? A laser pointer I can see through a scope?'

Chastity mimed incomprehension. 'Gotcha,' she said finally. 'Yep. I have a laser marker in my make-up bag. Like you do. No, dope, I don't. Do you? Mr Paranoia carries around a sniper scope?'

Stoner pulled a dirty, scuffed bag from under the

alleged bed in the back of the camper van. 'As it happens,' he remarked, 'I do. It came with the rifle.' He unwrapped a rifle and pointed at it. Pointed the rifle out the window, just in case. 'This,' he shared kindly, 'is a rifle.'

'It's an antique.'

'Choosers, beggars, helpful thoughts like that.' Stoner worked the rifle's action a couple of times, detached the scope with its attached laser light, and handed this to Chastity, who switched it on, experimentally. 'While you were seducing possibly innocent businessmen and changing their sad lives forever for the better, I was saving the country from over-tooled thugs. Decent gun though, in its day. Will still go bang, I expect.'

'We are the antiques roadshow,' she remarked, sorrowfully. She switched off the light. 'Can I guess your great plan, oh great planner, or do you get some sexual delight from revealing all to an appreciative audience?'

'Go ahead. I'll give you a grade at the end.' Stoner shrugged out of his jeans and into a pair of camo-pattern biker pants. 'Reinforced knees,' he revealed, pointing at his knees.

Chastity shrugged. 'Useful for aggressive praying I guess. Whatever. I take the van, don't collect the useful, accurate, modern ordnance provided for me. Instead, I find a decent vantage, identify the mark, light him up in laser colour, and you blow a hole in him with your elephant gun. Or the scenery. Or anyone unfortunate enough to be nearby. Maybe even me, if I'm particularly lucky.'

'Are you feeling lucky, punk?'

'Yeah. Right. How's my estimate of your great plan?'

'Perfect. You truly are the genius I always knew you were. Flaws? Objections?'

'Question. Why the paranoia?' There was a tinge of concern in Chastity's query.

'Answers later, once we've seen how this pans out. OK?'

'Written on a postcard to my new address in Hell, if your shooting isn't up to the job?'

'It's well up to it. Good gun. I'll be close, so it just needs not to jam during a little rapid fire. Bolt action, y'know. Very 1940.'

Chastity shook her head again. 'Do you add the cartridge and ball separately?'

'Probably could, if it made you happy, but not today.' Stoner pointed to the map. 'Drop me here. Drive until you can get an oversight, then do the identification thing.'

'OK.'

***

'No show. No target guy. Wonder what that was all about?' Chastity had returned to their drop-off point, where she found Stoner leaning casually against a tree, entirely visible despite his camo pants. 'I'll fire up the cell and give Charm a toot.'

Stoner held up a hand. 'No. I'll climb into the back of this thing, lie on the floor. You drive into the car park, check that the vehicle with your promised ordnance is present and correct, ignore it, go into the club, and order food, drink for two, explain to your waiter that you're waiting for a friend.'

'I am?'

'No. After you've cracked open a bottle of something hideously over-priced, call a waitress – a waitress, blonde as you if there is one – and reveal that you've left your purse and all your money in the car. Ask the waitress to leg out and get it for you – from the vehicle Charm left for you. Unlocked? Key on a wheel?'

Chastity nodded. 'Key on the wheel, driver side rear. This is sounding a little tense, JJ.'

'Just my typical paranoia. Don't worry about it.'

'What do I do when super waitress woman turns up without my purse? I have my money in my pocket, as you'd hope.'

'Act like a dim blonde, look embarrassed, over-tip insanely and leave. Try to look remorseful, can you do contrite as well as embarrassed? Do you have a Girl Guides badge for obvious contrition?'

'Fuck off, Stoner.'

'That's my girl. Let's go.'

***

The explosion took out four vehicles, shredded the hapless waitress, killed an adulterous couple having unimaginative and tedious sex in the car parked adjacent to the bombmobile, and caused an elderly golfer to suffer a fatal coronary in the club's bathroom when the windows blew in. An impressive bang. Over dramatic, if anything, but certainly impressive.

Chastity sat with Stoner in the camper van. He had collected her from the club's suddenly hectic car park, removed them from the running and the shouting and had driven to a convenient parking space further down the approach road. He'd also produced cold ginger beer for them to sip in a genteel English manner while waiting to see who arrived at the scene and whether they could recognise anyone. The black smoke cloud, oily and heavy, hung above the club. The silence was considerable.

'Fuck me,' suggested Chastity, faintly. 'How did you know? That was aimed at me, right? Just me?'

'Yep.' Stoner could do short answers when required. He reached behind the seats, extracted two pairs of binoculars, one of which he passed to Chastity.

'We watch the road, see if we recognise anyone heading super-rapido for the golf club? With or without flashing lights, bells, whistles, all that stealthy silent approach stuff?' She was becoming familiar with Stoner's plans.

'You got it.' Stoner surveyed the countryside through his own long lenses.

'You knew this was going to happen, didn't you?'

'Nope.'

'This is that "Elementary, my dear Watson" moment? You demonstrate your vast spook voodoo mind reading stuff while I do the simpering girlie bit?'

'Nope. Vehicle approaching, just one, very fast. Too soon for the plods. There won't be much local unmarked plod out here anyway, and the city scuffers will send a chopper. It's a drama thing. They watch too much TV.'

'Got it.' Chastity focused on the approaching vehicle. '4x4, single visible occupant. Male. Don't recognise him. Not even faintly.'

Stoner opened the van's door. 'Stay out of sight, but shout when another car appears, OK?' He stepped into the road, waved his arms vigorously, unmistakably signalling the snatch Land Rover to pull up. It didn't even slow, simply lit its headlights and carried on. Stoner revealed a micro-Uzi semi-automatic pistol and emptied its entire magazine into the front of the oncoming vehicle, shredding both tyres, changed mags without breaking eye contact with the driver and raised the smoking hot muzzle so the driver could see what was coming for him, put a short burst – maybe four shots, maybe five, neatly grouped – through the passenger-side windscreen. The Land Rover bounced off the road and into the ditch, stopping suddenly.

Stoner was by the driver's door before it opened, gestured with the hot gun barrel for the driver to dismount. Which he did, slowly.

'Holy crap, Stoner. What the big blue fuck was that about?'

'No time, Mince. Nice to see you. Long time. How's the wife? Keep your hands empty. Before I cut you in half with this animal, which is what happens as soon as my spotter tells me about fresh company approaching, tell me what you're doing and who sent you. Quick now, I need to get on with my knitting. Retirement is such fun.'

The arrival snapped to a perfect military at-ease posture, hands behind his back, no weapon in sight, stared straight ahead. He was shorter than Stoner, but not by much, more obviously muscled, and moved with almost gymnastic grace for such a large man.

'Sitrep, body count, body photos. In, out and back to Hereford. That's it.'

'There's more. Hurry now. Patience short, bullets cheap. Keep your eyes on the skies.'

'I rigged the device, no target ID, instructions through...' he faltered. 'Through the agency.'

'Which?'

'Temple Mask. You know it.' A statement, not a question.

Stoner paused. 'Relax,' he said. 'You have a call to make here, Mince. Think quick. One of the bodies was a woman, badly wrecked, three others – maybe four – collateral. That's actually what you'll find at the scene, mostly, so you can make with the happy snaps. Can you remember all that?'

Mince nodded, moving his posture slowly and unconsciously to full attention. His hands appeared at his side, thumbs in line with the seams of his denims. 'Got it.'

Stoner gestured towards the lopsided Land Rover. 'Can you fix this thing and...'

'Can lose it. Not a problem.'

'I'll know it if you report anything other than as instructed, Mince. I will ask the Mask. You understand that?'

'Got it.' Mince stared straight ahead, not looking at Stoner. 'You the target for this, Stoner? I know the rules – if I'd known it was you I'd have declined the gig. I was told it was a woman, identity unfamiliar and unnecessary. Was it actually you?'

'Nope. And you never saw me because I was never here. Old time rules, same as always, Mince. Temple Mask. Long long time since I had that quoted at me. Still applies. Semper fi, as the cousins have it.'

'Got it. Temple masks everything and everyone. Will we see you again after... whatever this is? At the temple?'

'You will. Be fast and be silent. Live on; I'm gone.' Stoner swung into the cab of the camper van, fired up its weary diesel and left, pottering slowly away through the Cotswolds countryside as though there was no hurry in the world. None.

'Chopper.' Stoner pointed.

Chastity nodded. 'Care to share? Mince? Temple Mask? Some boys' club?'

'Exactly that. Old boys' club. Old soldiers. They... we meet up from time to time to remember our heroism, neglected brilliance, to whine and whinge about how unappreciated we all were.'

'Oh yes. I'm sure.'

'And it's a decent enough self-help society. Old soldiers... lots of soldiers retire fully fit, often without wanting to retire. The ones who enjoy the action, the danger, the adrenaline, the bullet dodging, and the entire big boys' toys thing. Provides troops for a lot of what we should call private security. Freelance action men. That's a whole wide world of possibilities in itself.'

'Mince? He looked seriously hard, fit and ugly.'

'He's all of those. We served a couple of hard tours together. Hard as they come and none too bright. Perfect merc. I'd not tackle him without the Uzi. Maybe an RPG or two. Drone strike would be best.'

Chastity shifted her attention from the road ahead to Stoner, then back again. 'You think he'll report as you told him to?'

'Yep. He has no reason not to, and every reason to do so.'

'Don't understand, JJ. Why?'

Stoner glanced her way, swung the camper van onto a long, less winding road heading south. He sighed. 'OK,' he began, then stopped himself. He swallowed, banged both hands onto the wheel in a sudden, shocking split-second of violence, then calmed again, though it was plainly a struggle. 'Did you see how he looked straight ahead?'

'Yeah. Eye on the sky, like you said to him. Never once into the van or around him or anything. Not even at you, which was weird.'

'Nope. He didn't see you. Even if he was heavy-questioned – which isn't very likely and would certainly not be easy – he would only be able to reveal that he'd seen me. No one else. He'll change his wheels, go to the golf club, take his pics, skulk around like the freelance he is, then head home to report. And he'll report as instructed. By me.'

'Why? The Temple Mask thing?'

'Don't sound scornful. The old boys' network just saved your life. And whoever ordered the contract on you, that's you, Chastity Weise, not some no-mark no-show in a golf club, ordered it through the Temple, that person will think you're dead meat... at least for a while. Maybe forever, depends on who they are and how hard they look at the wreckage and remains.'

Chastity considered. The silent miles mounted, the roads grew steadily wider until they hit the motorway. After a while, as Stoner swung the camper van into a service area to fuel both the vehicle and its occupants, she asked the obvious question, her voice steady, restrained, toneless almost.

'Is Charm behind this?' It hung in the air like an obscure curse. Stoner parked up, switched off.

'Coffee. Cake.'

Chastity remained where she was, leaning slightly forward, as though coiled, ready to pounce. Her breathing was steady and her eyes were closed.

'Is she?' she asked. 'Is Charm behind this?'

Stoner pulled key from switch, bounced it in his hand, stared silently at her until she opened her eyes, turned her head and looked at him.

'I have no idea,' he said. 'She must be involved – connected – at some level. That's only what it feels like. No evidence.'

Chastity uncurled, like some hard female predator. 'She set me up. That's it.'

Stoner shook his head. 'Maybe so. Maybe not. She accepted the contract and whoever placed it relied on you following your usual procedure. So Charm, or whoever she uses to put the ordnance in place for you, did exactly that, Mince came along and rigged the device, just as he said. He's good. Boom, it went. An easy way to go. Clean. You'd have felt nothing.'

'Good to know. Like fuck it is. Who placed the contract?'

Stoner stepped out of the camper van. 'I don't know,' he said finally. 'And it's not the first time, is it? But unlike you, because I'm not officially dead, even temporarily, I can ask. And I will. Trust me. The Temple tells the truth to its Templars.' He waited while Chastity left the van, plipped its locks closed, and beckoned her to him. 'Do you trust me?' he asked, gently, almost softly. He focused his gaze somewhere an inch or two behind her eyes, staring into her head.

She nodded. Stared at the ground between them, not at him. Nodded again.

He offered her his arm, she took it. 'Let's go eat,' he suggested. 'Plotting and scheming is easier on a full stomach, and this has been a catastrophic day food-wise.'

***

They were into the road once more, still heading south. The radio reported no news at all about a fatal blast at a Cotswolds golf club. Maybe it was too common an occurrence to merit even a little hysteria. Footballer Stubs Toe, Horse Wins Race, Politician Tells Lie headlines and much weary discussion thereof. National radio at its best.

Chastity was aiming the camper van towards its spiritual home, the surflands of its ancestors, Stoner stretched out across the remaining space in the cockpit.

'Do you really think that Chas is not behind this?' Her voice was loud enough only to be heard over the weary wheeze and clatter of the engine, her tone calm, maybe restrained.

'No reason to think otherwise.' Stoner hefted himself into a more conventional sitting position, raised the back of the seat, checked his watch, the dashboard clock and the odometer. Habit, he supposed.

'It could be that we're supposed to jump to that conclusion. Could equally easily be the opposite. I can see advantage to whoever's actually behind this in either conclusion. Or in no conclusion at all. If the hit had taken, then you'd not be thinking anything, and whoever the puppet master is would still have nothing to worry about.'

Chastity gripped the wheel a little tighter. The van wandered slightly until she relaxed and corrected it. 'Your reasoning always makes my brain hurt. If this, then that; if the other thing then that other thing. Like a bleeding robot. An adding machine. Why would Chas... Charm want to take me out?'

'Don't know. How could I? You will know if it is actually the case. You might not know what it is that you know, but...'

Chastity smiled. A grim smile, but better than the shallow glower which had preceded it. 'And why would someone else want me to think she'd tried?'

Stoner reclined the seat again, unable to get comfortable, it seemed. 'A simple failsafe. You survive, you blame Charm, you are enraged beyond all reason, murder your last sister and leave the guilty party free to do... whatever. That whatever is another wide-open ocean of possibility. And speculating in that ocean is pointless, because without an understanding of the mission objective there's no hope of reaching any form of accurate conclusion.'

'You've done this before?'

'I have.' Stoner paused for a breath or two. 'Ask yourself where your glamorous band of lethal ladies get your contracts from? How close does Charm keep that side of it to her heaving bosom?'

Chastity considered her reply before delivering it. 'From those weird black'n'white Gothic guys, mostly. The techno prisoners. You know them.'

'Makes sense. Fits. From Menace, but not Mallis, I think. So the good sister Charm deals with them, not you?'

'Yeah.'

'And she doesn't talk about them to you?'

'Maybe she does. I don't have to listen. She talks about a lot of things. You, for example, the first time she got the benefit of your infamously mighty pork sword.'

'You're just distracting me here. Why?'

'I'm thinking. I've dealt with them both, but only remotely, and by phone talk and text, don't think I've done face to face at all. Not sure. Listened to lots of their stuff with Charm, thought. We usually put the phone onto speaker – more polite. Transparent. What's your take? More of your take.'

Stoner paused, watched the road ahead for a while, then the passing scenery for another, longer while. 'Think it all ties in with what went down last year. Think – know, in fact – that the Hard Man was terminating his network, me included, and I suspect that Menace, the potentially female half of the desperate duo, decided to take advantage of this, to fill an approaching vacuum and to maybe split from her... brother, Mallis. Mallis really doesn't seem to have been in the loop, because he was instrumental in me surviving the Hartmann encounter, then extracting you from Israel last year, and he even flew to the States to see me a couple weeks ago. It's hard to see why he'd do that if he was part of a plan to replace everyone in the old wetwork network. Make sense?'

'Only if I refuse to think about it. Wetwork network?'

'Everyone needs a silly name or two. Helps the sanity.'

'It does? So what happens next? What's your great new action plan?'

'Patience, Chastity. Patience.'

She laughed, gently. 'You mean you don't have a clue.'

'Exactly. Actually, no. I do. But I can't see how to make it happen. What I can reveal is that I'm a little sick of running and hiding.'

'You said that before.'

'I did?'

'You did.'

'OK.' Stoner lapsed back into broody silence. The drone of the VW diesel engine provided the least inspirational backing track in the history of soundtracks. Then, suddenly; 'Next junction, turn around. Head to The Smoke.'

'Fuck's sake.' Chastity's lack of amusement was unhidden.

'Belay that. Carry on to Cornwall.'

'For fuck's sake, Stoner. What is in your head?'

'I'm giving you a demonstration of indecision.'

Chastity's calm was restored, at least the appearance of calm. 'OK,' she said after a while. 'This demo. Explain it.' They had run out of motorway and were heading into the dark of Dartmoor.

'Loose ends. I hate them. One of the big screaming loose ends is Shard and Lissa. One trusted source tells me where they are, and that they're together. Another tells me they're somewhere else – or that Lissa is. Either or neither can be true. So I decided to go check. Then I realised there was no point to that, and changed my mind – hence the instruction to head to London, and then not. Shard would be a good gun, but his brain's already been melted too many times to make him reliable, and although Lissa is a lot – a whole lot – more than you think she is, I'm unsure of her connection to Blesses. That enough explanation, sweet Chastity?'

'Yes. So far as it goes. You believe Blesses is core to this?'

Stoner nodded, unwrapped a boiled sweet which he'd produced from nowhere and sucked it, noisily like a child. 'Yeah. It all makes sense seen from her perspective. So I need to think like she thinks.'

Chastity burst into sudden genuinely amused laughter, then calmed it. 'You don't know what you think yourself, JJ, so how the hell can you think like some psycho super-bitch killer dude voodoo hell-woman?'

'You make her sound attractive.'

'Don't think I ever met her, but the brochure looks nice.'

Stoner sucked on his sweet contemplatively. 'Yeah. Guess so. First time I met her I thought she was someone else. Next time I met her she tried to kill me.'

'A woman of great taste, then.'

'Exactly. And it's easier to understand most other people than it is to be honest with yourself about your own motives. Particularly if you're not sure what the end game you're after actually is. What you actually want. My view of the future changes from day to day.' He sighed, long and deep. 'I've always been a soldier, Chas. Always reported to an officer through a solid chain of command. Always, even when there was only one officer – the Hard Man – and the chain had only a single link – him and me. It feels seriously strange to look into the future without an objective, without a task. The only gig I can actually see is to sort out Blesses, once and forever. Apsart from staying alive... and not letting my friend... OK, friends, down. This is what Temple Mask is for. I wish... yeah... I do wish I'd thought of it before.'

Chastity nodded. Swung the camper through a series of ever smaller roads, finally entering the Principality of Cornwall. Night surrounded them, and the roads were quiet and dark.

Stoner again. 'Tonight we'll crash out in the camper. That OK with you? Look for a campsite and flash the cash and that glamorous girlie grin of yours.'

'Paranoia again, JJ?'

'Yep. Too many people still seem to know more of what we're doing than we do. And you're dead, at least for a little while. In any case, I need to chat with Charm. It's long overdue.'

***

'Thank Christ!' Charm's voice shouted from the cell phone's speaker. It made her sound shrill. Chastity and Stoner sat on opposite sides of the table in the van, curtains drawn, lights off, illumination provided only by the phone's screen. 'I was worried weak. What happened?'

Stoner replied, quietly, sombrely. 'It's only me,' he revealed, repeating the phrase quite possibly the least popular and most over used in the short history of cellular telephony. 'I've used Chastity's phone because it has your numbers.'

Silence followed for a while. Stoner was excellent at silences. As patient as snipers always are.

'JJ,' Charm found a voice, a weak voice, uncertain and uncharacteristically nervous. Quiet. 'Can I speak with Chas? Please.'

'Not easily. I've no idea where she is. I thought you'd know. I assume she has more than one phone. We were supposed to talk tonight. When I called her, this is the phone that rang. Interesting, huh?'

Charm sounded more nervous, if anything. 'How did you get her phone?'

'Long story. Nothing exciting. She's not with you?'

'No. Where are you?'

'I'll not say on the phone, if it's all the same with you.' Stoner paused. 'My usual preservative paranoia – y'know.' He laughed a quiet laugh, which produced an odd strangled response with no recognisable words. 'You OK? You sound pretty strange.'

'I think...' Charm's voice faded to silence, then returned a little stronger. 'Have you heard the news?'

'Excuse me?'

'Have you seen the news about a terrorist bombing near Hereford?'

'No.' Stoner's denial was emphatic and honest. 'Tell me. Do I need to check the news feeds? Terrorists? In Hereford? That's bold. Squaddies won't like that one little bit.' He inserted a dramatic pause. 'You telling me that Chastity's involved in a terror attack in Hereford? Say not; that would be one stupid stunt to pull. I mean that. I know a lot of guys in and around the city. What should I be asking them? Do you have other contact numbers for her?'

'She took a job.' Charm's struggle with her voice was either genuine or excellent acting. Stoner had no view on which it might be. Chastity remained silent, as she had throughout. 'Simple thing, routine. Easy for her. Drill is confirmation as soon as, simple exit. Now the news is reporting explosions, several deaths and no news here from Chas. Fuck.' She burst into sudden disastrous sobbing and hung up.

Stoner turned to the missing Chastity. 'Sounded genuine enough to me. Thoughts? You know her better than I do.'

'Only in some senses.' Chastity swung her feet up onto the cushion beside her. 'Hard to say. The being genuine, I mean. She's always been a brill actress. Hard, like I say, especially over a phone. Sounded straight enough to me, but I know her too well to believe everything she says.' She picked up the phone, logged on to a news service, scrolled around until she found the item she was looking for. Read it, then passed the phone to Stoner, who skimmed through it, then switched to a rival news service, read their own report, then on to a third. Shut down the device and stripped it, more out of habit than anything else, it seemed, providing work for his otherwise idle hands.

He produced the Uzi, as from a hat, laid it out on the cloth it had been wrapped in, and proceeded to strip it, clean it, oil it, reassemble it. Repeat. All the while in silence. Then: 'The trouble with our world is that beyond a point it's not possible to trust anyone. I've been at that point for too long. If I try to see beyond it, all I get is a headache. No clarity. When I'm here with you I can trust you because I can see you and because you've appeared straight in every one of your dealings with me. If you intended harm, you'd have done it by now, so I'm decently comfortable with you. If I couldn't see you, didn't know what you were up to, it would be just another worry. Another effort at trust. And I'm very low on trust right now.'

Chastity said nothing, seemingly listening to him and to her own inner dialogue at the same time.

Time passed. Stoner cleaned and reassembled the same weapon three more times, packed a half dozen magazines for it, wiping each shell with gun oil and checking their free movements in the company of their brother shells. 'Time to sleep,' he suggested. 'Things should look better in the morning, so they say.'

Chastity said nothing, rooted out a sleeping bag and disappeared inside it. Stoner stepped out of the van into the late evening. Stepped back, pulled the keys to the van from a pocket and placed them on the table in front of Chastity's silent open eyes. He packed a small bag with an assortment of items, slung it over a shoulder and returned to the side door. 'Going for a run. Few miles will do me good.' He looked at her shrouded form. 'I'd understand if you need to be somewhere else.' He slid the door shut behind him, and ran into the dark, almost silently.

25

TAKING IT EASY

The campsite was sparsely populated, the time of the season being a while past, but even so there was plenty of evidence of hearty breakfast activity. Small crowd, though, and certainly no crowding, although the still air managed to carry and share the welcoming odours of coffee brewing and pork products frying.

'You have a plan, then? Made up your mind about what's going to happen?' The fit blonde woman lazed back in a fragile chair while the darker, bearded man fixed a breakfast almost entirely devoid of healthy food.

'Party.'

'Say again?' Chastity sat upright. 'Did you say party?' She laughed, genuine amusement, a rare commodity.

Stoner shovelled butter-fried things onto a single plate, planted the plate onto the flimsy table, lifted a coarse loaf and a heavy knife and sliced the one with the other. 'In the meantime, while waiting for the funny hats, balloons, ribbons and stuff, a pot of coffee would be nice. Whatever's left on the plate after the coffee lands is yours.' He lifted blackened bacon onto heavy bread, added a hard fried egg, formed a sandwich and lifted the construction to his mouth. Bit deep and chewed with every appearance of happiness. Chastity dived inside the camper van, reappearing after only two bites with a pot of fresh coffee, two mugs and accoutrements.

'Two can play at planning,' she said, pouring for two.

Stoner wiped his face, spreading any residual greases more evenly around his facial hair, swallowed and reached for the coffee. 'Indeed. Let's share. What's your plan, o fabled angel of death? I always liked that. Suited you. Have you ever noticed how many angels are blondes, despite blondes being a little on the unusual side among the several tribes of Palestine?'

'Can't say I'd noticed.' Chastity had constructed an improbable sandwich of her own, and was contemplating it with either anticipation, relish or terror, depending. 'You're very happy, suddenly. Having a plan makes you happy?' She bit.

Stoner watched over her while she chewed. 'Yeah,' he agreed, finally. 'It does. Also cherubs.'

'What?'

'Cherubs are also notably blonde and have curly hair. They're also fat, inevitably. What does that tell you about Christianity?'

She laughed again. 'That you can't believe a word of it.'

'Exactly. Right then.' He leaned back, returned a waved greeting from a total stranger who plainly believed that spending nights in camper vans revealed a shared psyche or something, and scratched his beard. 'This needs to go,' he remarked.

'What? The beard? It suits you. Makes you look almost human, y'know?'

He smiled back, a picture of middle-aged happiness sitting outside a camper van in a field opposite a truly attractive and rather younger blonde woman with obvious athletic tendencies, while his inner man attempted to digest a week's worth of heavy calories. No passer-by would have looked twice. True security.

'Then it stays. I never did enjoy shaving. Who wants to kill you, angel of death?'

She grimaced around her mastication. Swallowed. Followed the swallow with a slip of her coffee. 'Seriously? I don't know. Which is the downside of rarely knowing who you've been contracted to take out and why. But you know all that, former sergeant Stoner. And I bet you have a theory.'

'I do.'

'Let's hear it, then. Stop dicking around.' There was a smile with the insult, but a marginal smile at best.

'It's a thing, isn't it? Here I go. Feel free to interrupt.' He drained his coffee mug, parked it on the fragile table between them. Rather to his surprise, Chastity refilled first his cup, then her own. 'You were set up last year, more than once. We'll never know why, probably, but we can work out who. That's what I've tried to do.' He sipped a little more.

'I'm a simple soul. I always look for a simple answer. In this case it would be just too easy to get distracted by the detail, so the first assumption is that as we share our working world, we should look at players known to us both who would have a motive. That's not many people, to be honest. At least, not that I can identify.'

'Your view is that whoever set me up for the bomb yesterday is the same person who set me up before? In Germany and in Israel?'

Stoner nodded. Sipped cautiously.

'If that's the case, why the gap? Why didn't your theoretical me-hater carry on and take me down any time over the last year? There've been several other jobs in that time.'

Stoner nodded again. 'I would imagine that the new attempt was because I've reappeared. I'd guess that you on your own aren't a danger to your anti-fan, and quite possibly I'm not either, though that's less likely. You'n'me together, though. A different beast. We are an effective team, us.'

Chastity smiled, a little grimly. 'I have seen the movie.'

'One of the best. Up there with Mary Poppins and Sin City. Much the same.' He paused, sipped, and picked up his own thread. 'I could spend an hour going through everything I thought, re-thought, re-re-thought, so forth, but there's no point. I'd defeat my own logic and send you running away, screaming. It's Menace.' He stopped talking abruptly and watched his companion's face.

'OK,' she said. 'Care to share some of your reasoning?'

'Not really. Not now. Later, maybe. Assuming there is a later.' He paused again. 'That bit was just for dramatic effect.'

'Hard luck. Try again.'

'Blesses is the key. Menace and Blesses make a superlative contract killing crew. Hard to fault. They'd clean up in the freelance market we all know and love.' He stopped again, sipped again, and watched her expression, again.

'OK so far.' Was all she said. Then: 'I'll think it through later, while driving or sleeping off breakfast, or something. OK?'

He nodded. 'The why of it could be so many reasons that only a woman could understand them all at once, we guys being a bit slow in the cognitive processing wossname, but what works best for me is the simple theory that the easiest way to boost a business like ours without government sponsorship is to take out all the serious opposition. That has several effects, all of them beneficial from a product marketing perspective.'

'Say again?'

'The crew who take me down are going to crow about it in their promotional campaign.'

'What?'

Stoner sighed. 'It's all about rep. Reputation. Top spenders buy top product. Top spenders are either governments – who have their own professional resources to take all credits and who rely on freelance labour to take the blame – or they're big corporations, who always prefer deniability, cut-outs and completely reliable contractors. Menace would be perfect for that. She simply needs to make with the regret that her longtime top buddy and associate, yadda yadda, Mallis has been cruelly ripped from her by a bunch of bastards upon whom she's already visited seriously heavy retribution – in other words, you'n'me are already daisy fodder by that point – for her customers, who were previously customers of her and Mallis, to take the logical path, the easy path, which is to continue to use her services until she screws up. Which she won't. Because, sweet Chastity, she has all the contacts which Mallis maintained and navigated so well. And she has Blesses, who knows an awful lot of the right people, to do the right thing when she needs them to do it. And has her own special talents, of course.' He paused. 'How'm I doing?'

Chastity shrugged. 'Sounds fine to me. But I don't know enough to argue with you. Charm might. But I can't talk to Charm because Charm thinks I'm dead. Doesn't she? Or do you think her performance on the phone was exactly that? A performance?'

Stoner shrugged. 'What goes in must always come out, otherwise we'd explode, which would be horrid.' He stood, surveyed the campsite. 'I'm off to a place where even angels of death fear to tread. While I'm there, attempting to lose a little body mass in a sanitary way, why don't you give her a call? Use one of the stolen phones and ask her how she is?'

If Chastity was surprised by his suggestion, she hid it well. 'OK. Should I be asking her anything else? Like who the fuck? And things like that?'

'No clue. Play it by ear. You can tell her you're with me if you want, just let me know what you've said once you've said it, so I don't appear even more prattish than usual. I do really need to take a long walk over there,' he gestured vaguely, 'but if you feel – believe – that she's on the level with you, that she didn't set you up, which I don't think she did, then tell her that I'd like to have a party, and it would be uber-cool if she arranged it. In the Blue Cube. That would be cool and confusing as all fuck. Excuse me.'

And he left at a brisk pace, marching like the military man towards the toilet block. Everyone stands aside for a man with a purpose.

26

SHAKE IT UP BABY

Sometimes the subtle approach is the best. Other times the better way is to knock on a door and ask for entry. Stoner had considered several of the options open to him, and had decided that the time for subtle, sly observation and careful situational analysis and preparation was over. He posted his only sentry, his security, muscle and back-up rolled into one at a suitable location, walked up to the main entrance to a house he owned, unlocked the door and let himself in. No one welcomed him home. No one attempted to deny him entry, either, thus proving once again that nothing is certain. Great quiet. Stoner looked around him, breathed in the background smell of the house, which should have been familiar but was not, as unfamiliar as the silence, in fact.

Although the house, old and rambling as it was, with sundry items of minor architectural interest, such as a red brick turret at one of its five corners, was divided up into apartments, all entirely self-contained, it still boasted both a common entry hallway and a large common kitchen. Stoner walked from the former into the latter. At least the visuals of the old house were familiar, along with the locations of the many items usually associated with a kitchen, especially a kitchen in a house populated by residents of several nationalities and ethnic groups, so a stack of woks shared space with saucepans, and hand-powered spice grinders rested alongside a decently proportioned electric blender. There were a lot of knives, too.

Stoner clattered around apparently happily and dug out a tin of coffee beans from a freezer. Shook his head and tutted quietly, hung his heavy biker jacket from the back of a sturdy wooden chair before walking to a cupboard, still the resting place of a coffee-scented hand grinder, and set about grinding the frozen beans. Every so often he would stop the grind, pause and inhale the gradually increasing aroma of the beans. Finally he fitted a fresh filter to an electric machine, loaded it with coffee and water from a tap, switched it on, and hefted himself up to perch on a work bench.

'Hey, Shard,' he remarked to the other man, the man silently standing in the doorway. 'Hey. How's it going, huh?' Stoner's tone was friendly, almost concerned, certainly genuine. A second figure appeared behind Shard. Female, as tall as the man, and black, very black, with harsh pale stubble sugar-coating her scalp. She pushed past the man Shard.

'JJ.' She walked into the kitchen, self-assured and upright. Stopped by the coffee machine and inspected its contents. 'Made enough for three?'

'Depends.' Stoner stretched out his legs as though contemplating the scuffed toes of his heavy Caterpillar boots. 'Care to join me? Am I welcome here?'

The black blonde walked across the room and swung herself up onto the worktop next to Stoner, rested her hand on his thigh. 'Better late than never, huh, JJ?' She squeezed his leg, not hard, far enough down the limb to be not quite provocative. 'How've you been, anyway?' The third party, Shard, the man in doorway, said nothing, observed in silence, resting and maybe relaxed against the door's framing wood.

Stoner sat silent for a beat, maybe several, turned to face the woman beside him. Looked closely, almost into her eyes. Lifted his hand and moved it to her face. Drew a finger lightly down the softly-lined skin below one deep black eye. Nine blue tears were tattooed in an irregular and incomplete pattern. His finger traced them. He nodded.

'You look well,' he said, quietly, almost conversationally. 'Very well. Better than I'd expected. That's good to see.' He took his hand back. 'Very good to see. Very good indeed.'

'You're thin, JJ. Skinny even. Not like the old days.' The Dirty Blonde gestured towards Shard; clean-shaven, broad-shouldered, buzz-cut Shard. 'Back then, you and he were almost identical. My toy soldiers. My own band of brothers.'

'We were like brothers.' Stoner directed his next comment to the man still standing silent in the doorway. 'Closer than brothers. Appearances can be misleading.'

The Dirty Blonde dropped smoothly, silently from the worktop, turned to face him. Slim, long-boned, dark clothing perfectly fitting, hanging perfectly from her tall black form. She did some things with her hands, shoulders, hips, and her clothes fell away, settling around her feet while she held his gaze, then looked down at herself, beautiful in her underwear. She took two steps towards Stoner, reached and caught his right hand in her left, pulled it towards her until his fingers traced the scar across her belly. An almost invisible scar, perfectly repaired, perfectly sealed and healed, the muscles beneath the near-black skin flat and toned and firm.

Stoner left his fingers in contact with her belly, breathed in her familiar scent like a predator would. His eyes held hers. 'No infection?'

She shook her head. 'None. The blade was clean and sharp. The hand holding it was steady and swift, the placing of it as precise as possible. Skilful.' She dressed again, smooth economy of muscular motion transforming a simple action into dance.

'How... how did you get away? How d'you get out?' Stoner sounded more confused, stumbling almost, than he would have preferred.

The Dirty Blonde sighed, deeply, a continental divide between them. 'Wrong question, JJ. Wrong question. Too often with you... you ask the wrong question.' Her composure, her self-control were excellent. 'The big question was... where were you? The whole thing was set up just for you. A two-man show for an audience of one, and that audience wasn't even present. So it became a one act play for the cameras. Because you weren't around. Were you?'

There was no accusation in her flat response, no levelling of guilt nor blame. Her poise was complete. She hopped up once again to the worktop, took Stoner's hand, the hand which had traced the long scar on her stomach. Squeezed it. 'It was a dangerous day, JJ. And it was all for your benefit. And you weren't there.' She turned to face him directly, let go of his hand.

Which drifted while both the Dirty Blonde and Stoner followed its apparently independent movement. It drifted to her face, to the pattern of tiny blue tears below her eye. Touched them. Hung there, holding the entire attention of at least two of the three people in the room.

'Tell me about it,' Stoner suggested, quietly. His hand fell back to the shared and neutral surface between them. 'Help me understand.' He looked up, measuring the other man, Shard, as though for the first time. Neither man spoke to the other. Shard stood, leaning still, Stoner sat, a seemingly permanent new arrangement.

The Dirty Blonde sat still and silent, eyes focused on something so very far away, too far away to even try to describe, maybe.

'Tell me about Blesses.' Stoner's quiet words lifted the haze from the Dirty Blonde's face. Her features seemed to sharpen, to gain focus, her eyes met his once again.

'Yes,' she said. 'Blesses. Long-time friend of yours, JJ, she said. She said... she implied much more, and she knows you completely. Up to a point. That became clear to me later. Too much later.' She laughed, suddenly, incongruously. 'A friend, she said. Tell me.' The Dirty Blonde's eyes shone with misplaced mischief. 'Tell me, JJ. Was she another lost lover?'

He shook his head. 'No.' It was his turn for introspection. 'No.' He looked up and spoke with conviction, firmly almost. 'No. And she cost me a life I didn't know I wanted until she killed it. And she did to me what I imagine she did to Shard over there, so I was incapable of stopping her.' He glanced over to the other man, who still hadn't moved, who still propped up the doorway. Stoner fell silent: the Dirty Blonde spoke again.

'Blesses introduced herself to me at your club, at the Blue Cube. You'd just done a disappearance. You'd cost me a life I didn't know I wanted until you killed it. Nearly killed him. Hartmann. Sinner and saviour.' The Dirty Blonde spoke gently, softly, as though mostly to herself. 'You thought you were defending me, somehow. You're a man, JJ. You think only in straight lines and you think almost only of yourself – of what you would want and how you might best get it – whatever it is. Women are better than that. We can think in curves. We can see how a change can improve everything for more than one person. You...' she rested her hand on his thigh again. 'You're smarter than most men. You almost killed the man who would have saved us – us, JJ, you and me – because you were jealous of him.'

Stoner rested his hand on hers, which was somehow once again on his thigh. 'No,' he said. 'I wasn't jealous. I tried to kill Hartmann – the Hard Man, or "that twat" as you were prone to call him – because he took out a contract on me. A fatal contract. A hit.' He lifted his hand from hers, which remained on his thigh. Resting.

'That true?' She stared at the floor, then up at the leaning Shard, then sidelong at Stoner. 'Is that the truth?'

Stoner nodded. 'Yep. Pretty much. There was betrayal everywhere. It was that time of year, or something. I... let him live for you, Lissa. If what he offered was what you wanted, then... then OK.'

'Have you spoken to him?'

'Yes.'

'And?' She was still gazing at him, eyes narrowed, thinking, or something very close to it.

'And nothing. He apologised. He talks very badly now. I don't understand how it's not repairable – most things are – but he leaves his voice sounding like a meat mincer.' He glanced over at Shard, but there was no change there, no reaction. 'He admits his error, his mistake, miscalculation. In his eyes, that's what it was; an error of judgement. He thought that Chastity – the killer, you must have met her – would take me out while

I was trying to figure out who the killer was, and why they were taking out the guys – all guys – who were dying. Was it only a year or so ago? Feels like a lifetime... several lifetimes.'

The Dirty Blonde moved her hand from Stoner's thigh to her own. 'Did it occur to you that maybe Hartmann wanted you out of the way so he could play housey-housey with me? So he could have me all to himself without you cluttering up the place?'

'No.' Stoner stood, stretched. 'You're a hooker. He bought your services just like any of your rich johns.' He lifted himself back onto the worktop beside her. 'No Mr Tran?' he wondered. 'Seems strange, the old house not smelling like a Chinese takeaway.'

'Vietnamese,' she corrected. 'And no. He's been away for some time now, on and off. Rarely speaks when he is here. Sometimes others of his...family appear, stay a while, leave. They're very quiet, they all have keys, they don't bother us.' She looked first at the leaning Shard then at the seated Stoner. 'He changed suddenly from the neighbourly, friendly guy I knew straight after the horror movie with Blesses, like he knew about it. Came to visit me in hospital, spoke with some of the staff there, asked me how I was, if I was OK for everything. Then zip. When I got back here he was already mostly gone. He came down here one afternoon, bearing tea – you remember how he loved his tea? – and apologised for Blesses. I was way up my own arse then, didn't care about anything and I hurt a lot, so I wasn't thinking. Mr Tran told me off, in that weird chiding friendly way, for not asking him how you were. Amazing. I told him I didn't care how you were. If you'd cared about me you'd have protected me from Blesses. Shit like that.'

She paused. The three of them shared a long silence.

'He told me that you were unwell, in America and that you might die. That I should think of others – of you.' The Dirty Blonde's tone of voice was more animated than before, although still quiet, controlled, subdued and spookily calm. 'He told me that you were the only good thing in my life and that I was a fool. That was the exact word. Fool.'

Stoner smiled then. 'I bet that went down well.'

'I told him to fuck off. That he was dead wrong, shit like that. He just smiled, smiled and bowed. The tea didn't make me dizzy, like it did whenever Blesses made it. When she was here the tea always made me feel drugged, good and stoned, and it sent Shard into a world beyond, or some shit like that.' She looked up at Shard, but that man was a study in statuary, impassive as carved stone on an island.

'Mr Tran visited me in the States.' Stoner spoke quietly, then drifted off into the silence again. 'He saved your black arse, Lissa. Didn't you know that?'

She stared at him. 'The fuck?'

'He did. He protected you, maybe that guy too...' he gestured at Shard in the doorway. 'Mr Tran did whatever it took to keep you safe while you got better. Who arranged the hospital?'

The Dirty Blonde shook her head slowly, looked over at Shard, who looked only at Stoner – at the distance between them. 'I'd thought... he had.' A gesture towards Shard again. 'Not Mr Tran. Why?'

'Don't know.' Stoner was also watching Shard, carefully. 'Ask him, why don't you? Mr Tran also told me that even he didn't know where you were, not exactly and until you got better, in case he got picked up and suffered information extraction, which is like dental extraction but less fun.'

The Dirty Blonde, nodded, slowly. 'It took about a month after the show before I was in any way actually really... aware. There were a lot of ambulances and then cars, and white rooms. I'd forgotten.'

Stoner rested his hand on her thigh now. 'Mr Tran apologised for introducing Blesses to you and to Shard. It was a mistake, not an act of violence.'

'Another mistake, huh? The world's filled with mistakes, suddenly.'

'He had no idea what she was capable of. That's what he says, and I believe him. No reason not to. If anything, you owe your life to him.'

The Dirty Blonde snorted. 'So I should feel gratitude to him? Not disgust at the stunt Blesses pulled? That's hard, even for you, JJ.'

Stoner shrugged, said nothing. He was mainly observing the stationary Shard, who was in turn observing him.

'What about us, JJ?' The Dirty Blonde had more to say, and rasped her long black fingers with their painted hooker nails through the short white stubble on her scalp as if for emphasis. 'Where are we now? You expect to take up where we left off? When you cleared off on your long vacation?'

Stoner stood. He considered the floor's tiling, then the still static Shard. 'There is no us,' he said, slowly and clearly. 'Maybe there never really was.' He heaved his shoulders and rolled them, swung his hips to ease them after their long time on the tough worktop. 'You're welcome to stay here while you decide what you want. I doubt Mr Tran will want to help move you much, but he's a secure guy, so if you feel threatened he'd be more help than I will.' He headed for the door.

The Dirty Blonde dropped to her feet. 'That's it?' she

said, a rare and savage expression clamped onto her features. 'Just like that?'

Stoner turned back to her, took the two paces necessary to bring them face to face, and rested his finger on the blue tattoo tears. 'More dead relatives, Lissa?' His hand fell away and his voice grew more quiet. 'Or more dead memories of your old country, babe? Maybe you could take a vacation back in the homelands, settle a few more scores? Be easier done from there than here, I'd imagine. There must be some of your old... friends that you'd like to watch meet their makers. Maybe Shard could help you, huh?' He turned to face that man in the doorway, but he'd gone. Stoner turned back to the Dirty Blonde.

'You're OK with Shard?' He sounded vaguely interested rather than concerned. 'With the guy who raped you and sliced out your insides?' He spread out his open palms before her. 'Excuse me for the question. I'd wondered whether you'd have killed the guy rather than set up home with him.' He smiled, suddenly. 'Home in my house, too. Wonders, they never cease.'

Mixed and conflicting expressions flittered like squalls across her beauty. 'He wasn't himself, JJ. You can have no idea of the man's remorse. His contrition and loyalty. And anger. Remember, you left him exposed. He had your back, and you left him behind. Where she found him.'

Stoner nodded. 'Question, then, Lissa, then I'll do what I have to do and leave you in peace. Maybe... see how it goes... maybe we'll catch up again. I would like that, somehow. But not yet.'

'Question?' she prompted him, not unkindly, her eyes holding his once more.

'You trust him?' He gestured to the empty doorway. 'Trust him with your life?'

She nodded, without hesitation. 'After what happened, I think he'd die for me. He... he helped with making the tears happen.' She smoothed a fingertip across the nine blue tattoos. 'Only one more tear and they're done. So, trust? Yes.'

'Would you trust him with mine? With my life?'

The Dirty Blonde shrugged, and a vast white shining smile of impossible beauty burst across her face, the blue tattoo tears glistened with light of their own. 'No,' she said. 'He'd kill you if I asked him to. You're too dangerous to everyone else. You are a disease.'

Stoner nodded, looked almost sad for a moment, then shrugged. 'Cool. Good answer. There would be far worse ways to go than being taken down by that man's hands around a long gun. Quick and silent. Amen to that.' He too smiled, two surprises – one for each of them – in a split second. 'I'll be having a party at the Blue Cube. You're invited. Both. I'll text as soon as I get date and time. How's that?'

'The man of a hundred surprises, JJ Stoner. I never miss a party. I will wear black – it'll be someone's funeral, right?'

Stoner leaned to her, rested his hands around her slim, hard waist, kissed her on the lips. It took some time. And then he left. Of Shard there was no sign. Only silence, and the silent memory of his presence.

27

YES WE'RE GOING TO A PARTY, PARTY

'That went well?' Chastity joined Stoner as soon as he was out of view of the house – his house – where so much of his own reasonably recent history had developed and was now closing down around him. He walked like a man without that well known care in the world, but he was in fact waiting for the shot. The shot to the back. The killing shot, the shot just below and to the right of his left shoulder blade. Worse, the disabling shot. Plenty of opportunities for those. Like to the head, where life destroying – rather than life ending – injuries were easy enough for a high calibre marksman wielding a high calibre rifle. Or to a limb, any major joint. Disabling – permanently disabling injuries are simple enough at short range for a decent and well-practised shooter. Which would describe Shard to a T.

No shot. Chastity punched him in the side, not very gently. He felt vaguely nauseous. Remote shock. 'Talk, soldier. Who was there, what went down? Where to next?'

Stoner demonstrated a fine ability to maintain his pace while sighing deeply at the same time. 'Lissa and Shard,' finally. 'It went as well as anything could in the circs. No one else. House like a morgue. No sign of wibbles watching me, but you can never be sure. Did you see anyone leave? Front or back, assuming you can be in two places at once, of course, wonder woman that you are.'

Chastity tapped a big fat cell phone, maybe it was a tablet, Stoner was unsure. 'There's two cams watching the rear, batteries good for up to forty-eight hours, depending on how often the motion sensor wibbles get activated. You can watch them on this. Two more at the front. No one left, no one entered. "Wibbles"?'

'Technical boy stuff that girls cannot hope to understand, like camshaft and catastrophe.'

'What's the score? In simple girl terms please. How is the previously gutted girlfriend? Has your own black whore maintained her stately attributes? Is she still your whore – if that's even possible – or has she sought out wallets new? Sorry... that should be pastures new. Silly me. Easy slip.'

Stoner shared the substance of his earlier two-way conversation. Chastity matched his pace and maintained her silence until he wound down. 'How do you feel about that?' she wondered.

'About what?'

'About the whore taking up again with your best mate? You're not so hot at choosing those best mates, if I may say so.'

'You may not.'

'OK. So you're sore as all hell about it?'

'Nope. There's a complete numbness in my own inner sore-as-hell system. Total failure in the soreness area. The more I think about it, the less I care. Let's get on. Did you get hold of your luscious pouting sister? The hydraulic Charm herself?'

'Yup.' Chastity tapped the pocket containing the phone, maybe a tablet device. 'I used your SIM card for it. Texted her as if I was you to ask for a meet.'

'Cool. She reply?'

'Yup. Called back inside one nanosecond, went straight to the voicemail and started demanding that you tell her where I was, what had happened to me, and the like. It was very moving, convincing, things like that. She was always a great actress, would have won Oscars for sure.'

Stoner shook his head. 'So little charity in what I'm hearing, lady.'

'She's dead. Charity is dead. So charity can share the grave with her. How come you're not phased by your whore shacking up with Shard, while I'm in a well of bitterness about Charity?'

'Guess I'm just a cold, miserable bastard with a heart of ice, or something stupid. Don't know, is the real answer. Lissa does what she does. It doesn't feel important anymore.' He stopped, maybe one hundred yards from the parked camper van. 'And isn't that just weird? I've been haunted by that fucking video for over a year. Now I've seen them, the movie stars, Lissa and Shard, I just could not care less. Like... like it's just over. Like...' he stretched out a vast sigh and started walking again, throwing the camper van's keys to Chastity and stopping by the passenger door. 'Like it never was important in the first place. I don't understand myself now, Chas. It's like that stuff in the bible about the old order passing, the centre cannot hold, the first shall be last, the last first, that stuff.'

'That's in the bible?'

'No idea. What did you – cunningly disguised as me – arrange with Charm? Whatever it is we'd best get it on before I completely lose the will to live.'

'You don't sound good, JJ.'

'I'm not good. Right now I wish I'd stayed in the States, shot things, bears and the like. Just waited around for the man with the long gun to come and close the book on me, whatever they do. Or maybe got a job, someone else's life entirely.'

Chastity keyed the engine into life, vocal diesel life. 'You don't sound like a man unconcerned, matey. You sound gutted. And it is OK. You can feel gutted. Your whore... sorry, JJ... Lissa must have meant a whole lot to you – you came back for her.'

'Is that how it looks? If I did feel like I should feel then I could have come back for her, but I don't so presumably I didn't.'

'Is that complicated boy stuff again?'

'Probably. I think I came back to kill Blesses. Possibly Hartmann, although I don't feel anything about him, either. Revenge is leaving me. It's exceeding strange.'

'But you do feel about Blesses?'

'You'd better believe that, sister. I am going to kill her. Me. Not cause her to be killed or anything subtle. I would like to pull a sharp blade across her throat and watch her bleed out. Better than shooting her. I can do mean things with a knife.' He suddenly looked across the cab at Chastity. 'And so can you, killer bitch from hell and angel of death.' He smiled suddenly. 'Screw them all, lady. Where're we going?'

'You're meeting Charm. I told her... your texts told her that you didn't know exactly where I was or exactly what state I was in, that you'd not heard from me for a little while but you were sure I was OK. Probably OK. You told her that you were going to have a party – a going-away party. That shut her up.'

'I bet.'

'You like that crap café where you met Hartmann so much that you're making whoopee with Charm there in about an hour.' She glanced at the dash clock. 'A little less. I've also been thinking.' She stopped, just shut up, forcing Stoner to demand that she say more. Which she did.

'Tomorrow night at the Blue Cube,' she announced. 'Tomorrow night's your leaving party, all friends invited.' She paused again. 'I've invited all your friends. Or rather you have, seeing as how it was your phone and its address book that did the invites. A pretty interesting address book too, even if I didn't recognise most of the names in it.' She pulled a SIM card from a pocket and handed it to Stoner. 'Hook up this little marvel of technology and see how many polite refusals and desperate lonely acceptances you've achieved. Are you really as popular a fellow as you think you are? Hmmm. Party time. Woo hoo, and joys like that.' There was no trace of a smile on her face or in her voice.

'Do you always drive so badly?' Stoner assembled a cell phone, plugged its charger into the dashboard somewhere and switched it on. Drummed his fingers while the device communicated in some incomprehensible manner with other devices overhead, underground, wherever. Finally, electronic hands shaken, codes exchanged and protocols synchronised, the screen revealed a collection of mixed messages.

'Stretch is still in the States,' he read out. 'He sends abuse, mostly. Guess that's OK. Proper pissed with me, too.' He scrolled around, swiping with his thumbs like a teenager. 'Fuck's sake, you invited Travis?'

'Don't know. Who's Travis? Is it a girl, a boy, what? Party pooper? Pill popper?'

'Bureau guy. You'd love him.'

'Wowza, then. How d'you know him?'

'How d'you think? I screwed his wife. Obviously. He says he'll come if I'm paying. That is seriously strange.'

'How so?' Chastity handled the lumbering camper van as though it was a sports car. Neither driver nor driven appeared happy with this motoring misunderstanding.

Stoner shook his head, continued scrolling around. 'He's far too senior to go swanning around at a moment's notice. He does serious saving the world shit. Not parties.'

'What's his wife like? Maybe he's after revenge?'

'She's a New York attorney. Gracious lady, cretin for a son.'

'Ain't it always the way?'

'You're talking rubbish. Watch the road.' He paused. 'Please.' More reading. 'I don't know half of these people. Where did you find them? Several are coming, they say.' Paused again. 'Including Lissa, but nothing from Shard. Charm is waiting for you. For me. Us. At the café. I'll tell her to get the cakes in.' Stoner swiped the cell phone into slumber, or its electronic equivalent. 'If half that shower turn up there'll be a war. Did you know you'd invited several Russians?'

'You can tell by the names, you know. Yuri G and Yuri B and Yuri H add up to a bit of a giveaway, and who is Svetlana K?'

'Can't remember. Probably some two hundred pound babushka with twelve kids and halitosis, only one of them Yuri's. Some Yuri or other.'

'The halitosis?'

'Idiot.'

'Blesses not on your party list, then?'

'Idiot. We're here.' And they were.

Chastity parked up, a short walk from the

unwelcoming café. 'I'll stay dead for a bit longer, if it's all the same to you.'

'Good move. You'll not get up to mischief while I'm gone?'

She laughed, insincerely, without obvious humour. 'The only ones likely to get up to mischief are you and my sister, huh? If you cut and run from the cake stakes and go find a room, send me a text, OK? There are some limits to my sisterly love, and to sit here – unfulfilled and unrequited, remember – while you guys get it on would stretch them.'

'Terminally?'

'Reckon so.'

'Your secret's safe with me. And so is your sister's virtue.'

'Fuck off and sow confusion, whatever it is you do. I imagine that Charm will sort out the party. She's really good at organising everything.'

'I'm banking on that. I've never organised a party in my life.'

'No surprises there. Go for it, soldier boy. Go do battle with Cotswolds cake. Killer stuff, they say...'

***

New day, new waitress. The café's cheap bell jingled as the door opened before Stoner, and it jingled again as it closed behind him. No silent stealthy entry, this.

'Ladies.' He pulled up a chair to join them. 'Bili, Charm. Thanks for coming.' The table was set for tea for three. The revised waitress hovered, inconclusively.

Charm leaned almost all the way over the table between them. 'Chas,' she said, neither pleasantries nor courtesies. Her pale face was tense, close to tears or anger. 'Where's Chas?' There was an urgency, a desperation almost, to her question.

'Nothing new from me. She told me she was on an op... a gig. Somewhere near Gloucester? Hereford? She was pretty vague and I wasn't paying too much attention. She did not mention terrorism, I swear. She not back yet? You guys have fail-safes? Retrieval systems? Maybe she's laying low.' He looked over at Bili, the petite bass player glowering at him in uncharacteristic silence from beneath her cascade curtain of blonde curls. 'You OK, friend of mine?' She ignored him and his question. Looked away.

Charm wasn't done. 'Something went tits-up at the gig. I got police reports...'

Stoner interrupted her. 'Who from?'

'The police and from Menace. Why?'

'Not Mallis?' Stoner appeared focused on this.

'No. He's not around... hasn't been for a while. Why?'

'Curiosity. I rarely deal with Menace.' He smiled in a heavily insincere way. 'Not my kind of girl, really. Overweight, mainly.'

'Menace set up the job.' Charm's distress was increasingly obvious, Bili reached out a hand and took one of hers, squeezed it. Still she said nothing, and her eyes were for Charm, not Stoner. 'Menace usually worked as our agent.' She looked away, away from Stoner and away from Bili. 'You know that,' she said. 'And I've apologised already.'

Stoner waved away the waitress, who vanished, leaving them alone – no other customers were in view, plainly another quiet day in tourist heaven. 'True,' he said. 'It still comes as a surprise. I don't want to know about the gig, and I'm fresh out of my good Samaritan costume, but if I hear from Chastity I'll tell her to get in touch. With you, not with Menace – if that's all OK with you.' He sipped some of Bili's tea, smiled at her. She ignored him. He turned back to Charm.

'You've heard nothing at all? Didn't you have eyes on the scene apart from Chastity? That's pretty sloppy. Sorry, but it's true.' Stoner spoke to Charm, but watched Bili, who in her turn watched either the table, the walls or Charm.

Charm, the focus of all current attention, shook her head, rapidly at first, then more slowly. 'No,' she said, quietly enough. 'Not really. Menace told me she'd have eyes there – a watcher of some kind, but they only arrived after the upfuck and...' Her voice simply faded out.

'And what? Buck up. You run a fucking hits for hire business, not a flower stall at the local vicarage. Christ's sake... Charm. Get a grip. What did Menace report to you?'

Charm shot explosively to her feet and shouted, no doubt causing considerable consternation far and wide – at least as far as the kitchen. 'She told me that her guy, her too-late guy, said there'd been an explosion and there'd been casualties. Fatalities.' She sat down again, subdued again. Careful observation suggested that she was on the edge of tears. Bili fussed around her in a blonde and ineffective way. Stoner, a man of stone during Charm's performance, leaned back in his chair and folded his hands behind his head.

'More specifically?' His voice was less aggressive now.

'A woman. Killed.' Tears then.

'OK. You think that was Chastity, your sister?' Stoner's voice was calm, rather than kind. He leaned forward again, rested his elbows on the table and his chin in his hands, gazed deep into Charm's eyes. She looked away, then back, finally holding his gaze. He nodded. 'Why don't you guys use cut-outs or fallbacks? Rhetorical question. Of course you don't. Did she even have back-up support? Of course not. You should retire.' He paused again, half risen from his seat and half turned towards the door. 'I would suggest that you get out while you're ahead. But you're not ahead. Not a bit. And I came here to invite you to a party tomorrow. But you've already had the invite.' He hooked a chair with his left foot, and observed it as he scooted it around the floor, making a fair amount of noise. 'See you tomorrow.' He stared suddenly at Bili. 'At the club.' Shook his head and looked away.

Both women stared at him, mute. He snapped the rest of the way upright, suddenly. A clatter from the kitchen suggested that he'd disturbed a listening ear. As if by magic, the waitress appeared, waved a notepad in a vague way, shook her head and disappeared again.

'Ah, Bili.' Stoner paused and looked at her. She said nothing, looked down, away from him, and he left, quietly. He even caught the door's idiot bell and twisted it silent for that little extra calm.

**

'That went well?' Chastity joined Stoner as soon as he was out of sight of the café.

'You were listening.' A statement, not a question. Another followed. 'Seems Charm is ambidextrous, after all.'

Chastity burst out laughing. 'What?'

'For a dead woman, you're surprisingly good humoured. And your sister really does swing both ways.' They were heading downhill, away from the café, the entire town doing that famous impression of a mausoleum so common to English settlements which claim to be historic.

Chastity calmed her laughter into a less gleeful grin. 'I'd not expected that.'

'No one does. It's a tradition. Has she had close girlfriends before?'

'I thought back after you explained about Bili. Not... not to my knowledge. Why's it important now?'

'It felt like she and Bili were very close, if you know what I mean. Damn nearly touching. They were touching. Damn.'

Chastity slowed her pace, almost to a standstill.

'She brought her new best girlfriend to a meet? For fuck's sake! The woman doesn't even know if I'm alive or dead or in between and she... she cares so much about her only remaining sister that she brought her totty along for afternoon tea?'

'It was a minor surprise for me too. Bili being there was not entirely expected. Bili being so close to Charm – she didn't even speak to me. Amazo. Really.'

'Is Bili solid gay, then? I'd always thought that you and she were... had been... maybe still were. Y'know. At it. Long-time lovers. I'm almost sure that you recently actually suggested that you love the woman. Though that might just be my over-active imagination or such.' She stopped. 'Is she really only into girls? Bili?'

Stoner matched her in the stationary stakes, thrust hands deep into his pockets. 'Yeah,' he managed after a moment. 'Mostly. I already told you that, super-brain. Is that famed memory slipping now?'

'I thought you and she...'

'Oh yeah. Several times. On and off. Varying degrees

of intensity and sometimes... sometimes with a whole lot of emotion. Bili loves the loving. The sex? Well, very variable, very moody. She's not alone in that. Likes to give physicals in return for emotionals.'

Chastity nodded. Calmer now, outrage at her sister subsiding. Spoke quietly as the afternoon wrapped up and died around them. 'That's why you didn't take up with her? You don't do emotion like that.'

'Whatever. Like I said before, she prefers tits and pussy to boy bits. If she wants penetration, plastic is more reliable, decent batteries are a fine invention, they say.' Stoner was moving again, briskly. The camper van was where they'd left it, in plain sight of anyone looking, nothing parked nearby. Stoner disarmed its alarm, reached for the door. Chastity grabbed his arm.

'You're not going to check it? You're not going to look to see whether your endless adversaries have found it and fucked it somehow?'

Stoner turned half-around to check her expression. 'I'm past caring, Chastity. Entirely past. One of the few people I still cared for is screwing the woman who screwed me, who maybe screwed you too. Go stand away a ways if you're concerned about the van. Detonation would do me a favour, right now.' He stood, stationary. 'Well?'

'Just open the thing up. Be romantic to go to hell together, huh?'

The camper van failed to surprise them by exploding, VW vehicles being of that stolid reliable tendency, and instead started instantly and carried them out of town, passing the confrontation café, where Bili and Charm could be seen through the quaintly awkward windows. They appeared to be arguing.

'They're arguing,' remarked Chastity, helpfully.

'Oh good,' Stoner replied without checking. 'Everyone should. Until it gets boring, then they should fight and maybe murder each other, so providing employment for armies of police. This is how society works.'

'You're full of shit.'

'That's true.'

'Where're we heading, bold warrior philosopher?'

'You'll see.'

***

'How much property do you own? Chastity was wandering around the dusty room. She picked up a magazine from a table, replaced it. 'American Vee Magazine,' she shook her head with no trace of amusement. 'You and your bloody Harleys. Why don't you get a good bike? Huh?'

Stoner looked away from the window, smiled at her, tolerantly. 'Tried them all. Clothes don't suit me.' His attention drifted back to the window. Then to its sill. He squatted before it, scraped the wooden surface with a too-long fingernail. 'Habit, I guess. You learn their ways, they learn yours. Like cats. Then you ignore each other and settle to a long time of contemptuous accommodation.' He looked more closely at the sill. 'Exactly like cats.' He stood up again. 'Interesting.' He angled himself to align himself with the scrapes on the sill, then backed slowly away from the window, all the while looking straight ahead. Looked suddenly at his companion, who was flicking through the pages of the bike magazine. 'You've not been here before, Chas?'

'No.' She met his gaze. 'Why?'

'Bipod feet.' He gestured at the window. 'Rifle, I

imagine. Could've been a camera, I suppose. Aimed straight at the club.'

Chastity ditched the magazine, came to stand at his side, shared his view. 'How many guys know about this place? And what is it anyway? Another of your hideaway knocking shops?' Her tone was friendly, her curiosity real and her attention to detail fine. 'There's a cleaned patch on the glass.'

'I see it.'

'Many of your guys know about this?' A question repeated deserves an answer.

'No. Hartmann could find out, I suppose, as could anyone looking hard. I've not been here for years. How old's the comic?'

'Four years.'

'It's a classic. Fetch a fortune on eBay.'

'You reckon?'

'Nope. But the window's been cleaned more recently than that. Well spotted, by the way. You get a prize.'

'Can't wait. Don't tell me. If I knew what my surprise prize was I might lose the will to live.' She continued to watch the window, with steady concentration. 'Shard know about it?'

Stoner shook his head, crossed the room and followed the view through the cleaned glass as he moved. 'I've never told him. Nor Bili. I don't use it. I don't own it, directly. A company does. A property company.'

Chastity lowered herself smoothly until she was sitting on her ankles, then rose all the way to tiptoe, also watching the changing perspectives through the cleared glass. 'And you own the company?'

'Not directly.' Stoner turned, suddenly, abruptly, ditched himself into an armchair, raising a small but visible dust cloud.

Chastity released her gaze from the glass, walked to his side and squatted beside him. 'You own a lot of places, then?'

'Yeah.'

'Investments? You're really very rich...' She purred like a contented, if large, cat, mockery in her voice. Not unkind.

Stoner slid his hand around her arm, rubbed it absently. 'In some ways. I guess. Somewhere to put the money. Some... I've lost a lot of friends over the years. Some of them left me their houses.' He took his hand back, used it to wipe his eyes, closed them and leaned back into the chair's dusty embrace. 'But not this one. I bought this so I could... observe the club. You can see both main entrances from here. And all the upper floors.' He released a long, tired sigh. 'You'd be surprised at how many people have come to the club to sort me out, fuck me up, whatever.'

'Not really. Bloody awful music deserves punishment.' She took his hand. 'You need to relax,' she offered, quietly. 'Get some sleep, maybe. I can help.' Her voice was uncharacteristically soft, her body motionless. 'It must be time... by now. The reward of virtue is exaggerated, JJ Stoner.'

He squeezed her hand. 'Not yet. Not... just yet. Give me something to look forward to.' He smiled, suddenly, sat upright, the small dust storm producing watering eyes. 'You always told me wild sex with you would be worth dying for. If it's worth dying for, it's surely worth waiting for?' To her complete surprise, he half-rose, leaned towards her and kissed her forehead. A long kiss. Not a peck. And quick as a snake, Chastity tilted her head, caught his lips with her own and held them. A stationary, chaste kiss which was remarkable mainly for its duration. Neither of them seemed to want to move. Stoner broke the moment.

'Promise not to kill me?' His voice was serious. Soft.

Chastity rose smooth as that snake to her full height, backed accurately across the dusty room to another dusty chair and subsided into it, raising no dust and holding his eyes with hers the whole time. 'Can't promise you won't die of it, old man, but we could consider it suicide.' She smiled, leaned smoothly forward until her elbows were resting on her knees, propped her head in her hands. 'I promise, then. Deal?'

'Deal.'

'We'd both better survive, then, huh?'

'Reckon so, Ms Chastity. Chastity Weise, huh? Cool.' His eyes closed. 'You're right. I need some sleep. Someone to watch over me, huh? See what the morrow brings.'

'I'll take the first watch.' Chastity glanced to the slowly dimming window, then back at Stoner, but he was already asleep.

28

SMILE FOR THE CAMERA

'No visitors, then?' Chastity unfolded herself from the dusty chair. Stoner was standing by a window, gazing into the dawn's chill light.

'Not last night.' He sounded distracted. 'There's some food in the freezer. And coffee beans. Blue Mountain, decent enough blend.'

'Great. You can rustle up something edible while I perform an ablution.' She stood upright, stretched at length and methodically.

Stoner continued to watch the streets, windows, doorways. 'You miss my point, I think.'

Chastity continued to stretch herself. 'Not really. You've not been here for years, rah, rah, rah, so someone else left the food. Someone who knows your taste for obscure coffee. Do I get a prize? Another Girl Guide merit badge for observation? Unless you seriously reckon the food's been poisoned, my suggestion that you flex your culinary skills still stands.' She lifted a foot until the leg was parallel to the carpet, leaned the foot onto the wall and began serious back and upper body exercises. Paused. 'Or would you rather I got some take-out? This is café land, no?'

Stoner looked at her. She dropped her leg, raised the other. 'Those exercises are twice as healthy if you do them naked,' he observed.

'You reckon?' Chastity stretched her arms, touching fingers to the toes of the foot on the wall. 'Did you read it in a book?'

Stoner pulled himself away from the wall, walked to her side. Stripped to his skin and threw his clothing into a dusty armchair. 'I need distraction,' he announced, sombrely. 'I think I might die today and the bloody organism is chiselling away at it. It needs to think about something else. Something positive.' He lifted a foot, reflecting her slow, firm movements back at her.

Chastity stepped back from the wall and studied him, closely. Shrugged. 'Back in a minute,' she said finally, and walked out of the room, returning in a few moments, preceded by the familiar morning sound of flushing water. She was of course nude and stood still facing Stoner, who dropped his foot to the floor, turned to face her. As one, they bowed to each other. Stoner tilted his head towards her through their shared silence. She nodded, and led the pair of them into a series of steps, stretches, bends, reaches, pulls and pushes, always in silence, moving together as if to a shared but inaudible music, the beat of an invisible drum. Eventually both bodies gleamed and both parties were panting.

'Impressive,' she said, finally. 'For an old man. Are you distracted enough? Can I go shower? Want to scrub my back? My front?' She grinned.

'One of us needs to watch.' Stoner turned back to the window. 'These walls have eyes,' he remarked with no particular stress, as though discussing the weather. 'Ears too, I'd imagine.'

'And you didn't put them there?'

'Nope.'

'Can you close them down? You've got that magic app on your phone...' Her voice trailed away. 'OK. If the guy who supplied the app fitted the ears and eyes, then you won't find them all. Correct?'

'Correct. But the same handy app suggests that there's no transmitting going on, so maybe they're dormant.' He grinned, flicked sweat from his face. 'Go shower before you chill. You're beautiful, by the way. And ferocious fit.'

'I bet you say that to all the girls.'

'Only if it's true. You should know that by now.' He smiled. 'Old habits die hard.'

'Unlike old men, so they say. Which old habits?'

'Paranoia. Simple, systemic paranoia. I am... under-gunned.'

'Out-gunned?' Chastity smiled at her own joke. 'Out-numbered also and always, I suppose?'

'No idea. Think I'm running out of fight, me.' He shook his head. 'Go shower. Chuck me a towel.'

Chastity tilted her head to one side, bird-like. 'Come shower with me. It's early. No-one will be coming for ages. I'll relieve your tension for you – unless you'd rather do it yourself, Mister Self-contained Military Man. I'll be shaving. It's that kind of day. You can do that for me if you want. I'd trust you with a sharp blade on my pussy.' No smile.

'Then I would indeed be fucked. Truly.'

'Only if you want. And you pretend you don't.' She stalked into the bathroom, flung a towel before latching the door almost noiselessly behind her. Stoner towelled down, hard, eyes on the other side of the main window. Mind elsewhere.

***

'Anyone arrive yet?' Time had vanished somehow, and Chastity was back, smelling good, damp and dressing rapidly.

'Nope.'

Chastity was complete in cotton, flimsy armour against the morning. Stoner dropped back into a dusty chair, played something distracting involving big loose knots with the towel.

'I need a decent gun.' He was almost mumbling, talking to himself maybe, inside his own head maybe, distracted certainly. Chastity said nothing, merely watched nothing at all interesting from the windows.

'Do you run errands, Miss?' Deceptive courtesy in the question.

'Yes.' No hesitation. 'What d'you want? Breakfast?'

Stoner nodded. 'Yeah, you're right. Food. Fresh and proper and honest. And ours. You choose.' He paused for a split moment. 'There's a long gun in the van. Between the folding top and the tin roof. In a hard case. Looks like a bass guitar case, long and thin.'

Chastity was on her feet already, sliding those feet into boots and lacing. 'Yep. Shells in the cold water tank, suppressor pretending to be a prop for the hood.'

Stoner looked up, surprise in his eyes.

'You say hood? You speak American? Golly and wow. What happened to bonnet? An anxious world awaits.'

Chastity nodded at his retrieval. 'Neat catch, soldier boy. Do I get my good Girl Guide's observer's merit badge yet?' A neat curtsey.

Stoner held out his hands to her, palms uppermost and open, empty. 'You do.'

Chastity was ready to face the world. 'No one's going

to be arriving yet. You need to check out the surrounding apartments. Or do you own them too? Either way...'

'Checked roughly last night.' Stoner was all matter of fact. 'No I don't own them. Picked my way in across the hall, locked up after me. Couldn't lift the locks on either of the verticals; above or below. Good locks, modern, no wish to do damage. No sign of occupants.'

'Isn't that a little... strange?'

'Not really. This is all commercial. What's residential is corporate, mostly. I did the searches a couple of years back. No sign of strangeness. All rentals, short-term. Nice and secure as neighbours go.'

'Laterals? Chastity was poised to leave. 'Either side? Up and down?'

'Look recently inhabited. Looks like no one home.'

She was stock still now. 'You trust that?'

He nodded. 'Don't be all day about getting breakfast. You're all the back-up I've got, now. Don't have an army. You and me. That's it.'

'No secret allies? Spies? Mysterious nuns with huge armouries? You've not got back-up? You, Mister Over-secure himself.'

Stoner shook his head, his face expressionless, mostly. 'What you see is what you get.' He looked up. 'This is All Cowards' Day. Get me the long gun, and I take the coward's shot. One shot. I take down Blesses – I don't miss – then we go party, you reunite with Charm, Bili still hates me, we see who else has accepted the mysterious party invite and...'

'And what, JJ?'

'I...' his voice wandered around with a will all its own. 'We'll see. Maybe it really is retirement.' He seemed a touch distressed at the notion. 'I feel old. Really old. This whole shitty scene is old. I'm... tired. Tired of it.'

Chastity was in his face. He'd not seen her move. 'Oh no, no you don't.' She stared into his eyes, hard, close up. 'No last hit for you yet, big boy. No topping yourself out of this. No long walk off a short roof for you. You're nowhere near that. We...' she paused, breathed audibly, almost a sigh. 'We have places to be. Many of them. You and me, JJ Stoner. We're not even started yet.'

Stoner rubbed his eyes with the heels of his hands. 'Yeah. Back to the States.' He paused as though a sudden thought had surprised him. 'You coming? You on for that?'

'You betcha. Teach me the blues, huh? I'll grow my hair long, maybe a beard. Wear denim, dungarees. Do God and hillbilly both. We could be brothers. Sanctified.' She smiled, it seemed genuine. 'You got brothers in the States? Brothers in arms?'

He nodded. 'I do. Where's breakfast? Where's that gun?'

***

'There.' It had been a long, long day. They'd worked together, the two solo artists, had built him a shooting platform, stable and exact. The long gun brooded on its bipod. Sights set, mechanism stripped, oiled, stripped and oiled again, dry-fired several times. The day was bright, traffic was mostly light and the air drifting through the open window was cold and clear, an infrared telescopic sight rested by the feet of the bipod, nothing obstructing the firing arc of the long gun itself. The street below had been deadly silent, then raucous for maybe an hour, maybe a little longer. A man had arrived and opened the side door to the Blue Cube, to JJ Stoner's own jazz bar and blues club. Chimp. Stoner identified the arrival as his barkeep. Another ex-military man, skin and bones and stubble and hair and long limbs working loose both below him and at his sides. Reliable. Solid. Indebted.

'There.' Stoner kept his eye holding whoever, whatever he'd seen through the long gun's telescopic sight. Chastity swung her squat binoculars slowly, steadily, calmly, shifting her field of vision to match his.

'Yes,' she said, finally. 'Charm.' They watched the street together, in a companionable and carefully stress-free silence, Stoner watching Charm, his focus total and complete; Chastity using her bins' greater field and sweeping her view over a wider area. Until... 'There,' she said, and again. Stoner lifted the long gun's reticule from its target – Charm's head, roughly central in the plane between eyes and ears, a favourite killing shot – and drifted away, searching, for something new.

'OK.' Finally. 'Menace.' He swung the long gun's foresight back to Charm, met her halfway in her walk towards Menace. 'Interesting,' he remarked, gently. 'Still no Mallis. An entertaining parallel in our wide game of Happy Families.'

'Say again?' Chastity's vision was on the prowl again, stalking cat-like between the slowly growing and slowly moving fragmented crowd below them.

'Menace without Mallis; Charm without Chastity. It's almost a symmetry. Sister without sister, sister without brother.'

'You making some kind of call, brother Stoner?'

'I am not, sister. I'm... interested. Patterns. Patterns in all things, always.'

'Madness lies in looking for patterns where there are only coincidences, JJ.'

'So you say. Madness lies in failing to recognise more than coincidence when it is in fact a pattern you're seeing.'

'You think?' Chastity was calm. Very calm. 'You see a pattern?'

'No. You shaved?'

'I did.'

'Close?'

'Exact.' She snorted softly through her nose. 'Precise.'

Stoner, finally and slowly, lifted his eyes from the rubber rest of the telescopic sight, closed them and sighed. 'Menace and Charm have entered the building. Together. It's probably time you came back from the dead. Resurrection is always a popular miracle among the true believers. Maybe you can convert your sister onto the side of the angels.'

'That may not be easy. Or even possible.' Chastity appeared untroubled by either outcome.

'Let's hope it is.' Stoner rested down again, settling his cheek to the familiar stock of the long gun, his eye back to the cushioning rubber of its sight. 'You should probably do it soon. The age of miracles may be passing. Again.' Chastity hefted the big bins back and shifted them slowly until they stopped again. Slowly, unbreathing, she shifted their focus.

'Hmm,' she managed, slowly, finally and after a respectful pause. 'That's your whore.' Maybe there was a question inside the statement.

Stoner confirmed the identity of the tall, slender black woman. 'No sign of Shard,' he observed.

'And the other woman? The woman your Dirty Blonde's talking to?' Chastity was static as a snake, coiled, waiting, a pounce ready to be sprung.

'You should be going.' Stoner had eased off the safety, so gently that Chastity had missed the delicate sound

of its mechanism. 'You should be seeing to Amanda...
to Charm. Making judgements, making decisions. I'll
accept and respect them all.'

'That's Blesses, then? Shorter than expected.'

'Don't be fooled. You'll never meet a greater presence
than that one. Watch it. Watch it carefully. Smell the
void, the voodoo. Watch her understand that I'm here,
if you want. It's impossible, but she'll know. And she'll
track me. She is my death. And how come the sanctified
fuck is she talking with Lissa? That's just... impossible.
There's hatred between them. Mutilation. Mind and
body. Body and soul.'

Chastity continued to observe the scenes below
them. 'You're rambling,' she said, in a carefully neutral
tone. 'You're scared. I've never seen that before.'

Stoner was controlling his breathing. Eye on the
target, finger on the trigger. 'I am. Yes. Yes I am. Look.
Look now.'

Chastity lowered the binoculars, squatted back onto
her heels, rubbed her eyes with the soft backs of her
scrubbed hands. 'Look at what?'

'Look at Blesses looking at me. She can't know we're
here. She doesn't know we're here, but she's watching
me. Fuck. You should go get Amanda. Charm. She's your
sister. If that's still important to you, you need to shift
your arse and sharpish.'

Chastity lifted the bins back to her eyes, watched for
maybe twenty seconds, lowered them once more. 'OK,'
she said, finally.

'OK what?' Stoner was unmoving. Full focus.

'Blesses is not looking at you. She's not looking
this way at all. She's scanning the street, road level, all
directions. She's not looking up.' She lifted the lenses
again. 'She's still not.' A pause. 'What do you see now, JJ?'

'She's watching me. Staring. Like...' his voice trailed away. 'She's not, is she?'

'No.' Chastity was living in the scene before her. 'She's just walked to the wall to our left of the entry. Sat down. What do you see?'

'The same walk to the wall, but she's still staring right at me.'

'No she's not. Put down the rifle, roll onto your back, close your eyes, tell me what you see.' She waited for maybe a five-count. 'Stand down, JJ. Do not do what she expects you to do.' Stoner closed his eyes, rested the rifle, released it carefully, like it might bite him, and did as he'd been told. He rolled onto his back, closed his eyes. Silent. Motionless. Speechless.

'Wow.' Chastity breathed the word, shaking her head slowly from side to side. 'She's really...' trailed away. 'You've really let her take hold of you, huh, JJ? You see what you want to see when she's there in your picture. And what you want to see is yourself, you at the centre of her attention. That's serious strange, soldier boy. Seriously sick stuff.'

Stoner maintained his quiet immobility.

'She... knows you. She's got you. Got you so tight you'll kill yourself when she wants it. Walk under her guns, which is the same thing.' Her attention all the while was on the view lost to her companion. 'Fuck.' Chastity rocked back on her heels, lowered the bins and turned to Stoner. 'Fuck,' she said once more, rose to her feet and walked slowly, deliberately to a chair. Collapsed like a broken puppet. Stared hard at Stoner. Shared her sudden understanding with him. 'She was pregnant, you know.' The words died in the air between them, pain like dust drifted in the dead room.

'Who?' Stoner's dead voice matched the crumbling dullness of their shared understanding.

'You know full well. Did you know before? Before the termination? Before the gutting? Before now?' She shook her head, then again, stared at him with wide, astonished eyes. 'That's what it was, wasn't it? The performance with Shard and your girl. An abortion, just for you, just for you to watch. Why does she hate you?'

'She doesn't.' Stoner lifted his arms as though in supplication, let them fall back, hard, onto the carpet around him. 'Didn't.' Another dusty drifting silence. 'Didn't.' He roused himself, raised himself to a more upright position, slumped now against the wall. 'No. I didn't know. She's a whore. Lissa. That's who she is. What she is. Whores do not get pregnant by accident. And if she'd decided to, then... then it would have been deliberate. You're saying she was, and you're saying it was mine?'

Chastity said nothing. Shrugged. Her eyes were closed, her gaze internal. Seconds died in their hundreds around them, the room fading as the daylight slowly ebbed.

Stoner hoisted himself to a squat. 'Can you take the shot, Chas? I doubt I can do it.' He held up a defensive hand. 'I know it's not your fight, but what you say feels... right. And it's...' His head fell forward into cupped hands. A long and aching pause. 'And it's all happened before.'

'How's that?'

'Ireland. In that beautiful country, too many years ago.' The weariness around him hung like a dull, dampening drape of sorrows. 'You met Bernadette, over in Germany. Remember?'

'Unforgettable, a Mother Superior with an arsenal. God's own divine warrior. Hit woman in a habit. Yeah, I remember her fine.'

Stoner produced a sigh so deep that Chastity looked

up, checking him for tears or other collapse. 'She was pregnant. A daughter. Blesses broke that one too. The same way.' He drifted once more into silence.

'She slit her gut with a blade?' Chastity's prod was gentle enough.

'No. She spooked some other sad fuck into shooting her right through her belly. Bye bye baby. Baby goodbye...' Stoner almost sang the line. Looked directly at Chastity for the first time in a while. 'I couldn't kill her then. Emptied a SIG magazine at close range and missed every fucking shot. Bernadette shot her through the knees. That stopped her. I thought the Hard Man would disappear Blesses forever, maybe inside a block of concrete, but no. Instead he recruited her.'

'Fuck.' A woman of few words this time.

'As you say. Can you take the shot, Chastity? Chas?' Stoner spread his hands between them. 'I will always owe you for that.'

'Yeah. Sure. I... want to.' Chastity hefted the rifle to her shoulder. 'Kill or wound?'

'Kill. It's the only reality left. Her or me.'

Chastity sat back. Raised her eyes heavenwards.

'What's up?' Stoner was on his feet and moving. 'I'll guess. She's vanished.'

'Hole in one. Sorry, JJ.' Chastity bent her eyes to the sight, Stoner scanned through the bins.

'Did you see her move?'

'No, but the entire group moved into the club. It's getting dim out there. Not entirely easy to see in detail.'

Stoner slung the bins into a chair, where they bounced, dustily, as he produced a black SIG Sauer from somewhere, checked it, cocked it, dropped it into a pocket of the big, heavy motorcycle rider's leather coat he was suddenly wearing. Movement all one, flowing, urgent. Chastity stared.

'Big coat, big man,' she said quietly. 'Heavy. Bulky.'

'Kevlar.' Stoner sounded so bright, so right, so confident in his fluid movement, now towards the door. He turned, nodded to her, eyes wide and bright. 'Check out your sister. Going to be hellish in there if there's a firefight. She up to that?' His short drive to the doorway paused as he waited for an answer.

'Doubt it. She'll expect...'

Stoner's hand turned the handle. 'Call her, then. Make an excuse, but get her out...'

Chastity shook her head. Made a decision. 'Safer for you if there's no warning, huh?'

'Yeah. You betcha.' And he was gone, the door slipping silently closed behind him.

29

DUST, SETTLING

Time to kill. Stoner ran down the stairs, passed the entrance lobby, with its unattended concierge station and air of dilapidation, swung instead into an Emergency! Fire! Exit! and dropped another floor, turned away from the garage access, the basement doors, and stopped in front of the slam-bar on the fire door. Paused as if in thought. Maybe prayer. Turned away from the fire door and pushed instead into the garage. Door locks and hinges were silent, oiled, maintained, as they should be. No lights, automatic or otherwise, illuminated his passage. His Caterpillar boots made almost no sound at all as he walked swiftly through the echoes towards the exit ramp, still lit by the outside evening, street lighting poised to change the colours and contours of everything. But not yet. Not quite yet.

He paused in the deep dark shadows around the door, surveying, assessing. Thinking. Forebrain stuff, less now of the terrified animal hindbrain. Autopilot disengaged. Cruise control disabled. All alert and calm, completely calm control. Breathing steady, just like in those long-ago army days. No excitement, simple relish and lust. He wanted to kill. No emotion-free contractual obligation, this. Passion. Anticipation. First clear shot. Stay away from her eyes. Take her from behind. No mistakes allowed.

The street was fading, streetlights easing into their shift, still dull and red, bright and white came later. Perfect cover. Traffic was steady, busy enough to distract, to hide. Peddies did what peddies do; walking with various degrees of conviction, direction, to wherever and whatever it was they were headed. No organised pattern in their random consistency. Nothing standing out. No watchers watching him, the practiced watcher watched, so far as he could see. And he could see clearly enough.

A van approached, anchored in the traffic stream on his own side of the road, and as it passed, Stoner slipped from shadow and matched its pace, roughly, absorbing the random rhythms of the pedestrian flow as he did so. Like everyone else, he walked hunched slightly against the approaching chill of evening, not checking for tails, not stopping and staring into random shop windows and using them as mostly ineffective mirrors, not stooping to tie tight shoelaces, not gazing about. Did the Light Brigade behave like paranoid schoolgirls as they rode onward into their own valley of death? Stoner doubted it. Buck up, man. Straight back, stiff lip.

Both the van and the man passed by the unlit unremarkable entrance to the Blue Cube, neither of them attracting any obvious interest. But then… anyone watching and waiting for Stoner was going to be as professional as he was himself. The darkness was arriving now, settling itself more convincingly than before, and the street's lighting was brightening accordingly. The air was condensing; a drizzle was approaching, maybe rain later. Stoner stopped, stepped back from the traffic, looked around. No haste, no urgency, no exaggerated calm either, just another peddie, anonymous apart from the heavy leather coat, and even that now looked more like a precaution against the weather than a protection against a bullet or a blade.

No lights above street level yet in the building on the opposite side of the street. Stoner looked around and up. No lights anywhere near the windows of the apartment he'd recently departed. He walked to the kerb, stopped, scanning for a gap in the traffic. A light rain was arriving, furtively. Cars flicked their wipers, greasing their screens, blurring their vision. A gap, an opening. Stoner checked again, he had little wish to be bounced off a car at this stage of proceedings. Stepped out into the gap, waving an acknowledgement to the approaching, slowing driver, who left him space to cross, and then Stoner stopped dead as a pedal cyclist, another invulnerable road rager, unlit in dark Lycra, appeared inside his own space, showing no sign of slowing. Hardy riders. Stoner stepped sharply back, waving a hand again at the accommodating car driver.

The unmistakeable tug, heave, pull, violence, energy, shock of a bullet spun him around, dropped him flat. Hard. He heard no shot.

Screams. Chaos. All stop. Man down.

Stoner bled. Hot, wet, aching. He could see only feet, wheels, legs, the wet road. Could hear only a wall of sound, none of it intelligible. His thinking felt perfect to him, although there was nothing to compare it with. He made to rise and fell back to the wet asphalt, doubled over himself. Part of him was loose, semi-detached, flapping around. Reason prevailed, and instead of reaching down to his side to investigate the injury, he pulled the heavy leather coat tight around him and started to shiver.

'Heart attack,' announced the first clear voice. Confident.

'Looked more like a stroke,' shared a second. 'I've called for an ambulance. They said not to move him until paramedics get here. Police on their way. Look at his colour. Stroke for sure.'

Voices. A dullard chorus drowning themselves in an ocean of jabber. Ages passed, achingly slowly and instantly somehow. Stoner stared at feet. Shoes, boots, crowding. 'Give him air,' someone commanded, but Stoner was breathing just fine. It was cold, though, and he wondered vaguely about the street lighting too, surely it should be less dark, even down here, surrounded by a stalking forest of feet. Sirens. He could hear a siren. Man down somewhere, then. Hope they get to him in time. Whoever he is. Godspeed, all that.

A familiar voice, then. 'Fuck,' it announced, breathing hard. 'JJ?' A question. He grumbled something he hoped would produce a smile. Somehow a smile seemed to be important.

'Stand back!' That familiar voice, a woman, commanding, taking no prisoners at all. The face behind the voice appeared in his vision, at an unusual angle. He smiled at the crazy geometry, understood that there were tears in his eyes and wondered why. Rain. Of course. It was raining. The familiar face applied the familiar voice again. A hand slipped inside his long leather coat, he shivered. It was too cold. He spoke, intending to ask her... Chastity... to leave him well wrapped. Chap could catch his death in this chill. Loud sirens.

'What d'you say, JJ?' She was sounding tense. No need for that. 'You're well fucked up inside there, soldier boy. Say some prayers.' She leaned in further, more voices were raising around them. 'What d'you say?' She was repeating herself. Stoner tried harder. A pair of male authority voices were intruding. Chastity told them to stand back, she was trying to hear what he had to say. Good girl. Brilliant woman.

'Three point three kilojoules,' he said, plainly.

'What!'

Stoner was pleased with their communication. At last he was getting somewhere. 'Eight hundred feet per second.' It was a horrible effort, but worth it, he was sure. But he was wrong. 'Metres per second,' he managed, and coughed. That felt dreadful, like a huge hand was inside him, gripping things and ripping them apart.

'Jesus, JJ, what are you on about?' Chastity sounded too stressed. He smiled at her, maybe, depending.

'Seven point six two,' he managed, and managed not to cough again. That was good. The chill was receding a little, and the feet were moving all around him. 'Ten grams, betcha.' Vision shut down as though a switch had been pulled, then brightened again.

Chastity had been shoved to one side and had her back to him. Two men rolled him onto a stretcher, tried to lay his legs flat, but Stoner kept them tented skywards, holding in his own guts. He knew what he was, where he was and that he was dying. That was OK. That was fine. Huge amount of noise, urgency, scissors trying to cut through the heavy leather Kevlar lined coat. They'd need to switch to bone forceps for that. He felt no need to share his understanding with the men who were lifting him, coat and everything. Chastity appeared at his side again. He could smell her. Wanted her to take his hand and hold it. Would have reached for her but couldn't, somehow. The lighting waxed and waned like a disco party with lots of drugs around. He was in a shrinking bubble, floating. Morphine, then.

Hurrah. Chastity leaned into him, he could breathe in her smile. She was smiling. Brilliant. Her. Brilliant. The light of life was in her eyes.

'JJ, you mad bastard.' Tears? Tears in her voice. 'Spouting ballistics when you've got a hole in you the size of Brazil?' He rolled his head, very slowly, in time to see her being pulled, levered away from his side by huge men in bright clothing.

'Kiss me,' he shouted. A real, honest to goodness shout. His world rocked and rolled insanely, the gurney was entering the vehicle. An ambulance. Chastity threw a man away from her, leaned in and kissed him, hard on the lips. He could see her, but felt little, floating, floating. 'Kill the bitch,' he said, suddenly and quite clearly. Laid his head down again, watching her, while the bright medics fussed around somehow. Chastity produced a cell phone, flicked it to life. Looked at Stoner. Keyed in a number. Looked at Stoner. He could see her tears streaming now, pouring. Hot, wet. He nodded. 'See you soon,' he said, and she pressed 'Send'.

The earth moved. A bottle fell and bounced. The ambulance, all the people – all those people – shook and shuddered and began to scream. Huge noise. Darkness and a howling impossible bounce and a shattering and a roar like a tidal wave on the biggest rocks imaginable in the wildest ocean's most mighty storm.

The doors slammed, lights dimmed and as the ambulance rocked and rolled away, Stoner and a medic, maybe two medics, in the back, a huge, dusty, broken silence grew outside their medical bubble. Stoner closed his eyes, nodded, welcoming peace as it descended. His legs fell slowly from their steepled knees-up protective posture until they lay flat on the stretcher at last.

30

THE OLD GOLDEN LAND

'He awake yet?' A deep southern American voice. Southern states. Mississippi, Louisiana. One of those. 'Trace says he's awake. He's just shammin', him. Listening to us. Laughing. Tell a joke and see if he giggles.'

Stoner raised a single finger. 'There y'go,' said the deep voice, conversationally. 'That's serious, heavyweight laughter. Don't get no funnier than that.'

A woman's voice, also American, further north. White, by the sound of it. Less familiar than the first, male voice, which was completely familiar – if unidentified as yet. 'Wipe his face down. Reckon his eyes are gummed shut.' The deed followed the word. Stoner opened an eye... two. Vision was very blurred. He blinked. This had no effect, so he closed his eyes again.

'Stretch.' His voice was a croak.

'Hey, man, that's one heroic guy voice you got now.' The deep south voice was filled with humour, entirely lacking in sympathy. 'You need a drink, and all we got is water, dammit. I come back later, I bring some medicine. Man medicine.' He drawled the last words, extending them beyond probability. Stoner smiled, a peculiarly cracking sensation.

'Fuck,' he said, distinctly, 'off.' Then, after a pause. 'Can someone sit me up a little?' No one moved, so he stayed where he was. 'OK, whoever's the boss torturer, then, can I have a drink?' His voice ground down into silence. Water in a tube reached his lips and he sipped, slowly, carefully. 'Whoa... that... that's weird. I can feel it inside me. Will it stay in there?'

'A mystery.' The woman again. 'How do you feel, Mr Stoner? Do you really want elevating?' He grunted an assent, and his head elevated along with part of his upper body. A deep, dark southern voice chuckled softly.

'Stoner, elevated. I like that.'

'OK,' the recumbent Stoner began, then silenced and sipped at the water again, opened both eyes and scanned the room. 'Bright,' he managed, before resting his eyes again. 'Where...' he paused, 'and when? I hurt a lot. Stretch. What're you doing here? Wherever here is.' Another grating cough, another sip of water. 'Bullet, huh?' His face contorted as he raised a hand to his side. 'Heavy and slow, or light and fast?' He opened his eyes again, blinked several times, then closed one eye and peered around with the other, repeating the process with the other. 'Both views the same,' he remarked. 'Not concussed, then. How long?'

Stretch McCann, huge and shiny and black, wearing a US military uniform with no insignia that Stoner could see, seated himself at Stoner's side. Other than the two of them, the wide white room was deserted, somehow.

'Ten days.' Stretch was as unhurried as ever. 'You know you were talking ballistics with your girlfriend when you went down?' Stoner stared at him, said nothing, blinked a little more. Raised his eyebrows, finally, and shook his head, very carefully.

'Ballistics? Girlfriend? Assume I remember nothing. Tell me everything.'

Stretch nodded, slowly and thoughtfully. 'Got that.' He stopped. Then: 'You toying with me, JJ? You got some kinda game a-playing here?'

Stoner shook his head. 'No. I sort-of left me for dead. I think. I took a slug.' His eyes folded closed again. 'Remember that. Ballistics? Yeah. Felt like a 7.62, nothing fancy. No idea why that was important. Girlfriend? You mean Chastity? Blonde, fit as a leopard, was at my side, had a... had a cell phone.' He opened his eyes, considered, and caught Stretch's attention. 'She called the cavalry?'

'Don't know, white boy. All is not clear, and these walls can certainly hear you, so rather than confuse the spooks with wild speculation I'll lay some facts on you. See how they feel. That sound OK to you, Mister Invalid? Tell me if I talk too fast for your addled Limey brain, huh? You are filled with drugs, many and various and expensive, I imagine.'

Stoner nodded.

'Right then. This is all very confused, so I'll start from the end, where all the best tales begin. You are in the US of A.' Stoner opened his eyes so wide they appeared in danger of rolling down his bearded cheeks and into the white folds of the bedding. 'Technically speaking.' Stretch leaned back in the flimsy hospital chair and folded his huge black hands behind his huge, shining bald black head. 'Less technically, we are both in Suffolk, a particularly flat region of the UK, also known as England. This is a USAF military hospital, and you may receive a billing for your treatment because that is how things work in your good-old, mom's apple pie United States. Mostly united, unlike your own Kingdom, buddy.'

'Cool. I like Suffolk. Windmills, cathedrals, oil rigs. I know my geography. How come this is a US Air Force sanatorium, huh? How come the envy of the world Brit National Health Service isn't putting Humpty together again? Why are you here? Nice to see you, but.'

Stretch grinned, a startling white array of large teeth. 'Picture this. The streets of London... OK, so it wasn't actually London, but I always liked that song. The mean streets...'

'Get on with this. I might die waiting.'

'You did that already, and more than once, so they say.' Stretch smiled again, a little bleakly. 'Guess you're one tough hombre, huh?' The smile faded. 'Man in a big biker coat collapses in the middle of the rainy street.' He looked up. 'How'm I doing?'

Stoner simply nodded, eyes closed once again. 'You're making it live for me, brother. The drama, all that. Get a move on.'

'All around you, innocent commuter Brits instantly spot that you've had a coronary, a seizure, been hit by a meteorite, whatever, crowd busy all around you to watch you die and then – as an afterthought – they all call 911.'

'999,' interrupted Stoner. 'We do it properly in Britland.'

'Whatever. Parameds, policemen, couple clergymen, an attorney or two, a fucking chopper, the whole nine yards all roll up to celebrate your passing. Fuck it, JJ, I've seen the movies – you're famous on YouTube – and there's this big crowd all around you, including – eventually – your own blonde bombshell. Chastity, the demon killer bitch from hell... or from your home counties, which sound similar.'

Stoner dived in. 'You should be on the radio, Stretch.

Never have I heard a more drawn out saga of agony. It could only have taken a minute and you've been talking for... days.'

'You should see the vids, my nearly departed amigo. Michael Bay could have made it into a movie. The chopper hovers about, making a god-awful noise, guys in dayglo appear and open your big old coat, then close it again and go pale, cross themselves. Maybe they puke, hard to see. Your demon blonde is talking to you, you talking to her, she makes a call on her cell, probably calling her mother or for divine intervention, and then the earth moves for you both. Remember how you used to have a club? Nice place. The Blue Cube. I had a piano there, me, and you had a groovy apartment and a famous ancient guitar or two. Remember?'

Stoner nodded, leaving his eyes closed.

'Well, short story long, brother, you don't need to worry about that old club no more, no more. The very moment your blonde bombshell taps her cell phone, the place just went away. Like being hit by a Hellfire from within. Very impressive. Building came down like a stack of dirty dishes. Whap. Military grade demolition. Professional. Took no prisoners.'

'Fuck.'

'Yeah. It gets better.' Stretch stretched, rose to his full height and paced to the far corner of the room, then back. 'You're off in the meat wagon, doing the heroic dying shit, seeking attention as usual for a Brit, your blonde has somehow gone away, and the TV crews are making like it's Armageddon, 9/11 and World War Three all rolled into one. They loved it. Top banana ratings, I can say.

'Next scene. Observant parameds observe that as well as dying and inconveniently bleeding out all over their floors, you're also carting artillery and appear to be connected to the fuck-off big bang that took out windows for miles around and nearly downed their very own chopper, so when they get you to a big hospital where men in scrubs are going to point and laugh and say "How we gonna fix that? Put this guy in a body bag now," there's a whole posse waiting for you. Lawmen, spooks, TV anchormen and even more scary, that crazed BBC reporter woman who only does serious disasters. She looks grave. You look like you should be in one. All very heavy indeed, and you go to theatre, die, recover, all that dramatic shit, and into a private guarded room, or suite, or whatever Brit hospitals do. Huge guards. Serious stuff. Politicians on the TV and like that.'

'You're enjoying this.'

'Damn right. Wish I'd been there. I only saw the movies. Lots of them. Had lots of time while you played the Sleeping Beauty crap. Your House of Parliament did debates, your Prime Minister talked a lot and said remarkably little, but what she did say made it plain that you – un-named somehow miraculously – were a terrorist. Probably Russian. You did look Russian. Maybe.'

'Russian?'

'Don't knock it. They're very good. They'll probably give you a job next.'

Stoner grunted, eased himself around, winced and paled. Subsided. 'And then. It's good so far. Who won? What's the score?'

Stretch suddenly laughed aloud, causing Stoner to start and stare, somehow groaning and grinning at the same time. 'What?'

'Well, sadly there's no vid of this, but a shiny suit from our embassy – that would be the US embassy,

US standing for United States, the special relationship and so on, goes to see your Prime Minister. Direct. No dicking about. Just sorta rolls up to Downing Street in the big armoured limo thing with about twelve regiments of marines to show how friendly we all are. Stopped all the traffic in Whitehall. Wish I'd been there, but history will show there were just the two of them and it never happened anyway. Our guy explains that you are also our guy – stop staring, you'll have a heart attack – and that you've prevented a...' Stretch paused to draw a theatrical breath '...a major terrorist attack on the fundamental fabric of western democratic society. I think I got that right. They did talk about it on the TV, but they lie, like you know. You are not only a big hero, but also an American big hero, and Uncle Sam wants to cradle your broken body to his manly bosom. Shit like that. I was here by then. Never flown so fast. Louisiana to Suffolk in about a half-hour. Awesome.'

'So you were here, and you saved the day. Great. I'm not American, and I'm certainly no hero.' Stoner held out the drained water glass for a refill. 'Go fetch, bro.'

'Hero is a no-no, we both know that. But it seems you are an American. Not only that, but you're an asset of some set of initials so scary that even the BBC can't get them wrong while not saying who they are.'

'No I'm not.'

'Oh yes you are, buddy boy. Uncle Sam is never wrong. Hellfire missiles say this, so it must be true. A fine man we both know by the name of Travis talked to me on the secure phone and assured me that you're an American now. And a Brit. You can be both. And as the Marines never leave a fallen brother to the scant mercies of the Brit health services, here you are. Fallen but about to rise again, broken and bloodied but unbent, and...'

'Shut up, Stretch.'

'Yassuh, massa.'

The air inside the room seethed suddenly as the double doors swung open and immediately closed themselves again behind a military medical officer of impressive rank. Stretch shot to his feet, standing to a full attention until the officer waved him back to his seat, with a casual but precise 'Stand down.'

He walked around the huge bed, flicked a glance over the chittering electronics surrounding it, leaned over the recumbent incumbent, and enquired after his general wellbeing. 'Tomorrow,' he said. 'Tomorrow you have two visitors, who you should see separately and in sequence, though they may try to visit you together, which would be taxing for you, then you're flying home.' He paused. 'To the States. Master Chief McCann here will escort you. We're providing a team of two field surgeons and the aircraft has a theatre should it be necessary.'

Stoner stared at him. 'I feel fine.' He looked again at the badges of rank. 'General.'

'You're not. Your insides have been mostly outside and need to be taken apart and fixed again soon so they work again, but we'll do that back home.' He smiled reassuringly, and pressed some buttons on a machine, which bleeped obligingly. 'And now you're going to sleep.'

'When did you get promoted...' Stoner spoke to Stretch, but unconsciousness stepped in.

***

The chemical awakening is rather less pleasant than the more natural kind. Stoner was entirely disoriented again. Life resumed in the middle of everything.

Snapped back into existence from nothing, nothing at all. No dreams, no gentle drift to the surface of awareness.

'...unwell and impossible to say.' Which did not sound especially encouraging. Despite his intention to stay quiet and listen a while, Stoner groaned. A hand descended onto his forehead, whether to estimate its temperature or to offer support, sympathy of some kind was unclear. 'Mister Stoner. You have visitors.' The hand vanished as Stoner opened his eyes. 'Gentlemen,' invited the voice. Stoner focused a little, with an effort. A door closed, hissing a little.

'How do you feel?' An English voice. Educated, probably a public school. Special Branch, then, not a common copper.

'Why would you care?' Stoner's voice was a rasp, he looked around for a glass of water. Found one, lifted a hand to collect it, groaned again at an eruption of pain in his insides, and let the hand fall back. The glass appeared at his lips, tilted, and he sipped.

'You can't have too much. Something to do with holes in your guts. Imagine you'd start leaking. Why would anyone want to kill you, Stoner?' A pause. 'Let me rephrase that. Why would someone try to kill you while crossing the street, then try to blow you up?'

'Outraged traffic vigilante. Probably a bloody push-bike pilot. They're all homicidal. Can I have some more water?'

'Your brain's working, then. That's good. Seriously, Mister Stoner. We need your help. It's plain you were the target of all this... excitement. We need to find out who it was and why. Public safety, public interest, all that. And you're back off across the pond tonight, so... can you help?'

Stoner nodded, encouragingly. 'I can't see well. can

you get a cloth or something and wipe my eyes so I can see who's talking to me?'

'Of course.' Vision restored, Stoner peered around the white room. One familiar face, one not. He caught the familiar eyes, the eyes above the mouth which had not been speaking to him. No response from the Hard Man, no recognition at all. Neutrality. Stoner responded in kind.

'You are the owner of the jazz club.' More a statement than a question from the public schoolboy. Stoner nodded a little, licked his lips carefully.

'Eleven people died in the explosion. Three more are in hospital and might make it. In a way, whoever shot you saved your life.'

'You think?' Stoner stared at his inquisitor, a bland, pinkly polished and unremarkable Brit face stared back.

'That probably wasn't the intention, then, in your view?'

'A quick call to tell me not to go to the club would have been easier all round.' Stoner coughed as carefully as he could, sipped a little more of the proffered water. He nodded towards the Hard Man. 'He dumb?'

'From a ministry,' explained the policeman, as though he was sharing a great and confidential truth. 'Just an observer. You two know each other?'

Stoner shook his head. 'Memory's not so good. Not sure. Does he know me? Mister Silent?' The Hard Man shook his head, silently, slowly, sadly.

It was time to fake a desire to be helpful. 'I was intending to have a party that night,' Stoner offered. 'A going-away party. Just a few friends. A few beers. Some music.' He took a theatrical and painful deep breath. 'Who was hurt... killed? It would be kind of you to tell me.'

The policeman pulled some photos from his pocket. 'Are you up to this?'

'I was a soldier for many years, Mr Policeman. I don't shock easily.' Which turned out to be untrue. The first morgue shot was Blesses, one eye wide and staring hate, the other missing entirely somehow. Stoner dropped the photos onto the bed, closed his eyes, eyes suddenly filling with brimming tears of their own. 'I'm sorry,' he whispered. 'I just can't do this. Not yet.' He lay back, wincing, and stared at the ceiling, far away and littered with lights and medical mysteries. 'If anyone wanted me dead, it was her.'

The policeman gathered the photos together, stored them somewhere out of sight. 'You know her?'

'Yes.'

A long pause. 'Are you going to tell me who she was?'

Stoner blinked, plainly in the grip of some profound emotion. 'I knew her only as Blesses. Irish. I knew her from my army days. She was connected with the paramilitaries. All sides, I think. I doubt she had any true belief. A foul woman. A hater. Worked for anyone who could provide a target for her hatred.' He glanced down, over to the Hard Man, who gazed back, impassive. 'She was one of the reasons I was leaving. I'm too old to be hated.'

The policeman appeared to be accepting this version. 'And she would have had the means to do... what? The bombing? The shooting?'

'Not herself. She'd not blow herself up, officer. She'd have contracted someone else to do that. Likewise the shooting. She was a woman who always got her way, got what she wanted. Got others to do her dirty work for her.' He was astonished to discover that tears were rolling down his cheeks, uncontrollably, stupidly, pointlessly.

The policeman stood, quietly and with every sign

of respect. 'The Irish have a long history of blowing themselves apart, Mr Stoner. I'm only sorry that you were involved – and the others, too. Innocents, I imagine.' Stoner said nothing, fascinated by the sheer volume of water, salt water, running down his face and into his beard. It began as a hot stream around his eyes, cooled rapidly until it brought a chill to the lower part of his face.

And the policeman said: 'The odd thing here is that the blast didn't kill her.' Stoner's eyes dried, miraculously. He pulled focus.

'No?' A peculiar, choking sound. Dry, like his eyes, suddenly.

'Shot.' The policeman sounded weary and frustrated. 'Something fast and automatic. Machine gun. Took out heart, lungs, ribs. Full magazine, maybe two. Something brutal, maybe an H&K...' Stoner, eyes closed, interrupted him.

'UMP9,' he said, words as dry as an African desert. '9x19 Parabellum.' Silence descended upon the room and all within. A packed, tense, shuddering silence, echoing to the sound of faraway fire.

'Maybe. Too soon to tell. But that sort of thing.' Both visitors were standing, shrugging their jackets to adjust them for their departure. 'We'll contact you through channels. Once you're feeling more like. And once we have DNA back and some fingerprints, dental records and the like. You're lucky to have survived this, Mr Stoner. Good luck.' He stopped, turned back. 'And thank you for your co-operation, and for what I understand has been a difficult piece of counter-terrorism work. I'll probably never know the whole story, but from what I've heard,' – a nod towards his silent companion – 'I gather it was bloody and bloody intense.' He walked to the door, swung it weightily open.

The Hard Man walked up to Stoner's bedside, leaned down and took one of Stoner's hands in both of his own. 'See you on the other side,' he said, quietly, turned and left.

ABOUT THE AUTHOR

Frank Westworth shares several characteristics with JJ Stoner: they both play mean blues guitar and ride Harley-Davidson motorcycles. Unlike Stoner, Frank hasn't deliberately killed anyone. Instead, he edits classic motorcycle magazines and has written extensively for the UK motoring press. Frank lives in Cornwall with his guitars, motorcycles, partner and cat.

***

Thanks for reading right to the very end. We hope you enjoyed *The Redemption Of Charm*. If you did, please take a few moments to review it on Amazon or Goodreads. Your feedback would be very much appreciated.

Although this is the final book in the Killing Sisters series, we don't think we've seen the last of JJ Stoner. If you'd like to stay in touch with JJ, then you'll find Frank Westworth and info about new short stories on Facebook and at www.murdermayhemandmore.net

ALSO BY FRANK WESTWORTH

A Last Act Of Charity: Killing Sisters Book 1

The Corruption Of Chastity: Killing Sisters Book 2

First Contract: a JJ Stoner short story

Two Wrongs: a JJ Stoner short story

Third Person: a JJ Stoner short story

Four Cornered: a JJ Stoner short story

Fifth Columnist: a JJ Stoner short story

DESPERATELY SEEKING JJ STONER?

A series of action-packed short stories reveal more about the earlier adventures of covert operative JJ Stoner, when he used sharp blades and blunt instruments to discreetly solve problems for the UK government

FIRST CONTRACT: JJ Stoner was a soldier. He killed people for a living and made no bones about it. On a scorching day in the Iraqi desert, when British blood stained the sand, he over-stepped the mark. Men died in compromising circumstances; too many men for an easy explanation. Faced with a dishonourable discharge and accusations of murder, Stoner accepted an offer from a stranger who represented an intelligence agency. Suddenly, Stoner found himself half a world away and about to execute his first private contract...

TWO WRONGS: starts with great sex and ends in sudden death. US Navy SEAL Stretch McCann believes he's met the girl of his dreams. Trouble is, she's married to someone else; another military man not inclined to suffer rivals lightly. Enter an altogether unusual Englishman, JJ Stoner, covert investigator and occasional assassin. Stoner offers Stretch an opportunity for action...

THIRD PERSON: A target is being stalked through rain-soaked city streets. Someone seeks JJ Stoner, independent operative, covert investigator and occasional contract killer. Caution is advised: with Stoner you often get more than you bargain for and this is Ireland, not so very long after the Good Friday agreement. Someone plans to put a cat among the peace process pigeons...

FOUR CORNERED: Stoner needs to prove to his boss that he's more than a one-trick pony whose only skill is delivering an abrupt ending. But when a static stake-out abruptly escalates into live fire, Stoner is distracted by two killer women. Suddenly, what should have been a 'routine conversation' with a disenchanted weapons inspector veers into violence with fatal consequences...

FIFTH COLUMNIST: A bent copper is compromising national security but none of the evidence will stand up in court. That's exactly why men like Stoner operate in the shadows, ready to terminate the target once an identity is confirmed...

SPECIAL RELATIONSHIP: When Stoner returns to the USA he's treading on sensitive territory. No Englishman is exactly welcome in Louisiana so soon after the international oil rig disaster. Stoner claims he's visiting New Orleans for the annual jazzfest, but the agents who meet him at the airport have a hard time believing this...

All the Stoner stories and earlier Killing Sisters novels are available at Amazon. Look out for the bumper ebook bundle which collects the first five Stoner stories into an all-action anthology